Praise for the novels of Laurell K. Hamilton featuring Anita Blake, Vampire Hunter

DANSE MACABRE

"It's an almost sure bet that there will be plenty of readers ready to enjoy the 'good parts'—sexual and otherwise—of each successive Anita Blake novel for years to come."
—*The Denver Post*

"Fans will find plenty here to sink their teeth into."
—*St. Louis Post-Dispatch*

"Her books outsell any other current vampire fiction."
—*Publishers Weekly*

"It just does not get more devilishly seductive than this...dark and chilling, hotter than hot, sexy, sensual, and incredibly intense."
—*Love Romances and More*

"Delivers some hot goods, Anita-style."
—*Fallen Angel Reviews*

"A fabulous action-packed story line filled with characters readers have come to think of as friends."
—*Midwest Book Review*

MICAH

"An exciting, erotic, and evocative paranormal romantic suspense thriller that will thrill her fans and send new readers scrambling for her backlist."
—*The Best Reviews*

"Highly palatable...equal portions hot sex and supernatural crime fighting—with a dollop of old-fashioned male-female melodrama."
—*Publishers Weekly*

continued...

INCUBUS DREAMS

"[A] thrill ride."   —*St. Louis Post-Dispatch*

"Hamilton maintains a terrific pace with suspense, revenge, and heart-pounding endings."   —*Detroit Free Press*

"Action-packed...The eroticism and the 'dramedy' of complicated relationships between shapeshifting lovers sets Hamilton's novels apart from the rest of the pack...[She] really does come off like the genre's answer to Henry Miller."   —*The Denver Post*

"A page-turning adventure...Fans of the series will not be disappointed."   —*Library Journal*

CERULEAN SINS

"Lavish...Fans won't want to miss this one...A great read."   —*St. Louis Post-Dispatch*

"The best Blake yet...hot stuff."   —*Publishers Weekly* (starred review)

"Hamilton's complex, enthralling world is utterly absorbing, and Anita's many fans will be thrilled to see her back in action."   —*Booklist*

"Anita's uncontrollable sexual energy has it's amusing (not to mention arousing) moments...This manages to go over the top while remaining a really compelling read."   —*Locus*

"Fresh and fun."   —*Metropole*

NARCISSUS IN CHAINS

"Laurell K. Hamilton's sexiest book... *Narcissus in Chains* hits the ground running and never stops... Hamilton just keeps getting better and better."
—*St. Louis Post-Dispatch*

"In [this novel], tough, sarcastic Anita Blake... torn between her inner vamp and wolf, makes a final mating choice that no fan will expect... Better pounce."
—*Kirkus Reviews*

"Interesting... compelling."
—*Locus*

"Amorous."
—*Publishers Weekly*

OBSIDIAN BUTTERFLY

"An erotic, demonic thrill ride. Her sexy, edgy, wickedly ironic style sweeps the reader into her unique world and delivers red-hot entertainment. Hamilton's marvelous storytelling can be summed up in three words: over the top. She blends the genres of romance, horror, and adventure with stunning panache. Great fun!"
—Jayne Ann Krentz

"Just when I think that Laurell K. Hamilton can't possibly get any farther out on the edge, along she comes with yet another eye-popping blend of hilarious sex, violence, and stuff that makes your hair stand on end. I've never read a writer with a more fertile imagination—and fewer inhibitions about using it!"
—Diana Gabaldon

"A monstrously entertaining read."
—*Publishers Weekly*

"An abundance of thrills, chills, violence, and sexual innuendo. Recommended."
—*Library Journal*

"An R-rated *Buffy the Vampire Slayer*... the action never stops... the climax is an edge-of-your-seat cliff-hanger... dessert for the mind, with sprinkles."
—*The New York Review of Science Fiction*

THE LUNATIC CAFE

Laurell K. Hamilton

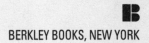
BERKLEY BOOKS, NEW YORK

THE BERKLEY PUBLISHING GROUP
Published by the Penguin Group
Penguin Group (USA) Inc.
375 Hudson Street, New York, New York 10014, USA
Penguin Group (Canada), 90 Eglinton Avenue East, Suite 700, Toronto, Ontario M4P 2Y3, Canada
(a division of Pearson Penguin Canada Inc.)
Penguin Books Ltd., 80 Strand, London WC2R 0RL, England
Penguin Group Ireland, 25 St. Stephen's Green, Dublin 2, Ireland (a division of Penguin Books Ltd.)
Penguin Group (Australia), 250 Camberwell Road, Camberwell, Victoria 3124, Australia
(a division of Pearson Australia Group Pty. Ltd.)
Penguin Books India Pvt. Ltd., 11 Community Centre, Panchsheel Park, New Delhi—110 017, India
Penguin Group (NZ), 67 Apollo Drive, Rosedale, North Shore 0632, New Zealand
(a division of Pearson New Zealand Ltd.)
Penguin Books (South Africa) (Pty.) Ltd., 24 Sturdee Avenue, Rosebank, Johannesburg 2196,
South Africa

Penguin Books Ltd., Registered Offices: 80 Strand, London WC2R 0RL, England

This book is an original publication of The Berkley Publishing Group.

PRINTING HISTORY
Ace mass market edition / January 1996
Berkley hardcover edition / March 2005
Berkley trade paperback edition / January 2008

Berkley trade paperback ISBN: 978-0-425-22111-2

The Library of Congress has cataloged the Berkley hardcover edition as follows:

Hamilton, Laurell K.
    The lunatic cafe / Laurell K. Hamilton.
        p. cm.
    ISBN 0-425-20137-6
    1. Blake, Anita (Fictitious character)—Fiction.   2. Werewolves—Fiction.   I. Title.

    PS3558.A443357L86 2005
    813'.54—dc22

                                                                        2004057496

PRINTED IN THE UNITED STATES OF AMERICA

10   9   8   7   6   5   4

To Trinity, my daughter,
If you had never come into my life, I would be a different person.
Less happy, less comfortable with myself.
You force me, every day, to look at the world with fresh eyes
and to throw my preconceptions to the wind.

Acknowledgments

Dr. Keith Nunnelee, who helped bring Trinity into the world ten years ago. No small task that. Sarah Sumner for food, comfort, and emergency runs to the doctor all those years ago; Mark Sumner for the same; John Sumner for worrying—nobody has better neighbors or better friends. Deborah Millitello, who took time out of her own writing schedule to help with Trinity when she was a baby so I could finish this book the first time. Marella Sands, congrats on selling your own series.

To all the Alternate Historians: Tom Drennan, N. L. Drew, and Rett McPherson, who made sure this book stood alone.

1

IT WAS TWO weeks before Christmas. A slow time of year for raising
the dead. My last client of the night sat across from me. There had been
no notation by his name. No note saying zombie raising or vampire slay-
ing. Nothing. Which probably meant whatever he wanted me to do was
something I wouldn't, or couldn't, do. Pre-Christmas was a dead time of
year, no pun intended. My boss, Bert, took any job that would have us.

George Smitz was a tall man, well over six feet. He was broad shoul-
dered, and muscular. Not the muscles you get from lifting weights and
running around indoor tracks. The muscles you get from hard physical
labor. I would have bet money that Mr. Smitz was a construction worker,
farmer, or something similar. He was shaped large and square with grime
embedded under his fingernails that soap would not touch.

He sat in front of me, crushing his toboggan hat, kneading it in his
big hands. The coffee that he'd accepted sat cooling on the edge of my
desk. He hadn't taken so much as a sip.

I was drinking my coffee out of the Christmas mug that Bert, my
boss, had insisted everyone bring in. A personalized holiday mug to add a
personal touch to the office. My mug had a reindeer in a bathrobe and
slippers with Christmas lights laced in its antlers, toasting the merry season with champagne and saying, "Bingle Jells."

Bert didn't really like my mug, but he let it go, probably afraid of what else I might bring in. He'd been very pleased with my outfit for the evening. A high-collared blouse so perfectly red I'd had to wear makeup to keep from looking pale. The skirt and matching jacket were a deep forest green. I hadn't dressed for Bert. I had dressed for my date.

. The silver outline of an angel gleamed in my lapel. I looked very Christmasy. The Browning Hi-Power 9mm didn't look Christmasy at all, but since it was hidden under the jacket, that didn't seem to matter. It might have bothered Mr. Smitz, but he looked worried enough to not care. As long as I didn't shoot him personally.

"Now, Mr. Smitz, how may I help you today?" I asked.

He was staring at his hands and only his eyes rose to look at me. It was a little-boy gesture, an uncertain gesture. It sat oddly on the big man's face. "I need help, and I don't know who else to go to."

"Exactly what kind of help do you need, Mr. Smitz?"

"It's my wife."

I waited for him to continue, but he stared at his hands. His hat was wadded into a tight ball.

"You want your wife raised from the dead?" I asked.

He looked up at that, eyes wide with alarm. "She's not dead. I know that."

"Then what can I possibly do for you, Mr. Smitz? I raise the dead, and am a legal vampire executioner. What in that job description could help your wife?"

"Mr. Vaughn said you knew all about lycanthropy." He said that as if it explained everything. It didn't.

"My boss makes a lot of claims, Mr. Smitz. But what does lycanthropy have to do with your wife?" This was the second time I'd asked about his wife. I seemed to be speaking English, but perhaps my questions were really Swahili and I just didn't realize it. Or maybe whatever had happened was too awful for words. That happened a lot in my business.

He leaned forward, eyes intense on my face. I leaned forward, too, I couldn't help myself. "Peggy, that's my wife, she's a lycanthrope."

I blinked at him. "And?"

"If it came out, she'd lose her job."

I didn't argue with him. Legally, you couldn't discriminate against lycanthropes, but it happened a lot. "What sort of work is Peggy in?"

"She's a butcher."

A lycanthrope that was a butcher. It was too perfect. But I could see why she'd lose her job. Food preparation with a potentially fatal disease. I don't think so. I knew, and the health department knew, that lycanthropy can only be transferred by an attack in the animal form. Most people don't believe that. Can't say I blame them entirely. I don't want to be fuzzy, either.

"She runs a specialty meat store. It's a good business. She inherited it from her father."

"Was he a lycanthrope, too?" I asked.

He shook his head. "No, Peggy was attacked a few years back. She survived . . ." He shrugged. "But, you know."

I did know. "So your wife is a lycanthrope and would lose her business if it came out. I understand that. But how can I help you?" I fought the urge to glance at my watch. I had the tickets. Richard couldn't go in without me.

"Peggy's missing."

Ah. "I am not a private detective, Mr. Smitz. I don't do missing persons."

"But I can't go to the police. They might find out."

"How long has she been missing?"

"Two days."

"My advice is to go to the police."

He shook his head stubbornly. "No."

I sighed. "I don't know anything about finding a missing person. I raise the dead, slay vampires, that's it."

"Mr. Vaughn said you could help me."

"Did you tell him your problem?"

He nodded.

Shit. Bert and I were going to have a long talk. "The police are good at their job, Mr. Smitz. Just tell them your wife is missing. Don't mention the lycanthropy. See what they turn up." I didn't like telling a client to withhold information from the police, but it beat the heck out of not going at all.

"Ms. Blake, please, I'm worried. We've got two kids."

I started to say all the reasons I couldn't help him, then stopped. I had an idea. "Animators, Inc., has a private investigator on retainer. Veronica Sims has been involved in a lot of preternatural cases. She might be able to help you."

"Can I trust her?"

"I do."

He stared at me for a long moment, then nodded. "All right, how do I get in touch with her?"

"Let me give her a call, see if she can see you."

"That would be great, thank you."

"I want to help you, Mr. Smitz. Hunting missing spouses just isn't my specialty." I dialed the phone as I talked. I knew Ronnie's number by heart. We exercised at least twice a week together, not to mention an occasional movie, dinner, whatever. Best friends, a concept that most women never outgrow. Ask a man who his best friend is and he'll have to think about it. He won't know right off the top of his head. A woman would. A man might not even be able to think of a name, not for his best friend. Women keep track of these things. Men don't. Don't ask me why.

Ronnie's answering machine clicked in. "Ronnie, if you're there, it's Anita, pick up."

The phone clicked, and a second later I was talking to the genuine article. "Hi, Anita. I thought you had a date with Richard tonight. Something wrong?"

See, best friends. "Not with the date. I've got a client here who I think is more up your alley than mine."

"Tell me," she said.

I did.

"Did you recommend he go to the police?"

"Yep."

"He won't go?"

"Nope."

She sighed. "Well, I've done missing persons before but usually after the police have done everything they can. They have resources I can't touch."

"I'm aware of that," I said.

"He won't budge?"

"I don't think so."

"So it's me or . . ."

"Bert took the job knowing it was a missing person. He might try giving it to Jamison."

"Jamison doesn't know his butt from a hole in the ground on anything but raising the dead."

"Yeah, but he's always eager to expand his repertoire."

"Ask him if he can be at my office . . ." She paused while she leafed through her appointment book. Business must be good. "At nine tomorrow morning."

"Jesus, you always were an early riser."

"One of my few faults," she said.

I asked George Smitz if nine o'clock tomorrow was all right.

"Couldn't she see me tonight?"

"He wants to see you tonight."

She thought about that for a minute. "Why not? It's not like I have a hot date, unlike some people I could mention. Sure, send him over. I'll wait. Friday with a client is better than Friday night alone, I guess."

"You've just hit a dry spell," I said.

"And you've hit a wet spell."

"Very funny."

She laughed. "I'll look forward to Mr. Smitz's arrival. Enjoy *Guys and Dolls*."

"I will. See you tomorrow morning for our run."

"You sure you want me over there that early in case dream boat wants to stay over?"

"You know me better than that," I said.

"Yeah, I do. Just kidding. See you tomorrow."

We hung up. I gave Mr. Smitz Ronnie's business card, directions to her office, and sent him on his way. Ronnie was the best I could do for him. It still bothered me that he wouldn't go to the police, but hey, it wasn't my wife.

I've got two kids, he'd said. Not my problem. Really. Craig, our nighttime secretary, was at the desk, which meant it was after six. I was running late. There really wasn't time to argue with Bert about Mr. Smitz, but . . .

I glanced at Bert's office. It was dark. "Boss man gone home?"

Craig glanced up from his computer keyboard. He has short, baby-fine brown hair. Round glasses to match a round face. He's slender and taller than I am, but then who isn't? He's in his twenties with a wife and two babies.

"Mr. Vaughn left about thirty minutes ago."

"It figures," I said.

"Something wrong?"

I shook my head. "Schedule me some time to talk to the boss tomorrow."

"I don't know, Anita. He's booked pretty solid."

"Find some time, Craig. Or I'll barge in on one of the other appointments."

"You're mad," he said.

"You bet. Find the time. If he yells about it, tell him I pulled a gun on you."

"Anita," he said with a grin, as if I were teasing.

I left him riffling through the appointment book trying to squeeze me somewhere. I meant it. Bert would talk to me tomorrow. December was our slowest season for raising zombies. People seemed to think you couldn't do it close to Christmas, as if it were black magic or something. So Bert scheduled other things to take up the slack. I was getting tired of clients with problems I could do nothing about. Smitz wasn't the first this month, but he was going to be the last.

With that cheerful thought I bundled into my coat and left. Richard was waiting. If traffic cooperated, I might just make it before the opening number. Traffic on a Friday night, surely not.

2

THE 1978 NOVA that I'd been driving had died a sad and tragic death. I was now driving a Jeep Cherokee Country. It was a deep, deep green that looked black at night. But it had four-wheel drive for winter and enough room to carry goats in the back. Chickens were what I used for zombie raising most of the time, but occasionally you needed something bigger. Carrying goats in the Nova had been a bitch.

I pulled the Cherokee into the last parking space in the lot on Grant. My long, black winter coat billowed around me because I had only buttoned the bottom two buttons. If I buttoned all the buttons I couldn't get to my gun.

My hands were shoved into the coat pockets, arms huddling the cloth around me. I didn't wear gloves. I've never been comfortable shooting with gloves on. The gun is a part of my hand. Cloth shouldn't interfere.

I ran across the street in my high-heeled pumps, careful on the frosty pavement. The sidewalk was cracked, with huge sections broken out of it, as if someone had taken a sledgehammer to it. The boarded-up buildings were as dilapidated as the sidewalk. I'd missed the crowd, being nearly late, so I had the shattered street to myself. It was a short but lonely walk on a December night. Broken glass littered the ground and in heels I had to be very careful where I stepped. An alley cut the buildings. It looked like the natural habitat of *Muggerus americanus*. I watched the darkness carefully. Nothing moved. With the Browning I wasn't too worried, but still . . . You didn't have to be a genius to shoot someone in the back.

The wind gusted cold enough to take my breath away as I neared the corner and relative safety. I wore a lot of sweaters in the winter, but tonight I'd wanted something dressier, and I was freezing my patooties off, but I was hoping that Richard would like the red blouse.

At the corner there were lights, cars, and a policeman directing traffic in the middle of the street. You never saw this many police in this section of St. Louis unless the Fox was on. A lot of wealthy people came down here in their furs, diamonds, Rolex watches. Wouldn't do for a friend of the city council to get mugged. When Topol came to reprise his role in *Fiddler on the Roof*, the audience was very crème de la crème and the place crawled with cops. Tonight there was just the usual. Mostly in front of the theater, mostly doing traffic, but also taking peeks at the seedy backs of buildings in case someone with money wandered away from the light.

I went through the glass doors into the long, narrow entryway. It was brightly lit, shiny somehow. There's a little room to the right where you can pick up your tickets. People streamed out of it, hurrying to the inner glass doors. I wasn't as late as I thought if there were this many people still getting tickets. Or maybe everyone else was as late as I was.

I caught a glimpse of Richard standing in the far right corner. At six foot one he is easier to spot across a crowded room than I am, at my own five foot three. He stood quietly, eyes following the crowd's movement. He didn't seem bored or impatient. He seemed to be having a good time watching the people. His eyes followed an elderly couple as they walked through the glass doors. The woman used a cane. Their progress was painfully slow. His head turned slowly with them. I scanned the crowd. Everyone else was younger, moving with confident or hurried stride. Was Richard looking for victims? Prey? He was, after all, a werewolf. He'd gotten a bad batch of lycanthropy vaccine. One of the reasons I never get the shots. If my flu shot accidentally backfires, that's one thing, but being furry once a month . . . No, thanks.

Did he realize he was standing there searching the crowd like a lion staring at a bunch of gazelles? Or maybe the elderly couple had reminded him of his grandparents. Hell, maybe I was giving him motives that were only in my suspicious little brain. I hoped so.

His hair was brown. In sunlight it gleamed with strands of gold, hints of copper. I knew the hair was shoulder length, nearly my length, but he'd done something to it, pulled it back somehow so it gave the illusion of being very short and close to his head. Not easy with hair as wavy as his.

His suit was some rich shade of green. Most men would have looked like Peter Pan in a green suit, but on him it looked just right. As I walked closer, I could see his shirt was a pale almost gold, tie a darker green than the suit, with tiny Christmas trees done in red. I would have made a smart remark about the tie, but dressed in red and green with a Christmas angel on my lapel, who was I to complain?

He saw me and smiled. The smile was very bright against his permanently tanned skin. His last name, Zeeman, is Dutch, but somewhere back in his ancestry was something not European. Not blond, not fair, not cold. His eyes were a perfect, chocolate brown.

He reached out and took my hands, gently, drawing me to him. His lips were soft against my mouth, a brief, nearly chaste kiss.

I stepped back, taking a breath. He kept hold of my hand, and I let him. His skin was very warm against my cold hand. I thought about asking him if he'd been thinking about eating that elderly couple, but didn't. Accusing him of murderous intent might spoil the evening. Besides, most lycanthropes weren't aware of doing nonhuman things. When you pointed it out, it always seemed to hurt their feelings. I didn't want to hurt Richard's feelings.

As we went through the inner doors into the crowded lobby, I asked, "Where's your coat?"

"In the car. Didn't want to carry it, so I made a dash for it."

I nodded. It was typical Richard. Or maybe lycanthropes didn't get cold. From the back I could see he'd braided his hair tight to his scalp. The tip of the braid trailed over his collar. I couldn't even figure out how he'd done it. My idea of fixing my hair is to wash, smear a little hair goop through it, then let it dry. I was not into high-tech hair design. Though it might be fun to figure out the knots in a leisurely fashion after the show. I was always willing to learn a new skill.

The main lobby of the Fox is a cross between a really nice Chinese restaurant and a Hindu temple, with a little Art Deco thrown in for flavor. The colors are so dazzling, it looks like the painter ground up stained glass with bits of light trapped in them. Pit bull–size Chinese lions with glowing red eyes guard a sweep of stairs that lead up to the Fox Club balcony, where for fifteen thousand dollars a year you can eat wonderful meals and have a private box. The rest of us peons mingled nearly shoulder to shoulder in the carpeted lobby, with offerings of popcorn, pretzels, Pepsi, and on some nights, hot dogs. A far cry from chicken cordon bleu or whatever they were serving up above.

The Fox treads that wonderfully thin line between gaudiness and the fantastic. I've loved the building since I first saw it. Every time I come, there is some new wonder. Some color, or carving, or statue that I didn't notice before. When you realize that it was originally built to be a movie theater, you realize how much things have changed. Movie theaters now have the souls of unwashed socks. The Fox is alive as only the best buildings are alive.

I had to let go of Richard's hand to unbutton my coat the rest of the way, but hey, we weren't attached at the hip. I stood close to him in the crowd without touching, but I could feel him, like a line of warmth against my body.

"We're going to look like the Bobsey twins when I take my coat off," I said.

He raised his eyebrows.

I spread the coat like a flasher, and he laughed. It was a good laugh, warm and thick like Christmas pudding.

" 'Tis the season," he said. He gave me a one-armed hug, quick like you'd give a friend, but his arm stayed over my shoulders. It was still early enough in our dating that touching each other was new, unexpected, exhilarating. We kept looking for excuses to touch each other. Trying to be nonchalant about it. Not fooling each other. Not sure we cared. I slipped my arm around his waist and leaned just a bit. It was my right arm. If we were attacked now, I'd never draw my gun in time. I stayed there for a minute thinking it just might be worth it. I moved around him, offering my left hand to him.

I don't know if he caught a glimpse of the gun or just figured it out, but his eyes widened. He leaned close to me, whispering against my hair. "A gun here, at the Fox? You think the ushers will let you in?"

"They did last time."

He got a strange look on his face. "You always go armed?"

I shrugged. "After dark, yes."

His eyes were puzzled, but he let it go. Before this year I'd sometimes gone out after dark unarmed but it had been a rough year. A lot of different people had tried to kill me. I was small even for a woman. I jogged, lifted weights, had a black belt in judo, but I was still outclassed by most professional bad guys. They tended to also lift weights, know martial arts, and outweigh me by a hundred pounds or more. I couldn't arm-wrestle them, but I could shoot them.

Also a lot of this year I'd been up against vampires, and other preternatural creepie-crawlies. They could lift large trucks with a single hand or worse. Silver bullets might not kill a vampire, but it certainly slowed them down. Enough for me to run like hell. To get away. To survive.

Richard knew what I did for a living. He'd even seen some of the messy parts. But I still expected him to blow it. To start playing the male protector and bitch about the gun or something. It was almost a permanent tightness in my gut, waiting for this man to say something awful. Something that would ruin it, destroy it, hurt.

So far, so good.

The crowd started flowing towards the stairs, parting on either side to the corridors leading into the main theater. We shuffle-stepped with the crowd, holding hands to keep from being separated. Sure.

Once free of the lobby, the crowd flowed towards the different aisles like water searching for the quickest route downstream. The quickest route was still pretty slow. I dug the tickets out of the pocket of my suit jacket. I didn't have a purse. There was a small brush, a lipstick, lipliner, eye shadow, ID, and my car keys stuffed in my coat pockets. My beeper was tucked in the front of my skirt, discreetly to one side. When not dressed up, I wore a fanny pack.

The usher, an older woman with glasses, shone a tiny flashlight on our tickets. She took us to our seats, motioned us in, and went back up to assist the next group of helpless people. The seats were good, near the middle, sort of close to the stage. Close enough.

Richard had scooted in to sit on my left without being asked. He's a quick study. It's one of the reasons we're still going out. That and the fact that I lust after his body something terrible.

I spread my coat over the seat, spreading it out so it wouldn't be bulky. His arm snaked across my chair, fingers touching my shoulder. I fought the urge to lay my head on his shoulder. Too hokey, then thought, what the hell. I snuggled into the bend of his neck, just breathing in the scent of his skin. His aftershave was clean and sweet, but underneath was the smell of his skin, his flesh. It made it so the aftershave would never smell the same on anyone else. Frankly, without a drop of aftershave I loved the smell of Richard's neck.

I straightened up, pulling just a little away from him. He looked at me questioningly. "Something wrong?"

"Nice aftershave," I said. No need to confess that I'd had an almost irresistible urge to nibble his neck. It was too embarrassing.

The lights dimmed and the music began. I'd never actually seen *Guys and Dolls* except in the movies. The one with Marlon Brando and Jean Simmons. Richard's idea of a date was caving, hiking, things that required your oldest clothes and a pair of good walking shoes. Nothing wrong with that. I like the outdoors, but I wanted to try a dress-up date. I wanted to see Richard in a suit and let him see me in something frillier than jeans. I was after all a girl, whether I liked to admit it or not.

But having proposed the date, I didn't want to do the usual dipsy-duo of dinner and a movie. So I'd called up the Fox to see what was playing and asked Richard if he liked musicals. He did. Another point in his favor. Since it was my idea, I bought the tickets. Richard had not argued, not even to pay half. After all, I hadn't offered to pay for our last dinner. It hadn't occurred to me. I was betting paying for the tickets occurred to Richard, but he'd let it go. Good man.

The curtain came up and the opening street scene paraded before us, bright colors, stylized, perfect and cheerful, and just what I needed. "The Fugue for Tinhorns" filled the bright stage and flowed out into the happy dark. Good music, humor, soon to be dancers, Richard's body next to mine, a gun under my arm. What more could a girl ask for?

3

A TRICKLE OF people had slipped out before the end of the musical, to beat the crowd. I always stayed until the very end. It seemed unfair to slink away before you could applaud. Besides, I hated missing the end of anything. I was always convinced that the bit I'd miss would be the best part.

We joined in enthusiastically with a standing ovation. I've never lived in any city that gives so many standing Os. Admittedly sometimes, like tonight, the show was wonderful, but I've seen people stand on productions that didn't deserve it. I don't stand unless I mean it.

Richard sat back down after the lights came up. "I'd rather wait until the crowd thins out. If you don't mind." There was a look in his brown eyes that said he didn't think I would.

I didn't. We'd driven separate cars. When we left the Fox, the evening was over. Apparently, neither of us wanted to leave. I knew I didn't.

I leaned on the seats in front of us, gazing down at him. He smiled up at me, eyes gleaming with lust, if not love. I was smiling, too. Couldn't seem to help myself.

"You know this is a very sexist musical," he said.

I thought about that a moment, then nodded. "Yep."

"But you like it?"

I nodded.

His eyes narrowed a bit. "I thought you might be offended."

"I have better things to worry about than whether *Guys and Dolls* reflects a balanced worldview."

He laughed—a short, happy sound. "Good. For a minute there I thought I'd have to get rid of my Rodgers and Hammerstein collection."

I studied his face, trying to decide if he was teasing me. I didn't think so. "You really collect Rodgers and Hammerstein sound tracks?"

He nodded, eyes bright with laughter.

"Just Rodgers and Hammerstein, or all musicals?"

"I don't have them all, but all."

I shook my head.

"What's wrong?"

"You're a romantic."

"You make it sound like a bad thing."

"That happy-ever-after shit is fine on stage, but it doesn't have a lot to do with life."

It was his turn to study my face. Evidently, he didn't like what he saw, because he frowned. "This date was your idea. If you don't approve of all this happy stuff, why'd you bring me?"

I shrugged. "After I asked you on a dress-up date, I didn't know where to take you. I didn't want to do the usual. Besides, I like musicals. I just don't think they reflect reality."

"You're not as tough as you pretend to be."

"Yes," I said, "I am."

"I don't believe that. I think you like that happy-ever-after shit as much as I do. You're just afraid to believe in it anymore."

"Not afraid, just cautious."

"Been disappointed too many times?" He made it a question.

"Maybe." I crossed my arms on my stomach. A psychologist would have said I was closed off, uncommunicative. Fuck them.

"What are you thinking?"

I shrugged.

"Tell me, please."

I stared into his sincere brown eyes and wanted to go home alone. Instead. "Happy ever after is just a lie, Richard, and has been since I was eight."

"Your mother's death," he said.

I just looked at him. I was twenty-four years old and the pain of that first loss was still raw. You could deal with it, endure it, but never escape it. Never truly believe in the great, good place. Never truly believe that the bad thing wasn't going to come swooping down and take it all away. I'd rather fight a dozen vampires than one senseless accident.

He pried my hand from its grip on my arm. "I won't die on you, Anita. I promise."

Someone laughed, a low chuckle that brushed the skin like fingertips. Only one person had that nearly touchable laugh—Jean-Claude. I turned, and there he was, standing in the middle of the aisle. I hadn't heard him come. Hadn't sensed any movement. He was just there like magic.

"Don't make promises you can't keep, Richard."

4

I PUSHED AWAY from the seats, taking a step forward to give Richard room to stand. I felt him at my back, a comforting presence if I hadn't been more worried about his safety than my own.

Jean-Claude was dressed in a shiny black tux, complete with tails. A white vest with minute black dots bordered the gleaming whiteness of his shirt. The collar was high and stiff, with a cravat of soft black cloth tied around it and tucked into the vest as if ties had never been invented. The stickpin in his vest was made of silver-and-black onyx. His shoes had spats on them, like the ones Fred Astaire used to wear, though I suspected the entire outfit was of a much older style.

His hair was fashionably long, the nearly black curls edging the white collar. I knew what color his eyes were, but I didn't look at them now. They were midnight blue, the color of a really good sapphire. Never look a vampire in the eyes. It's a rule.

With the master vampire of the city standing there, waiting, I realized how empty the theater was. We'd waited out the crowd, all right. We were alone in the echoing silence. The distant murmur of the departing crowd was like white noise. It meant nothing to us. I stared at the shiny mother-of-pearl buttons on Jean-Claude's vest. It was hard to be tough when you couldn't meet someone's eyes. But I'd manage.

"God, Jean-Claude, don't you ever wear anything but black and white?"

"Don't you like it, *ma petite*?" He gave a little spin so I could get the whole effect. The outfit suited him beautifully. Of course, everything he wore seemed made to order, perfect, lovely, just like him.

"Somehow I didn't think *Guys and Dolls* would be your cup of tea, Jean-Claude."

"Or yours, *ma petite*." The voice was rich like cream, with a warmth that only two things could give it: anger or lust. I was betting it wasn't lust.

I had the gun, and silver bullets would slow him down, but it wouldn't kill him. Of course, Jean-Claude wouldn't jump us in public. He was much too civilized for that. He was a business vampire, an entrepreneur. Entrepreneurs, dead or alive, didn't go around tearing people's throats out. Normally.

"Richard, you're unusually quiet." He stared past me. I didn't glance back to see what Richard was doing. Never take your eyes off the vampire in front of you to glance at the werewolf in back of you. One problem at a time.

"Anita can speak for herself," Richard said.

Jean-Claude's attention flicked back to me. "That is certainly true. But I came to see how the two of you enjoyed the play."

"And pigs fly," I said.

"You don't believe me?"

"Not hardly," I said.

"Come, Richard, how did you enjoy your evening?" There was an edge of laughter to his voice but under that was still the anger. Master vampires are not good to be around when they're angry.

"It was wonderful until you showed up." There was a note of warmth to Richard's voice, the beginnings of anger. I'd never seen him angry.

"How could my mere presence spoil your . . . date?" The last was spit out, scalding hot.

"Why are you so pissed tonight, Jean-Claude?" I asked.

"Why, *ma petite*, I never get . . . pissed."

"Bullshit."

"He's jealous of you and me," Richard said.

"I am not jealous."

"You're always telling Anita how you can smell her desire for you. Well, I can smell yours. You want her so bad you can"—Richard gave an almost bitter sound—"taste it."

"And you, Monsieur Zeeman, you don't lust after her?"

"Stop talking like I'm not here," I said.

"Anita asked me out on a date. I said yes."

"Is this true, *ma petite*?" His voice had gone very quiet. Scarier than anger, that quietness.

I wanted to say no, but he'd smell a lie. "It's true. What of it?"

Silence. He just stood there utterly still. If I hadn't been looking right at him, I wouldn't have known he was there. The dead make no noise.

My beeper went off. Richard and I jumped as if we'd been shot. Jean-Claude was motionless as if he hadn't heard it.

I hit the button, and the number that flashed made me groan.

"What is it?" Richard asked. He laid his hand on my shoulder.

"The police. I've got to find a phone." I leaned back against Richard's chest. His hand squeezed my shoulder. I stared at the vampire in front of me. Would Jean-Claude hurt him after I'd gone? I wasn't sure.

"You got a cross on you?" I didn't bother to whisper. Jean-Claude would have heard me anyway.

"No."

I half turned. "No! You're out after dark without a cross?"

He shrugged. "I'm a shapeshifter. I can take care of myself."

I shook my head. "Getting your throat ripped out once wasn't enough?"

"I'm still alive," he said.

"I know you heal from almost anything, but for God's sake, Richard, you don't heal from everything." I started pulling the silver chain of my crucifix out of my blouse. "You can borrow mine."

"Is that real silver?" Richard asked.

"Yes."

"I can't. I'm allergic to silver, remember."

Ah. Stupid me. Some preternatural expert offering silver to a lycanthrope. I tucked the chain back in my blouse.

"He's no more human than I am, *ma petite*."

"At least I'm not dead."

"That can be remedied."

"Stop it, both of you."

"Have you seen her bedroom, Richard? Her collection of toy penguins?"

I took a deep breath and let it out. I was not going to stand here and explain how Jean-Claude had managed to see my bedroom. Did I really have to say, out loud, that I didn't sleep with the walking dead?

"You're trying to make me jealous, and it won't work," Richard said.

"But there is that worm of doubt in you, Richard. I know it. You are my creature to call, my wolf, and I know you doubt her."

"I don't doubt Anita." But there was a defensiveness in his voice that I didn't like at all.

"I don't belong to you, Jean-Claude," Richard said. "I'm second in line to lead the pack. I come and go where I please. The alpha rescinded his orders about obeying you, after you nearly got me killed."

"Your pack leader was most upset that you survived," Jean-Claude said sweetly.

"Why would the pack leader want Richard dead?" I asked.

Jean-Claude looked past me at Richard. "You haven't told her that you're in a battle of succession?"

"I will not fight Marcus."

"Then you will die." Jean-Claude made it sound very simple.

My beeper sounded again. Same number. "I'm coming, Dolph," I muttered.

I glanced at Richard. Anger glittered in his eyes. His hands were balled into fists. I was standing close enough to feel the tension coming off him like waves.

"What's going on, Richard?"

He gave a quick shake of his head. "My business, not yours."

"If someone's threatening you, it is my business."

He stared down at me. "No, you aren't one of us. I won't involve you."

"I can handle myself, Richard."

He just shook his head.

"Marcus wants to involve you, *ma petite*. Richard refuses. It is a . . . bone of contention between them. One of many."

"How do you know so much about it?" I asked.

"We leaders of the preternatural community must deal with each other. For everyone's safety."

Richard just stood staring at him. It occurred to me for the first time that he seemed to look Jean-Claude in the eyes, with no ill effects. "Richard, can you meet his eyes?"

Richard's eyes flicked down to me, then back to Jean-Claude. "Yes. I'm a monster, too. I can look him in the eyes."

I shook my head. "Irving can't look him in the eyes. It's not just being a werewolf."

"As I am a master vampire, so our handsome friend here is a master werewolf. Though they do not call them that. Alpha males, is it not? Pack leaders."

"I prefer pack leader."

"I'll just bet you do," I said.

Richard looked hurt, his face crumbling like a child's. "You're angry with me, why?"

"You've got all this heavy shit going on with your pack leader, and you don't tell me. Jean-Claude keeps hinting your leader wants you dead. That true?"

"Marcus won't kill me," Richard said.

Jean-Claude laughed. The sound had a bitter undertaste to it, as if it hadn't been laughter at all. "You are a fool, Richard."

My beeper went off again. I checked the number, and turned it off. It wasn't like Dolph to call this many times, this close together. Something bad was happening. I needed to go. But . . .

"I don't have time to get the full story right this second." I poked a finger into the middle of Richard's chest. I gave Jean-Claude my back. He'd already done the damage he'd intended. "You are going to tell me every last bit of what's going on."

"I don't . . ."

"Save it. You either share this problem, or we don't date anymore."

He looked shocked. "Why?"

"Either you kept me out to protect me, which I'm going to hate. Or you have some other reason. It better be a damn good reason and not just some male ego shit."

Jean-Claude laughed again. This time the sound wrapped me around like flannel, warm and comforting, thick and soft next to naked skin. I shook my head. Just Jean-Claude's laughter was an invasion of privacy.

I turned to him, and there must have been something in my face because the laughter died as if it had never been. "As for you, you can get the hell out of here. You've had your fun for the night."

"Whatever do you mean, *ma petite*?" His beautiful face was as pure and blank as a mask.

I shook my head and stepped forward. I was leaving. I had work to do. Richard's hand gripped my shoulder.

"Let me go, Richard. I'm mad at you right now." I didn't look at him. I didn't want to see his face. I was afraid if he looked hurt, I'd forgive him anything.

"You heard her, Richard. She doesn't want you touching her." Jean-Claude had taken a gliding step closer.

"Leave it alone, Jean-Claude."

Richard's hand squeezed gently. "She doesn't want you, Jean-Claude." There was anger in his voice, more anger than should have been there. As if he were trying to convince himself more than Jean-Claude.

I stepped forward, shaking his hand off. I wanted to reach for it, but didn't. He'd been keeping major shit from me. Dangerous shit. It wasn't allowed. Worse yet, he thought in some dark corner of his soul that I might have given in to Jean-Claude. What a mess.

"Fuck you both," I said.

"So you have not had that pleasure?" Jean-Claude said.

"That's Anita's question to answer, not mine," Richard said.

"I would know it if you had."

"Liar," I said.

"No, *ma petite*. I would smell him on your skin."

I wanted to slug him. The desire to smash that beautiful face was physical. It tightened my shoulders, made my arms ache. But I knew better. You don't volunteer for slugfests with vampires. It shortens your life expectancy.

I walked up very close to Jean-Claude, bodies nearly touching. I stared him in the nose, which ruined some of the effect, but his eyes were drowning pools and I knew better.

"I hate you." My voice was flat with the effort not to scream. In that moment I meant it. And I knew Jean-Claude would sense it. I wanted him to know.

"*Ma petite . . .*"

"No, you've done enough talking. It's my turn. If you harm Richard Zeeman, I'll kill you."

"He means that much to you?" There was surprise in his voice. Great.

"No, you mean that little." I stepped away from him, around him. Gave him my back and walked away. Let him sink his fangs into that bit of truth. Tonight, I meant every word.

5

THE NUMBER ON my beeper was the car phone of Detective Sergeant Rudolf Storr. A Christmas present from his wife last year. I'd sent her a thank-you note. Police radio made everything sound like a foreign language. Dolph picked up on the fifth ring. I knew he'd get to it eventually.

"Anita."

"What if I'd been your wife?" I asked.

"She'd know I was working."

I let it go. Not every wife would appreciate her husband answering the phone with another woman's name. Maybe Lucille was different.

"What's up, Dolph? This was supposed to be my night off."

"Sorry, the murderer didn't know that. If you're too busy, we'll muddle through without you."

"What's got your panties in a twist?"

I was rewarded with a small sound that might have been a laugh. "Not your fault. We're out towards Six Flags on Forty-four."

"Where exactly on Forty-four?"

"Out near the Audubon Nature Center. How soon can you get here?"

"Problem, I don't know where the hell you are. How do I get to the nature center?"

"It's across the road from the St. Ambrose Monastery."

"Don't know it," I said.

He sighed. "Hell, we're out in the middle of fucking nowhere. Those are the only landmarks."

"Just give me directions. I'll find it."

He gave me directions. There were too many of them, and I didn't have pen and paper. "Hold on, I've got to get something to write with." I laid the phone down and snatched a napkin from the concession area. I begged a pen from an older couple. The man was wearing a cashmere overcoat. The woman wore real diamonds. The pen was engraved, and might have been real gold. He did not make me promise to bring it back. Trusting, or above such petty concerns. I was going to have to start stocking my own writing materials. It was getting embarrassing.

"I'm back, Dolph, go ahead."

He didn't ask what took so long. Dolph isn't big on extraneous questions. He gave the directions again. I read them back to him to be sure I had them right. I did.

"Dolph, this is at least a forty-five minute drive." I'm usually the last expert to be called in. After the victim has been photographed, videotaped, poked, prodded, etc. . . . After I come, everyone gets to go home, or at least leave the murder scene. People were not going to like cooling their heels for two hours.

"I called you as soon as I figured out nothing human did it. It'll take us at least forty-five minutes to finish up and be ready for you."

I should have known Dolph would have planned ahead. "Okay, I'll be there as soon as I can."

He hung up. I hung up. Dolph never said good-bye.

I gave the man back his pen. He accepted it graciously as if he'd never doubted its return. Good breeding.

I went for the doors. Neither Jean-Claude nor Richard had made it to the lobby. They were in public so I didn't really think they'd have a fistfight, angry words but not violence. So the vampire and the werewolf could take care of themselves. Besides, if Richard wasn't allowed to worry about me when I was off on my own, the least I could do was return the favor. I didn't think Jean-Claude really wanted to push me that far. Not really. One of us would die, and I was beginning to think, just maybe, it wouldn't be me.

6

THE COLD WRAPPED around me outside the doors. I hunched my shoulders, tucking my chin inside my collar. A laughing foursome walked a few yards ahead of me. They hung on each other, huddling against the cold. The women's high heels made a sharp theatrical clatter. Their laughter was too high, too shrill. A first double date that had gone well, so far. Or maybe they were all deeply in love and I was feeling bitchy. Maybe.

The foursome parted like water around a stone, revealing a woman. The couples came back together on the other side of her, laughing as if they hadn't seen her. Which they probably hadn't.

I felt it now, a faint stirring in the cold air. A sensation that had nothing to do with the wind. She was pretending to be unseen. Until the couples had noticed her, by not noticing her, I hadn't noticed her, either. Which meant she was good. Very, very good.

She stood under the last streetlight. Her hair was butter yellow and thick with waves. Longer than mine, nearly to her waist. The coat she wore, buttoned all the way up, was black. The color was too harsh for her. It bleached the color from her skin even with makeup.

She stood in the center of the sidewalk, arrogant. She was about my size, not physically imposing. So why did she stand there as if nothing in the world could hurt her? Only three things give you that kind of confidence: a machine gun, stupidity, or being a vampire. I didn't see a machine gun, and she didn't look stupid. She did look like a vampire now that I realized what I was looking at. The makeup was good. It made her look almost alive. Almost.

She caught me staring at her. She stared back, trying to catch my eyes with her own, but I was an old hand at this little dance. Staring at someone's face while not staring at their eyes is a trick that gets easier with practice. She frowned at me. Didn't like the eyes not working.

I stood about two yards from her. Feet apart, as balanced as I was going to get in high heels. My hands were already out in the cold, ready to go for my gun if I had to.

Her power crept over my skin like fingers touching here and there, trying to find a weakness. She was very good, but she was also only a little over a hundred. A hundred years wasn't old enough to cloud my mind. All animators had a partial natural immunity to vampires. Mine seemed to be higher than most.

Her pretty face was blank with concentration like a china doll's. She flung a hand outward as if throwing something at me. I flinched, and her power caught me like an invisible wave, slamming into my body. It staggered me.

I pulled my gun. She didn't try and jump me. She tried to concentrate me out of it. She was at least two hundred years old. I'd underestimated her age by a century. I didn't make mistakes like that often. Her power beat along my skin like tiny clubs, but it never came close to touching my mind. I was almost as surprised as she looked when I pointed the gun at her. It had been too easy.

"Hey," came a voice from behind us. "Put the gun down, now!" A policeman, just when I needed one. I pointed the gun at the sidewalk.

"Put the gun on the sidewalk, right now," his voice growled out, and without turning around I knew his own gun was out. Cops take guns very seriously. I held the Browning out to my right, one-handed, left hand in the air, and squatted to lay the gun gently on the sidewalk.

"I do not need this interruption," the vampire said. I glanced up at her as I stood, slowly, putting my hands atop my head, fingers laced. Maybe I'd get points for knowing the drill. She was staring past me at the approaching cop. It wasn't a friendly look.

"Don't hurt him," I said.

Her eyes flicked back to me. "We are not allowed to attack the police." Her voice was thick with scorn. "I know the rules."

I wanted to say, "What rules?" but didn't. It was a good rule. The policeman could live with a rule like that. Of course, I wasn't a cop, and I was betting the rules didn't apply to me.

The cop came into view out of the corner of my eye. His gun was pointing at me. He kicked my gun out of reach. I saw it hit the building. A hand shoved into my back, getting my attention. "You don't need to know where the gun went."

He was right, for now. He frisked me one-handed. It wasn't very thorough, and I wondered where his partner was.

"Enough," the vampire said.

I felt the cop step back from me. "What's going on here?"

Her power slithered past me, like a great beast had brushed me in the dark. I heard the policeman gasp.

"Nothing is happening here," the vampire said. There was a flavoring of accent in her voice. German or Austrian, maybe.

I heard his voice say, "Nothing is happening here."

"Now go back to directing traffic," she said.

I turned, slowly, hands still on my head. The cop was standing there, face empty, eyes wide. His gun was pointed at the ground, as if he'd forgotten he was holding it.

"Go away," she said.

He stood there frozen. He was wearing his cross tie tack. He was wearing his blessed cross, just like he was supposed to, and it wasn't doing much good.

I backed away from both of them. If she stopped paying attention to the cop, I wanted to be armed. I lowered my arms slowly, watching the cop. If she took her control off suddenly, and I wasn't where I was supposed to be, he might shoot me. Probably not, but maybe. If he saw me with the gun in my hand a second time, almost certainly.

"I don't suppose you would remove his cross so I could order him about?"

My eyes flicked to the vampire. She was looking at me. The cop stirred, struggling like a dreamer in the grip of a nightmare. She turned her eyes back to him, and the struggles ceased.

"I don't think so," I said. I knelt, trying to keep my attention on both of them. I touched the Browning, and wrapped cold fingers around it. My hands were stiff from being exposed to the cold for so long. I wasn't sure how fast I could draw right at that moment. Maybe I should look into some gloves. Maybe ones with the fingertips cut out.

I shoved the Browning in my coat pocket, hand still gripping it. My hand would warm up, and I could shoot through my coat if I had to.

"Without the cross I could make him go away. Why can't I control you like that?"

"Just lucky, I guess."

Her eyes flicked to me. Again, he stirred. She had to stare at him while she talked to me. It was interesting to see how much concentration it took. She was powerful but it had its limits.

"You are the Executioner," she said.

"What of it?"

"I didn't believe the stories. Now I believe some of the stories."

"Bully for you. Now, what do you want?"

A slight smile curled her lipsticked mouth. "I want you to leave Jean-Claude alone."

I blinked, not sure I'd heard right. "What do you mean, leave him alone?"

"Don't date him. Don't flirt with him. Don't talk to him. Leave him alone."

"Glad to," I said.

She turned to me, startled. You don't get to surprise a two-hundred-year-old vamp often. Her face looked very human with its wide eyes and little *o* of surprise.

The cop gave a snort and looked around wildly. "What the hell?" He looked at both of us. We looked like two petite women out for the evening. He glanced down at his gun and seemed embarrassed. He didn't remember why it was out. He put the gun away, muttering apologies and backing away from us. The vampire let him go.

"You'd leave Jean-Claude alone, just like that?" she asked.

"You bet."

She shook her head. "I do not believe you."

"Look, I don't care what you believe. If you have the hots for Jean-Claude, more power to you. I've been trying to get him off my back for years."

Again that shake of the head, sending her yellow hair flying about her face. It was a very girlish gesture. It would have been cute if she hadn't been a corpse.

"You are lying. You desire him. Anyone would."

I couldn't argue that. "You got a name?"

"I am Gretchen."

"Well, Gretchen, I wish you joy of the Master. If you need any help sinking your fangs into him, let me know. I would love for him to find a nice little vampire to settle down with."

"You mock me."

I shrugged. "A little, but it's habit, nothing personal. I mean what I said. I don't want Jean-Claude."

"You don't think he's beautiful?" Her voice was soft with surprise.

"Well, yeah, but I think tigers are beautiful. I still don't want to sleep with one."

"No mortal could resist him."

"This one can," I said.

"Stay away from him, or I'll kill you," she said.

Gretchen wasn't listening to me, not really. She heard the words, but the meaning didn't sink in. Reminded me of Jean-Claude.

"Look, he chases me. I'll stay away from him if he'll let me. But don't threaten me."

"He's mine, Anita Blake. Come against me at your peril."

It was my turn to shake my head. Maybe she didn't know I had a gun pointed at her. Maybe she didn't know it had silver-plated bullets in it. Maybe she had lived for a couple of centuries and had grown arrogant. Yeah, that was probably it.

"Look, I don't have time for this right now. Jean-Claude is yours, great, fine. I'm thrilled to hear it. Keep him away from me, and I will be the happiest woman alive or dead." I didn't want to turn my back on her, but I had to go. If she wasn't going to jump me here and now, Dolph was waiting at a murder scene. I had to go.

"Gretchen, what are you and Anita talking about?" Jean-Claude stalked towards us. He was wearing, I kid you not, a black cape. It was a Victorian style with a collar. A top hat with a white silk band completed the look.

Gretchen gazed at him. It was the only word for it. The naked adoration in her face was sickening, and very human. "I wanted to meet my rival."

I wasn't her rival, but I didn't think she'd believe that.

"I told you to wait outside so you would not meet her. You knew that." The last three words were spat out, thrown at her like rocks.

She flinched. "I meant no harm this night."

That was almost a lie, but I didn't say anything. I could have told him that she'd threatened me, but somehow it seemed like tattling. She'd gone to a lot of trouble to get me alone. To warn me off. Her love for him was so naked. I could not enlist his help against her. Foolish, but true. Besides, I didn't like owing Jean-Claude favors.

"I'll leave you two lovebirds alone."

"What lies did you tell her about us?" His words scalded the air. I could feel myself choking on his rage. Jesus.

She fell to her knees, hands held upward, not to avoid a blow, but beseeching, reaching for him. "Please, I only wanted to meet her. To see the mortal that would steal you from me."

I did not want to see this, but it was like a car crash. I couldn't quite bring myself to leave.

"She steals nothing. I have never loved you."

The pain was raw on her face, and even under the makeup she looked less human. Her face was thinning out, bones growing more apparent, as if her skin were shrinking.

He grabbed her arm and pulled her roughly to her feet. His white-gloved fingers dug into her arm. If she'd been human, there would have been bruises. "Get hold of yourself, woman. You are losing control."

Her thinning lips drew back from fangs. She hissed at him, jerking free of his hand. She covered her face with hands that were almost claws.

I'd seen vampires show their true form, but never by accident, never in the open, where anyone might see. "I love you." The words came out muffled and twisted, but the feeling in those three words was very real. Very . . . human.

"Get out of sight before you disgrace us all," Jean-Claude said.

She raised a face that was no longer human to the light. The pale skin glowed with an inner light. The makeup sat on that glowing surface. The blush, eye shadow, lipstick seemed to float above the light, as if her skin would no longer absorb them. When she turned her head, I could see the bones in her jaws like shadows inside her skin. "This is not over between us, Anita Blake." The words fell out from between fangs and teeth.

"Leave us!" Jean-Claude's words were an echoing hiss.

She launched herself skyward, not a leap, not levitation, just upward. She vanished into the darkness with a backwash of wind.

"Sweet Jesus," I whispered it.

"I am sorry, *ma petite*. I sent her out here so this would not happen." He walked towards me in his elegant cape. A gust of icy wind whistled around the corner, and he had to make a grab for the top hat. It was nice to know that at least his clothing didn't obey his every whim.

"I've got to go, Jean-Claude. The police are waiting for me."

"I did not mean for this to happen tonight."

"You never mean for anything to happen, Jean-Claude. But it happens anyway." I put a hand up to stop his words. I didn't want to hear any more of them.

"I've got to go." I turned and walked towards my car. I transferred my gun back to its holster when I was safely across the icy street.

"I am sorry, *ma petite*." I whirled to tell him to get the hell away from me. He wasn't there. The streetlight glowed down on empty sidewalk. I guess he and Gretchen hadn't needed a car.

7

THERE IS A glimpse of stately old homes to the right just before you turn onto Highway 44. The houses hide behind a wrought-iron fence and a security gate. When the homes were built, they were the height of elegance and so was the neighborhood. Now the town houses are an island in a rising flood of project housing and dead-eyed children who shoot each other over a scuffed sneaker. But the old money stayed, determined to be elegant, even if it kills them.

In Fenton the Chrysler plant is still the largest employer. A side road runs past fast-food restaurants and local businesses. But the highway bypasses them all. A straight line going onward and not looking back. The Maritz building spans the highway with a covered crosswalk that looks big enough to hold offices. It gets your attention like an overly aggressive date, but I know the name of the business, and I can't say that about many other buildings along 44. Sometimes aggressive works.

The Ozark Mountains rise on either side of the road. They are soft and rounded. Gentle mountains. On a sunny autumn day, with the trees blazing color, the mountains are startling in their beauty. On a cold December night with only my own headlights for company, the mountains sat like sleeping giants pressing close to the road. There was just enough snow to gleam white through the naked trees. The black shapes of evergreens were permanent shadows in the moonlight. A limestone cliff shone white where the mountains had been cracked open for a gravel pit.

Houses huddled at the base of the mountains. Neat farmhouses with front porches just made for sitting on. Not-so-neat houses made of unpainted wood with rusty tin roofs. Corrals sat in empty fields without a farmhouse near. A single horse stood in the icy cold, head down searching the tops of the winter-killed grass. A lot of people kept horses out past Eureka—people who couldn't afford to live in Ladue or Chesterfield, where houses cost over half a mil a piece, but you did get barns, exercising pens, and a corral in your backyard. Here all you got was a shed, a corral, and miles to drive to visit your horse, but at least you had one. A lot of trouble to go to for a horse.

The white head of a road sign flashed in the headlights. I slowed down. A car had run into the pole and crumbled it like a broken flower stem. The sign was hard to read from a sixty-degree angle. Which was probably why Dolph had told me to look for the smashed sign rather than the street name.

I pulled onto the narrow road. In St. Louis we'd gotten about a three-inch snowfall. Here it looked more like six. The road hadn't been plowed. It angled sharply upward, climbing into the hills. Tire tracks like wagon wheels made two lines through the snow. The police cars had gotten up the hill. So could my Jeep. In my old Nova I might have been wading fresh snow in high heels. Though I did have a pair of Nikes in the trunk. Still, jogging shoes weren't a big improvement. Maybe I should buy a pair of boots.

It just didn't snow that much in St. Louis. This was one of the deepest snowfalls I'd seen in four years. Boots seemed sort of unnecessary.

The trees curled over the road, naked branches bouncing in the headlights. Wet, icy trunks bent towards the road. In summertime the road would be a leafy tunnel, now it was just black bones erupting from the white snow.

At the crest of the hill there was a heavy stone wall. It had to be ten feet tall, and effectively hid anything on the left-hand side of the road. It had to be the monastery.

About a hundred yards further there was a plaque set in the wall next to a spiked gate. St. Ambrose Monastery was done in raised letters, metal on metal. A driveway curved up and out of sight around a curve of hill. And just across from the entrance was a smaller gravel road. The car tracks climbed into the darkness ahead of me and vanished over the next hill. If the gate hadn't been there for a landmark, I might have missed it. It was only when I turned the Jeep to an angle that my lights caught the tire tracks leading off to the right.

I wondered what all the heavy traffic was up ahead. Not my problem. I eased onto the smaller road. Branches scraped at the Jeep, scratching down the gleaming paint job like fingernails on a chalkboard. Great, just great.

I'd never had a brand-new car before. That first ding, where I'd run over a snow-covered tombstone, had been the hardest. After the first damage the rest was easy to take. Riiight.

The land opened up to either side of the narrow road. A large meadow with winter-killed weeds waist high, weighted down with snow. Lightning flashes of red and blue strobed over the snow, chasing back the darkness. The meadow stopped abruptly in a perfect straight line where the mower had cut it. A white farmhouse, complete with screened-in porch, sat at the end of the road. Cars were everywhere, like a child's spilled toys. I hoped the road formed a turn around under the snow. If not, the cars were parked all over the grass. My grandmother Blake had hated it when people parked on the grass.

A lot of the cars had their motors running, including the ambulance. There were people sitting in the cars, waiting. But for what? By the time I got to a crime scene, all the work was usually done. Someone would be waiting to take the body away after I'd finished looking at it, but the crime-scene people should have been done and gone. Something was up.

I pulled in next to a St. Gerard County Sheriff car. One policeman was standing in the driver's side door, leaning on the roof. He'd been staring at the knot of men near the farmhouse, but he turned to stare at me. He didn't look happy with what he saw. His Smokey Bear hat shielded his face but left his ears and the back of his head open to the cold. He was pale and freckled and at least six foot two. His shoulders were very broad in his dark winter jacket. He looked like a large man who had always been large, and thought that made him tough. His hair was some pale shade that absorbed the colors of flashing lights, so his hair looked alternately blue and red. As did his face, and the snow, and everything else.

I got out of the car very carefully. Snow spilled in around my foot, soaking my hose, filling the leather pump. It was cold and wet, and I kept a death grip on the car door. High heels and snow do not mix. The last thing I wanted to do was fall on my ass in front of the St. Gerard County Sheriff Department. I should have just grabbed my Nikes from the back of the Jeep and put them on in the car. It was too late now. The deputy sheriff was walking very purposefully towards me. He had boots on and was having no trouble with the snow.

He stopped within reach of me. I didn't let strange men get that close to me normally but to back up I'd have to let go of the car door. Besides he was the police, I wasn't supposed to be afraid of the police. Right?

"This is police business, ma'am, I'll have to ask you to leave."

"I'm Anita Blake. I work with Sergeant Rudolf Storr."

"You're not a cop." He seemed very certain of that. I sort of resented his tone.

"No, I'm not."

"Then you're going to have to leave."

"Can you tell Sergeant Storr that I'm here . . . please." Never hurts to be polite.

"I've asked you real nice twice now to leave. Don't make me ask a third time."

All he had to do was reach out and grab my arm, shove me into the Jeep, and away we went. I certainly wasn't going to draw my gun on a cop with a lot of other cops within shouting distance. I didn't want to get shot tonight.

What could I do? I shut the car door very carefully and leaned against it. If I was careful and didn't move around too much, I might not fall down. If I did, maybe I could claim police brutality.

"Now, why did you do that?"

"I drove forty-five minutes and left a date to get here." Try to appeal to his better nature. "Let me talk to Sergeant Storr and if he says I need to leave, I'll leave."

"I don't care if you flew in from outta state. I say you leave. Right now."

He didn't have a better nature.

He reached for me. I stepped back, out of reach. My left foot found a patch of ice and I ended up on my ass in the snow.

The deputy looked sort of startled. He offered me a hand up without thinking about it. I climbed to my feet using the Jeep's bumper, moving farther away from Deputy Sullen at the same time. He figured this out. The frown lines on his forehead deepened.

Snow clung in wet clumps to my coat and glided in melting runnels down my legs. I was getting pissed off.

He strode around the Jeep.

I backpedaled using my hands on the car as traction. "We can play ring-around-the-Rosie if you want to, Deputy, but I'm not leaving until I've talked to Dolph."

"Your sergeant isn't in charge here." He stepped a little closer.

I backed away. "Then find someone who is."

"You don't need to talk to anyone but me," he said. He took three rapid steps towards me. I backed up faster. If we kept this up we'd be running around the car like a Marx brothers movie, or would that be the Keystone Kops?

"You're running from me."

"In these shoes, you've got to be kidding."

I was almost around the back of the Jeep, we'd be back where we started soon. Over the crackle of police radios you could hear angry voices. One of them sounded like Dolph. I wasn't the only one having trouble with the local cops. Though I seemed to be the only one being chased around a car.

"Stop, right where you are," he said.

"If I don't?"

He unclicked the flap on his holster. His hand rested on the butt of his gun. No words necessary.

This guy was crazy.

I might be able to get to my gun before he could draw his, but he was a cop. He was supposed to be one of the good guys. I try not to shoot the good guys. Besides, try explaining to other cops why you shot a cop. They get testy as hell about stuff like that.

I couldn't draw my gun. I couldn't outrun him. Arm wrestling seemed to be out. I did the only thing I could think of. I yelled "Dolph, Zerbrowski! Get your butts over here."

The shouting stopped as if someone had clicked a switch. Silence and the crackle of radios were the only sounds. I glanced towards the men. Dolph was glancing my way. At six foot eight inches, Dolph towered over everyone else. I waved a hand at him. Not frantically, but I wanted to be sure he saw me.

The deputy drew his gun. It took everything I had not to go for mine. But this bugnut was looking for an excuse. I wasn't going to give it to him. If he shot me anyway, I was going to be pissed.

His gun was a .357 Magnum, great for whale hunting. It was overkill for anything on two legs. That was human. I felt very human staring down that gun barrel. My eyes flicked up to his face. He wasn't frowning anymore. He looked very determined, and very sure of himself, as if he could pull the trigger and not get caught.

I wanted to yell for Dolph again, but didn't. The fool might pull the trigger. At this distance with that caliber of weapon I was dead meat. All I could do was stand there in the snow, my feet going slowly numb, hands gripping the car. At least he hadn't asked me to put my hands up. Guess he didn't want me to fall down again until he splattered my brains all over the new paint job.

It was Detective Clive Perry who walked towards us. His dark face reflected the lights like ebony. He was tall, though not as tall as the deputy from hell. His slender frame was enclosed in a pale camel's-hair coat. A hat that matched it perfectly sat atop his head. It was a nice hat and couldn't be pulled low enough to cover his ears. Most nice hats couldn't be. You had to get a toboggan hat, something knit that would ruin your hair to keep your ears warm. Not stylish. Of course, I wasn't wearing a hat at all. Didn't want to muss my hair.

Dolph had gone back to yelling at someone. I couldn't tell exactly what color uniform he was yelling at, there were at least two flavors to choose from. I caught a glimpse of a wildly gesturing arm, the rest of the man lost behind the small crowd. I'd never seen anybody wave their fists in Dolph's face. When you're six foot eight and built like a wrestler, most people are a little afraid of you. Probably wise.

"Ms. Blake, we're not quite ready for you," Perry said.

He always called everyone by title and last name. He was one of the most polite people I'd ever met. Soft-spoken, hardworking, courteous, so what had he done to end up on the Spook Squad?

The squad's full title was the Regional Preternatural Investigation Team. They handled all preternatural-related crime in the area. A sort of permanent floating special task force. I don't think anyone planned on the squad actually solving cases. Their success rate was high enough that Dolph had been invited to lecture at Quantico. Lecturing to the FBI's preternatural research branch was not shabby.

I kept staring at the deputy and his gun. I wasn't going to glance away a second time. I didn't really believe he'd shoot me, but I wasn't sure. There was something in his face that said he'd do it, that maybe he wanted to do it. You give some people a gun and they turn into bullies. Legally armed bullies.

"Hello, Detective Perry. The deputy here and I seem to have a problem."

"Deputy Aikensen, do you have your gun out?" Perry's voice was soft, calm, a voice to talk jumpers off of ledges, or madmen out of hostages.

Aikensen turned his head, glancing back at Perry. "No civilians allowed at a murder scene, sheriff's orders."

"I don't think Sheriff Titus meant for you to shoot the civilians, Deputy."

He glanced back at Perry. "You making fun of me?"

There was enough time. I could have pulled my gun. I wanted to shove it in his ribs. I wanted him disarmed, but I behaved myself. It took more willpower than was pretty, but I didn't draw my gun. I wasn't ready to kill the son of a bitch. If you draw guns, there is always the chance someone will end up dead. Unless you want someone dead, you don't draw, simple as that. But it hurt something deep down inside when the deputy turned back to me with his gun still out. So far my ego was taking a lot of bruising, but I could live with that, and so could Deputy Aikensen.

"Sheriff said I wasn't to let anybody but police into the perimeter."

"Perimeter" was a pretty fancy word for someone this stupid. Of course, it was a military term. He'd probably been dying to use it in conversation for years.

"Deputy Aikensen, this is our preternatural expert, Anita Blake."

He shook his head. "No civvies, unless the sheriff okays it."

Perry glanced back towards Dolph, and what I now assumed was the sheriff. "He's not even allowing us near the body, Deputy. What do you think the chances are of Sheriff Titus saying a civilian can see the body?"

Aikensen grinned then, most unpleasant. "Slim and none." He still held the gun very steady on the middle of my body. He was enjoying himself.

"Put the gun away and Ms. Blake will leave," Perry said.

I opened my mouth to say, The hell I will, but Perry gave a small shake of his head. I kept quiet. He had a plan, better than what I had.

"I don't take orders from no nigger detective."

"Jealous," I said.

"What?"

"That he's a big city detective and you're not."

"I don't have to take crap from you, either, bitch."

"Ms. Blake, please, let me handle this."

"You can't handle shit," Aikensen said.

"You've been totally uncooperative and rude, you and your sheriff. You can call me all the names you like, if that makes you feel better, but I can't let you point a gun at one of our people."

A look passed over Aikensen's face. I could see the thought flicker into life. Perry was a cop, too. He probably had a gun, and Aikensen had his back to him. The deputy whirled, bringing the gun up as he moved. His hand flexed.

I went for my gun.

Perry's empty hands were held out from his body, showing he was unarmed.

Aikensen was breathing hard. He raised the gun to head level, two-handed, steady, no hurry.

Someone noticed us and yelled, "What the fuck?" Indeed.

I pointed the Browning at Aikensen's back. "Freeze, Aikensen, or I will blow you away."

"You're not armed."

I clicked the hammer back. On a double-action you don't need to do that before you fire, but it makes a nice dramatic sound. "You didn't frisk me, asshole."

People were running towards us, shouting. But they wouldn't get here in time. It was just the three of us in the psychedelic snow, waiting.

"Put the gun down, Aikensen, now."

"No."

"Put it down or I'll kill you."

"Anita, you don't need to shoot. He's not going to hurt me," Perry said. It was the only time he'd ever used my first name.

"I don't need no nigger protecting me." His shoulders tensed. I couldn't see his hands well enough to be sure, but I thought he was pulling the trigger. I started to squeeze the trigger.

A bellowing voice yelled, "Aikensen, put that damn gun down!"

Aikensen pointed the gun skyward, just like that. He hadn't been pulling the trigger at all. He was just jumpy. I felt a giggle at the back of my throat. I'd almost shot him for being twitchy. I swallowed the laugh and eased off the trigger. Did Deputy Numb-nuts know how close he'd come? The only thing that had saved him was the Browning's trigger. It was stiff. There were a lot of guns out there where a tiny squeeze was all you needed.

He turned towards me, gun still out, but not pointed. Mine was still pointed. He started to lower his weapon to point it back at me. "If that barrel drops another inch, I'm going to shoot you."

"Aikensen, I said put the damn gun up. Before you get somebody killed." The man that went with the voice was about five foot six and must have weighed over two hundred pounds. He looked perfectly round like a sausage with arms and legs. His winter jacket strained over his round little tummy. A clear, grey stubble decorated his double chins. His eyes were small, nearly lost in the doughiness of his face. His badge glittered on his jacket front. He hadn't left it inside on his shirt. He'd pinned it outside, where the big city detectives couldn't miss it. Sort of like unzipping your fly so company could see you were well-endowed.

"This nigger . . ."

"We don't hold with talk like that, Deputy, you know that."

From the look on Aikensen's face you'd have thought the sheriff had told him there was no Santa Claus. I was betting the sheriff was a good ol' boy in the worst sense of the word. But there was intelligence in those beady little eyes, more than you could say for Aikensen.

"Put it away, boy, that's an order." His southern accent was getting thicker, either for show, or because he was getting teed off at Aikensen. A lot of people's accents got stronger under stress. It wasn't a Missouri accent. Something further south.

Aikensen finally, reluctantly, put up the gun. He didn't snap the holster closed, though. He was cruising for a bruising. I was just glad I hadn't been the one to give it to him. Of course if I'd pulled the trigger before Aikensen had raised his gun skyward, I'd never have known he wasn't pulling his trigger, too. If we'd all been cops with Aikensen as a criminal, it would have gone down as a clean shoot. Jesus.

Sheriff Titus put his hands in the pockets of his jacket and looked at me. "Now, miss, you can put your gun away, too. Aikensen here isn't going to shoot nobody."

I just stared at him, gun pointed skyward, held loose. I had been ready to put the gun away until he told me to do it. I'm not big on being told anything. I just stared at him.

His face still looked friendly, but his eyes lost their shine. Angry. He didn't like being defied. Great. Made my night.

Three other deputies gathered at Titus's back. They all looked sullen and ready to do anything their sheriff asked them to do. Aikensen stepped over to them, hand hovering near his freshly holstered gun. Some people never learn.

"Anita, put the gun away." Dolph's usual pleasant tenor was harsh with anger. Like what he wanted to say was shoot the son of a bitch, but it would be hard to explain to his superiors.

Though not officially my boss, I listened to Dolph. He'd earned it.

I put the gun away.

Dolph was made up of blunt angles. His black hair was cut very short, leaving his ears naked to the cold. His hands were plunged into the pockets of a long black trench coat. The coat looked too thin for the weather, but maybe it was lined. Though he was a little too bulky to leave room for him and a lining in the same coat.

He beckoned Perry and me to one side, and said softly, "Tell me what happened."

We did.

"You really think he was going to shoot you?"

Perry stared down at the trampled snow for a moment, then looked up. "I'm not sure, Sergeant."

"Anita?"

"I thought he was, Dolph."

"You don't sound sure now."

"The only thing I'm sure of is that I was going to shoot him. I was squeezing down on him, Dolph. What the hell is going on? If I end up killing a cop tonight, I'd like to know why."

"I didn't think anybody was stupid enough to pull a weapon," Dolph said. His shoulders hunched, the cloth of his coat straining to hold the movement.

"Well, don't look now," I said, "but Deputy Aikensen has still got his hand right over his weapon. He's just aching to draw it again."

Dolph drew a large breath in through his nose and let it out in a white whoosh of breath from his mouth. "Let's go talk to Sheriff Titus."

"We've been talking to the sheriff for over an hour," Perry said. "He isn't listening."

"I know, Detective, I know." Dolph kept walking towards the waiting sheriff and his deputies. Perry and I followed. What else could we do? Besides, I wanted to know why an entire crime-scene unit was standing around twiddling their thumbs.

Perry and I took a post to either side of Dolph, like sentries. Without thinking about it we were both a step back from him. He was, after all, our leader. But the automatic staging irked me. Made me want to step forward, be an equal, but I was a civvie. I wasn't equal. No matter how much I hung around or did, I wasn't a cop. It made a difference.

Aikensen's hand was gripping the butt of his gun tight. Would he actually draw down on all of us? Surely, even he wasn't that stupid. He was glaring at me, nothing but anger showed in his eyes. Maybe he was that stupid.

"Titus, tell your man there to get his hand away from his gun," Dolph said.

Titus glanced at Aikensen. He sighed. "Aikensen, get your damned hand away from your damn gun."

"She's a civilian. She drew on a policeman."

"You're lucky she didn't shoot your ass," Titus said. "Now, fasten the holster and tone it down a notch, or I'm going to make you go home."

Aikensen's face looked even more sullen. But he fastened his holster and plunged his hands into the pockets of his coat. Unless he had a derringer in his pocket, we were safe. Of course, he was just the sort of yahoo that would carry a backup weapon. Truthfully, sometimes so did I, but only when the alligator factor was high. Neck deep instead of ass deep.

Footsteps crunched through the snow behind us. I turned halfway so I could keep an eye on Aikensen and see the new arrivals.

Three people in navy blue uniforms came to stand on the other side of us. The tall man in front had a badge on his hat that said police chief. One of his deputies was tall, so thin he looked gaunt, and too young to shave. The second deputy was a woman. Surprise, surprise. I'm usually the only female at a crime scene. She was small, only a little taller than I, thin, with close-cropped hair hidden under her Smokey Bear hat. The only thing I could tell in the flashing lights was that everything on her was pale, from her eyes to her hair. She was pretty in a pixielike way, cute. She stood with her feet apart, hands on her Sam Brown belt. She was carrying a gun that was a little too big for her hands. I was betting she wouldn't like being called cute.

She was either going to be another pain in the ass, like Aikensen, or a kindred spirit.

The police chief was at least twenty years older than either deputy. He was tall, not as tall as Dolph, but then who was? He had a salt-and-pepper mustache, pale eyes, and was ruggedly handsome. One of those men who might not have been very attractive as a young man, but age had given his face character, depth. Like Sean Connery who was better looking at sixty than he had been at twenty.

"Titus, why don't you let these good people get on with their work? We're all cold and tired and want to go home."

Titus's small eyes flared to life. A lot of anger there. "This is county business, Garroway, not city business. You and your people are out of your jurisdiction."

"Holmes and Lind were on their way into work when the call came over the radio that somebody had found a body. Your man Aikensen here said he was tied up and couldn't get to the body for at least an hour. Holmes offered to sit with the body and make sure the crime scene stayed pure. My deputies didn't touch anything or do anything. They were just baby-sitting the crime scene for your people. What is wrong with that?" Garroway said.

"Garroway, the murder was found on our turf. It was our body to take care of. We didn't need any help. And you had no right to call in the Spook Squad without clearing it with me first," Titus said.

Police Chief Garroway spread his hands in a push-away gesture. "Holmes saw the body. She made the call. She thought the man hadn't been killed by anything human. Protocol is we call in the Regional Preternatural Investigation Team anytime we suspect supernatural activity."

"Well, Aikensen and Troy here don't think it was anything supernatural. A hunter gets eaten up by a bear and your little lady there jumps the gun."

Holmes opened her mouth but the chief held up a hand. "It's all right, Holmes." She settled back down, but she didn't like it.

"Why don't we ask Sergeant Storr here what he thinks killed the man?" Garroway said.

I was close enough to hear Dolph sigh.

"She had no right to let people near the body without us there to supervise," Titus said.

Dolph said, "Gentlemen, we have a dead body in the woods. The crime scene is not getting any younger. Valuable evidence is being lost, while we stand here and argue."

"A bear atttack is not a crime scene, Sergeant," Titus said.

"Ms. Blake is our preternatural expert. If she says it was a bear attack, we'll all go home. If she says it was preternatural, you let us do our job, and treat it as a crime scene. Agreed?"

"Ms. Blake, Ms. Anita Blake?"

Dolph nodded.

Titus squinted at me, as if trying to bring me into focus. "You're the Executioner?"

"Some people call me that, yeah."

"This little bit of a girl has over a dozen vampire kills under her belt?" There was laughter in his voice, disbelief.

I shrugged. It was actually higher than that now, but a lot of them were unsanctioned kills. Not something I wanted the police to know about. Vampires have rights, and killing them without a warrant is murder. "I'm the legal vampire executioner for the area. You got a problem with that?"

"Anita," Dolph said.

I glanced at him, then back at the sheriff. I wasn't going to say anything more, honest, but he did.

"I just don't believe a little thing like yourself coulda done all the things I've heard."

"Look, it's cold, it's late, let me see the body and we can all go home."

"I don't need a civilian woman to tell me my job."

"That's it," I said.

"Anita?" Dolph said. That one word told me not to say it, not to do it, whatever it was.

"We have licked enough jurisdictional butt for one night, Dolph."

A man appeared, offering us steaming mugs on a tray. The smell of coffee mingled with the scent of snow. The man was tall. There was a lot of that going around tonight. A lock of white-blond hair obscured one eye. He wore round metal-framed glasses that made his face look even younger than it was. A dark toboggan hat was pulled low over his ears. Thick gloves, a multicolored parka, jeans, and hiking boots completed his outfit. He didn't look fashionable but he was dressed for the weather. My feet had gone numb in the snow.

I took a mug of coffee gratefully. If we were going to stand out here and argue, hot anything sounded like a great idea. "Thanks."

The man smiled. "You're welcome." Everybody was taking a mug but not everybody was saying thank you. Where were their manners?

"I've been sheriff of this county since before you were born, Ms. Blake. It's my county. I don't need any help from the likes of you." He sipped his coffee. He had said thank you.

"The likes of me? What's that supposed to mean?"

"Let it go, Anita."

I looked up at Dolph. I didn't want to let it go. I sipped at the coffee. The smell alone made me feel less angry, more relaxed. I stared into Titus's little piggy eyes and smiled.

"What's so funny?" he asked.

I opened my mouth to say, you, but the coffee man interrupted. "I'm Samuel Williams. I'm the caretaker here. I live in the little house behind the nature center. I found the body." He held his now-empty tray down at his side.

"I'm Sergeant Storr, Mr. Williams. These are my associates, Detective Perry, and Ms. Blake."

Williams dunked his head in acknowledgment.

"You know all of us, Samuel," Titus said.

"Yes, I do," Williams said. He didn't seem too excited about knowing them all.

He nodded at Chief Garroway and his deputies. "I told Deputy Holmes that I didn't think it was a natural animal. I still don't, but if it is a bear, it slaughtered that man. Any animal that'll do that once will do it again." He looked down at the snow, then up, like a man rising from deep water. "It ate parts of that man. It stalked him and treated him like a prey animal. If it really is a bear, it needs to be caught before it kills somebody else."

"Samuel here has a degree in biology," Titus said.

"So do I," I said. Of course, my degree was in preternatural biology, but hey, biology is biology, right?

"I'm working on my doctorate," Williams said.

"Yeah, studying owl shit," Aikensen said.

It was hard to tell, but I think Williams blushed. "I'm studying the feeding habits of the barred owl."

I had a degree in biology. I knew what that meant. He was collecting owl shit and regurgitated pellets to dissect. So Aikensen was right. Sort of.

"Will your doctorate be in ornithology or strigiology?" I asked. I was proud of myself for remembering the Latin name for owls.

Williams looked at me with a sense of kinship in his eyes. "Ornithology."

Titus looked like he'd swallowed a worm. "I don't need no college degree to know a bear attack when I see it."

"The last reported bear sighting in St. Gerard County was in 1941," Williams said. "I don't think there's ever been a bear attack reported." The implication just sat there. How did Titus know a bear attack from beans if he'd never seen one?

Titus threw his coffee out on the snow. "Listen here, college boy—"

"Maybe it is a bear," Dolph said.

We all looked at him. Titus nodded. "That's what I've been saying."

"Then you better order up a helicopter and get some dogs out here."

"What are you talking about?"

"An animal that'd slice up a man and eat him might break into houses. No telling how many people the bear might kill." Dolph's face was unreadable, just as serious as if he believed what he was saying.

"Now, I don't want to get dogs down here. Start a panic if people thought there was a mad bear loose. Remember how crazy everyone got when that pet cougar got loose about five years ago. People were shooting at shadows."

Dolph just looked at him. We all looked at him. If it was a bear, he needed to treat it like a bear. If it wasn't . . .

Titus shifted uncomfortably in his heavy boots in the snow. "Maybe Ms. Blake ought to have a look." He rubbed the cold tip of his nose. "Wouldn't want to start a panic for the wrong reasons."

He didn't want people to think there was a rampaging bear on the loose. But he didn't mind people thinking there was a monster on the loose. Or maybe Sheriff Titus didn't believe in monsters. Maybe.

Whatever, we were on our way to the murder scene. Possible murder scene. I made everyone wait while I put on my Nikes and the coveralls that I kept for crime scenes and vampire stakings. Hated getting blood on my clothes. Besides, tonight the coveralls were warmer than hose.

Titus made Aikensen stay with the cars. Hoped he didn't shoot anybody while we were gone.

8

I DIDN'T SEE the body at first. All I saw was the snow. It had pooled into a deep drift in one of those hollows that you find in the woods. In spring the holes fill with rain and mud. In fall they pile deep with leaves. In winter they hold the deepest snow. The moonlight carved each footprint, every scuff mark into high relief. Every print filled like a cup with blue shadows.

I stood at the edge of the clearing staring down at the mishmash of tracks. Somewhere in all this were the murderer's tracks, or a bear's tracks, but unless it was an animal I didn't know how anyone was going to figure out which tracks were significant. Maybe all crime scenes were tracked up this much, the snow just made it obvious. Or maybe this scene had been screwed over. Yeah.

Every track, cop or not, led to one thing—the body. Dolph had said the man had been sliced up, eaten. I didn't want to see it. I'd been having a very good time with Richard. A pleasant evening. It wasn't fair to end the night by looking at partially eaten bodies. Of course, the dead man probably thought being eaten hadn't been much fun either.

I took a deep breath of the cold air. My breath fogged as I exhaled. I couldn't smell the body. If it'd been summer, the dead man would have been ripe. Hurrah for the cold.

"You planning to look at the body from here?" Titus said.

"No," I said.

"Looks like your expert is losing her nerve, Sergeant."

I turned to Titus. His round, double-chinned face was smug, pleased with itself.

I didn't want to see the body, but losing my nerve, never. "You better hope this isn't a murder scene . . . Sheriff, because it has been fucked twenty ways to Sunday."

"You're not helping anything, Anita," Dolph said softly.

He was right, but I wasn't sure I cared. "You got any suggestions for preserving the crime scene, or can I just march straight in like the fifty billion people before me?"

"There were only four sets of footprints when I was ordered to leave the scene," Officer Holmes said.

Titus frowned at her. "When I determined it was an animal attack, there was no reason to keep it secure." His southern accent was getting thicker again.

"Yeah, right," I said. I glanced at Dolph. "Any suggestions?"

"Just walk in, I don't think there's much to preserve now."

"You criticizing my men?" Titus said.

"No," Dolph said, "I'm criticizing you."

I turned away so Titus wouldn't see me smile. Dolph doesn't suffer fools gladly. He'll put up with them a little longer than I will, but once you've reached his limit, run for cover. No bureaucratic ass will be spared.

I stepped into the hollow. Dolph didn't need my help to hand Titus his head on a platter. The snow collapsed at the edge of the hole. My feet slid on the leaves underfoot. I ended on my butt for the second time to-night. But I was on a slope now. I slid almost all the way to the body. Laughter bubbled up behind me.

I sat on my ass in the snow and stared at the body. They could laugh all they wanted; it was funny. The dead man wasn't.

He lay on his back in the snow. The moonlight shone down on the body, reflecting on the snow, and giving the luster of midday to objects below. I had a penlight in one of the coverall's pockets, but I didn't need it. Or maybe didn't want it. I could see enough, for now.

Ragged furrows ran down the right side of his face. One claw had sliced over the eye, spilling blood and thick globs of eyeball down his cheek. The lower jaw was crushed, as if some great hand had grabbed it and squeezed. It made the face look unfinished, only half there. It must have hurt like hell, but it hadn't killed him. More's the pity.

His throat had been torn out; that had probably killed him. The flesh was just gone. His spine shone a dull white, like he'd swallowed a ghost and it hadn't gotten away. His camouflage coveralls were ripped away from his stomach. Some trick of the moonlight threw a thick shadow inside that ripped cloth. I couldn't see the damage inside. I needed to.

I prefer night kills. Darkness steals the color. Somehow it just isn't as real at night. Shine some light on it and the colors explode: the blood is crimson; the bone sparkles; fluids are not just dark but green, yellow, brown. Light lets you differentiate. A mixed blessing, at best.

I slipped the surgical gloves on. They were a cool second skin. Even riding in my inner pocket, the gloves were cooler than my skin. The penlight snapped on. Its tiny yellowish beam was dimmed by the bright moonlight, but cut through the shadows like a knife. The man's clothing had been peeled away like the layers of an onion; coveralls, pants and shirt, thermal underwear. The flesh was torn. The light glinted on frozen blood and gobbets of icy flesh. Most of the internal organs were gone. I shone the light on the surrounding snow, but there was nothing to see. The flesh, organs, were gone.

The intestine had leaked dark fluid all over the cavity, but it was frozen solid. I smelled no odor as I leaned over. Cold was a wonderful thing. The edges of the wound were ragged. No knife had done this. Or if it had, it was like no blade I'd ever seen. The medical examiner could tell for sure. A rib had been broken. It pointed upward like an exclamation mark. I shone the light on the bone. It was chipped, but not claws, not hands . . . teeth. I would have bet a week's pay that I was looking at tooth marks.

The throat wound was crusted with frozen snow. Reddish ice crystals had frozen to his face. The remaining eye was frozen shut with bloody ice. There were tooth marks at each side of the throat wound, not claws. The crushed jaw bore clear imprint of teeth. It certainly wasn't human teeth. Which meant it wasn't ghouls, vampires, zombies, or any other human undead. I had to hike my coat up to fish the tape measure out of the coverall pocket. It would have looked better if I'd taken the time to unbutton my coat, but, hey, it was cold.

The claw marks on the face were wide ripping things. Wider than a bear's claws, wider than anything natural. Monstrously large. There was a nearly perfect imprint of teeth on either side of the jaw. As if the creature had bitten down hard, but not tried to tear. Biting to crush, biting to . . . stop the screaming. Can't make a lot of noise with the entire bottom half of your mouth crushed. There was something very deliberate about that one bite. The throat was torn away, but again not as bad as it could be. Just enough to kill. It was only when you got to the stomach that the creature had lost control. The man was dead before the stomach was opened. I'd have bet on that. But the creature took the time to eat the stomach. To feed. Why?

There was an imprint in the snow, near the body. The imprint showed where people had knelt in it, me included, but the light picked up blood drained into the snow. He'd been facedown when someone rolled him over.

The footprints had tracked through nearly every inch of snow except for the blood splatters. Given a choice, people won't walk through blood. Crime scene or not. There wasn't nearly as much blood as you'd expect. Slicing a throat is messy business. But, of course, this throat hadn't been sliced. It had been ripped out by teeth. The blood had gone into the mouth, not onto the snow.

The blood had soaked into the clothing. If we could find our creature, it would be covered in blood, too. The snow was surprisingly clean for the amount of carnage. There was a thick pool of blood to one side, at least a yard from the body, but right next to the body-size impression. The dead man had lain by that stain long enough to bleed quite a bit, then been rolled over on its stomach, where it had lain long enough for the skin to freeze to the snow. More blood had pooled underneath the body while it lay facedown. Now here the body lay faceup, but no fresh blood. The body hadn't been turned over the last time until after he was very dead.

I called up, "Who rolled the body over?"

"It was just like that when I came on the scene," Titus said.

"Holmes?" Chief Garroway made her name a question.

"He was faceup when we got here."

"Did Williams move the body?"

"I didn't ask," she said.

Great. "Someone moved him. It'd be good to know if it was Williams."

"I'll go ask him," Holmes said.

"Patterson, you go with her," Titus said.

"I don't need . . ."

"Holmes, just go," Garroway said.

The two deputies left.

I went back to looking at the body. Had to think of it as a body, couldn't call it a "him." If I did that, I'd begin to wonder if he had a wife, kids. I didn't want to know. It was just a body, so much meat. Don't I wish.

I shone the penlight on the mishmashed snow. I stayed on my knees, nearly crawling on the snow. Me and Sherlock Holmes. If the creature had come up behind the man, there should have been some mark in the snow. Maybe not a whole print but something. Every print I found wore shoes. Whatever had done this hadn't worn shoes. Even with a herd of squabbling cops trampling through there should have been some imprint of claws and animal tracks. I couldn't find any. Maybe the crime techs would have better luck. I hoped so.

If there were no prints, could it have flown in? A gargoyle, maybe? It was the only large winged predator that attacked man. Except for dragons, but they weren't native to this country, and it would have been a hell of a lot messier. Or maybe a lot neater. A dragon would simply have swallowed the man whole.

Gargoyles will attack and kill a man, but it's rare. Besides the nearest pack was in Kelly, Kentucky. The Kelly gargoyles were a small subspecies that had attacked people but never killed. They were mostly carrion eaters. In France there were three species of gargoyles that were man-sized or better. They'd eat you. But there'd never been anything that large in America.

What else could it be? There were a few lesser eastern trolls in the Ozarks, but not this close to St. Louis. Besides I'd seen pictures of troll kills, and this wasn't it. The claws were too curved, too long. The stomach looked like it had been cleaned out by something with a muzzle. Trolls looked frightfully human, but then they were primates.

A lesser troll wouldn't attack a human if it had a choice. A greater mountain troll might have, but they had been extinct for more than twenty years. Also they had a tendency to snap off trees and whap people to death, then eat them.

I didn't think it was anything as exotic as trolls or gargoyles. If there'd been tracks leading up to the body, I'd have been sure it was a lycanthrope kill. Trolls had been known to wear castoff clothing. So a troll could have tramped through the snow, or a gargoyle could have flown up, but a lycanthrope . . . they had to walk on naked feet that wouldn't fit any human shoe. So how?

I would have slapped my forehead, but didn't. If you do that at murder scenes, you got blood in your hair. I looked up. Humans almost never look up. Millions of years of evolution had conditioned us to ignore the sky. Nothing was big enough to take us from above. But that didn't mean something couldn't jump on us.

A tree branch snaked out over the hollow. The penlight picked out fresh white scars against the black limb. A shapeshifter had crouched on the bark, waiting for the man to walk underneath. Ambush, premeditation, murder.

"Dolph, could you come down here a minute?"

Dolph walked carefully down the snow-covered slope. Didn't want to repeat my performance, I guess. "You know what it is?"

"Shapeshifter," I said.

"Explain." He had his trusty notebook out, pen poised. I explained what I'd found. What I thought.

"We haven't had a rogue lycanthrope since the squad was formed. Are you sure about this?"

"I'm sure it's a shapeshifter, but I didn't say it was a lycanthrope."

"Explain."

"All lycanthropes are shapeshifters by definition, but not all shapeshifters are lycanthropes. Lycanthropy is a disease that you catch from surviving an attack or getting a bad batch of lycanthropy vaccine."

He looked at me. "You can get it from the vaccine?"

"It happens."

"Good to know," he said. "How can you be a shapeshifter and not a lycanthrope?"

"Most often an inherited condition. The family guardian dog, beast, giant cat. Mostly European. One person a generation has the genes and changes."

"Is that tied to the moon like normal lycanthropy?"

"No. A family guardian comes out when the family needs it. War, or some kind of physical danger. There are swanmanes. They are tied to the moon, but it's still an inherited condition."

"That it?"

"You can be cursed, but that's really rare."

"Why?"

I shrugged. "You've got to find a witch or something with magic powerful enough to curse somebody with shapeshifting. I've read spells for personal shapeshifting. The potions are so full of narcotics that you might believe you were an animal. You might also believe you were the Chrysler building, or you might just die. Real spells for it are a lot more complex and usually require a human sacrifice. A curse is a step up from a spell. It's not really a spell at all."

I tried to think how to explain it. In this area Dolph was the civvie. He didn't know the lingo. "A curse is like the ultimate act of will. You just gather all your power, magic, whatever, and focus it on one person. You will them to be cursed. You always do it in person, so they know it's been done. Some theories think it takes the victim's belief to make a curse work. I'm not sure I buy that."

"Are witches the only people that can curse people?"

"Occasionally somebody will run afoul of a fairy. One of the old Daoine sidhe, but you'd have to be in Europe for that. England, Ireland, parts of Scotland. In this country it'd be a witch."

"So a shapeshifter, but we don't know what kind or even how they got to be a shapeshifter."

"Not from a few marks and tracks, no."

"If you saw the shifter face-to-face could you tell what kind they were?"

"What animal?" I asked.

"Yeah."

"Nope."

"Could you tell if they'd been cursed or if it was a disease?"

"Nope."

He just looked at me. "You're usually better than this."

"I'm better with the dead, Dolph. Give me a vamp or a zombie and I'll tell you their Social Security number. Some of that is natural talent, but a lot of it is practice. I haven't had as much experience with shapeshifters."

"What questions can you answer?"

"Ask and find out," I said.

"You think this is a brand-new shapeshifter?" Dolph asked.

"Nope."

"Why not?"

"The first time you change on the night of the full moon. It's too early for a brand-new shifter. But it could be a second, or third month, but . . ."

"But what?"

"If this is still a lycanthrope that can't control itself, that kills indiscriminately, it should still be here. Hunting us."

Dolph glanced out into the darkness. He held his notebook and pen in one hand, right hand free for his gun. The movement was automatic.

"Don't sweat it, Dolph. If it was going to eat more people, it would have taken Williams or the deputies."

His gaze searched the darkness, then came back to me. "So the shapeshifter could control itself?"

"I think so."

"Then why kill the man?"

I shrugged. "Why does anyone kill? Lust, greed, rage."

"The animal form used as a murder weapon then," Dolph said.

"Yeah."

"Is it still in animal form?"

"This was done by a half-and-half form, sort of a wolfman."

"A werewolf."

I shook my head. "I can't tell what sort of animal it is. The wolfman was just an example. It could be any sort of mammal."

"Just a mammal?"

"These wounds, yeah. I know there are avian weres, but they don't do this sort of damage."

"So werebirds?"

"Yeah, but that's not what did this."

"Any guesses?"

I squatted beside the body, stared at it. Willed it to tell me its secrets. Three nights from hence, when the soul had finally flown far away, I might have tried to raise the man and ask what did this. But his throat was gone. Even the dead can't talk without the proper equipment.

"Why did Titus think it was a bear kill?" I asked.

Dolph thought about that for a minute. "I don't know."

"Let's ask him."

Dolph nodded. "Be my guest." He sounded just a wee bit sarcastic. If I'd been arguing with the sheriff for hours, I'd have been a large chunk o' sarcastic.

"Come on, Dolph. We can't know less than we do right now."

"If Titus has any say in it, we might."

"Do you want me to ask him or not?"

"Ask."

I called up to the waiting men. "Sheriff Titus."

He looked down at me. He'd gotten out a cigarette but hadn't lit it yet. He paused with a lighter halfway to his mouth. "You want something, Ms. Blake?" The cigarette bobbed in his lips as he spoke.

"Why do you think this is a bear attack?"

He snapped the lid on his lighter, and took the unlit cig out of his mouth with the same hand. "Why do you want to know?"

I wanted to say, just answer the damn question, but I didn't. Brownie point for me. "Just curious."

"It wasn't a mountain lion. A cat would have used its claws more. Scratched him up some."

"Why not a wolf?"

"Pack animal. Looks like only one animal to me."

I had to agree with all the above. "I think you've been holding out on us, Sheriff. You seem to know a lot about animals that aren't native to this area."

"I go hunting now and then, Ms. Blake. Need to know the habits of your prey if you want to bag one."

"So a bear by process of elimination?" I asked.

"You might say that." He put the cig back in his mouth. Flame flared, pulsing against his face. When he flipped the lighter closed, the darkness seemed thicker.

"What do you think it was, Ms. Expert?" The smell of his cigarette carried on the cold air.

"Shapeshifter."

Even in the darkness I could feel the weight of his eyes. He blew a ghostly cloud of smoke moonward. "You think so."

"I know so," I said.

He gave a sharp *hmph* sound. "Awful sure of yourself, ain't ya?"

"You want to come down here, Sheriff. I'll show you what I've found."

He hesitated, then shrugged. "Why not?" He came down the slope like a bulldozer, heavy boots forming snowy wakes. "Okay, Ms. Expert, dazzle me."

"You are a pain in the ass, Titus."

Dolph sighed a white cloud of breath.

Titus thought that was real funny, laughed, doubled over, slapping his leg. "You are just a laugh a minute, Ms. Blake. Now, tell me what you got."

I did.

He took a long drag on his cig. The end flared bright in the darkness. "Guess it wasn't a bear, after all."

He wasn't going to argue. Bliss. "No, it wasn't."

"Cougar?" he said, sort of hopefully.

I stood carefully. "You know it wasn't."

"Shapeshifter," he said.

"Yeah."

"There hasn't been a rogue shapeshifter in this county for ten years."

"How many did it kill?" I asked.

He took in a lungful of smoke and blew it out slowly. "Five."

I nodded. "I missed that case. It was before my time."

"You'da been in junior high when it happened?"

"Yeah."

He threw his cigarette in the snow and ground it out with his boot. "I wanted it to be a bear."

"Me, too," I said.

9

THE NIGHT WAS a hard, cold darkness. Two o'clock is a forsaken time of night, no matter what the season. In mid-December two o'clock is the frozen heart of eternal night. Or maybe I was just discouraged. The light over the stairs leading up to my apartment shone like a captured moon. All the lights had a frosted, swimming quality. Slightly unreal. There was a haze in the air, like an infant fog.

Titus had asked me to stick around in case they found someone in the area. I was their best bet for figuring out if the person was a lycanthrope or some innocent schmuck. Beat the heck out of cutting off a hand to see if there was fur on the inside of the body. If you were wrong, what did you do, apologize?

There had been some lycanthrope tracks leading up to the murder scene. Plaster casts had been made, and at my suggestion, copies were being sent to the biology department at Washington University. I had almost addressed it to Dr. Louis Fane. He taught biology at Wash U. He was one of Richard's best friends. A nice guy. A wererat. A deep, dark secret that might be jeopardized if I started addressing lycanthrope paw prints to him. Addressing it to the entire department pretty much guaranteed Louie would see it.

That had been my greatest contribution of the night. They were still searching when I drove off. I had my beeper on. If they found a naked human in the snow, they could call. Though if my beeper went off before I got some sleep, I was going to be pissed.

When I shut my car door, there was an echo. A second car door slammed shut. I was tired, but it was automatic to search the small parking lot for that second car. Irving Griswold stood four cars down, bundled in a Day-Glo orange parka with a striped muffler trailing around his neck. His brown hair formed a frizzy halo to his bald spot. Tiny round glasses perched on a button nose. He looked jolly and harmless, and was a werewolf, too. Seemed to be my night for it.

Irving was a reporter on the *St. Louis Post-Dispatch*. Any story about me and Animators, Inc., usually had his byline on it. He smiled as he walked towards me. Just your friendly neighborhood reporter. Yeah, right.

"What do you want, Irving?"

"Is that any way to greet someone who has spent the last three hours in his car waiting for you?"

"What do you want, Irving?" Maybe if I just kept repeating the question over and over, I'd wear him down.

The smile faded from his round little face. He looked solemn and worried. "We've got to talk, Anita."

"Will this be a long story?"

He seemed to think about that for a moment, then nodded. "Could be."

"Then come upstairs. I'll fix us both some real coffee."

"Real coffee as opposed to fake coffee?" he asked.

I started for the stairs. "I'll fix you a cup of java that'll put hair on your chest."

He laughed.

I realized I'd made a pun and hadn't meant to. I know Irving is a shapeshifter. I've even seen his wolf form. But I forget. He's a friend and doesn't seem the least preternatural in human form.

We sat at the small kitchenette table, sipping vanilla nut creme coffee. My suit jacket was draped over the back of the kitchen chair. It left my gun and shoulder holster exposed. "I thought you were on a date tonight, Blake."

"I was."

"Some date."

"A girl can never be too careful."

Irving blew on his cup, sipping it delicately. His eyes had flicked from side to side, taking in everything. Days from now he'd be able to describe the room completely, down to the Nike Airs and jogging socks in front of the couch.

"What's up, Irving?"

"Great coffee." He wouldn't meet my eyes. It was a bad sign.

"What's wrong?"

"Has Richard told you anything about Marcus?"

"Your pack leader, right?"

Irving looked surprised. "He told you?"

"I found out tonight that your alpha is named Marcus. There's a battle of succession going on. Marcus wants Richard dead. Richard says he won't fight him."

"Oh, he fought him, all right," Irving said.

It was my turn to be surprised. "Then why isn't Richard pack leader?"

"Richard got squeamish. He had him, Blake, claws at Marcus's throat." Irving shook his head. "He thought when Marcus recovered they could talk, compromise." He made a rude sound. "Your boyfriend is an idealist."

Idealist. It was almost the same thing as fool. Jean-Claude and Irving agreed. They didn't agree on much.

"Explain."

"You can move up in the pack hierarchy by fighting. You win, you go up a notch. You lose, you stay where you are." He took a long sip of coffee, eyes closed as if drinking in the warmth. "Until you fight for pack leader."

"Let me guess. It's a fight to the death."

"No killie, no new leader," he said.

I shook my head, coffee sitting untouched in front of me. "Why are you telling me all this, Irving? Why now?"

"Marcus wants to meet you."

"Why didn't Richard tell me that himself?"

"Richard doesn't want you involved."

"Why not?" Irving kept answering my questions, but the answers weren't helping much.

Irving shrugged. "Richard won't give Marcus a freaking inch. If Marcus said black, Richard would say white."

"Why does Marcus want to see me?"

"I don't know," Irving said.

"Yeah, right."

"Honest, Blake, I don't know what's going on. Something big is up, and no one's talking to me."

"Why not? You're a shapeshifter."

"I'm also a reporter. I made the mistake years back of printing an article. The lycanthrope I talked to lied, said he never gave me permission to quote him. He lost his job. Some of the others wanted to out me, too, let me lose my job." He huddled around his coffee mug. Eyes distant with remembering. "Marcus said no, said I was more valuable to them as a reporter. No one's really trusted me since."

"Not a forgiving bunch," I said. I sipped my coffee and found it cooling. If I drank it fast enough, it would be drinkable, barely.

"They never forgive and they never forget," Irving said.

Sounds like a bad character trait, but it's one of my founding principles, so I couldn't complain much. "So Marcus sent you out here to talk to me. About what?"

"He wants to meet you. To talk some kind of business."

I got up and refilled my mug. A little less sugar this time. I was beginning to wake up just from frustration. "Let him make an appointment to come to my office."

Irving shook his head. "Marcus is some hotshot surgeon. You know what would happen if even a hint of what he is got out?"

I could understand that. You might get away with being a shapeshifter on some jobs. Doctor was not one of them. There was still the dentist in Texas that was being sued by a patient. Said she contracted lycanthropy from him. Nonsense. You didn't get it from having human hands in your mouth. But the case hadn't been thrown out. People didn't have a lot of sympathy for fur balls treating their kid's sparkling teeth.

"Okay, send someone else to the office. Surely, Marcus must trust someone."

"Richard has forbidden anyone to contact you."

I just looked at him. "Forbidden?"

Irving nodded. "Anyone lower in the pack order contacts you at their peril."

I started to smile and stopped. He was serious. "You're not kidding."

He raised a three-fingered salute. "Scout's honor."

"So how come you're here? You looking to move up in the pack?"

He paled. Honest to God, he paled. "Me? Fight Richard? Hell no."

"Then Richard won't mind you talking to me?"

"Oh, he'll mind."

I frowned. "Is Marcus going to protect you?"

"Richard gave a specific order. Marcus can't interfere."

"But he ordered you to come see me," I said.

"Yep."

"What's to stop Richard from busting your chops about this?"

Irving grinned. "I thought you'd protect me."

I laughed. "You son of a bitch."

"Maybe, but I know you, Blake. You won't like that Richard's been keeping things from you. You certainly won't like him protecting you. Besides, I've been your friend for years. I don't think you'll stand by while your boyfriend beats the hell out of me."

Irving knew me better than Richard did. It was not a comforting thought. Had I been fooled by a handsome face, a nice sense of humor? Had I not seen the real Richard? I shook my head. Could I be fooled that completely? I hoped not.

"Do I have your protection?" He was still smiling, but there was something in his eyes. Fear, maybe.

"You need me to say it out loud for it to be official?"

"Yeah."

"That a rule in the lycanthrope underground?"

"One of them," he said.

"You have my protection, but I want information in return."

"I told you I don't know anything, Blake."

"Tell me what it's like to be a lycanthrope, Irving. Richard seems determined to keep me in the dark. I don't like being in the dark."

Irving smiled. "I heard that."

"You be my guide to the world of the furry, and I'll keep Richard off your back."

"Agreed."

"When does Marcus want to meet?"

"Tonight." Irving had the grace to look embarrassed.

I shook my head. "No way. I'm going to bed. I'll meet with Marcus tomorrow, but not tonight."

He looked down into his coffee, fingertips touching the mug. "He wants it to be tonight." He looked up at me. "Why do you think I've been camped out in my car?"

"I am not at the beck and call of every monster in town. I don't even know what Fur Face wants to meet about." I leaned back in the chair and crossed my arms. "No way am I going out tonight to play with shapeshifters."

Irving squirmed in his chair, rotating the coffee cup slowly on the table. He wouldn't meet my eyes again.

"What's wrong now?"

"Marcus told me to set up a meeting with you. If I refused, he'd have me . . . punished. If I come here, Richard gets pissed. I'm trapped between two alpha males, and I ain't up to it."

"Are you asking me to protect you from Marcus, as well as Richard?"

"No," he said, shaking his head, "no. You're good, Blake, but you aren't in Marcus's league."

"Glad to hear it," I said.

"Will you meet with Marcus tonight?"

"If I say no, do you get in trouble?"

He stared into his coffee. "Would you believe no?"

"Nope."

He looked at me, brown eyes very serious. "He'll get mad, but I'll live."

"But he'll make you hurt." It wasn't a question.

"Yeah." That one word so soft, so tentative. It wasn't like Irving.

"I'll see him on one condition. That you're present at the meeting."

His face bloomed into a grin that spread from pole to pole. "You are a true friend, Blake." All the sadness was gone, washed away in the rosy glow of finding out what the hell was going on. Even ass deep in alligators, Irving was a reporter. It was who and what he was, more than the lycanthropy.

The smile alone was worth a meeting. Besides, I wanted to know if Richard was really in danger. Meeting the man who was threatening him was the only real way to find out. Also, I didn't really care for someone threatening one of my friends. Silver-plated bullets only slowed down a vampire, unless you can take out the head and heart. Silver bullets will kill a werewolf, no second chances, no healing, just dead.

Marcus might remember that. If he pushed it, I might even remind him.

10

IRVING HAD CALLED Marcus from my apartment. Again Irving didn't know why, all he did know was Marcus said to call before we came. I went into the bedroom. Hung up my dry-clean-only suit, and changed clothes. Black jeans, red polo shirt, black Nikes with a blue swoosh, and real socks. I abandoned jogging socks for everyday wear once winter set in.

I reached for the bulky green sweater I had laid out on the bed. I hesitated. It wasn't the fact that the sweater had stylized Christmas trees on it, and it might not be the coolest thing to wear. I didn't give a damn about that. I was debating on whether to carry a second gun. A fashion accessory nearer and dearer to my heart than any piece of clothing.

No lycanthrope had threatened me yet, but ol' Gretchen the vamp had. She might not be a master vampire but she was close. Besides, the memory of the cop taking the Browning away was still fresh. I had too many preternatural enemies to go unarmed. I got out my Uncle Mike's sidekick inner-pants holster. A comfy fit that didn't ruin the line of your jeans unless someone was really looking.

My main backup gun is a Firestar 9mm. Small, light, pretty to look at, and I could wear it at my waist and still be able to sit down. The sweater hung to midthigh. The gun was invisible unless you frisked me. The gun was set in front, ready for a cross-draw. Probably wouldn't need it. Probably.

The sweater bulked up around the straps of the shoulder holster. I've seen people wear shoulder rigs underneath bulky sweaters or sweatshirts, but you lose a few seconds groping under the cloth. I'd rather look less than fashion perfect and live.

The sweater was too long for my leather jacket, so I was back in my black trench coat. Me and Phillip Marlowe. I didn't take any extra ammo. I figured twenty-one rounds was enough for one night. I even left my knives at home. I almost talked myself out of the Firestar. I usually didn't start carrying two guns until after people had tried to kill me. I shrugged. Why wait? If I didn't need it, I'd feel silly tomorrow. If I did need it, I wouldn't feel silly at all.

Irving was waiting for me. Sitting on the couch like a good little boy. He looked like a schoolboy whom the teacher had made stand in the corner.

"What's wrong?"

"Marcus wanted me to just give you directions. He doesn't want me at the meeting. I said, you wouldn't come without me. That you didn't trust him." He looked up at me. "He's pretty pissed."

"But you stood your ground," I said.

"Yeah."

"Why don't you sound happier about that?"

He shrugged. "Marcus in a bad mood is not a pleasant experience, Blake."

"I'll drive, you give directions."

"Marcus said we both should drive. He said that I'd need to stay after the meeting, for a little talk."

"Come on, Irving, I'm driving, you're giving directions, and when I leave, you leave."

"I appreciate the offer, Blake, but you don't want Marcus mad at you."

"If I'm protecting you from Richard, I might as well throw in Marcus."

He shook his head. "No, you follow my car." He held up a hand. "No more arguing, Blake. I am a werewolf. I have to live in the community. I can't afford to make a stand against Marcus, not over one little talk."

I wanted to argue some more, but I didn't. Irving knew his problems better than I did. If fighting Marcus over this would make things worse, then I'd let it go. But I didn't like it.

The Lunatic Cafe was located in University City. Its sign was a glowing crescent moon with the restaurant name done in soft blue neon. Except for the name, and the nifty sign, the place didn't look much different from all the other shops and restaurants in the college district.

It was Friday night and there was no parking. I was beginning to think Marcus would have to come out to my car, when a wine dark Impala pulled out of the two spaces it had been hogging. My Jeep slipped in with room for a second car on one side.

Irving waited in front of the restaurant. His hands were shoved deep into his pockets. The ridiculous muffler trailed nearly to the ground. He looked distracted and not a bit happy.

I walked towards him with the trench coat flapping around me like a cape. Even like this, most people wouldn't see the gun. They'd see a small woman with a bright Christmas sweater. People see what they expect to see most of the time. The people that I was wearing the gun for would notice, and know I was armed.

Irving pushed the door in without a word. Irving, quiet? I didn't like seeing him subdued, almost beaten, like a kicked dog. It made me not like Marcus, and I hadn't even met him.

Noise poured around us just inside the door. A murmur of voices so thick it was like ocean noise. Silverware clinked, someone laughed high and bright like a hand rising from the noise, to be swallowed back again and lost. There was a bar along one wall, polished dark wood, old and lovingly cared for. The rest of the room held small, round tables that could comfortably seat about four. Every seat was full, and then some. Three doorways opened up; one beside the bar, one to the right, one in the middle. More tables were shoved into the smaller rooms.

The cafe had started life as someone's home. We were standing in the living room. Through the doorways leading to the other rooms were open archways, as if someone had knocked down a few walls. Even with that, the place was claustrophobic. People were three deep at the bar waiting for a table. The place was jammed to bursting with happy, smiling people.

One of the women behind the bar came around, wiping her hands on a towel tucked into the tie of her apron. She gave a wide, welcoming smile. She had a pair of menus in her one hand.

I started to say, but we don't need . . . when Irving gripped my arm. Tension vibrated through his hand. He'd grabbed my right arm. I turned to tell him not to do that, but the look on his face stopped me. He was staring at the smiling woman as if she had sprouted a second head. I turned back to the woman, and looked at her. Really looked at her.

She was tall, slender, with long, straight hair. It was a rich, reddish auburn that gleamed under the lights. Her face was a soft triangle, chin maybe a little too pointed, but overall she was lovely. Her eyes were a strange amber-brown that matched her hair perfectly.

Her smile widened, just a lift of lips. I knew what I was looking at. Lycanthrope. One that could pass for human. Like Richard.

I looked out over the room, and realized why it felt so tight. It wasn't just the crowd. A majority of the happy, smiling people were shapeshifters. Their energy burned in the air like the weight of a thunderstorm. I had thought the crowd was boisterous, too loud, but it was the shapeshifters. Their energy boiled and filled the room, masquerading as the energy of any crowd. As I stood there at the door, a face lifted here and there. Human eyes looked at me, but the glance wasn't human.

The glance was considering, testing. How tough was I? How good would I taste? It reminded me of the way Richard had been watching the crowd at the Fox. I felt like a chicken at a coyote convention. I was suddenly glad of the second gun.

"Welcome to the Lunatic Cafe, Ms. Blake," the woman said. "I'm Raina Wallis, proprietor. If you'll follow me. Your party is waiting for you." She said it all with a smile and a warm glow in her eyes. Irving's grip on my arm was nearly painful.

I leaned into him, and whispered, "That's my right arm."

He blinked at me. His eyes flicked to the Browning, and he let go, muttering, "Sorry."

Raina leaned closer. Irving flinched. "I won't bite, Irving, not yet." She gave a low laugh that was rich and bubbling. The kind of laugh that was meant for bedrooms and private jokes. The laugh gave her eyes and body a different look. She suddenly seemed more voluptuous, more sensual than just a second ago. Nicely weird.

"Mustn't keep Marcus waiting." She turned and began threading her way through the tables.

I glanced at Irving. "Something you want to tell me?"

"Raina's our alpha female. If the punishment's going to be really bad, she does it. She's a lot more creative than Marcus."

Raina was motioning to us by the archway near the bar. Her lovely face was frowning, looking a little less lovely, and a lot more bitchy.

I patted his shoulder. "I won't let her hurt you."

"You can't stop it."

"We'll see," I said.

He nodded, but not as if he believed me. He started between the tables. I followed. A woman touched his hand as he walked past. Gave him a smile. She was about my size, and dainty, with straight black hair cut short that framed her face like black lace. Irving squeezed her fingers and kept walking. Her large, dark eyes met mine. The eyes told me nothing. They had smiled at Irving; for me they were neutral. Like the eyes of a wolf I'd seen once in California. I'd walked around a tree and there it had stood. I had never really understood what neutral meant until that moment. Those pale eyes stared at me, waiting. If I threatened it, it would attack. If I left it alone, it would run. My choice. The wolf hadn't given a damn which way it turned out.

I kept walking, but the space between my shoulder blades was itching. I knew if I turned around that nearly every eye would be on me, on us. The weight of their gaze was physical.

I had an urge to whirl and say boo, but fought it off. I had a feeling they were all staring at me with neutral inhuman eyes, and I didn't want to see it.

Raina led us to a closed door at the back of the dining room. She pushed it open and motioned us through with a theatrical wave of her arm. Irving just walked through. I walked through but kept my eyes on her. I was nearly close enough for her to have hugged me. Close enough that with her reflexes she could probably take me.

Lycanthropes are just faster than a normal human. It isn't mind tricks like with vampires. They are just flat out better. I wasn't sure how much better in human form, though. Staring up into Raina's smiling face, I wasn't sure I wanted to find out.

We stood in a narrow hallway. There was a door at either end, one showing the cold night through its glass window, the other closed, a question mark.

Raina closed the door behind us, leaning on it. She seemed to collapse against it, head hanging down, hair spilling forward.

"Are you all right?" I asked.

She took a deep, shuddering breath and looked up at me.

I gasped. I couldn't help myself.

She was gorgeous. Her cheekbones were high and sculpted. Her eyes wider and more centered in her face. She looked like what might have been her sister, a family resemblance but not the same person.

"What did you just do?"

She gave that rich, bedroom laugh again. "I am alpha, Ms. Blake. I can do a great many things that most shifters cannot."

I was willing to bet that. "You moved your bones around, on purpose, like do-it-yourself cosmetic surgery."

"Very good, Ms. Blake, very good." Her amber-brown eyes flashed to Irving. The smile left her face. "Do you still insist on this one being at the meeting?"

"Yes, I do."

Her lips pursed, as though she'd tasted something sour. "Marcus said to ask, then to bring you." She shrugged, and stood away from the door. She was taller by about three inches. I wished I'd paid more attention to her hands. Had they changed, too?

"Why the body sculpting?" I asked.

"The other form is my day form. This is real."

"Why the disguise?"

"In case I have to do something nefarious," she said.

Nefarious?

She stalked down the hall towards the other closed door. Her walk was a gliding, athletic movement like a big cat's. Or would that be big wolf's?

She knocked on the door. I heard nothing, but she opened the door. She stood there, arms crossed over her stomach, cradling her breasts, smiling at us. I was beginning not to like Raina's smiles.

The room was a banquet hall with cloth-covered tables grouped in a horseshoe. A raised platform with four chairs and a lectern closed the mouth of the horseshoe. Two men stood on the platform. One was at least six feet tall, slender but muscled like a basketball player. His hair was black, cut short with a matching finger-thin mustache and goatee beard. He stood with one hand gripping his opposite wrist. A jock pose. A bodyguard pose.

He wore a skintight pair of black jeans, and a sweater with a black-on-black design clung to wide shoulders. There was a fringe of dark chest hair just above the scooped neckline. Black tooled cowboy boots and a large blocky watch completed the badass look.

The other man was no more than five foot seven. His hair was that funny shade of blond that has brown highlights in it, but still manages to be blond. The hair was short but styled and blow-dried, and would have been lovely to look at if it had been a little longer. His face was clean-shaven, square jawed, with a dimple in his chin. The dimple should have made the face look fun, but it didn't. It was a face for rules. Those thin lips were built for saying, my way or else.

He wore a pale blue linen suit jacket over black pants. A pale blue turtleneck that matched the jacket to perfection completed the outfit. His shoes were black and polished to a shine.

It had to be Marcus. "Alfred." One word, but it was an order. The bigger man stepped-leaped off the platform. It was a graceful, bounding movement. He moved in a cloud of his own vitality. It rolled and boiled around him almost like heat rising off pavement. You couldn't see it with the naked eye, but you could sure as hell feel it.

Alfred came at me as though he had a purpose. I put my back to the wall, keeping Raina in sight, along with everybody else. Irving moved back with me. He stood a little away from all of us, but closer to me than anyone.

I put the trench coat back so the gun showed plainly. "Your intentions better be friendly, Alfred."

"Alfred," the other man said. One word, even the tone sounded the same, but this time Alfie stopped in his tracks. He stood, staring at me. His eyes weren't neutral, they were hostile. People don't usually dislike me on sight. But hey, I wasn't too thrilled with him, either.

"We have not offered you violence, Ms. Blake," Marcus said.

"Yeah, right. Alfie there is contained violence in motion. I want to know what his intentions are before he comes closer."

Marcus looked at me as if I'd done something interesting. "A very apt description, Ms. Blake. You can see our auras, then?"

"If that's what you want to call it," I said.

"Alfred's intentions are not hostile. He will merely search you for weapons. It is standard procedure for nonshifters. It is nothing personal, I assure you."

The very fact that they didn't want me armed made me want to keep my weapons. Stubbornness, or a strong survival instinct.

"Maybe I'd agree to being searched if you explained why I'm here first." Stall, until I could decide what to do.

"We don't discuss business in front of the press, Ms. Blake."

"Well, I'm not talking to you without him."

"I will not jeopardize all of us to satisfy idle curiosity." He was still standing on the platform like a general surveying his troops.

"The only reason I'm here at all is because Irving is a friend. Insulting him isn't going to endear you to me."

"I do not wish to endear myself to you, Ms. Blake. I wish your aid."

"You want my help?" I didn't try to keep the surprise out of my voice. He gave a brief nod.

"What kind of help?"

"He must leave."

"No," I said.

Raina pushed away from the wall and stalked around us, just out of reach, but circling like a shark. "Irving's punishment could begin now." Her voice was low and purring around the edges.

"I didn't know wolves purred," I said.

She laughed. "Wolves do a lot of things, as I'm sure you're aware."

"I don't know what you mean."

"Oh, come now, woman to woman." She leaned one shoulder against the wall, arms crossed, face friendly. I was betting she could bite my finger off and smile just like that the entire time.

She bent close as if we were sharing secrets. "Richard is as good as he looks, isn't he?"

I stared into her amused eyes. "I don't kiss and tell."

"I'll tell you my juicy tidbit, if you'll tell me yours."

"Raina, enough." Marcus had moved forward to the edge of the stage. He didn't look happy.

She gave him a lazy smile. She was baiting him more than me, and enjoying it very much.

"Irving must leave, and Alfred must search you for weapons. There is no negotiating those two points."

"I'll make you a deal," I said. "Irving leaves now, but he goes home. No punishment."

Marcus shook his head. "I have decreed he will be punished. My word is law."

"Who died and made you king?"

"Simon," Raina said.

I blinked at her.

"He fought and killed Simon. That's who died and made him pack leader."

Ask a silly question . . . "You want my help, Irving goes free and untouched. No punishment."

"Don't do this, Anita," Irving said. "You'll just make things worse."

Raina stayed leaning beside me. Just a little girl talk. "He's right, you know. Right now he's mine to play with, but if you make Marcus really angry he'll give him to Alfred. I'll torture his mind and body. Alfred will break him."

"Irving goes free, no punishment. I stay and let Alfred search me for weapons. Otherwise we walk."

"Not we, Ms. Blake. You are free to go, but Irving is mine. He will stay, and with or without you he will be taught his lesson."

"What did he do wrong?" I asked.

"That is our business, not yours."

"I'm not going to help you do shit."

"Then go," he leaped gracefully off the stage, walking towards us as he spoke, "but Irving stays. You are only among us for this one night. He must live with us, Ms. Blake. He cannot afford your bravado."

The last sentence brought him just a little behind Alfred. Close up there were fine lines around his eyes and mouth, a slackness to the skin of his neck and jaws. I added ten years to his age. Fifties.

"I can't leave Irving here, knowing what you'll do to him."

"Oh, you have no idea what we'll do to him," Raina said. "We heal so well." She pushed away from the wall and walked to Irving. She paced round him in a tight circle, shoulder, hip, brushing against him, here and there as she moved. "Even the weakest of us can take so very much damage."

"What do you want to guarantee Irving's safety?" I asked.

Marcus looked at me, face careful, neutral. "You promise to aid us, and let Alfred frisk you. He is my bodyguard. You must let him do his job."

"I can't promise to help you without knowing what it is."

"Then we have no bargain."

"Anita, I can take it, whatever they dish out. I can take it. I've done it before."

"You asked for my protection from Richard, just call it a package deal," I said.

"You asked her for her protection?" Raina stepped away from him, surprise plain on her pretty face.

"Just against Richard," Irving said.

"It's clever," Raina said, "but it does have certain implications."

"She's not a pack member. It only works on Richard because they're dating," Irving said. He looked a little worried.

"What implications?" I asked.

Marcus answered, "To ask pack members for their protection is to acknowledge they are of higher rank without having to fight them. If they give their protection, then you have agreed to help them fight their battles. If they are challenged you are honor bound to aid them."

I glanced at Irving. He looked ill. "She's not one of us. You can't hold her to the law."

"What law?" I asked.

"Pack law," Marcus said.

"I forfeit her protection," Irving said.

"Too late," Raina said.

"You place us in a quandary, Ms. Blake. A pack member has acknowledged you as higher rank than he is. Acknowledged you as dominant. By our laws we must accept that as binding."

"I can't be a pack member," I said.

"No, but you can be dominant."

I knew what the word meant in the real world. Marcus was using it as if it meant more. "What does it mean to be dominant?"

"It means you can stand as Irving's protector against all comers."

"No," Irving said. He brushed past Raina and stood in front of Marcus. He stood tall and stared him in the eye. It was not a submissive display.

"I won't let you use me like this. It's what you intended all along. You knew I'd ask her protection from Richard. You counted on it, didn't you, you smug bastard."

A low growl trickled out from between Marcus's perfect white teeth. "I would watch my tongue if I were you, youngling."

"If it offends you, I will cut it out." Alfred's first words were not comforting.

This was getting out of hand. "Irving is under my protection, Alfred. If I understand the law. You have to go through me to hurt Irving, is that right?"

Alfred turned cold, dark eyes to me. He nodded.

"If you kill me, then I can't help Marcus."

This seemed to puzzle the big fella. Great, confusion to my enemies.

Marcus smiled. "You have found a flaw in my logic, Ms. Blake. If you truly intend to protect Irving, to the letter of the law, then you would indeed die. No mere human could withstand one of us. Even the lowliest would kill you."

I let that comment go. Why argue when I was winning anyway?

"Since you cannot accept challenges, and you won't let us harm Irving, he is safe."

"Great, now what?"

"Irving can go, and he will not be harmed. You stay and hear our plea. You may decide to aid us or not, Irving will not suffer for your choice."

"That's mighty generous of you."

"Yes, Ms. Blake, it is." There was a look in his eyes that was very serious. Raina might play sadistic games. Alfred might hurt you in an eager rush. But Marcus, it was just business. He was a mob boss with fur.

"Leave us, Irving."

"I won't leave her."

Marcus turned on him with a snarl. "My patience is not endless!"

Irving dropped to his knees, head bowed, spine bent low. It was a submissive display. I grabbed Irving's arm, and lifted him to his feet. "Get up, Irving. The nice werewolf isn't going to hurt you."

"And why is that, Ms. Blake?"

"Because Irving's under my protection. If Alfred can't fight me, then you sure as hell can't."

Marcus threw back his head, and gave a sharp, barking laugh. "You are clever, and brave. Traits we admire." The laughter died from his face, lingering in his eyes like a pleasant dream. "Do not challenge me too openly, Ms. Blake. It wouldn't be healthy."

The last of the laughter died out of his eyes. I was left staring into human eyes, but there was no one home to talk to. It looked like a human being, talked like a human being, but it wasn't one.

I dug my fingers into Irving's parka-clad shoulder. "Go on, Irving. Get out of here."

He touched my arm. "I would never leave you in a tough spot."

"I'm safe tonight, you're not. Now go, please, Irving."

I watched the struggle on his face. But finally after another dirty look from Marcus, he left. The door closed and I was alone with three werewolves. Down from four. The night was looking up.

"Alfred must search you now."

So much for the night looking up. "Then do it," I said. I just stood there. I didn't put my arms out. I didn't lean against the wall. I wasn't going to help him, not unless he asked.

He took the Browning, then patted down my arms, legs, even the small of my back. He didn't pat down the front center of my body. Maybe he was being a gentleman, or maybe he was just careless. Whatever, he missed the Firestar. I had eight silver bullets and they didn't know it. The night was looking up.

11

MARCUS TOOK A seat on the platform. Alfred stood just behind him like a good bodyguard. "Join us, Ms. Blake. It may be a long meeting to stand through."

I didn't want to sit with Alfred at my back, so I moved to the last chair. The empty chair between us looked unsociable, but I was out of Alfred's reach. Safety before good manners.

Raina sat on Marcus's right, hand on his knee. Marcus sat in the same manner he did everything—rigid. Posture that would have made my Aunt Mattie proud. But he didn't move Raina's hand. In fact, he laid his hand over hers. Love? Solidarity? They didn't strike me as a really compatible couple.

A woman came through the door. Short blond hair styled and held in place with gel. Her business skirt suit was red with pinkish undertones, like a rose petal. Her white blouse had one of those blousy ties that made the suit seem feminine, and a little silly.

"Christine, it's good of you to come," Marcus said.

The woman nodded, and took the seat at the end of the horseshoe of tables, nearest the stage. "What choice did I have? What choice did you give any of us?" she asked.

"We must have a united front on this, Christine."

"As long as you're in charge, right?"

Marcus started to say more but the crowd was growing. People drifted through the door in ones, twos, threes. He let the argument go. They could argue later, and I was betting they would. The woman's complaint sounded like an old one.

I recognized one person. Rafael the Rat King. He was tall, dark, and handsome with short-cut black hair, strong Mexican features, and an arrogant expression. He would have looked as stern as Marcus except for his lips. They were soft and sensuous, and ruined some of the effect.

Rafael nodded at me. I nodded back. He had two wererats with him, in human form. I didn't recognize either of them.

There were about a dozen people sitting along the tables when Marcus stood and walked to the podium. "My friends, I have asked you here tonight to meet Anita Blake. The vampires call her the Executioner. I believe she can help us."

"What can a vampire hunter do for us?" This from a tall man who sat alone, chairs on either side acting as walls. He had short white hair, cut in a strange Mia Farrow sixties cut, but gentler. He wore a white dress shirt, pale pink tie, white sport jacket, and cream-colored pants. He looked like the Good Humor man with money. But he had a point.

"We don't need a human to help us." This from a man who sat with one other. He had hair cut just above his collar, so curly it looked like fur, or maybe . . . Naw. He had thick eyebrows over dark eyes, with heavy, sensual features. The Rat King's lips may have seemed kissable, but this man seemed made for nefarious deeds done in dark places.

His clothing matched his face. The boots that he had propped on the table were of soft, velvety leather. His pants were of shiny black leather. The shirt he was almost wearing was a muscle tank top that left most of his upper body bare. His right arm was covered from elbow to fingers in leather straps. The knuckles had spikes coming out of them. The hair on his chest was as curly and dark as the hair on his head. A black duster coat was thrown across the table beside him.

The woman on his right rubbed her cheek along his shoulder as if it were a cat scent marking. Long, dark hair formed waves around her shoulders. What I could see of her outfit looked tight, black, and mostly of leather.

"We are human here, Gabriel," Marcus said.

Gabriel made a rude noise. "You believe what you want to, Marcus. But we know what we are, and what she isn't." He pointed at me with his gauntleted fist. It didn't seem a particularly friendly gesture.

Rafael stood. The gesture stopped the argument. There was something about the way he stood there in his ordinary street clothes that made you stare at him as if he were wearing a crown. His presence was more commanding than that of a ton of black leather. Marcus made the lowest of growls. Too many kings in this room.

"Does Marcus speak for Anita Blake as he speaks for the wolves?"

"Yes," Marcus said. "I speak for Ms. Blake."

I stood up. "I don't know what's going on, but I can speak for myself."

Marcus turned like a small blond storm. "I am pack leader. I am law."

Alfred moved to face me, big hands flexing.

"Chill out, fur face. You're not my leader, and I'm not a pack member."

Alfred stalked forward. I hopped off the stage. I had the gun, but I might need it more later. If I drew it now, I might not have it later. He leaped off the stage, a high bounding as if he'd had a trampoline to jump from. I dropped to the ground and rolled. I felt the air of his passage. I ended up against the stage. I went for the Firestar, and he was on me. Faster than a speeding bullet, faster than anything I'd ever seen.

His hand gripped my throat and squeezed. His lips drew back from his teeth, and made a low, rolling growl, like the sound a Rottweiler would make.

My hand was on the Firestar, but I still had to lift up, point it, and pull the trigger. I'd never make it. He'd rip my throat out long before I could manage it.

He drew me to my feet using my throat as a handle. His fingers dug in just enough to let me feel the strength in his hands. All he had to do was clench his fist, and the front of my throat would come with it. I kept my hand on the Firestar. I'd be clinging to it when I died.

"Does Alfred fight your battles for you now?" It was Christine of the blousy tie. "Pack leaders must fight all challenges to their dominance personally or forfeit leadership. It's one of your own laws, Marcus."

"Do not quote my laws back to me, woman."

"She challenged your authority over her, not Alfred's. If he kills her, is he the new pack leader?" There was soft derision in her voice.

"Release her, Alfred."

Alfred's eyes flicked to Marcus, then back to me. His fingers tensed, digging in and raising me to my tiptoes.

"I said, let her go!"

He dropped me. I staggered back against the stage and aimed Firestar in one movement. It wasn't pretty, but the gun was out and pointed at Alfred. If he tried me again, I was going to kill him, and I'd enjoy it.

"I thought you checked her for weapons," Marcus said.

"I did." Alfred was backing away, hands held in front of him as if to ward off a blow.

I scooted along the stage so I could keep an eye on Marcus. I caught sight of Raina, still sitting, looking amused.

I backed away from everyone, working to put a wall at my back. If Marcus was faster than Alfred, I needed distance, like a hundred miles, but I'd have to settle for the far wall.

"Have him disarm her," Raina said. She sat there, legs crossed, hands resting on her knee, smiling. "It was Alfred's oversight. Let him correct it."

Marcus nodded. Alfred turned his eyes back to me.

I pressed my back more solidly into the wall, as if I could make a door if I pressed hard enough. Alfred stalked towards me, slow, like a movie maniac. I pointed the gun at his chest. "I will kill him," I said.

"Your little bullets cannot hurt me," Alfred said.

"Silver-plated Glaser safety rounds," I said. "It'll blow a hole in your chest big enough to put a fist through."

He hesitated. "I can heal any wound, even silver."

"Not if it's a killing blow," I said. "I take out your heart and you're dead."

He glanced back at Marcus. Marcus's face was all squeezed down with anger. "You let her bring a gun among us."

"If you're afraid of the gun, Marcus, take it away from her yourself." Christine again. This time I wasn't sure she was helping me.

"We intend you no harm, Ms. Blake. But I promised the others you would bring no weapons among us. I gave my word. If you will give Alfred your gun, this can end."

"No way."

"You are defying me, Ms. Blake. I cannot let anyone contest my authority." He had come to stand at the end of the stage, closest to me. He was closer to me than Alfred. I wasn't sure it was an improvement.

"You step off that stage and I'll shoot."

"Alfred." Just the name again, but it was enough. Alfred moved up beside him, eyes on Marcus's face. "Master?"

"Take it from her, Alfred. She cannot defy us."

"You're going to get him killed, Marcus."

"I don't think so."

Alfred took a step forward, in front of Marcus. His face was neutral, eyes unreadable. "This is a stupid thing to die over, Alfie."

"He gives orders. I obey. It is the way of things."

"Don't do this," I said.

Alfred took a step forward.

I took a slow, steadying breath. I had a peripheral sense of everyone else, but I was looking only at Alfred. At a spot in the center of his chest. "I am not bluffing."

I felt him tense, knew he was going to do it. He was confident that he could move faster than I could pull the trigger. Nothing was that fast. I hoped.

He leaped in that wide, arching roll that he'd used earlier. I dropped to one knee, aiming as I moved. The bullet hit him in midair. He jerked and crumbled to the floor.

The gunshot echoed into silence. I got to my feet, the gun still pointed at him. I eased forward. He never moved. If he was breathing, I couldn't see it. I knelt until the gun was shoved into the back of his spine. No movement. I felt for a pulse in his neck. Nothing. I pulled the Browning out of his waistband left handed. I kept the Firestar pointed at everybody. I wasn't as good left handed, and I didn't want to take the time to switch hands.

Marcus stepped off the stage. "Don't," I said. He froze, staring at me. He looked shocked, as if he hadn't thought I'd do it.

Rafael came up through the tables. "May I look at him?"

"Sure." But I backed away. Theoretically out of reach.

Rafael turned him over. Blood had pooled on the floor from the hole in his chest. Bright crimson rivulets trailed down his lips to mingle with his beard. Not faster than a speeding bullet, after all.

Marcus looked at me over the body. I had expected to see anger, but all I saw was pain. He mourned Alfred's passing. I may have pulled the trigger, but he had pushed Alfred into it. He knew it, I knew it. We all knew it.

"You didn't have to kill him," he said, softly.

"You gave me no choice," I said.

He glanced down at Alfred's body, then back to me. "No, I suppose I didn't. We killed him together, you and I."

"For future reference, so there will never be another misunderstanding between us, Marcus. I never bluff."

"So you said."

"But you didn't believe me."

He watched the blood spread across the floor. "I believe you now."

12

WE HAD A body on the ground. The age-old question remained. What do you do with a dead body? There was the traditional approach. "I'll call the cops," I said.

"No," Marcus said. That one word had more force in it than anything he'd said since Alfred hit the ground.

"He's dead, folks. If I'd hit him with a regular bullet he'd heal, but it was silver. We've got to call the cops."

"Are you so eager to go to jail?" This from Rafael.

"I don't want to go to jail, but I killed him."

"I think you had a little help on that." Christine had moved up beside us. She stood there in her rose-petal suit with her sensible black pumps, staring down at the body. A line of blood trickled towards her shoes. She had to see it, snaking its way towards her. She didn't move out of the way. The blood seeped around the toe of her shoe and kept going.

Raina came up behind Marcus. She put her arms around his shoulders, leaning her face against his neck, close enough to whisper in his ear. Those lips did not move, but it had been her one needling comment that had pushed things over the edge. One little remark.

Marcus rubbed his hand along her arm, lowering his face to kiss her wrist.

I looked around at them. Rafael was still kneeling by the body. A line of blood was making for the knee of his slacks. He stood up quickly, fingertips brushing the bloody floor. He raised the fingers to his mouth. I wanted to say, don't, but didn't. He stuck the fingers in his mouth and sucked them clean.

His dark eyes flicked to me. He lowered his hand as if he were embarrassed, as if I'd caught him in an intimate bodily function. Maybe I had.

The two leather-clad shapeshifters drifted up behind the tables, as if they'd circle me. I backed away. I still had the guns naked in my hands. The one with the spiked glove looked at me, a smile playing at the edge of his mouth. His eyes were a strange liquid grey. His curly black hair had fallen in a tangle over his eyes. They bore a startling luminosity peering from behind that black hair. He made no move to push his hair from his eyes. It would have driven me nuts. But then maybe I wasn't accustomed to staring out through fur.

He stepped closer to the body, which was closer to me. I raised the guns. At this range you didn't really have to aim. I did not feel more confident with a gun in each hand. Fact was, I felt silly, but I didn't want to lose the time to holster one of them. To holster the Firestar, I had to scoot my sweater up and shove the gun in the inner-pants holster. I could probably do it without glancing down, but I wasn't sure. Habit might take over. Like driving a car. You don't realize how long you glanced down until that semi truck looms into view. If Gabriel was as fast as Alfred, a fraction of a second would be enough.

His smile widened, the tip of his tongue traced his full lips. His gaze had heat in it. Nothing magical, just the heat that any man could put into his eyes. That look that said they were wondering what you looked like naked, and if you'd give a good blow job. Crude, but accurate. That look was not wanting to make love to anyone. The look was pure fucking. Even sex was too mild a term.

I fought the urge to turn away. I didn't dare take my eyes off of him. But I wanted to. My skin crawled under his gaze. I felt heat creeping up my face. I couldn't meet his eyes and not blush. My Daddy'd raised me better than that.

He took a step forward, a small movement, but it put him almost in arm's reach. With Alfred's body still warm, he was playing with me. I raised the guns a little more firmly, pointed at him. "Let's not do this again," I said.

"Gabriel, leave her alone," Christine said.

He glanced back at her. "|'Tyger! Tyger! burning bright/ In the forests of the night/ What immortal hand or eye/ Could frame thy fearful symmetry?'|"

"Stop it, Gabriel," she said. She was blushing. One stanza of Blake and she was embarrassed. Why that poem? A weretiger maybe? But who was the kitty cat? Maybe both.

He turned back to me. I watched something slide behind his eyes. Some streak of perversity that made him want to take that next step.

"Try me tonight, and you're going to join your friend on the floor."

He laughed, mouth wide, exposing pointed canines, top and bottom like a cat. Not fangs, but not human, either.

"Ms. Blake is under my protection," Marcus said. "You will not harm her."

"You let Alfred nearly throttle me, then you goad him into attacking me. I don't think much of your protection, Marcus. I think I do just fine on my own."

"Without those little guns you wouldn't be so tough." This from the brunette biker chick. Brave words, but she was standing on the other side of the little crowd.

"I'm not going to offer to arm wrestle you. I know I'm outclassed without a gun. That's why I've got them."

"You refuse my protection?" Marcus asked.

"Yeah," I said.

"You are a fool," Raina said.

"Maybe, but I'm still the one with the guns."

Gabriel laughed again. "She doesn't believe you can protect her, Marcus, and she's right."

"You question my dominance?"

Gabriel turned, giving me his back, staring at Marcus. "Always."

Marcus moved forward, but Raina tightened her grip on him. "We've aired enough dirty laundry in front of Ms. Blake for one night. Don't you think?"

He hesitated. Gabriel just stared at him. Finally Marcus nodded.

Gabriel gave a purring laugh and knelt down by the body. He smeared his fingers through the blood. "It cools so fast." He wiped his hand on Alfred's sweater and touched the open chest wound. He ran his hand around the edge as though he were scooping icing from a bowl. His hand came out crimson. He raised it to his mouth, blood dripping down his arm. His tongue licked along his bloody fingers.

"Stop it," Marcus said.

The woman knelt on the other side of the body. She knelt, lowering her torso, butt in the air, like lions drinking at watering holes. She lapped up the blood from the floor with quick, sure movements of her tongue.

"Jesus," I whispered.

There was movement in the room like a wind over a field of wheat. They were all out of their seats. They were all moving towards the body.

I stepped back, put the wall at my back, and began working my way towards the door. If there was going to be a feeding frenzy, I didn't want to be the only non-shapeshifter in the room. Didn't seem healthy.

"No!" Marcus's voice roared through the room. He stalked to the body, pushing everyone back without a gesture. Even Gabriel rolled back onto his left side, propped up, sitting in the blood. The woman crawled back, out of reach. Gabriel stayed within touching distance of the master werewolf. He gazed up at Marcus, but there was no fear on his face.

"We are not animals to feed on our dead."

"We are animals," Gabriel said. He raised his bloody hand towards Marcus. "Smell the blood, and tell me you don't want it."

Marcus jerked his head away, swallowing hard enough for me to hear it. Gabriel rose to his knees, pressing the blood close to Marcus's face.

He slapped the hand away, but stepped away from the body, too. "I smell the blood." His voice was very harsh when he said it, every word squeezed out through a low growl. "But I am a human being. That means I do not have to give in to my urges." He turned his back on the body, pushed his way through the crowd, having to step up on the stage to find a clear place to stand. His breathing was hard and fast, as if he'd been running as fast as he could.

I was about halfway behind the podium. I could see his face. Beads of sweat touched his skin. I had to get out of here.

The white-haired man who had spoken first, wondering what good a vampire executioner would be to them, was standing apart from the others. He was leaning against a table, arms crossed. He was watching me. From across the room, he could watch all he wanted to. I had the guns out and pointed at everybody. There wasn't anyone in this room that I wanted to be around unarmed.

I was almost at the door. I needed a free hand for the door. I was nearly the length of the room away from them. It was as far away as I could get without opening the door. I holstered the Firestar. Transferred the Browning to my right hand. I slid my left hand behind me along the wall, until I touched the doorknob. I turned the knob and opened the door a crack. I was far enough away from all of them, that I gave the room my back and opened the door wide. And stopped.

The hallway was four deep with lycanthropes. They were all staring at me with wide, haunted eyes. I pressed the Browning into the chest of the nearest one. "Back up."

He just stared at me as if he didn't understand what I'd said. His eyes were brown and perfectly human, but it reminded me of the look a dog gets when it's trying to understand English. It wants to understand, but just doesn't quite get it.

There was movement behind me. I slammed my back against the door, pressing it flat to the wall, gun scanning the room. If the shapeshifters in the hallway surged forward, I was gone. I could shoot some of them, but not all of them.

It was the man who'd been leaning against the table. He put his hands up to show himself unarmed, but that didn't really help. What helped was there was no sweat on his face. He didn't look glassy eyed, like the ones in the hall. He looked very . . . human.

"My name is Kaspar Gunderson. Do you need a little help?"

I glanced at the waiting horde and back to him. "Sure."

Kaspar smiled. "You'll take my help, but not Marcus's?" He seemed amused.

"Marcus doesn't offer help. He gives orders."

"Too true."

Rafael moved up beside him. "None of us takes orders from Marcus. Though he would like us to."

A sound somewhere between a moan and a howl broke from the crowd in the hall. I scooted a little farther down the wall, pointing the gun at the crowd. There were too many possible dangers, I had to pick someone to trust. Rafael and the other man seemed a better choice than the crowd.

A high ragged scream broke from inside the room. I shoved my back into the wall, and turned back to the room. What now?

I caught a glimpse of thrashing limbs through the huddled lycanthropes. The dark-haired woman threw back her head and shrieked.

"She's fighting it," the pale man said.

"Yes, but she will not win unless a dominant steps in to help her," Rafael said.

"Gabriel won't help."

"No," Rafael said, "he enjoys the show."

"It's not full moon yet, what the hell's happening?" I said.

"The scent of blood started it. Gabriel fed it. He and Elizabeth. Now, unless Marcus can control them, they may all turn and feed," Rafael said.

"And this is a bad thing?" I asked.

Rafael just looked at me. His hands gripped his forearms so tightly the skin paled. His short-clipped fingernails bit into the skin, and tiny little half circles of blood formed under his hands. He took a deep, cleansing breath and nodded. He removed his fingers from his arms. The cuts filled with blood but only a few trickled. Minor cuts, minor pain. Pain sometimes helped keep a vamp from controlling your mind.

His voice came out strained, but clear, each word pronounced with great care, as if it took great effort just to speak. "One of the old wives' tales that is true is that a lycanthrope has to feed after shapeshifting." His eyes stared at me, drowning deep. The black had eaten all the white. His eyes sparkled like jet buttons.

"Are you about to go all furry on me?"

He shook his head. "The beast does not control me. I control myself."

The other man stood there, calmly.

"Why aren't you having problems?"

"I'm not a predator. Blood doesn't bother me."

A whimper came in from the hallway. A young man who couldn't have been more than twenty was crawling on hands and knees into the room. A low whimper was rising from his throat like a mantra.

He raised his head, sniffing the air. His head turned with a jerk, eyes staring at me. He crawled towards me. His eyes were the color of spring skies, innocent as an April morning. The look in them was not. He looked at me as if he were wondering what I tasted like. In a human I'd have thought he was thinking of sex, now . . . maybe he was just thinking of food.

I pointed the gun at his forehead. His eyes looked past the gun, at me. I wasn't even sure he saw the gun. He touched my leg. I didn't shoot him. He hadn't offered to hurt me. I wasn't sure what the hell was going on, but I couldn't shoot him for touching me. Not just for that. He had to do something to deserve a bullet in the brain. Even from me.

I moved the gun slightly from side to side in front of his eyes. They didn't track.

His hands gripped my jeans, pulling him to his knees. His head was a little above my waist, blue eyes staring up at my face. His arms wrapped around my waist. He buried his face in my stomach, sort of nuzzling.

I tapped his head with the barrel of the gun. "I don't know you well enough for you to nuzzle me, fella. Get up."

His head buried under my sweater. His mouth bit gently into my side. He stiffened, arms rigid. His breathing was suddenly ragged.

And I was suddenly afraid. One man's foreplay was another man's appetizer. "Get him off of me before I hurt him."

Rafael yelled, voice roaring over the mounting chaos, "Marcus!" That one word rang out and silence fell. Faces turned to him. Faces smeared with blood. Elizabeth, the dark-haired woman, was nowhere in sight. Only Marcus remained clean. He stood on the stage rigid, but there was a vibration to him like a struck tuning fork. His face was gaunt with some great effort. He looked at us with the eyes of a drowning man, who was determined not to scream on the last trip down.

"Jason is having some difficulty controlling himself," Rafael said. "He is your wolf. Call him off."

Gabriel stood up, his face coated in blood. He bared his flashing teeth with a laugh. "I'm surprised Ms. Blake hasn't killed him yet."

Raina stood from the kill, a patch of blood on her chin. "Ms. Blake refused Marcus's protection. She is dominant. Let her discover what it means to refuse our help."

Jason was still rigid against me. His arms locked tight, face pressed against my stomach. I could feel his breath through my shirt, hot and too heavy for what was happening.

"You asked me here for my help, Marcus. Your hospitality sucks."

He glared at me. But even from across the room I could see a nervous tic jumping in his face. A twitching, as though something alive were trying to come out.

"It is too late for business tonight, Ms. Blake. Things are out of hand."

"No joke. Get him off of me, Marcus. One dead tonight is enough."

Raina went to him, holding up a bloody hand to him. "Let her acknowledge your dominance over her. Acknowledge that she needs your help."

Marcus stared at me. "Acknowledge my dominance, and I will call Jason off."

"If he starts to shapeshift, I'll kill him. You know I'll do it, Marcus. Call him off."

"If I am to give you my protection, you must acknowledge me."

"Fuck you, Marcus. I'm not asking you to save me. I'm asking you to save him. Or don't you care about your pack members?"

"Rafael is a king," Raina said, "let him save you."

A shudder ran through the man. His grip tightened painfully. He stood, arms still locked behind my back. If he'd held me any closer, I'd have come out the other side. He was about my height, which put our faces very close. His eyes were full of a great hunger, a need. He bent his head as if to kiss me, but another shudder ran through him. He buried his face in my hair, lips touching my neck.

I pressed the barrel of the Browning into his chest. If he tried to take a bite out of me, he was dead. But where Alfred had been a bully, this one, Jason, seemed unable to help himself, like a compulsion. If I waited too long I'd be just as dead. But until he hurt me it made me not want to hurt him. Besides, I was feeling a wee bit gun happy for killing Alfred. Not a lot, but a little. It cut Jason some slack.

His teeth brushed along my neck, drawing an edge of skin into his mouth. He had just about reached the end of my patience even if he didn't turn furry.

A low, rumbling growl vibrated along my skin. My pulse thudded into my throat. I squeezed down on the trigger. I couldn't wait for him to bite my throat out.

I heard Kaspar say, "Rafael, no!"

Jason's head jerked up, eyes wild. Rafael stood beside us, holding his arm in front of Jason's face. Blood ran down it from deep scratches.

"Fresh blood, my wolf," Rafael said.

Jason jerked away from me so fast, he threw me into the wall. My head smacked the wall after my shoulders made impact, which was the only thing that saved me from passing out. I ended up with my butt on the floor, gun in my hand only by instinct. The strength in that one movement left my gut hollow with fear. I had let him nuzzle my neck, as if he were human. He could have torn me apart with his human hands. I might have killed him first, but I'd have been just as dead.

Jason crouched in front of Rafael. A ripple ran through his back like a wave of water driven by wind. Jason fell into a little ball, his back pulsing under his shirt.

Rafael stood over him, blood dripping onto the floor. "I hope you understand what I have done for you," he said.

I had enough air back to speak. "You want me to shoot him?"

A strange look came over his face, leaving his black button eyes dead. "You offer your protection."

"Protection, smetection. You helped me. I'll help you."

"Thank you, but I have started it, and I must finish it, but I think you must go before you run out of silver bullets."

Kaspar offered me a hand up; I took it. His skin was unusually warm, but that was all. He didn't seem to have the urge to touch me or eat me. A nice change.

The crowd was coming in the door, in twos and threes and tens. Some moved like sleepwalkers towards the body at the far side of the room. That was dandy. Some went for Rafael and the writhing Jason. He'd said he could handle himself. But about six of them turned to me and Kaspar.

They stared at us with hungry eyes. One, a girl, dropped to her knees and began to crawl towards me. "Can you do anything about this?" I asked.

"I'm a swan, they consider me food."

It took every ounce of self-control not to glance at him. I stared at the crawling lycanthrope, and said, "A swan, great. You got any suggestions?"

"Wound one of them. They respect pain."

The girl was reaching out for me. I stared at her slender arm and didn't fire. Glazer safety rounds could take off an arm. I wasn't sure lycanthropes could heal amputations. I pointed over her head at the large male behind her. I gut-shot him. He fell screaming to the floor, blood pouring between his fingers. The girl turned on him, burying her face in his stomach.

He slapped her away. The others surged forward.

"Let's get out while we can," Kaspar said. He motioned for the door.

Didn't have to ask me twice. Marcus was suddenly there. I hadn't seen him come, too busy concentrating on the immediate threat. He pulled two men off the wounded one, tossing them like toys. He drew a manila file folder from under his blue linen jacket and handed it to me. In a voice that was more growl than anything, he said, "Kaspar can answer your questions."

He turned with a snarl, tearing into the lycanthropes, protecting the one I'd wounded. Kaspar pushed me out the door, and I let him.

I had one last glimpse of Jason. He was a mass of flowing fur and naked dripping bones. Rafael was once again the slick, black ratman I'd met months ago. The crown-shaped burn in his forearm, the mark of kingship for the rats, showed clean. He was no longer bleeding. The change had healed him.

The door slammed shut. I wasn't sure who had done it. Kaspar and I stood in the hallway, alone. There were no sounds from behind the door. The silence was so heavy, it thrummed in my head.

"I can't hear them?"

"Soundproof room," he said.

Logical. I stared down at the file folder. There was a bloody handprint on it. I held it gingerly at the edge, waiting for the blood to dry.

"Are we supposed to sit down and have a business meeting?"

"Knowing Marcus, the information will be complete. He's a very good bureaucrat."

"But not a very good pack leader."

He glanced at the door. "I'd say that somewhere else if I were you."

He had a point. I stared up at him. His baby-fine hair was nearly white, almost feathery. I shook my head. It couldn't be.

He grinned at me. "Go ahead. Touch it."

I did. I brushed fingers through his hair, and it was soft and downy like the under feathers on a bird. Heat rose from his scalp like fever. "Jesus."

Something heavy smacked into the door. I felt the vibrations through the floor. I backed away, hesitating about putting the Browning away. I compromised and put my hand in the pocket of my trench coat. It was the only coat I owned with pockets deep enough to swallow the Browning.

Kaspar opened the door to the dining rooms. There were still people eating. Humans out for a night on the town. Carving their steaks, eating their veggies, oblivious to the potential destruction just two doors away.

I had a horrible urge to yell, Flee, flee for your lives. But they wouldn't have understood. Besides the Lunatic Cafe had been here for years. I'd never heard of an incident here. Of course, I'd killed one man, werewolf, whatever. I didn't think there was going to be enough evidence to turn over to the cops. Maybe a few well-gnawed bones.

Who knew what disasters had been covered up here?

Kaspar handed me a business card. It was white and shiny with Gothic script that said, KASPAR GUNDERSON, ANTIQUES AND COLLECTIBLES.

"If you have any questions, I will try to answer them."

"Even if the questions are about what the hell you are?"

"Even that," he said.

We were walking as we talked. He offered me his hand beside the bar in the outer dining room. The outside door was in sight, fun almost over for the night. Thank God.

My smile froze on my face. I knew one of the men at the bar. Edward was sitting there sipping a tall, cold drink. He never glanced at me, but I knew he saw me. Kaspar cocked his head to one side. "Is anything wrong?"

"No," I said, "no." My words were too fast, even I didn't believe myself. I tried my best professional smile. "It's just been a long night."

He didn't believe me, and I didn't care. I wasn't good at spur-of-the-moment lying. Kaspar let it go, but his eyes scanned the crowd as he walked out, looking for whatever or whoever had bothered mc.

Edward looked like a nice, ordinary man. He was five foot eight, of slender build, with short blond hair. He had on a nondescript black winter jacket, jeans, and soft-soled shoes. He looked a little like Marcus, and in his own way, was just as dangerous.

He was ignoring me, effortlessly, which meant he might not want to be noticed. I walked past him, wanting to ask what the hell he was doing here, but not wanting to blow his cover. Edward was an assassin who specialized in vampires, lycanthropes, and other preternatural humanoids. He'd started out killing humans, but it had been too easy. Edward did love a challenge.

I stood in the cold dark wondering what to do. I had the bloody file folder in one hand. The other was still gripping the Browning. Now that the adrenaline was seeping away, my hand was cramping around the gun. I'd held it too long without firing it. I tucked the folder under my arm and put the gun away. All the shapeshifters were busy eating each other. I could probably walk to my car without having a gun naked in my hands.

Edward didn't come out. I had half expected him to. He was hunting someone, but who? After what I'd seen tonight, I wasn't sure hunting them was such a bad idea.

Of course, Richard was one of them. I didn't want anyone hunting him. I would have to ask Edward what he was doing, but not tonight. Richard wasn't inside. The rest of them could take their chances. I had a momentary thought about Rafael, but let it go. He knew what Edward looked like, if not exactly what he did for a living.

I stopped halfway down the sidewalk. Should I warn Edward that Rafael might recognize him and tell the others? My head hurt. For this one night let Death take care of himself. The vampires called me the Executioner, but they called Edward Death. After all, I'd never used a flamethrower on them.

I kept walking. Edward was a big, scary boy. He could take care of himself. And everyone else in the back room certainly didn't need my help.

Even if they did, I wasn't sure I wanted to give it to them. Which brought me back to the file folder. What could they need my help for? What could I do that they couldn't? I almost didn't want to know. But I didn't throw the folder in the nearest trash can. Truth was, if I didn't read it, it would bug me. Curiosity killed the cat. Here was hoping it didn't do the same for animators.

13

AT 5:35 THAT morning I was tucked in bed with the file folder. My favorite stuffed toy penguin, Sigmund, was sitting next to me. It used to be that I used Sigmund only when people were trying to kill me. Lately, I'd been sleeping with him most of the time. It'd been a rough year.

The Browning Hi-Power was in its second home, a holster on the headboard of the bed. I sometimes slept without the penguin, but never without the gun.

The folder consisted of a half dozen sheets of paper. All neatly typed, double spaced. The first was a list of eight names with an animal designation beside them. The last two pages were an explanation of the names. Eight lycanthropes had gone missing. Vanished. No bodies, no signs of violence. Nothing. Their families knew nothing. None of the lycanthropes knew anything.

I went back over the names. Margaret Smitz was number seven. Designation wolf. Could it be George Smitz's wife? Peggy was a nickname for Margaret. Don't ask me how you get Peggy from Margaret, but you do.

The last few pages were suggestions about who Marcus thought I should talk to. Controlling little bastard. He did offer an explanation for why he asked me for help. He thought that the other shapeshifters would talk more freely to me than to him or any of his wolves. No joke. I was sort of a compromise. They didn't trust the police. And who else do the lunarly disadvantaged go to for help? Why, your friendly neighborhood animator.

I wasn't sure what I could do for them. I had sent George Smitz to Ronnie for a reason. I was not a detective. I'd never handled a missing-person case in my life. When I met Ronnie the next day, cancel that, that morning, I'd fill her in. George's wife missing was one thing, but eight lycanthropes missing was a pattern. They needed to go to the police. But they didn't trust human law. As late as the 1960s, lycanthropes were still being mobbed and burned at the stake. Couldn't blame them for being leery.

I put the folder in the drawer of the nightstand. I got a plain white business card out of the drawer. The only thing on it was a phone number. Edward had given me the card only two months ago. It was the first time I'd ever been able to contact him. Before he'd just shown up. Usually when I didn't want him to.

The number was a twenty-four-hour phone message service. A mechanized voice said, "At the tone leave your message." A long, low beep sounded. "This is Anita. What the hell are you doing in town? Call me soon." I wasn't usually that blunt on a phone message, but hey, it was Edward. He knew me. Besides, he didn't appreciate social niceties.

I set the alarm, turned off the light, and cuddled into the blankets, my faithful penguin at my side. The phone rang before I'd gotten warm. I waited for the machine to pick up; after the eighth ring I gave up. I'd forgotten to turn on the machine. Great.

"This better be important," I said.

"You said to call soon." It was Edward.

I pulled the receiver under the blankets with me. "Hi, Edward."

"Hi."

"Why are you in town? And why were you at the Lunatic Cafe?"

"Why were you?"

"It is nearly six in the freaking morning, I haven't been to sleep yet. I don't have time for games."

"What was in the folder you had? There was fresh blood on it. Whose blood was it?"

I sighed. I wasn't sure what to tell him. He might be a great deal of help, or he could kill people that I was supposed to be helping. Choices, choices.

"I can't tell you shit until I know if I'm endangering people."

"I never hunt people, you know that."

"So you are on a hunt."

"Yes."

"What this time?"

"Shapeshifters."

Figures. "Who?"

"I don't have any names yet."

"Then how do you know who to kill?"

"I've got film."

"Film?"

"Come to my hotel room tomorrow and I'll show you the film. I'll tell you everything I know."

"You're not usually this obliging. What's the catch?"

"No catch. You might be able to identify them, that's all."

"I don't know a lot of shapeshifters," I said.

"Fine, just come, see what I have."

He sounded so sure of himself, but then he always did. "Okay, where are you staying?"

"Adams Mark. Do you need directions?"

"No, I can get there. When?"

"Do you work tomorrow?"

"Yeah."

"Then at your convenience, of course."

He was being too damn polite. "How long will your little presentation take?"

"Two hours, maybe less."

I shook my head, realized he couldn't see it, and said, "It'll have to be after my last zombie appointment. I'm booked until then."

"Name the time."

"I can be there between twelve-thirty and one." Even saying it made me tired. I wasn't going to get any sleep again.

"I'll be waiting."

"Wait. What name are you registered under?"

"Room 212, just knock."

"You do have a last name, don't you?"

"Of course. Good night, Anita." The phone line went dead, buzzing in my hand like an unquiet spirit. I fumbled the receiver into its cradle and switched on the answering machine. I turned the sound down as low as it would go and snuggled back under the covers.

Edward never shared information unless forced to. He was being too helpful. Something was up. Knowing Edward, it was something unpleasant. Lycanthropes disappearing without a trace. It sounded like a game that Edward would enjoy. But somehow I didn't think it was him. He liked taking credit for his kills as long as the police couldn't tie him to them directly.

But somebody was doing it. There were bounty hunters who specialized in rogue lycanthropes. Edward might know who they were and if they'd condone murder. Because if all eight were dead, then it was murder. None of them was wanted, as far as I knew. The police would know, but I wasn't going to involve the police. Dolph should know if lycanthropes were disappearing in his territory.

I felt sleep sucking at the edges of the world. I flashed on the murder victim. I saw his face frozen in the snow, one eye ripped open like a grape. The crushed jaw tried to move, to speak. One word hissed out of his ruined mouth: "Anita." My name, over and over. I woke up enough to roll over, and sleep washed over me in a heavy, black wave. If I dreamed again, I never remembered.

14

EVERY YEAR I wondered what to buy Judith, my stepmother, for Christmas. You'd think after fourteen years I'd get better. Of course, you'd think she'd get better at buying for me. Judith and I always end up staring at each other across this chasm of misunderstanding. She wants me to be this perfect feminine daughter, and I want her to be my dead mother. Since I can't have what I want, I've made sure Judith doesn't get her wish, either. Besides, she's got Andria, who is perfect. One perfect kid in the family is enough.

Ronnie and I were Christmas shopping. We had jogged on the slick wintery streets at nine that morning. I'd managed about three hours of sleep. The running helped. The freezing wind slapping my face helped even more. I was wide awake and temporarily energized when we hit the mall, hair still damp from the shower.

Ronnie is five foot nine. Her short blond hair is cut in a sort of pageboy. It's the same haircut she's had since I met her, but then my hairstyle hasn't changed, either. She was wearing jeans, cowboy boots with purple tooling, a short winter coat over a lilac crewneck sweater. She was not wearing a gun. Didn't think the mall elves would get that out of hand.

I was dressed for the office, because I'd need to go straight there from shopping. The skirt was a standard navy blue, with a black belt for my shoulder holster to slip through. The skirt was about two inches higher than I was comfortable with, but Ronnie had insisted. She's a tad more fashion conscious than I am. Then, who isn't? The jacket was a rich midnight blue, the color of Jean-Claude's eyes. Darker blue designs, nearly black, traced it in a vaguely Oriental pattern. The open-necked blouse was a blue that matched the jacket. With black high-heel pumps, I looked pretty snazzy. Ronnie had picked out the jacket, too. Its only fault was that it didn't hide the Browning as well. You got little flashes of it as I moved. So far no one had run screaming to the mall cops. If they had known I was wearing a knife on each forearm under the pretty jacket, maybe they would have.

Ronnie was staring into a jewelry case at Krigle's, and I was staring at her eyes. They were grey. The same color that Gabriel's eyes had been last night, but there was something different. Her eyes were human. Even in human form Gabriel's eyes weren't human.

"What's wrong?"

I shook my head. "Thinking about last night."

"How do you feel about loverboy after last night?" The jewelry store was three deep in people. We'd forced our way to the case, but I knew I wasn't buying anything here, so I sort of stood beside Ronnie, scanning the crowd. All the faces looked hostile, but it was nothing personal. They were Christmas shopping with two weeks to the big day. Ho, ho, ho.

The store was a mass of shoving, jostling people. I was getting claustrophobic. "Are you going to buy something?"

Ronnie looked up at me. "You never answered my question."

"Get me out of this mess and maybe I will."

She stood up and motioned me forward. I cleared us a path to the open mall. I'm small and was dressed too pretty to be intimidating, but people cleared a path. Maybe they saw the gun. When we were in the main open space, I took a deep breath. It was crowded but nothing like the stores. At least here, people weren't actually brushing against me. If they did it out here, I could yell at them.

"You want to sit down?" There were miraculously two seats open on a bench. Ronnie had made the offer because I was dressed for work, which meant heels. In her comfy cowboy boots she didn't need to sit. My feet didn't hurt yet. Maybe I was getting used to wearing heels. Eeek.

I shook my head. "Let's hit the Nature Company. Maybe I'll find Josh something there."

"How old is he now, eleven?" Ronnie asked.

"Thirteen," I said. "My baby brother was my height last year. He'll be gigantic this year. Judith says he's outgrowing his jeans faster than she can buy them."

"A hint to buy him jeans?" Ronnie said.

"If it is, I'm ignoring it. I'm buying Josh something fun, not clothes."

"A lot of teenagers would rather have clothes," Ronnie said.

"Not Josh, not yet anyway. He seems to have taken after me."

"What are you going to do about Richard?" she asked me.

"You're not going to let it go, are you?"

"Not a chance."

"I don't know what I'm going do. After what I saw last night. After what Jean-Claude told me. I just don't know."

"You know that Jean-Claude did it deliberately," she said. "To try and drive a wedge between you."

"I know, and it worked. I feel like I don't know Richard. Like I've been kissing a stranger."

"Don't let fang-face break you up."

I smiled at that. Jean-Claude would love being referred to as fang-face. "I won't."

She punched my shoulder softly. "I don't believe you."

"It won't be Jean-Claude that breaks us up, Ronnie. If Richard's been lying to me for months . . ." I didn't finish the sentence. I didn't have to.

We were outside the Nature Company. It was crawling with people like a jar of lightning bugs abuzz with activity, but not half as bright.

"What exactly has Richard lied about?"

"He didn't tell me about this battle he's got going with Marcus."

"And you tell him everything," she said.

"Well, no."

"He hasn't lied to you, Anita. He just didn't tell you. Let him explain. Maybe he's got a good reason."

I turned and looked full at her. Her face was all soft with concern. It made me look away. "He's been in danger for months, and didn't tell me. I needed to know."

"Maybe he couldn't tell you. You won't know until you ask him."

"I saw lycanthropes last night, Ronnie." I shook my head. "What I saw last night wasn't human. It wasn't even close."

"So he's not human. No one's perfect."

I looked at her then. She was smiling at me. I had to smile back. "I'll talk to him."

"Call him before we leave the mall and set up a dinner for today."

"You are so pushy," I said.

She shrugged. "I've learned from the best."

"Thanks," I said. "What have you learned from George Smitz?"

"Nothing new to add to the folder you showed me. Except he doesn't seem to know that his wife is one of eight missing shapeshifters. He thinks she's the only one. I got a picture of her. You need pictures of the others. First thing you need in a missing-person case is a picture. Without a picture you could pass them on the street and not know it."

"I'll ask Kaspar about pictures."

"Not Richard?"

"I'm sort of mad at him. I don't want to ask him for help."

"You're being petty."

"It's one of my best traits."

"I'll check out the usual channels for a missing person, but if they're all lycanthropes, I bet it isn't a missing person."

"You think they're dead?"

"Don't you?"

"Yeah."

"But what could take out eight shapeshifters without a trace?" she asked.

"That's got me worried, too." I touched her arm. "You wear your gun from now on."

She smiled. "I promise, Mommy."

I shook my head. "Shall we brave one more store? If I can get Josh's gift, I'll be halfway done."

"You'll have to buy Richard a present, you know."

"What?"

"You have to buy your steady a gift. It's traditional."

"Shit." I was halfway mad at him, but she was right. Fighting or not, I had to buy him something. What if he bought me something, and I didn't? I'd feel guilty. If I bought something and he didn't, then I could feel superior. Or angry. I was almost hoping he wouldn't buy me anything.

Was I looking for an excuse to dump Richard? Maybe. Of course, maybe after we talked he'd give me a good excuse on a silver, excuse me, golden platter. I was ready for a knock-down, drag-out fight. It did not bode well.

15

My ONE O'CLOCK appointment was with Elvira Drew. She sipped her coffee, elegant fingernails curled around the mug. Her nail polish was clear, making her fingertips glint like abalone shell; colorless until the light hit it. The rest of her was just as tasteful. Her dress was that interesting color that looked blue one minute and green the next. Blue-green they called it, but it wasn't accurate. The dress was almost green. For cloth to have that shimmer, almost a life of its own like fur, it had to be expensive. The dress was probably worth more than my entire wardrobe.

Her long yellow hair spilled down her back in an elegant line. It was the only thing that didn't match. That dress, the manicure, the dyed-to-match shoes, the nearly invisible makeup should have gone with a tasteful but complicated hairdo. I liked her better for the hair being free and nearly untouched.

When she raised her eyes to meet mine, I knew why she'd spent so much on the dress. Her eyes were the same startling blue-green. The combination was breathtaking.

I sat across from her, sipping my coffee, happy I'd dressed up. Most days she'd have made me feel like a country cousin. Today I could hold my own.

"What can I do for you today, Ms. Drew?"

She smiled, and the smile was all it should have been. She smiled like she knew the effect it had on most people. I was almost afraid to see her near a man. If she lit up this much for me, the thought of what she'd do around Jamison or Manny was kind of frightening.

"I'm a writer. I'm working on a book about shapeshifters."

My smile wilted around the edges. "Really. And what brings you to the offices of Animators, Inc.?"

"The book is set up with each chapter being a different animal form. I give history, any well-known shapeshifters of that form from history, then a personal profile of a present-day shapeshifter."

My face was beginning to hurt, and I knew my smile was more a baring of teeth than anything else. "Sounds like an interesting book. Now, how can I help you?"

She blinked gorgeous eyes at me and looked puzzled. She was good at looking puzzled. I'd seen the intelligence in her eyes a moment ago. The dumb-blonde routine was an act. Would it have worked if I were a man? I hoped not.

"I'm missing one interview. I need to find a wererat. The interview can be strictly confidential." The dumb blonde was gone as quickly as it had come. She'd seen I wasn't buying it.

The interview can be—not would—be confidential. I sighed and gave up on the smile. "What made you think I could find you a wererat?"

"Mr. Vaughn assured me that if anyone in this area could help me, it would be you."

"Did he really?"

She smiled, eyes glittering. "He seemed very sure you could help me."

"My boss promises a lot of things, Ms. Drew. Most of which he doesn't have to deliver." I stood. "If you could wait here for just a moment, I want to confer with Mr. Vaughn."

"I'll wait right here for you." Her smile was just as sweet, but something in her eyes let me know she knew exactly what kind of conferring I had in mind.

The outer office was done in pale greens, from the wallpaper, with its thin Oriental designs, to the foamy carpet. Plants flourished in every unoccupied niche. Bert thought the plants gave the office a homey touch. I thought it looked like a cheap jungle set.

Mary, our daytime secretary, glanced up from her computer keyboard with a smile. Mary was over fifty, with blond hair that was a little too yellow to be natural. "You need something, Anita?" Her smile was pleasant. I'd almost never seen her in a bad mood. It was a good personality trait for a receptionist.

"Yeah, to see the boss."

She cocked her head to one side, eyes suddenly wary. "Why?"

"I should have an appointment to see Bert today, anyway. I told Craig to schedule it."

She glanced through the appointment book. "Craig did, and Bert canceled it." The smile was gone. "He really is very busy today."

That was it. I went for Bert's door.

"He's with a client right now," Mary said.

"Peachy," I said. I knocked on the door and opened it without waiting for permission.

Bert's desk took up most of the pale blue office. It was the smallest of the three offices, but it was permanently his. The rest of us had to rotate. He'd played football in college and it still showed. Broad shoulders, strong hands, six feet four inches tall and aware of every inch. His boater's tan had washed away with the winter weather. His white crew cut seemed a little less dramatic against the paler skin.

His eyes are the color of dirty window glass, sort of grey. Those eyes glared at me now. "I'm with a client, Anita."

I spared a glance for the man sitting across from him. It was Kaspar Gunderson. He was dressed all in white today, and it emphasized everything. How I could have ever looked at him and thought him human was beyond me. He smiled. "Ms. Blake, I presume." He put out a hand.

I shook it. "If you could wait outside for just a few moments, Mr. . . ."

"Gunderson," he said.

"Mr. Gunderson, I need to speak with Mr. Vaughn."

"I think it can wait, Anita," Bert said.

"No," I said, "it can't."

"Yes," he said, "it can."

"Do you want to have this particular talk in front of a client, Bert?"

He stared at me, his small grey eyes looking even smaller as he squinted at me. It was his mean look. It had never worked on me. He gave a tight smile. "Are you insisting?"

"You got it."

He took a long, deep breath and let it out slowly, as if he were counting to ten. His flashed his best professional smile on Kaspar. "If you will excuse us for a few minutes, Mr. Gunderson. This won't take long."

Kaspar stood, nodded at me, and left. I closed the door behind him.

"What the hell are you doing coming in here while I'm talking to a client?" He stood up, and his broad shoulders nearly touched from wall to wall.

He should have known better than to try and intimidate me with size. I've been the smallest kid on the block for as long as I can remember. Size hadn't been impressive for a very long time.

"I told you no more clients that are outside my job description."

"Your job description is anything I say it is. I'm your boss, remember?" He leaned over his desk, palms flat.

I leaned into the desk on the other side. "You sent me a missing person's case last night. What the fuck do I know about missing persons?"

"His wife's a lycanthrope."

"And that means we should take his money?"

"If you can help him, yes."

"Well, I gave it to Ronnie."

Bert leaned back. "See, you did help him. He would never have found Ms. Sims without your help."

He was looking all reasonable again. I didn't want him reasonable. "I've got Elvira Drew in my office right now. What the hell am I supposed to do with her?"

"Do you know any wererats?" He had sat down, hands crossed over his slightly bulging middle.

"That's beside the point."

"You do, don't you?"

"And if I say yes?"

"Set up an interview. Surely one of them wants to be famous."

"Most lycanthropes go to a lot of trouble to hide what they are. Being outed endangers their jobs, marriages. There was that case in Indiana last year where a father lost his kids to his ex-wife after five years, because she found out he was a shapeshifter. No one wants to risk that kind of exposure."

"I've seen shifters interviewed on live television," he said.

"They're the exceptions, Bert, not the rule."

"So you won't help Ms. Drew?"

"No, I won't."

"I won't try and appeal to your sense of greed, though she has offered us a lot of money. But think what a positive book on lycanthropy would do to help your shapeshifting friends. Good press is always welcome. Before you turn her down, talk to your friends. See what they say."

"You don't give a damn about good exposure for the lycanthrope community. You're just excited about the money."

"True."

Bert was an unscrupulous bastard and didn't care who knew it. It was hard to win a fight when you couldn't insult someone. I sat down across from him. He looked pleased with himself, like he knew he'd won. He should have known better.

"I don't like sitting down across from clients and not knowing what the hell they want. No more surprises. You clear clients with me first."

"Anything you say."

"You're being reasonable. What's wrong?"

His smile widened, setting his little eyes sparkling. "Mr. Gunderson has offered us a lot of money for your services. Twice the normal fee."

"That's a lot of money. What does he want me to do?"

"Raise an ancestor from the dead. He's under a family curse. A witch told him if he could talk to the ancestor that the curse originated with, she might be able to lift it."

"Why double the fee?"

"The curse started with one of two brothers. He doesn't know which one."

"So I have to raise them both."

"If we're lucky, only one."

"But you keep the second fee anyway," I said.

Bert nodded vigorously, happy as a greedy clam. "It's even your job description, and besides, even you wouldn't let a fellow go through his life with feathers on his head if you could help him, now would you?"

"You smug bastard," I said, but my voice sounded tired even to me.

Bert just smiled. He knew he'd won.

"You'll clear clients with me that aren't zombie raisings or vampire slayings?" I said.

"If you have the time to read up on every client I see, then I certainly have time to write up a report."

"I don't need to read about every client, just the ones you're sending my way."

"But, Anita, you know it's just luck of the draw which of you is on duty on any given day."

"Damn you, Bert."

"You've kept Ms. Drew waiting long enough, don't you think?"

I stood up. It was no use. I was outmaneuvered. He knew it. I knew it. The only thing left was a graceful retreat.

"Your two o'clock canceled. I'll have Mary send Gunderson in."

"Is there anything you wouldn't schedule in as a client, Bert?"

He seemed to think about that for a minute, then shook his head. "If they could pay the fee, no."

"You are a greedy son of a bitch."

"I know."

It was no use. I wasn't winning this one. I went for the door.

"You're wearing a gun." He sounded outraged.

"Yeah, what of it?"

"I think you can meet clients in broad daylight at our offices without being armed."

"I don't think so."

"Just put the gun in the desk drawer like you used to."

"Nope." I opened the door.

"I don't want you meeting clients armed, Anita."

"Your problem, not mine."

"I could make it yours," he said. His face was flushed, voice tight with anger. Maybe we were going to get to fight after all.

I closed the door. "You mean fire me?"

"I am your boss."

"We can argue about clients, but the gun is not negotiable."

"The gun frightens clients."

"Send the squeamish ones to Jamison," I said.

"Anita"—he stood up like an angry storm—"I don't want you wearing the gun in the office."

I smiled sweetly. "Fuck you, Bert." So much for a graceful exit.

16

I CLOSED THE door and realized I had accomplished nothing but pissing Bert off. Not a bad hour's work, but not a great accomplishment. I was going to tell Ms. Drew that I might be able to help her. Bert was right about good press. I nodded at Gunderson as I passed him. He smiled back. Somehow I didn't think he really wanted me to raise the dead. I'd find out soon enough.

Ms. Drew was sitting legs crossed, hands folded in her lap. The picture of elegant patience.

"I may be able to help you, Ms. Drew. I'm not sure, but I may know someone who can help you."

She stood up, offering me a manicured hand. "That would be wonderful, Ms. Blake. I certainly appreciate your help."

"Does Mary have a number where I can reach you?"

"Yes." She smiled.

I smiled. I opened the door, and she walked past me in a cloud of expensive perfume. "Mr. Gunderson, I can see you now."

He stood, laying the magazine he'd been leafing through on the small table beside the *Ficus benjium*. He didn't move with that dancelike grace that the other shapeshifters had. But then swans weren't particularly graceful on land.

"Have a seat, Mr. Gunderson."

"Please, Kaspar."

I leaned on the edge of the desk, staring down at him. "What are you doing here, Kaspar?"

He smiled. "Marcus wants to apologize for last night."

"Then he should have come in person."

His smiled widened. "He thought that offering a sizable monetary reward might make up for our lack of hospitality last night."

"He was wrong."

"You aren't going to give an inch, are you?"

"Nope."

"Are you not going to help us?"

I sighed. "I'm working on it. But I'm not sure what I can do. What or who could take out eight shapeshifters without a struggle?"

"I have no idea. None of us do. That is why we have come to you."

Great. They knew less than I did. Not comforting. "Marcus gave me a list of people to question." I handed it to him. "Any thoughts, or additions?"

He frowned, eyebrows arching together. The white eyebrows were not hair. I blinked, trying to concentrate. The fact that he was feathery seemed to bother me a lot more than it should have.

"These are all rivals for Marcus's power. You met most of them at the cafe."

"Do you really think he suspects them, or is he just making trouble for his rivals?" I asked.

"I don't know."

"Marcus said you could answer my questions. Do you actually know anything that I don't?"

"I would say that I know a great deal more about the shapeshifting community than you do," he said. He sounded a trifle offended.

"Sorry, I think it's just wishful thinking on Marcus's part that his rivals are the bad guys. Not your fault he's playing games."

"Marcus often tries to manage things. You saw that last night."

"His management skills haven't impressed me so far."

"He believes that if there were one ruler for all shapeshifters, we would be a force to rival the vampires."

He might be right on that. "He wants to be that ruler," I said.

"Of course."

The intercom buzzed. "Excuse me a minute." I hit the button. "What is it, Mary?"

"Richard Zeeman on line two. He says he's returning your message."

I hesitated, then said, "I'll take it." I picked up the phone, very aware that Kaspar was sitting there listening. I could have asked him to step outside, but I was getting tired of playing musical clients.

"Hi, Richard."

"I got your message on my answering machine," he said. His voice was very careful, as if he were balancing a glass of water filled to the very brim.

"I think we need to talk," I said.

"I agree."

My, weren't we being cautious this afternoon. "I'm supposed to be the one that's mad. Why does your voice sound so funny?"

"I heard about last night."

I waited for him to say more, but the silence just stretched to infinity. I filled it. "Look, I have a client with me right now. You want to meet and talk?"

"Very much." He said it as though he weren't really looking forward to it.

"I have a dinner break around six. You want to meet at the Chinese place on Olive?"

"Doesn't sound very private."

"What did you have in mind?"

"My place."

"I only get an hour, Richard. I don't have time to drive that far."

"Your place, then."

"No."

"Why not?"

"Just no."

"What we need to say to each other isn't going to go over well in public. You know that."

I did. Dammit. "All right, we'll meet at my place a little after six. Do you want me to pick up something?"

"You're at work. It'll be easier for me to pick up something. You want mooshu pork and crab ragoon?"

"Yeah." We'd dated enough that he could order food for me without asking. But he asked anyway. Brownie point for him.

"I'll see you at about six-fifteen then," he said.

"See you."

"Bye, Anita."

"Bye." We hung up. My stomach was one hard knot of dread. If we were going to have "the" fight, the breakup fight, I didn't want to have it at my apartment, but Richard was right. We didn't want to be screaming about lycanthropes and killing people in a public restaurant. Still, it was not going to be a good time.

"Is Richard angry about last night?" Kaspar asked.

"Yeah."

"Is there anything I can do to help?"

"I need the complete stories about the disappearances: struggles, who last saw them, that sort of thing."

"Marcus said all questions directly about the disappearances should be answered only by him."

"You always do what he says?"

"Not always, but he's quite adamant about this, Anita. I am not a predator. I cannot defend myself against Marcus at his worst."

"Would he really kill you for going against his wishes?"

"Perhaps not kill me, but I would be hurting for a very, very long time."

I shook my head. "He doesn't sound any better than most master vampires I know."

"I don't personally know any master vampires. I am forced to take your word for that."

I had to smile. I knew more monsters than the monsters did. "Would Richard know?"

"Perhaps, and if not, he could help you find out."

I wanted to ask him if Richard was as bad as Marcus. I wanted to know if my sweetie was really a beast at heart. I didn't ask. If I wanted to know about Richard, I should ask Richard.

"Unless you have more information, Kaspar, I have work to do." It sounded grumpy even to me. I smiled to try to soften it but didn't take it back. I wanted this whole mess to go away, and he was a reminder of it.

He stood. "If you need any assistance, please call."

"You'll only be able to give me the assistance Marcus okays, right?"

A slight flush colored his pale skin, a pink glow like colored sugar. "I am afraid so."

"I don't think I'll be calling," I said.

"You don't trust Marcus?"

I laughed, but it was harsh, not amused. "Do you?"

He smiled, and gave a slight nod of his head. "I suppose not." He moved for the door.

I had my hand on the doorknob when I turned and asked, "Is it really a family curse?"

"My affliction?"

"Yeah."

"Not a family one, but a curse, yes."

"Like in the fairy tale?" I said.

"Fairy tale sounds like such a gentle thing. The original stories are often quite gruesome."

"I've read some of them."

"Have you read *The Swan Princess* in its original Norse?"

"Can't say I have."

"It's even worse in the original language."

"Sorry to hear that," I said.

"So am I." He stepped closer to the door, and I had to open it to let him go. I dearly wanted to hear the story from his own lips, but there was a pain in his eyes that was raw enough to cut skin. I couldn't press against that much pain.

He stepped past me. I let him go. I was really going to have to find my textbook on fairy tales as truth from that comparative literature class. It had been a long time since I'd read *The Swan Princess*.

17

IT WAS MORE like six-thirty by the time I walked down the hallway to my apartment. I had half expected to see Richard sitting in the hall, but it was empty. The tightness in my stomach eased just a bit. A reprieve, even of a few minutes, was still a reprieve.

I had my keys in the door when the door behind me opened. I dropped the keys, leaving them dangling. My right hand went for the Browning. It was instinct, not something I thought about. My hand was on the butt, but I hadn't drawn it when Mrs. Pringle appeared in the door. I eased my hand away from the gun and smiled. I don't think she realized what I was doing because her smile never faltered.

She was tall and thin with age. Her white hair was wrapped in a bun at the nape of her neck. Mrs. Pringle never wore makeup and never apologized for being over sixty. She seemed to enjoy being old.

"Anita, you're running a little late tonight," she said. Custard, her Pomeranian, yapped in the background like a stuck record.

I frowned at her. Six-thirty was early for me to get home. Before I could say anything, Richard appeared behind her in the doorway. His hair fell around his face in a mass of rich brown waves. He was wearing one of my favorite sweaters. It was solid forest green and squishy soft to the touch. Custard was barking at him, inches away from his leg, as if working up courage for a quick nip.

"Custard, stop that," Mrs. Pringle said. She looked up at Richard. "I've never seen him behave like this around anyone. Anita can tell you that he likes almost everyone." She looked to me for support, embarrassed about her dog being rude to a guest.

I nodded. "You're right. I've never seen him act like this before." I was looking at Richard. His face was as closed and careful as I'd ever seen it.

"He acts like this around other dogs sometimes, tries to boss them," she said. "Do you have a dog, Mr. Zeeman? Maybe Custard smells him on you."

"No," Richard said, "I don't have a dog."

"I found your beau sitting in the hall with his sack of food. I thought he might like to wait inside. I'm sorry that Custard has made the visit so unpleasant."

"I always enjoy talking shop with another teacher," he said.

"So polite," she said. Her face had broken into a wonderful smile. She'd only met Richard once or twice in the hall, but she liked him. Even before she found out he was a teacher. Snap judgment.

Richard stepped around her into the hall. Custard followed him, yipping furiously. The dog looked like an overly ambitious dandelion. But it was a pissed dandelion. The dog bounced forward on tiny feet, giving a little hop with each bark.

"Custard, get back in here."

I held the door open for Richard. He had a white take-out sack and a coat in his arms. The dog gave a running bound, darting in to nip his ankle. Richard looked down at the dog. Custard stopped a nose away from his pants leg. He rolled eyes upward, a look in his doggy eyes that I'd never seen before. A considering look as if he wondered if Richard really would eat him.

Richard slipped through the door. Custard just stood there in the hallway, as subdued as I'd ever seen him. "Thanks for looking after Richard, Mrs. Pringle."

"My pleasure. He's a nice young man," she said. Her tone of voice said more than the words. "Nice young man" meant marry him. My stepmother, Judith, would agree with her. Except that Judith would have said it out loud, no hinting.

I smiled and closed the door. Custard started yapping at the door. I locked the door out of habit and turned to face the music.

Richard had draped his leather coat across the back of the couch. The take-out sack was sitting on the small kitchenette table. He lifted out cartons of food. I put my coat on the back of the couch by his and slipped off the high heels. I lost about two inches of height and felt much better.

"Nice jacket," he said. His voice was still neutral.

"Thanks." I had been going to take the jacket off, but he liked it, so I kept it on. Silly, but true. We were both being so careful. The tension in the room was choking.

I got plates out of the cabinet. I got a cold Coke from the fridge for me and poured a glass of water for Richard. He didn't like carbonated beverages. I'd taken to keeping a jug of cold water in the fridge just for him. My throat felt tight as I set the drinks on the table.

He set out silverware. We moved around my minuscule kitchen like dancers, knowing where each would be, never bumping unless it was on purpose. Tonight there was no touching. We left the lights off. The only light was from the living room, leaving the kitchen in semidarkness like a cave. It was almost as if neither one of us wanted to see clearly.

We sat down at last. We stared at each other over the food on the plates: mooshu pork for me, cashew chicken for Richard. The smell of hot Chinese food filled the apartment. Warm and comforting on most occasions. Tonight it nauseated me. A double order of crab ragoon sat on a plate between us. He had filled a saucer with sweet-and-sour sauce. It was the way we always ate Chinese, sharing a bowl of sauce.

Damn.

His chocolate brown eyes stared at me. I was the one who looked away first. I didn't want to do this. "So, do all dogs react like that to you?"

"No, just the dominant ones."

I looked up at that. "Custard is dominant to you?"

"He thinks so."

"Unhealthy," I said.

He smiled. "I don't eat dogs."

"I didn't mean . . . oh, shit." If we were going to do this, might as well do it right. "Why didn't you tell me about Marcus?"

"I didn't want to involve you."

"Why not?"

"Jean-Claude involved you with Nikolaos. You told me how much you hated that. Resented it. If I brought you in to help me with Marcus, what would be the difference?"

"It's not the same," I said.

"How? I won't use you like Jean-Claude did. I won't do it."

"If I volunteer, you're not using me."

"What are you going to do? Kill him?" There was a bitterness in his voice, anger.

"What's that supposed to mean?"

"You might as well take your jacket off. I saw the gun."

I opened my mouth to protest and closed it. Explaining in the middle of a fight that I wanted to look good for him sounded silly. I stood up and took the jacket off. I draped it carefully over the back of the chair, taking a lot of time with it. "There. Happy?"

"Is that gun your answer to everything?"

"Why do you suddenly have a problem with me carrying a gun?"

"Alfred was my friend."

That stopped me. It hadn't even occurred to me that Richard might like Alfred. "I didn't know he was your friend."

"Would it have made a difference?"

I thought about that. "Maybe."

"You didn't have to kill him."

"I had this conversation with Marcus last night. They left me no choice, Richard. I warned him, more than once."

"I heard all about it. The pack's buzzing with it. How you wouldn't back down. You rejected Marcus's protection. You shot another one of us." He shook his head. "Oh, everyone's real impressed."

"I didn't do it to impress them."

He took a deep breath. "I know, that's what scares me."

"You're scared of me?"

"For you," he said. The anger was seeping out of his eyes, what was replacing it was fear.

"I can handle myself, Richard."

"You don't understand what you did last night."

"I am sorry if Alfred was your friend. Frankly, he didn't strike me as someone you'd hang out with."

"I know he was a bully, and Marcus's dog to call, but he was mine to protect."

"Marcus wasn't doing a lot of protecting last night, Richard. He was more interested in his little power struggle than in keeping Alfred safe."

"I stopped by Irving's place this morning." He let the statement hang there in the air between us.

It was my turn to get angry. "Did you hurt him?"

"If I did, it was my right as beta male."

I stood up, hands pressed on the tabletop. "If you hurt him, we are going to have more than just words."

"Are you going to shoot me, too?"

I looked at him, with his wonderful hair, looking scrumptious in his sweater, and nodded. "If I had to."

"You could kill me, just like that."

"No, not kill, but wound, yeah."

"To keep Irving safe, you'd pull a gun on me." He was leaning back in the chair, arms crossed on his chest. His expression was amazed and angry.

"Irving asked for my protection. I gave it."

"So he told me this morning."

"Did you hurt him?"

He stared at me for a long time, then finally said, "No, I didn't hurt him."

I let out a breath I hadn't known I was holding and eased back into my chair.

"You'd really pit yourself against me to protect him. You really would."

"Don't sound so amazed. Irving was caught in the middle of the two of you. Marcus would have hurt him if he didn't contact me, and you said you'd hurt him if he did. Didn't seem very fair."

"A lot of things in the pack aren't fair, Anita."

"So is life, Richard. What of it?"

"When Irving told me that he was under your protection, I didn't hurt him, but I didn't really believe you'd hurt me."

"I've known Irving a lot longer than I've known you."

He leaned forward, hands on the tabletop. "But he's not dating you."

I shrugged. I didn't know what else to say. Nothing seemed like a safe bet.

"Am I still your sweetie or did your baptism by fire last night make you not want to date me anymore?"

"You're in a life-or-death struggle and you didn't tell me. If you hide things like that from me, how can we have a relationship?"

"Marcus won't kill me," he said.

I just stared at him. He seemed sincere. Shit. "You really believe that, don't you?"

"Yes."

I wanted to call him a fool, but I closed my mouth and tried to think of something else to say. Nothing came to mind. "I've met Marcus. I've met Raina." I shook my head. "If you really believe that Marcus doesn't want you dead, you're wrong."

"One night and you're an expert," he said.

"Yeah, on this I am."

"That's why I didn't tell you. You'd kill him, wouldn't you? You'd just kill him."

"If he was trying to kill me, yeah."

"I have to handle this myself, Anita."

"Then handle it, Richard. Kill his ass."

"Or you'll do it for me."

I sat back in my chair. "Shit, Richard, what do you want from me?"

"I want to know if you think I'm a monster."

The conversation was moving too fast for me. "You're accusing me of being a murderer. Shouldn't that be my question?"

"I knew what you were when we first met. You thought I was human. Do you still think I'm human?"

I stared at him. He looked so uncertain. In my head I knew he wasn't human. But I'd still never seen him do any of the otherworldly stuff. Looking at him here in my kitchen, brown eyes brimming with sincerity, he just didn't seem very dangerous. He believed that Marcus wouldn't kill him. It was too naive for words. I wanted to protect him. To keep him safe somehow.

"You're not a monster, Richard."

"Then why haven't you touched me tonight, not even a hello kiss."

"I thought we were mad at each other," I said. "I don't kiss people that I'm mad at."

"Are we mad at each other?" His voice was soft, hesitant.

"I don't know. Promise me something."

"What?"

"No more hiding. No more lying, not even by omission. You tell me the truth, and I'll tell you the truth."

"Agreed, if you promise not to kill Marcus."

I stared across at him. How could anybody be a master werewolf and be so goody-two-shoes? It was both charming and liable to get him killed. "I can't promise that."

"Anita . . ."

I held up a hand. "I can promise not to kill him unless he attacks me, or you, or a civilian."

It was Richard's turn to stare at me. "You could kill him, just like that?"

"Just like that."

He shook his head. "I don't understand that."

"How can you be a lycanthrope and never have killed anybody?"

"I'm careful."

"And I'm not?"

"You're almost casual about it. You killed Alfred last night, and you don't seem sorry."

"Should I be?"

"I would be."

I shrugged. Truth was, it did bother me a little. There might have been a way out without Alfred ending up in a body bag. Or in the stomachs of his friends. But I'd killed him. There it was. No going back. No changing it. No apologizing.

"It's the way I am, Richard. Live with it or get out. I'm not going to change."

"One of the reasons I wanted to date you to begin with was I thought you could take care of yourself. You've seen them now. I think I can get out of it alive, but a regular person—an ordinary human being—what chance would they have?"

I just looked at him. I flashed on him with his throat torn out. Dead. But he hadn't been dead. He'd healed. He'd lived. There'd been another man. Another human being that hadn't healed. I never wanted to love anyone and lose them like that. Ever.

"So you got what was advertised. What's the problem?"

"I still want you. I still want to hold you. Touch you. Can you stand to touch me after what you saw last night?" He wouldn't meet my eyes. His hair fell forward, hiding his face.

I stood up and took the step that left me looking down at him. He raised his face to me, his eyes glittered with unshed tears. The fear in his face was raw. I had thought that what I saw last night would make a difference between us. I flashed on Jason's unnatural strength, the sweat on Marcus's face, Gabriel with his blood-coated mouth. But staring into Richard's face, with him close enough to touch, none of that was real. I trusted Richard. Besides, I was armed.

I leaned over him, bending down to kiss his lips. The first kiss was gentle, chaste. He made no move to touch me, hands in his lap. I kissed his forehead, hands combing through his long hair, so I could feel the warmth of him against my fingers. I kissed his eyebrows, the tip of his nose, each cheek, finally his lips again. He sighed, the breath pouring into my mouth, and I pressed my lips against his like I'd eat him from the mouth down.

His arms wrapped around my back, hands hesitating at my waist, fingers slightly lower. His hands jumped to my thighs, skipping all those questionable areas. I put one leg on either side of his knees, and found the short skirt did have its uses. I straddled his lap, didn't have to raise the skirt an inch. Richard made a small sound of surprise. He stared at me, and his eyes were drowning deep.

I raised his sweater off his stomach, running hands against his bare flesh. "Off," I said.

He raised the sweater over his head in one movement, dropping it to the floor. I sat in his lap, staring at his bare chest. I should have stopped right there, but I didn't want to.

I pressed my face in the bend of his neck, breathing in the smell of his skin, his hair covering my face like a veil. I ran just the tip of my tongue in a thin line of wetness down his neck, across his collarbone.

His hands kneaded the small of my back, sliding downward. His fingers danced over my buttocks, then up to my back. Point for him. He hadn't groped me.

"The gun, can you take it off?" He asked with his face buried in my hair.

I nodded, slipping out of the shoulder straps. I couldn't get the rest off without removing the skirt's belt. My hands didn't seem to want to work.

Richard took my hands and placed them gently to either side. He undid the buckle and began to slide the belt out a loop at a time. Each pull made me move just a little. I held the holstered gun while he drew the belt free. He let the belt drop to the floor. I folded the shoulder holster carefully and laid it on the table behind us.

I turned back to him. His face was startingly close. His lips were soft, full. I licked the edges of his mouth. The kiss was quick and messy. I wanted to run my mouth over other things. Down his chest. We'd never let it go this far. Not even close.

He pulled my blouse out of the skirt, running hands over my bare back. The feel of his naked skin on places he'd never touched before made me shudder.

"We have to stop now." I whispered it into his neck, so it wasn't completely convincing.

"What?"

"Stop." I pushed a little back from him, enough to see his face. Enough to breathe just a little. My hands were still playing with his hair, touching his shoulders. I dropped my hands. Made myself stop. He was so warm. I raised my hands to my face, and could smell him on my skin.

I did not want to stop. From the look on his face, the feel of his body, neither did he. "We should stop now."

"Why?" His voice was almost a whisper.

"Because if we don't stop now, we might not stop at all."

"Would that be such a bad thing?"

Staring into his lovely eyes from inches away, I almost said, no. "Maybe, yes."

"Why?"

"Because one night is never enough. You either have a regular diet of it or you go cold turkey."

"You can have this every night," he said.

"Is that a proposal?" I asked.

He blinked at me, trying to draw himself back up. To think. I watched the effort and struggled with it myself. It was hard to think sitting in his lap. I stood up. His hands were still under my shirt, on my bare back.

"Anita, what's wrong?"

I stood looking down at him, hands on his shoulders for balance, still too close for clear thinking. I backed away, and he let me go. I leaned my hands against the kitchen counter, trying to think enough to make sense.

I tried to think how to say a couple of years' worth of pain in one mouthful. "I was always a good girl. I didn't sleep around. In college I met someone, we got engaged, we set a date, we made love. He dumped me."

"He'd done all that just to get you in bed?"

I shook my head and turned to look at him. He was still sitting there with his shirt off, looking scrumptious. "His family disapproved of me."

"Why?"

"His mother didn't like my mother being Mexican." I leaned my back against the cabinets, arms crossed, hugging myself. "He didn't love me enough to go against his family. I missed him in a lot of ways, but my body missed him, too. I promised myself I'd never let that happen again."

"So you're waiting for marriage," he said.

I nodded. "I want you, Richard, badly, but I can't. I promised I'd never let myself get hurt like that again."

He stood up and came to stand in front of me. He stood close but didn't try to touch me. "Then marry me."

I looked up at him. "Yeah, right."

"No, I mean it." He put his hands on my shoulders, gently. "I've thought about asking before, but I was afraid. You hadn't seen what a lycanthrope could do, what we could be. I knew you needed to see that before I could ask, but I was afraid for you to see it."

"I still haven't seen you change," I said.

"Do you need to?"

"Standing here like this, I say no, but realistically, if we're serious, probably."

"Now?"

I stared up at him in the near dark and hugged him. I folded against him and shook my head, cheek sliding along his naked chest. "No, not now."

He kissed the top of my head. "Is that a yes?"

I raised my head to look at him. "I should say no."

"Why?"

"Because life is too complicated for this."

"Life is always complicated, Anita. Say yes."

"Yes." The minute I said it, I wanted it back. I lusted after him a lot. I even loved him maybe more than a little. Did I suspect him of eating Little Red Riding Hood? Hell, he couldn't even bring himself to kill the Big Bad Wolf. Of the two of us, I was the more likely to slaughter people.

He kissed me, his hands pressing against my back. I drew back enough to breathe, and said, "No sex tonight. The rule still stands."

He lowered his mouth and spoke with our lips almost touching. "I know."

18

I WAS LATE to my first zombie appointment. Surprise, surprise. Being late to the first meeting made me late to the other two. It was 2:03 by the time I got to Edward's room.

I knocked. He opened the door and stepped to one side. "You're late."

"Yeah," I said. The room was nice but standard. A single king-sized bed, nightstand, two lamps, a desk against the far wall. The drapes were closed over the nearly wall-to-wall windows. The bathroom light was on, door open. The closet door was half-open, showing that he'd hung up his clothes. He planned to stay for a while.

The television was on, sound turned off. I was surprised. Edward didn't watch television. A VCR sat on top of the TV. That was not standard hotel issue.

"You want something from room service before we get started?"

"A Coke would be great."

He smiled. "You always did have champagne tastes, Anita." He went to the phone and ordered. He asked for a steak, rare, with a bottle of burgundy.

I took off my coat and laid it on the desk chair. "I don't drink," I said.

"I know," he said. "You want to freshen up while we wait for the food?"

I glanced up and caught a distant look at myself in the bathroom mirror. Chicken blood had dried to a sticky, brick color on my face. "I see your point."

I shut the bathroom door and looked at myself in the mirror. The lighting was that harsh, glaring white that so many hotel bathrooms seem to have. It's so unflattering that even Ms. America wouldn't look good in it.

The blood stood out like reddish chalk against my pale skin. I was wearing a white Christmas sweatshirt that had Maxine from the Shoebox Hallmark commercials on it. She was drinking coffee with a candy cane in hand, saying, "This is as jolly as I get." Bert had asked us to wear Christmasy-type things for the month. Maybe the sweatshirt wasn't exactly what he had in mind, but hey, it was better than some of the ones I had at home. There was blood on the white cloth. Figures.

I took the sweatshirt off, draping it on the bathtub. There was blood smeared over my heart. I'd even gotten a little on my silver cross. I'd put the blood there along with the stuff on my face and hands. I'd killed three chickens tonight. Raising zombies was a messy job.

I got one of the white washrags from the little towel rack. I wondered how Edward would explain the bloodstains to the maid. Not my problem, but sort of amusing anyway.

I ran water into the sink and started scrubbing. I caught a glimpse of myself with blood running down my face in watery rivulets. I stood up and stared. My face looked fresh scrubbed and sort of surprised.

Had Richard really proposed? Had I really said yes? Surely not. I had said yes. Shit. I wiped at the blood on my chest. I played with monsters all the time. So I was engaged to one. That stopped me. I sat down on the closed lid of the stool, bloody washrag gripped in my hands. I was engaged. Again.

The first time he'd been so white bread that even Judith had liked him. He'd been Mr. All-American, and I hadn't been good enough for him, according to his family. What had hurt most was that he hadn't loved me enough. Not nearly as much as I'd loved him. I'd have given up everything for him. Not a mistake to make twice.

Richard wasn't like that. I knew that. Yet there was that worm of doubt. Fear that he'd blow it. Fear he wouldn't blow it. Damned if you do, damned if you don't.

I looked down and realized I was dripping bloody water on the linoleum. I knelt and wiped it up. I was scrubbed as clean as I was going to get until I showered at home. If I'd brought clean clothes, I might have done it here, but I hadn't thought of it.

Edward knocked on the door. "Food's here."

I got dressed, put the rag in the sink, and ran cold water over it. I made sure the cloth wasn't blocking the drain and opened the door. The smell of steak hit me. It smelled wonderful. I hadn't eaten for more than eight hours, and truthfully I hadn't eaten all that much then. Richard had distracted me.

"Do you think room service would shoot us if we asked for another order?"

He made a small hand motion at the room-service cart. There were two orders on the cart.

"How did you know I'd be hungry?"

"You always forget to eat," he said.

"My, aren't we being mother of the year."

"The least I can do is feed you."

I looked at him. "What's up, Edward? You're being awfully considerate."

"I know you well enough to know you won't like this. Call the meal a peace offering."

"Won't like what?"

"Let's eat, watch the movie, and all will be revealed."

He was being cagey. It wasn't like him. He'd shoot you, but he wouldn't be cute about it. "What are you up to, Edward?"

"No questions until after the movie."

"Why not?"

"Because you'll have better questions." With that inscrutable answer he sat down on the edge of the bed and poured a glass of red wine. He cut his meat, which was raw enough to bleed in the center.

"Please tell me my steak isn't bloody."

"It isn't bloody. You like your meat well dead."

"Ha, ha." But I sat down. It seemed odd sharing a meal in Edward's hotel room, like we were two business people traveling together, just a working dinner. The steak was well done. Thick house fries suitably spiced took up almost as much room as the steak. There was a side order of broccoli, which could be slid to one side and ignored.

The Coke came in a chilled wineglass, which seemed a little excessive, but it looked nice.

"The movie's going to start near the end. I don't think you'll have any trouble picking up the plot." He hit the remote control, and the TV screen flickered, jumping from a game show to a bedroom.

A woman with long brown hair lay on her back in a round bed. She was nude, or at least what I could see of her was nude. Below the waist she was hidden behind the furiously pumping buttocks of a dark-haired man.

"This is pornography." I didn't even try to keep the disbelief from my voice.

"It certainly is."

I glanced at Edward. He was cutting his steak with neat, precise hand movements. He chewed a bite of steak, sipped his wine, and watched the screen.

I glanced back at the "movie." A second man had joined the couple on the bed. He was taller than the first man, with shorter hair, but beyond that it was a little hard to tell, mainly because I was trying not to look.

I sat on the edge of Edward's bed with our nice steak dinners, and for the first time felt awkward around Edward. There had never been any sexual tension between us. We might kill each other someday, but we'd never kiss. But I was still in a man's hotel room watching a porno movie, and good girls just didn't do that.

"Edward, what the hell is going on?"

He hit the remote control. "Here, a face shot."

I turned back to the screen. The frozen image stared out at me. It was the second man. It was Alfred.

"Oh, my, God," I said.

"You know him?" Edward asked.

"Yeah." No sense denying it. Alfred was dead. Edward couldn't hurt him anymore.

"Name?"

"Alfred. I don't know the last name."

He hit fast forward. The images on the screen moved at a furious pace, doing intimate things that would have been obscene at any speed. At fast forward it seemed sadder. Ridiculous as well as degrading.

He hit the pause again. The woman was full face to the camera, mouth open, eyes heavy lidded with sexual languor. Her hair was spread artfully over the silken pillow. It should have been provocative. It managed not to be.

"Do you know her?"

I shook my head. "No."

He hit the button again. "We're near the end."

"What about the other man?"

"He wears a face mask throughout."

The masked man had mounted the woman from behind. His hips cupped her butt, the line of his thigh matching hers. He leaned his upper body over her nude torso, hands massaging the flesh of her upper arms. He seemed to be draping himself on top of her more than anything else. There seemed to be very little sex going on.

She was supporting his full weight on her hands and knees. Her breath came in pants. A low growl trickled through the room. The camera did a close-up of the man's back. The skin was rippled, as if a hand had rubbed the under surface of his skin, then vanished. More ripples, as if something small were trying to punch its way out.

A wider-angle shot showed him still draped over the woman. The ripples on his back were growing. You could see things pushing against his skin, movements large enough you could have seen them even if he'd been dressed. Like those I had seen on Jason last night.

I had to admit this part was fascinating. I'd seen people shapeshift, but never like this. Not in minute detail, not with the loving eye of a camera on it.

The skin split along his back, and he reared upward, hands hugging her waist, screaming. Clear liquid flowed down his back in a wash that soaked the bed and the woman underneath him.

The woman gave a little encouragement, moving her buttocks against him, thrusting against him, head bowed to the bed.

Black fur flowed outward from his back. His hands shot to his sides, spasming. He leaned over her again, hands digging into the bed. The hands were just hands, then those human fingers sliced into the bed, ripping white stuffing from great clawed furrows.

The man seemed to shrink. The fur flowed faster and faster, almost liquid in its speed. The mask dropped away. The face was the wrong shape for it now. The camera did a close shot of the fallen mask. A bit of art in all this . . . oh, hell. I didn't have a word for it.

The man was gone. A black leopard mounted the woman and seemed very happy with the arrangement. The leopard bent over the woman, lips spread to reveal glistening teeth. The leopard nipped her back, drawing a small amount of blood. She gave a low moan, a shudder sweeping her body.

Alfred came back into view. He was still in human form. He crawled up to the bed and kissed the woman. It was a long, complete kiss, full of probing tongues. He rose on his knees, still kissing her, rocking his body with the movements. He seemed very excited to see her.

His back rippled, and he tore away from her, hands clutching the sheets. The change seemed to go a lot faster for him. The camera did a close-up of one of his hands. Bones slid out of the skin with wet, sucking noises. Muscles and ligaments crawled and rearranged. The skin tore and that same clear liquid poured out. The hand changed into a naked claw before the dark fur flowed over it.

He stood on bent legs, half wolf, half man, but all male. He threw back his head and howled. The sound had a deep, resonating quality that filled the room.

The woman looked up at him, eyes wide. The leopard jumped off her, rolling on the bed, for all the world like a big kitten. It rolled itself in the silken sheet, until only its black-furred face peeked out.

The woman lay on her back, legs spread-eagled. She held out her hands to the wolfman, tongue flicking out along her lips as if she were really enjoying herself. Maybe she was.

The werewolf thrust into her, and it wasn't gentle. She gave a gasping moan, as if it were the best thing she'd ever felt.

The woman was making noises. Either she was a very good actor or she was coming close to climax. I wasn't sure which I preferred. Good acting, I think.

She came with a sound between a scream and a shout of joy. She lay back gasping on the bed, body liquid. The werewolf gave one last shuddering thrust and drew claws down the length of her naked body.

She screamed then, no acting required. Blood poured down her body in scarlet rivulets. The leopard gave a startled scream and jumped off the bed. The woman put her hands up in front of her face, and the claws smashed her arms to one side. Blood poured, and there was a glimpse of bone in one arm where the claws had torn all the flesh away.

Her screams were high and continuous, one loud ragged shriek after another, as fast as she could draw air. The werewolf's pointed muzzle lowered towards her face. I had an image of the murder victim's crushed jaw. But he went for her throat. He bit her throat out, spraying a great gout of blood.

Her eyes stared sightless at the camera, wide and shiny, dull with death. The blood had somehow left her face untouched. The werewolf reared back, blood dripping from its jaws. A gob of blood fell on her staring face, running between her eyes.

The leopard leaped back onto the bed. It licked her face clean with long, sure strokes of its tongue. The werewolf licked its way down her body, stopping over her stomach. It hesitated, one yellow eye staring at the camera. It began to feed. The leopard joined the feast.

I closed my eyes, but the sounds were enough. Heavy, wet, tearing sounds filled the room. I heard myself say, "Turn it off." The sounds stopped, and I assumed that Edward had turned the tape off, but I didn't look up to see. I didn't look up until I heard the whir of the tape rewinding.

Edward cut a bite of steak.

"If you eat that right now, I will throw up on you."

He smiled, but he put down his silverware. He looked at me. His expression was neutral, as it was most of the time. I couldn't tell if he'd enjoyed the film or been disgusted by it. "Now you can ask me questions," he said. His voice was like it always was, pleasant, unaffected by external stimuli.

"Jesus, where did you get that thing?"

"A client."

"Why give it to you?"

"The woman was his daughter."

"Oh, God, please, tell me he didn't watch this."

"You know he saw it. You know he watched it to the end or why hire me? Most men don't hire people to kill their daughter's lovers."

"He hired you to kill the two men?"

Edward nodded.

"Why did you show this to me?"

"Because I knew you'd help me."

"I'm not an assassin, Edward."

"Just help me identify them. I'll do the rest. Is it all right if I drink some wine?"

I nodded.

He sipped his wine. The dark liquid rolled around the glass, looking a lot redder than it had before the movie. I swallowed hard and looked away. I would not throw up. I would not throw up.

"Where can I find Alfred?"

"Nowhere," I said.

He set his wineglass carefully on the tray. "Anita, you disappoint me. I thought you'd help me after seeing what they did to the girl."

"I'm not being uncooperative. That film is one of the worst things I've ever seen, and I've seen a hell of a lot. You're too late to find Alfred."

"How too late?"

"I killed him last night."

A smile spread across his face, beautiful to behold. "You always make my job easier."

"Not on purpose."

He shrugged. "Do you want half the fee? You did do half the work."

I shook my head. "I didn't do it for money."

"Tell me what happened."

"No."

"Why not?"

I looked at him. "Because you hunt lycanthropes and I don't want to give someone to you by accident."

"The wereleopard deserves to die, Anita."

"I'm not arguing that. Though, technically, he didn't kill the girl."

"The father wants them both. Do you blame him?"

"No, I guess I don't."

"Then you'll help me identify the other man?"

"Maybe." I stood up. "I need to call someone. I need for someone else to see this film. He might be able to help you more than I could."

"Who?"

I shook my head. "Let me see if he'll come first."

Edward gave a long nod, almost a bow with just his neck. "As you like."

I dialed Richard's number by heart. I got his machine. "This is Anita, pick up if you're there. Richard, pick up. This is important." No one picked up the phone.

"Damn," I said.

"Not home?" Edward asked.

"Do you have the number for the Lunatic Cafe?"

"Yes."

"Give it to me."

He repeated the number slowly, and I dialed it. A woman picked up the phone. It wasn't Raina. I was thankful for that. "Lunatic Cafe, Polly here, how may I help you."

"I need to speak with Richard."

"I'm sorry we don't have any waiters by that name."

"Look, I was a guest of Marcus's last night. I need to speak with Richard. It's an emergency."

"I don't know. I mean, like, they're all busy in the back room."

"Look, get Richard on the phone now."

"Marcus doesn't like to be disturbed."

"Polly, is it? I have been on my feet for over thirteen hours. If you do not put Richard on the phone right now, I am going to come down there personally and bust your ass. Am I making myself clear?"

"Who is this?" She sounded a little miffed, and not in the least afraid.

"Anita Blake."

"Oh," she said. "I'll get Richard for you, right away, Anita, right away." There was an edge of panic to her voice that hadn't been there before. She put me on hold. Someone with a sick sense of humor had compiled the Muzak. "Moonlight and Roses," "Blue Moon," "Moonlight Sonata." Every song was a moon theme. We were halfway through "Moon over Miami" when the phone clicked back to life.

"Anita, it's me. What's wrong?"

"I'm all right, but I've got something you need to see."

"Can you tell me what it is?"

"I know this sounds corny, but not over the phone."

"You sure you're not just looking for an excuse to see me again?" There was a note of teasing in his voice.

It had been too long a night. "Can you meet me?"

"Of course. What's wrong? Your voice sounds awful."

"I need a hug and to erase the last hour of my life. The first you can take care of when you get here, the second I'll just have to live with."

"Are you home?"

"No." I glanced at Edward, putting my hand over the mouthpiece. "Can I give him the hotel room?"

He nodded.

I gave Richard the hotel room, and directions. "I'll be there as soon as I can." He hesitated, then said, "What did you say to Polly? She's nearly hysterical."

"She wouldn't put you on the phone."

"You threatened her," he said.

"Yeah."

"Was it an idle threat?"

"Pretty much."

"Dominant pack members don't make idle threats to subordinates."

"I'm not a pack member."

"After last night you're a dominant. They're treating you like a rogue dominant lycanthrope."

"What does that mean?"

"It means when you say you're going to bust someone's ass, they believe you."

"Oh, sorry."

"Don't apologize to me, apologize to Polly. I'll be there before you get her calmed down."

"Don't put her on, Richard."

"That's what you get for being trigger happy. People get scared of you."

"Richard . . ." A sobbing female voice came on the line. I spent the next fifteen minutes convincing a crying werewolf that I wasn't going to hurt her. My life was getting too strange, even for me.

19

RICHARD WAS WRONG. He didn't knock on the door while I was on the phone calming Polly down. She was so grateful that I had forgiven her for her rudeness, that it was embarrassing. Waves of submissiveness poured out of the phone. I hung up.

Edward was grinning at me. He had moved to one of the soft chairs. "Did you just spend nearly twenty minutes convincing a werewolf that you weren't going hurt her?"

"Yes."

He laughed, a wide, abrupt sound. The smile vanished, leaving a sort of shimmering glow to his face. His eyes glittered with something darker than humor. I wasn't sure what he was thinking, but it wasn't pleasant.

He slid down in the chair, base of his skull resting on the back, hands clasped over his stomach, ankles crossed. He looked utterly comfortable. "How did you come to be the terror of good little werewolves everywhere?"

"I don't think they're used to people shooting and killing them. At least not on first acquaintance."

His eyes simmered with some dark joke. "You went in there and killed someone your first night? Hell, Anita, I've been down three times and haven't killed anyone yet."

"How long have you been in town?"

He looked at me for a long moment. "Is that an idle question or do you need to know?"

It had occurred to me that Edward could take out eight lycanthropes and leave no trace. If any human could do it, it was him.

"I need to know," I said.

"A week, tomorrow." His eyes had gone empty. They were as cool and distant as any of the shapeshifters' last night. There's more than one way to become a predator. "Of course, you'll have to take my word for it. You can check with registration, but I could have changed hotels."

"Why would you lie to me?"

"Because I enjoy it," he said.

"It's not the lie you enjoy."

"What do I enjoy?"

"Knowing something I don't."

He gave a small shrug, not easy for him, slid down in the chair as he was. He made it look graceful. "Egotistical of you."

"It's not just from me. You like keeping secrets for the pure hell of it."

He smiled then, a slow, lazy smile. "You do know me well."

I started to say, we're friends, but the look in his eyes stopped me. His stare was a little too intense. He seemed to be studying me as if he'd never really seen me before.

"What are you thinking, Edward?"

"That you might be able to give me a run for my money."

"What's that supposed to mean?"

"You know how I like a challenge."

I stared at him. "You're talking about coming against me, seeing who's better?" I made it a question. He didn't give me the answer I wanted.

"Yes."

"Why?"

"I won't do it. You know me—no money, no killing—but it would be . . . interesting."

"Don't go all spooky on me, Edward."

"It's just for the very first time I'm wondering if you would win?"

He was scaring me. I was armed, and he didn't seem to be, but Edward was always armed. "Don't do this, Edward."

He sat up in one liquid movement. My hand jumped to my gun. The gun was halfway out of its holster when I realized he hadn't done anything but sit up. I let out a shaky breath and eased the gun back into the holster. "Don't play with me, Edward. One of us will get hurt if you do."

He spread his hands wide. "No more games. I would like to know which of us was best, Anita, but not enough to kill you."

I let my hand relax. If Edward said he would kill me tonight, he meant it. If we ever did do this for real, he'd tell me first. Edward liked to be sporting about these things. Surprising your victim made things too easy.

There was a knock on the door. I jumped. Nervous—who, me? Edward sat there as though he hadn't heard, still staring at me with his spooky eyes. I went to the door. It was Richard. He put his arms around me, and I let him. I folded against his chest and was very aware that I couldn't pull a gun very fast clasped to Richard's body.

I drew back first and pulled him into the room. He looked questioningly at me. I shook my head. "You remember Edward?"

"Anita, you didn't tell me you were still dating Richard." Edward's voice was pleasant, normal, as if he hadn't been wondering what it would be like to kill me. His face was open, friendly. He walked across the room with his hand outstretched. He was a superb actor.

Richard shook his hand, looking a little puzzled. He glanced at me. "What's happening, Anita?"

"Can you set up the movie?"

"If you'll let me eat during it. My steak is getting ice cold," Edward said.

I swallowed hard. "You've seen the movie before, and you still ordered steaks. Why?"

"Maybe to see if you could eat after watching it."

"You competitive bastard."

He just smiled.

"What movie?" Richard asked.

"Eat your steak, Edward. We'll watch after you're done."

"It bothered you that much?"

"Shut up and eat."

He sat down on the edge of the bed and started cutting meat. The meat was red. Blood oozed out of it. I walked towards the bathroom. I wasn't going to be sick, but if I watched him eat that piece of meat I would be.

"I'm going to hide in the bathroom. You want an explanation, come join me," I said.

Richard glanced at Edward, then back to me. "What is going on?"

I pulled him into the bathroom and shut the door behind us. I ran cold water in the sink and splashed it on my face.

He gripped my shoulders, massaging. "Are you all right?"

I shook my head, water dripping down my face. I fumbled a towel and pressed it to my face, holding it there a minute. Edward hadn't warned me because he liked to shock people. And a warning would have lessened the impact. How much impact did I want Richard to endure?

I turned to him, towel still clutched in my hands. He looked worried, all tender concern. I didn't want him to look like that. Had I really said yes, just eight hours ago? It seemed less and less real.

"The movie is a porno flick," I said.

He looked startled. Good. "Porno? Are you serious?"

"Deadly," I said.

"Why do I need to see it?" A thought seemed to occur to him. "Why did you watch it with him?" There was the tiniest bit of anger in his voice.

I laughed then. I laughed until tears ran down my face, and I was too breathless to speak.

"What's so funny?" He sounded a little indignant.

When I could speak without gasping, I said, "Be afraid of Edward, but never be jealous of him."

The laughter had helped. I felt better, less dirty, less embarrassed, even a little less horrified. I stared up at him. He was still wearing the green sweater that had ended up on my kitchen floor earlier. He looked wonderful. I realized I didn't. In my oversize sweatshirt, complete with bloodstain, jeans, and sneakers, I had lost several notches in the cuteness game. I shook my head. Did it matter? No, I was delaying. I didn't want to go back out there. I didn't want to watch the movie again. I certainly didn't want to sit in the same room with the man I might marry and watch him watch a porno film. Should I spoil the ending?

Would it excite him before it went wrong? I looked at his very human face, and wondered.

"It's lycanthropes and a human in the film."

"They're already for sale?" he said.

It was my turn to look surprised. "You know about the film? You said 'they.' There are more of them?"

"Unfortunately," he said. He leaned against the door, sliding down to sit Indian fashion on the floor. If he'd stretched his legs out, there wouldn't have been room for both of us.

"Explain this, Richard."

"It was Raina's idea," he said. "She convinced Marcus to order some of us to participate."

"Did you . . ." I couldn't even say it.

He shook his head. Something tight in my chest eased. "Raina tried to get me in front of the cameras. For those that need to hide their identity they use masks. I wouldn't do it."

"Did Marcus order you to?"

"Yes. These damn films are one of the main reasons I started rising in the pack. Everyone higher in the structure could order me around. If Marcus okays it, they can order you to do almost anything, as long as it's not illegal."

"Wait. The films aren't illegal?"

"Bestiality is against the law in some states, but we sort of slip through the cracks on the law."

"Nothing else illegal goes on in these films?" I asked.

He stared up at me. "What's on that film that makes you look so scared?"

"It's a snuff film."

He just stared at me, no change of expression, as if waiting for me to say more. When I didn't, he said, "You cannot be serious."

"I wish I wasn't."

He shook his head. "Even Raina wouldn't do that."

"Raina wasn't in the film as far as I saw."

"But Marcus wouldn't approve of that, not that." He stood up, using only his legs and the wall. He paced to the edge of the bathtub and back. He brushed past me, slamming his hand into the wall. It gave a resounding thunk.

He turned, and I'd never seen him so angry. "There are other packs around the country. It doesn't have to be us."

"Alfred was in it."

He leaned his back against the far wall, and slammed his palms into the wall again. "I can't believe it."

Edward knocked on the door. "The film's ready."

Richard yanked the door open and poured into the other room like a crackling storm. For the first time I felt some of that otherworldly energy radiating from him.

Edward's eyes widened. "You gave him a preview?"

I nodded.

The room was in darkness except for the television. "I'll give you two lovebirds the bed. I'll sit over here." He sat down in the chair again, upright, watching us. "Don't mind me if the mood strikes you."

"Shut up and start the movie," I said.

Richard had sat down on the edge of the bed. The room-service cart was gone, along with its offending meat. Great, one less reason to upchuck. Richard seemed to have calmed down. He seemed normal enough sitting there. That wash of energy was gone so cleanly that I wondered if I'd imagined it. I glanced at Edward's face. He was watching Richard as if he had done something interesting. I hadn't imagined it.

I thought about turning on the lights but didn't. Darkness seemed better for this.

"Edward."

"Showtime," he said. He hit the button, and it began again.

Richard stiffened at the first image. Did he recognize the other man? I didn't ask, not yet. Let him see it, then questions.

I didn't want to sit on the bed with my sweetie while this filth played. Maybe I hadn't really thought about what sex might mean to Richard. Did it mean shapeshifting? Bestiality? I hoped not, and wasn't sure how to find out without asking, and I didn't want to ask. If the answer was yes to the bestiality, the wedding was off.

I finally walked across the screen and sat down in the other chair, beside Edward. I didn't want to see the film again. Apparently neither did Edward. We both watched Richard watch the film. I wasn't sure what I expected to see, or even what I wanted to see. Edward's face gave nothing away. His eyes closed about halfway through. He'd slid down in the chair again. He looked asleep, but I knew better. He was aware of everything in the room. I wasn't sure Edward ever really slept.

Richard watched alone. He sat on the very edge of the bed, hands clasped together, shoulders hunched. His eyes were bright, reflecting the light of the television set. I could almost watch the action playing over his face. Sweat glistened on his upper lip. He wiped it away, catching me looking at him. He looked embarrassed, then angry.

"Don't watch me, Anita." His voice was choked tight with something more than emotion, or less.

I couldn't pretend sleep like Edward. What the hell was I supposed to do? I got up and walked towards the bathroom. I studiously did not look at the screen, but I had to cross in front of it. I felt Richard track me as I moved. His eyes on my back made my skin itch. I wiped suddenly sweating palms on my jeans. I turned, slowly, to look at him.

He was looking at me, not the movie. There was rage on his face—anger was too mild a word—and hatred. I didn't think it was me he was angry with. That left who? Raina, Marcus . . . himself?

The woman's scream jerked his head around to the film. I watched his face while his friend killed her. The rage blossomed on his face, spilling out his mouth in an inarticulate cry. He slid off the bed to his knees, covering his face with his hands.

Edward was standing. I caught the movement on the edge of my vision and found him holding a gun that had magically appeared. I was holding the Browning. We stared at each other over Richard's kneeling body.

Richard had rolled into an almost fetal position, rocking slowly back and forth on his knees. The sounds of tearing flesh came from the screen. He raised a shocked face, caught one glimpse of the screen, and scrambled towards me. I stepped out of the way and he let me. He was going for the bathroom.

The door slammed shut, and a few seconds later the sound of his retching came through the door.

Edward and I stood out in the room, looking at each other. We still had our guns out. "You go for your gun as quickly as I do. That wasn't true two years ago."

"It's been a rough two years," I said.

He smiled. "Most people wouldn't have seen me move in the dark."

"My night vision is excellent," I said.

"I'll remember that."

"Let's call a truce tonight, Edward. I'm too tired to screw with it tonight."

He gave one nod, and tucked the gun at the small of his back. "That wasn't where the gun started out," I said.

"No," he said, "it wasn't."

I holstered the Browning and knocked on the bathroom door. Admittedly, I didn't turn completely around. I just wasn't easy with Edward at my back right that moment.

"Richard, are you all right?"

"No." His voice sounded deeper, hoarse.

"Can I come in?"

There was a long pause, then, "Maybe you better."

I pushed the door open carefully, didn't want to smack him with it. He was still kneeling over the toilet, head down, long hair hiding his face. He had a bunch of toilet paper crumbled in one hand. The sharp, sweet smell of vomit hung in the air.

I closed the door and leaned against it. "Can I help?"

He shook his head.

I smoothed his hair back on one side. He jerked away from me as if I'd burned him. He ended up huddled in the corner, trapped between the wall and the bathtub. The look on his face was wild, panicked.

I knelt in front of him.

"Don't touch me, please!"

"Okay, I won't touch you. Now what's wrong?"

He wouldn't look at me. His eyes wandered the room, not settling on anything, but definitely avoiding me.

"Talk to me, Richard."

"I can't believe Marcus knows. He can't know. He wouldn't allow it."

"Could Raina do it without his knowing?"

He nodded. "She's a real bitch."

"I noticed."

"I have to tell Marcus. He won't believe it. He might need to see the film." His words were almost normal, but his voice was still breathy, thin, panicked. If he kept this up, he was going to hyperventilate.

"Take a slow, deep breath, Richard. It's all right."

He shook his head. "But it isn't. I thought you'd seen us at our worst." He gave a loud, spitting laugh. "Oh, God, now you really have."

I reached for him, to comfort, to do something. "Don't touch me!" He screamed it at me. I backed up and ended sitting with my back pressed against the far wall. It was as far away as I could get without leaving the room.

"What the hell is wrong with you?"

"I want you, right now, here, after seeing that."

"It excited you?" I made it a question.

"God help me," he said.

"Is that what sex means to you, not the killing but before?"

"It can, but it isn't safe. In animal form we're contagious. You know that."

"But it's a temptation," I said.

"Yes." He crawled towards me, and I felt myself recoil. He sat back on his knees and just looked at me. "I am not just a man, Anita. I am what I am. I don't ask you to literally embrace the other half, but you have to look at it. You have to know what it is or it's not going to work between us." He studied my face. "Or have you changed your mind?"

I didn't know what to say. His eyes didn't look wild anymore. They had gone dark and deep. There was a heat to his gaze, to his face, that had nothing to do with horror. He rose on all fours, the movement was enough to bring him close to me. I stared at his face from inches away.

He gave a long, shuddering sigh, and energy prickled along my skin. I was left gasping. His otherness beat against my skin like a crashing wave. The wash of it pressed me against the wall like an invisible hand.

He leaned into me, lips almost touching, then moved past. His breath was hot against the side of my face. "Think how it could be. Making love like this, feeling the power crawl over your skin while I was inside you."

I wanted to touch him, and I was afraid to touch him. He drew back enough to look me in the face, close enough to kiss. "It would be so good." His lips brushed mine. He whispered the next words into my mouth like a secret. "And all this lust comes from me seeing blood and death and imagining her fear."

He was standing, as if someone had pulled him upright with strings. It was magically quick. It made Alfred last night look slow. "This is what I am, Anita. I can pretend to be human. I'm better at it than Marcus, but it's just a game."

"No." But my voice was just a whisper.

He swallowed hard enough for me to hear it. "I've got to go." He offered me his hand. I realized he couldn't open the door with me sitting there, not without banging me with it.

I knew if I refused his hand that that would be it. He would never ask again, and I would never say yes. I took his hand. He let out a long breath. His skin was hot to the touch, almost burning hot. His skin sent little shock waves through my arm. Touching him with all his power loose in the room was too amazing for words.

He raised my hand to his mouth. He didn't so much kiss my hand as nuzzle it, rub it along his cheek, trace his tongue over my wrist. He dropped it so abruptly, I stumbled back. "I have to get out of here, now." There was sweat on his face again.

He stepped out into the room. The lights were on this time. Edward was sitting in the chair, hands loose in his lap. No weapon in sight. I stood in the bathroom door, feeling Richard's power swirl out and fill the outer room like water too long imprisoned. Edward showed great restraint, not going for a gun.

Richard stalked to the door and you could almost feel the waves of his passing in the air. He stopped with his hand on the doorknob. "I'll tell

Marcus if I can get him alone. If Raina interferes, we'll have to think of something else." He gave one last glance at me, then he was gone. I almost expected him to run down the hallway, but he didn't. Self-restraint at its best.

Edward and I stood in the doorway and watched him vanish around the corner. He turned to me. "You're dating that."

Minutes ago I would have been insulted, but my skin was vibrating with the backwash of Richard's power. I couldn't pretend anymore. He'd asked me to marry him, and I'd said yes. But I hadn't understood, not really. He wasn't human. He really, truly wasn't.

The question was, how big a difference did that make? Answer: I hadn't the foggiest.

20

I SLEPT SUNDAY morning and missed church. I hadn't gotten home until nearly seven o'clock in the morning. There was no way to make a ten o'clock service. Surely God understood the need for sleep, even if he didn't have to do it himself.

Late afternoon found me at Washington University. I was in the office of Dr. Louis Fane, Louie to his friends. The early-winter evening was filling the sky with soft purple clouds. Strips of sky like a lighted backdrop for the clouds showed through his single office window. He rated a window. Most doctorates didn't. Doctorates are cheap on a college campus.

Louie sat with his back to the window. He had turned on the desk lamp. It made a pool of golden warmth against the coming night. We sat in that last pool of light, and it seemed more private than it should have. A last stand against the dark. God, I was melancholy today.

Louie's office was suitably cluttered. One wall was ceiling-to-floor bookshelves, filled with biology textbooks, nature essays, and a complete set of James Herriot books. The skeleton of a Little Brown Bat was laid behind glass and hung on his wall by his diploma. There was a bat identification poster on his door like the ones you buy for bird feeders. You know, "Common Birds of Eastern Missouri." Louie's doctoral thesis had been on the adaptation of the Little Brown Bat to human habitation.

His shelves were lined with souvenirs; seashells, a piece of petrified wood, pinecones, bark with dried lichen on it. All the bits and pieces that biology majors are always picking up.

Louie was about five foot six, with eyes as black as my own. His hair was straight and fine, growing a little below his shoulders. It wasn't a fashion statement as it was with Richard. It sort of looked as though Louie had just not gotten around to cutting his hair in a while. He had a square face, a slender build, and looked sort of inoffensive. But muscles worked in his forearms as he tented his fingers and looked at me. Even if he hadn't been a wererat, I might not have offered to arm-wrestle him.

He had come in specially to talk to me on a Sunday. It was my day off, too. It was the first Sunday that Richard and I hadn't at least talked to each other in months. Richard had called and canceled, saying it was pack business. I hadn't been able to ask questions because you can't argue with your answering machine. I didn't call him back. I wasn't ready to talk to him, not after last night.

I felt like a fool this morning. I'd said yes to a proposal from someone I didn't know. I knew what Richard had shown me, his outward face, but inside was a whole new world that I had just begun to visit.

"What did you and the rest of the professors think of the footprints the police sent over?"

"We think it's a wolf."

"A wolf? Why?"

"It's certainly a big canine. It isn't a dog, and other than wolves that's about it."

"Even allowing for the fact that the canine foot is mixed with human?"

"Even allowing."

"Could it be Peggy Smitz?"

"Peggy could control herself really well. Why would she kill someone?"

"I don't know. Why wouldn't she kill someone?"

He leaned back in his chair. It squeaked under his weight. "Fair question. Peggy was as much a pacifist as the pack would let her be."

"She didn't fight?"

"Not unless forced into it."

"Was she high in the pack structure?"

"Shouldn't you be asking Richard these questions? He is next in line to the throne, so to speak."

I just looked at him. I wouldn't look away as if I were guilty of something.

"I smell trouble in paradise," he said.

I ignored the hint. Business, we had business to discuss. "Peggy's husband came to see me. He wanted me to look for her. He didn't know about the other missing lycanthropes. Why wouldn't Peggy have told him?"

"A lot of us survive in relationships by pretending as hard as we can that we aren't what we are. I bet Peggy didn't talk pack business with her husband."

"How hard is it to pretend?"

"The better you control, the easier it is to pretend."

"So it can be done."

"Would you want to go through your life pretending you didn't raise zombies? Never talking about it? Never sharing it? Having your husband embarrassed by it, or sickened by it?"

I felt my face burn. I wanted to deny it. I wasn't embarrassed by Richard, or sickened, but I wasn't comfortable, either. Not comfortable enough to protest. "It doesn't sound like a very good way to live," I said.

"It isn't."

There was a very heavy silence in the room. If he thought I was going to spill the beans, he was wrong. When all else goes to hell, concentrate on business. "The police were all over the area where the body was found today. Sergeant Storr said they didn't find anything but a few more footprints, a little blood." Truth was, they had found some fresh rifle slugs in the trees near the kill area, but I wasn't sure I was free to share that with the lycanthrope community. It was police business. I was lying to both sides. It didn't seem like a good way to run a murder investigation, or a missing-person case.

"If the police and the pack would share information, we might be able to solve this case."

He shrugged. "It's not my call, Anita. I'm just an Indian, not a chief."

"Richard's a chief," I said.

"Not as long as Marcus and Raina are alive."

"I didn't think Richard had to fight her for pack dominance. I thought it was Marcus's fight."

Louie laughed. "If you think Raina would let Marcus lose without helping him, you haven't met the woman."

"I have met her. I just thought her helping Marcus was against pack law."

He shrugged again. "I don't know about pack law, but I know Raina. If Richard would play footsie with her, she might even help him defeat Marcus, but he's made it very clear that he doesn't like her."

"Richard said she had this idea about lycanthrope porno movies?"

Louie's eyes widened. "Richard told you about that?"

I nodded.

"I'm surprised. He was embarrassed about the whole idea. Raina was hot and heavy to have him be her costar. I think she was trying to seduce him, but she misjudged her boy. Richard is too private to ever have sex for a camera."

"Raina's starred in some of the movies?"

"So I'm told."

"Have any of the wererats appeared in the flicks?"

He shook his head. "Rafael forbid it. We're one of the few groups that refused it flat."

"Rafael's a good man."

"And a good rat," Louie said.

I smiled. "Yeah."

"What's up with you and Richard?"

"What do you mean?"

"He left a message on my answering machine. Said he had big news concerning you. When I saw him in person, he said it was nothing. What happened?"

I didn't know what to say. Not a new event lately. "I think it has to be Richard's news."

"He said something about it being your choice and he couldn't talk about it. You say it's his business and you can't talk about it. I wish one of you would talk to me."

I opened my mouth, closed it, and sighed. I had questions that I needed answers to, but Louie was Richard's friend before he was mine. Loyalty and all that. But who the hell else could I ask? Irving? He was in enough trouble with Richard.

"I've heard Richard and Rafael talk about controlling their beasts. Does that mean the change?"

He nodded. "Yes." He looked at me, eyes narrowing. "If you've heard Richard talk about his beast, you must have seen him close to changing. What happened last night?"

"If Richard didn't tell you, Louie, I don't think I can."

"The grapevine says you killed Alfred. Is that true?"

"Yes."

He looked at me as if waiting for more, then shrugged. "Raina won't like that."

"Marcus didn't seem too pleased, either."

"But he won't jump you in a dark alley. She will."

"Why didn't Richard tell me that?"

"Richard is one of the best friends I have. He's loyal, honest, caring, sort of the world's furriest boy scout. If he has a flaw, it's that he expects other people to be loyal, honest, and caring."

"Surely after what he's seen from Marcus and Raina, he doesn't still think they're nice people?"

"He knows they aren't nice, but he has trouble seeing them as evil. When all is said and done, Anita, Marcus is his alpha male. Richard respects authority. He's been trying to work out some sort of compromise with Marcus for months. He doesn't want to kill him. Marcus doesn't have the same qualms about Richard."

"Irving told me Richard defeated Marcus, could have killed him, and didn't. Is that true?"

" 'Fraid so."

"Shit."

"Yeah, I told Richard he should have done it, but he's never killed anyone. He believes all life is precious."

"All life *is* precious," I said.

"Some life is just more precious than others," Louie said.

I nodded. "Yeah."

"Did Richard change for you last night?"

"God, you are relentless."

"You said it was one of my better qualities."

"It is normally." It was like being picked at by Ronnie. She never gave up, either.

"Did he change for you?"

"Sort of," I said.

"And you couldn't handle it." It was a flat statement.

"I'm not sure, Louie. I'm just not sure."

"Better to find out now," he said.

"I guess so."

"Do you love him?"

"None of your damn business."

"I love Richard like a brother. If you're going to slice his heart up and serve it on a platter, I'd like to know now. If you leave, I'll be the one helping him pick up the pieces."

"I don't want to hurt Richard," I said.

"I believe you." He just looked at me. There was a great peacefulness to his expression, as if he could wait all night for me to answer the question. Louie had more patience than I would ever have.

"Yes, I love him. Happy?"

"Do you love him enough to embrace his furry side?" His eyes were staring at me as if they'd burn a hole through my heart.

"I don't know. If he were human . . . Shit."

"If he were human, you'd marry him maybe?" He was kind enough to make it a question.

"Maybe," I said. But it wasn't a maybe. If Richard had been human, I'd be a very happily engaged woman right now. Of course, there was another male that wasn't human that had been trying to get me to date him for a while. Jean-Claude had said that Richard wasn't any more human than he was. I hadn't believed him. I was beginning to. It looked like I owed Jean-Claude an apology. Not that I would ever admit it to him.

"A writer came to my office yesterday, Elvira Drew. She's doing a book on shapeshifters. It sounds legit and could be good press." I explained the format of the book.

"Sounds good, actually," he said. "Where do I come in?"

"Guess."

"She's missing a wererat interview."

"Bingo."

"I can't afford to be exposed, Anita. You know that."

"It doesn't have to be you. Is there anyone among you that would be willing to meet with her?"

"I'll ask around," he said.

"Thanks, Louie." I stood.

He stood and offered me his hand. His grip was firm but not too strong, just right. I wondered how fast he really was, and how easy it would be for him to crush my hand into pulp. It must have shown on my face, because he said, "You might want to stop dating Richard. Until you get this sorted out."

I nodded. "Yeah, maybe."

We stood there in silence for a moment. There didn't seem to be anything left to say, so I left. I was all out of clever repartee, or even a good joke. It was barely dark, and I was tired. Tired enough to go home and crawl into bed and hide. Instead, I was on my way to the Lunatic Cafe. I was going to try and convince Marcus to let me talk to the police. Eight missing, one dead human. It didn't have to be connected. But if it was a werewolf, then Marcus would know who did the killing, or Raina would know. Would they tell me? Maybe, maybe not, but I had to ask. They'd come closer to telling me the truth than they would to the police. Funny how all the monsters talked to me and not to the police. You had to begin to wonder why the monsters were so damn comfortable around me.

I raised zombies and slew vampires. Who was I to throw stones?

21

I WALKED ALONG the campus sidewalk towards my car. I walked from one pool of light to the next. My breath fogged in the glow of the street-lights. It was my night off so I was dressed all in black. Bert wouldn't let me wear black to work. Said it gave the wrong impression—too harsh—associated with evil magic. If he'd done any research, he'd have found that red, white, and a host of other colors are used in evil rituals. It depends on the religion. It was very Anglo-Saxon of him to outlaw only black.

Black jeans, black Nike Airs with a blue swoosh, a black sweater, and a black trench coat. Even my guns and holsters were black. I was just monochrome as hell tonight. I was wearing silver, but it was hidden under the sweater; a cross, and a knife on each forearm. I was headed for the Lunatic Cafe. I was going to try to persuade Marcus to let me share information with the police. The missing lycanthropes, even the ones like Peggy Smitz who didn't want their secret known, were safe from bad publicity now. They were dead. They had to be. There is no way to hold eight shapeshifters against their will for this long. Not alive.

It couldn't hurt them to tell the cops, and it might save any other shapeshifters from going missing. I had to talk to the people who had last seen the missing ones. Why had none of them put up a fight? That had to be a clue. Ronnie was better at this sort of thing than I was. Maybe we could go out detecting tomorrow.

Would Richard be there? If so, what was I supposed to say to him? It made me stop walking. I stood in the cold dark, trapped between street-lights. I wasn't ready to see Richard again. But we had a dead body, maybe more. I couldn't chicken out just because I didn't want to see Richard. It would be pure cowardice.

Truth was, I would rather have faced down a herd of vampires than one would-be fiancé.

The wind whistled at my back as if a blizzard were moving up behind me. My hair streamed around my face. The trees were icy still, no wind. I whirled, Browning in my hand. Something slammed into my back, sending me smashing into the sidewalk. I tried to save myself, arms slamming into the concrete first. My arms went numb and tingling. I couldn't feel my hands. My head snapped downward.

There is that moment after a really good head blow that you can't react. A frozen moment when you wonder if you'll ever be able to move again.

Someone was sitting on my back. Hands jerked my coat on the left side. I heard the cloth rip. The feeling was coming back in my arms. I'd lost the Browning. I tried to roll over on my side to go for the Firestar. A hand slammed my head into the sidewalk again. Light exploded inside my head. My vision went dark, and when I could see again, I caught Gretchen's face rearing above me.

She had a handful of my hair, pulled painfully to one side. My sweater was ripped away from my shoulder. Gretchen's mouth was stretched wide, fangs shimmering in the dark. I screamed. The Firestar was trapped under my body. I went for one of the knives, but it was under the sleeve of my coat, the sleeve of my sweater. I wasn't going to get there in time.

There was a high scream, and it wasn't me. A woman was standing at the end of the sidewalk screaming. Gretchen raised her head and hissed at them. The man with her grabbed her shoulders and pushed her off the path. They ran. Wise.

I plunged the knife into her throat. It wasn't a killing blow and I knew it, but I thought she'd rear. Give me a chance at the Firestar. She didn't. I shoved the knife in to its hilt; blood poured down my hand, splattered my face. She darted downward, going for my throat. The knife had done as much damage as it could. There was no time to go for the second blade. I was still pinned over the gun. I had forever to watch her mouth coming for me, to know I was going to die.

Something dark smashed into her, rolling her off me with the impact. I was left gasping on the sidewalk, blinking. I had the Firestar in my hand. I didn't remember getting it out. Practice, practice, practice.

There was a wererat on top of Gretchen. The dark muzzle darted downward, teeth glimmering. Gretchen grabbed his muzzle, holding those snapping teeth from her throat. A furred claw slashed her pale face. Blood flowed. She screamed, punching one hand into his stomach. It raised him in the air, just enough for her to get her legs under him. She lifted with her legs and shoved him into the air. The wererat went tumbling like a thrown ball.

Gretchen was on her feet like magic. I sighted down the barrel of the gun, still on the ground. But she was gone into the bushes, after the wererat. I'd missed my chance.

Snarls and snapping branches came from the darkness. It had to be Louie. I didn't know that many wererats that would come to my rescue.

I stood up and the world swam. I stumbled, and it took everything I had to stay standing. For the first time I wondered how badly I was hurt. I knew I was scraped up some because I could feel that sharp, stinging pain that taking off the first layer of skin will get you. I raised a hand to my head and it came away with blood. Some of it was mine.

I tried another step, and I could do it. Maybe I'd just tried to stand too fast. I hoped so. I didn't know if a wererat could take a vampire or not. But I wasn't standing out here in the clear and waiting to find out.

I was at the edge of the trees when they rolled out of the darkness and over me. I lay on the pavement for the second time, but there was no time to get my wind back. I rolled onto my right side, sighting down my arm towards the noise. The movement was too sudden, my vision swam. When I could focus again, Gretchen had sunk fangs into Louie's neck.

He gave a high, wild squeal. I couldn't shoot her lying down, all I could see from here was the rat's body, her arms and legs riding him, but the only shot I had that might kill her was a line of her blond head. I didn't dare try it. I might kill Louie, too. Even clear-headed, it would have been an iffy shot.

I got to my knees. The world shifted, and nausea rolled at the back of my throat. When the world was still again, there was still nothing to shoot at. Some trick of a distant streetlight flashed on the blood pouring from his throat. If she'd had the teeth Louie had, he'd be dead.

I fired into the ground near them, hoping it would scare her off. It didn't. I aimed at a tree just above her head. It was as close to Louie as I dared get. The bullet exploded in the tree. One blue eye looked at me while she fed off of him. She was going to kill him while I watched.

"Shoot her," it was Louie's voice twisted around furry jaws, but his voice. His eyes glazed and closed, while I watched. Last words.

I took a deep, steadying breath and aimed two-handed, one hand cupping the other in a teacup grip. I sighted on that one pale eye. Darkness swam over my vision. I waited on my knees, blind, for my vision to clear and me to pull that trigger. If my vision went while I was firing, I'd hit Louie. I was out of options.

Or maybe not. "Richard asked me to marry him and I said yes. You can smell a lie. I said yes to marrying someone else. We don't have to do this."

She hesitated. I stared into her eye. My vision was clear. Arm steady, I pressed on the trigger. She released his throat, sliding her head into his neck fur, hiding. Her voice came muffled but clear enough: "Put down your little gun, and I will let him go."

I took a breath and raised the gun skyward. "Let him go."

"The gun first," she said.

I didn't want to give up my only gun. That seemed like a really bad idea. But what choice did I have? If I were Gretchen, I wouldn't want me armed. I did still have the second knife, but from this distance it was useless. Even if I could throw well enough to put it through her heart, it would have to be a very solid blow. She was too old for a glancing blow to do much good. I'd shoved a knife hilt-deep into her throat and it hadn't slowed her down. It had impressed me.

I laid the Firestar on the sidewalk and raised my hands to show myself unarmed. Gretchen rose slowly from behind Louie's limp body. Without her propping him up, his body rolled onto its back. There was a looseness to the movement that unnerved me. Was it too late? Could a vampire's bite kill like silver?

The vampire and I stared at each other. My knife was sticking out of her throat like an exclamation mark. She hadn't even bothered to take it out. Jesus. I must have missed the voice box or she wouldn't have been able to talk. Even vampirism has its limits. I was meeting her eyes. Nothing was happening. It was like looking into anyone's eyes. That shouldn't have been. Maybe she was holding her power in check? Naw.

"Is he still alive?"

"Come closer and see for yourself."

"No, thanks." If Louie was dead, my being dead wouldn't help that.

She smiled. "Tell me again, this news of yours."

"Richard asked me to marry him, and I said yes."

"You love this Richard?"

"Yes." This was no time for hesitation. She accepted it with a nod. I guess it was true, surprise, surprise.

"Tell Jean-Claude and I will be content."

"I plan on telling him."

"Tonight."

"Fine, tonight."

"Lie. When I leave you will tend your wounds, and his, and not tell Jean-Claude."

I couldn't even get away with a little white lie, shit. "What do you want?"

"He is at Guilty Pleasures tonight. Go there and tell him. I will be waiting for you."

"I have to tend to his wounds before I do anything," I said.

"Tend his wounds, but come to Guilty Pleasures before dawn, or our truce is over."

"Why not tell Jean-Claude yourself?"

"He would not believe me."

"He could tell you were telling the truth," I said.

"Just because I believed it was truth would not make it so. But he will smell the truth on you. If I am not there, wait for me. I want to be there when you tell him you love another. I want to see his face fall."

"Fine, I'll be there before dawn."

She stepped over Louie's body. She had the Browning in her right hand, held palm over the barrel and grip, not to fire but to keep me from it. She stalked to me and picked up the Firestar, eyes never leaving me.

Blood dripped down the knife hilt in her throat. The blood fell in a heavy, wet splat. She smiled as my eyes widened. I knew it didn't kill them, but I'd thought it hurt. Maybe they only took the blades out from habit. It certainly didn't seem to bother Gretchen.

"You can have these back after you tell him," she said.

"You're hoping he kills me," I said.

"I would shed no tears."

Great. Gretchen took a step backwards, then another. She stopped at the edge of the trees, a pale form in the dark. "I await you, Anita Blake. Do not disappoint me this night."

"I'll be there," I said.

She smiled, flashing bloody teeth, stepped back again, and was gone. I thought it was a mind trick, but there was a backwash of air. The trees shook as if a storm were passing. I looked up and caught a glimpse of something. Not wings, not a bat, but . . . something. Something my eyes couldn't or wouldn't make sense of.

The wind died, and the winter dark was as still and quiet as a tomb. Sirens wailed in the distance. I guess the coeds had called the cops. Couldn't say I blamed them.

22

I STOOD, CAREFULLY. The world didn't spin. Great. I walked to Louie. His rat-man form lay very still and dark on the grass. I knelt, and another wave of dizziness took me. I waited on all fours for it to pass. When the world was steady once more, I put my hand on his fur-covered chest. I let out a sigh when his chest rose and fell under my palm. Alive, breathing. Fantastic.

If he'd been in human form, I'd have checked his neck wound. I was pretty sure that just touching his blood in animal form wouldn't give me lycanthropy, but I wasn't one hundred percent. I had enough problems without turning furry once a month. Besides, if I had to pick an animal, a rat wouldn't be it.

The sirens were getting closer. I wasn't sure what to do. He was badly hurt, but I'd seen Richard worse off and he had healed. But had he needed some medical attention to get healed? I didn't know. I could hide Louie in the bushes, but would I be leaving him to die? If the cops saw him like this, his secret was out. His life would be in a shambles around him, just because he'd helped me. It didn't seem fair.

A long sigh rose from his pointed muzzle. A shudder ran through his body. The fur began to recede like the tide pulling back. The awkward, ratlike limbs began to straighten. His bent legs straighted. I watched his human form rise from the fur like a shape caught in ice.

Louie lay there on the dark grass, pale and naked and very human. I'd never seen the process in reverse before. It was just as spectacular as the change to animal form, but it wasn't as frightening, maybe because of the end product.

The wound on his neck was more like an animal bite than a vampire, skin torn, but two of the marks were deeper, fangs. There was no blood on the wound now. As I watched, blood started to flow. I couldn't tell for sure in the dark, but it looked like the wound was already beginning to heal. I checked his pulse. It was steady, strong, but what did I know? I wasn't a doctor.

The siren was silent, but lights strobed the darkness just over the trees like colored lightning. The cops were coming, and I had to decide what to do. My head was feeling better. My vision was clear. The dizziness seemed to be gone. Of course, I hadn't tried to stand again. I could carry him in a fireman's carry; not too fast and not too far, but I could do it. The bite marks were shrinking. Hell, he'd be healed by morning. I couldn't let the cops see him, and I couldn't leave him here. I didn't know if lycanthropes could freeze to death, but I didn't feel lucky tonight.

I covered him with my coat, wrapping it around him as I lifted. Wouldn't do for him to get frostbite on certain delicate places. You lose a toe and there you are.

I took a deep breath and stood with him across my shoulders. My knees didn't like lifting him. But I got to my feet, and my vision wavered. I stood there, bracing against a suddenly moving world. I fell to my knees. The extra weight made it hurt.

The police were coming. If I didn't get out of here right now, I might as well give it up. Giving up wasn't one of my better things. I got to one knee and gave that last push. My knees screamed at me, but I was standing. Black waves passed over my eyes. I just stood there letting it sway over me. The dizziness wasn't as bad this time. The nausea was worse. I'd throw up later.

I stayed on the sidewalk. I didn't trust myself in the snow. Besides, even city cops could follow prints in the snow. A planting of trees hid me from the direction of the flashing lights. The sidewalk led around a building. Once around that I could backtrack to my car. The thought of driving while my vision kept sweeping in and out was a bad idea, but if I didn't get some distance between me and the cops, all this effort would be wasted. I had to get to the car. I had to get Louie out of sight.

I didn't look back to see if there were flashlights sweeping the area. Looking back wouldn't help, and with Louie on my shoulders it was a lot of effort to turn. I put one foot in front of the other, and the edge of the building curved around us. We were out of sight, even if they cleared the trees. Progress. Great.

The side of the building stretched like some dark monolith to my left. The distance around the building seemed to be growing. I put one foot in front of the other. If I just concentrated on walking, I could do this. Louie seemed to be getting lighter. That wasn't right. Was I about to pass out and just didn't know it yet?

I looked up and found the edge of the building right beside me. I'd lost some time there. It was a bad sign. I was betting I had a concussion. It couldn't be too bad or I'd pass out, right? Why didn't I believe that?

I peered around the corner, concentrating on not whacking Louie's legs into the building. It took a lot more concentration than it should have.

The police lights strobed the darkness. The car was parked on the edge of the lot with one door open. The radio filled the night with garbled squawking. The car looked empty. Squinting at something that far away brought a wave of blackness across my eyes. How the hell was I going to drive? One problem at a time. Right now, just get Louie to the Jeep, out of sight.

I stepped away from the sheltering building. It was my last refuge. If the cops came now with me walking across the parking lot, it was over.

On a Sunday night there weren't a lot of cars in the visitors' parking lot. My Jeep sat under one of the streetlights. I always parked under a light if I could. Safety rule number one for women traveling alone after dark. The Jeep looked like it was in a spotlight. The light was probably not that bright. It just looked that way because I was trying to be sneaky.

Somewhere about halfway to the Jeep, I realized that the head injury wasn't the only problem. Sure I could lift this much weight, even walk with it, but not forever. My knees were trembling. Every step was getting slower and took more effort. If I fell down again, I wasn't going to be able to pick Louie back up. I wasn't even sure I'd be able to get me back up.

One foot in front of the other, just one foot in front of the other. I concentrated on my feet until the Jeep's tires came into view. There, that wasn't so hard.

The car keys were, of course, in the coat pocket. I hit the button on the key chain that unlocked the doors. The high-pitched beeping noise that signaled them open only sounded loud enough to wake the dead. I opened the middle doors, balancing Louie one handed. I let him fall into the backseat. The coat fell open, revealing a naked line of body. I must have been feeling better than I thought because I took the time to fling the coat over his groin and lower chest. It left one arm flung outward, limp and awkward, but that was all right. My sense of propriety could live with a naked arm.

I closed the door and caught a glimpse of myself in the sideview mirror. One side of my face was a bloody mask, the clean parts had bloody scrapes. I slid into the Jeep, and got a box of aloe and lanolin baby wipes from the floorboard. I'd started carrying the wipes to help with the blood from zombie raisings. It worked better than the plain soap and water that I had been carrying. I wiped enough blood off that I wouldn't get stopped by the first cop that drove by, then slid behind the wheel.

I glanced in the rearview mirror. The police car still stood there alone, like a dog waiting for its master. The motor kicked. I put the car in gear and hit the gas. The Jeep weaved towards a streetlight as if it were a magnet. I slammed the brakes on and was glad I'd worn my seat belt.

Okay, so I was just a bit disoriented. I hit the light on my sunshade that's supposed to let you check your makeup, and checked my eyes instead. The pupils were even. If one pupil had been blown, that might have meant I was bleeding inside my head. People died from things like that. I'd have turned us in to the cops and gotten a ride to the hospital. But it wasn't that bad. I hoped.

I clicked the light off and eased the Jeep forward. If I drove very slowly, the car wouldn't want to kiss the streetlight. Great. I inched out of the parking lot, expecting to hear shouts behind me. Nothing. The street was dark and lined with cars on either side. I crawled down the street at about ten miles per hour, afraid to go faster. It looked like I was driving through cars on one side. Illusion but unnerving as hell.

A bigger street and headlights stabbed at my eyes. I put my hand up to shield my eyes and nearly ran into a parked car. Shit. I had to pull over before I hit something. Four more blocks before I found a gas station with pay phones outside. I wasn't sure how rough I looked. I didn't want some overzealous clerk to call the police after I'd gone to all the trouble of getting away undetected.

I eased the Jeep into the parking lot. If I overcorrected and took out the gas pumps, they might call the cops anyway. I pulled the Jeep in front of the phone bank. I put it in park and was very relieved to be standing still.

I fumbled a quarter out of the ashtray. It had never held anything but change. When I left the car, for the first time I was aware of how cold it was without my coat. There was a line of cold going down my back where the sweater had been ripped away. I dialed Richard's number without thinking about it. Who else could I call?

The answering machine kicked in. "Dammit, be home, Richard, be home."

The beep sounded. "Richard, this is Anita. Louie's hurt. Pick up if you're there. Richard, Richard, dammit, Richard, pick up." I leaned my forehead against the cool metal of the phone booth. "Pick up, pick up, pick up. Richard. Dammit."

He picked up, sounding out of breath. "Anita, it's me. What's wrong?"

"Louie got hurt. His wound's healing. How do you explain that to a hospital emergency room?"

"You don't," he said. "We have doctors that can tend him. I'll give you an address to go to."

"I can't drive."

"Are you hurt?"

"Yeah."

"How bad?"

"Bad enough that I don't want to drive."

"What happened to the two of you?"

I gave him a very abbreviated version of the night's events. Just a vampire attack, no specific motive. I wasn't ready to tell him I had to tell Jean-Claude about our engagement, because I wasn't sure we still had one. He'd asked, I said yes, but now I wasn't sure. I wasn't even sure Richard was sure anymore.

"Give me the address." I did. "I know the gas station you're talking about. I stop there when I visit Louie sometimes."

"Great. When can you be here?"

"Are you going to be all right until I can get there?"

"Sure."

"Because if you're not, call the police. Don't risk your life just to keep Louie's secret. He wouldn't want that."

"I'll keep that in mind."

"Don't get macho on me, Anita. I don't want anything to happen to you."

I smiled with my forehead pressed against the phone. "Macho's the only way I got this far. Just get here, Richard. I'll be waiting." I hung up before he could get mushy on me. I was feeling too pitiful to withstand much sympathy.

I got back into the Jeep. It was cold inside the car. I'd forgotten to turn on the heater. I turned the heater on full blast. I knelt on the seat and checked on Louie. He hadn't moved. I touched the skin of his wrist, checking for the pulse. It was strong and steady. For the heck of it, I lifted his hand and let it flop back. No reaction. I hadn't really expected one.

Usually, a lycanthrope stayed in animal form for eight or ten hours. Changing back early took a lot of energy. Even if he hadn't been hurt, Louie would be asleep for the rest of the night. Though sleep was too mild a word for it. You couldn't wake them from it. It wasn't a great survival method. Just like sleeping during the day didn't help vampires much. Evolution's way of helping us puny humans out.

I slid down in my seat. I wasn't sure how long it would take for Richard to get here. I glanced at the station building. The man behind the counter was reading a magazine. He wasn't taking any notice of us at the moment. If he'd been watching, I would have moved out of the lights. Didn't want him wondering why I was sitting here, but if he wasn't paying attention, we'd just sit here.

I leaned back, putting my head against the headrest. I wanted to close my eyes, but didn't. I was pretty sure I had a concussion. Going to sleep wasn't a good idea. I'd had one head injury worse than this, but Jean-Claude had cured it. But a vampire mark was a little harsh for a mild concussion.

This was the first time I'd been badly hurt since I lost Jean-Claude's marks. They had made me harder to hurt, faster to heal. Not a bad side effect. One of the other effects had been an ability to meet a vampire's eyes without them being able to bespell me. Like I had met Gretchen's eyes.

How had I met her eyes with impunity? Had Jean-Claude lied to me? Was there some lingering mark? Another question to ask him when I saw him. Of course, after I told him the news bulletin, all hell would break loose and there would be no more questions. Well, maybe one question. Would Jean-Claude try to kill Richard? Probably.

I sighed, closing my eyes. I was suddenly tired, so tired I didn't want to open my eyes. Sleep sucked at me. I opened my eyes and slid up in the seat. Maybe it was just tension, adrenaline draining away, or maybe it was a concussion. I clicked on the overhead light and checked on Louie again. Breathing and pulse were steady. His head was to one side, neck stretched in a long line that showed the wound. The bite marks were healing. I couldn't see it happening, but every time I looked it was better. Like trying to watch a flower bloom. You see the effect, but you never actually see it happening.

Louie was going to be all right. Would Richard be all right? I'd said yes because in the heat of the moment I meant it. I could see spending my life with him. Before Bert found me and showed me how to use my talent for money, I'd had a life. I'd gone hiking, camping. I'd been a biology major and thought I'd go on for my master's and doctorate and study preternatural creatures for the rest of my life. Sort of the preternatural Jane Goodall. Richard had reminded me of all that, of what I'd originally thought my life would be like. I hadn't planned on spending my life ass deep in blood and death. Really.

If I gave in to Jean-Claude, it would be admitting that there was nothing but death, nothing but violence. Sexy, attractive, but death all the same. I'd thought with Richard I had a chance at life. Something better. After last night I wasn't even sure of that.

Was it too much to ask for someone who was human? Hell, I knew a lot of women in my age bracket that couldn't get a date at all. I'd been one of them until Richard. All right, Jean-Claude would have taken me out, but I was avoiding him. I couldn't imagine dating Jean-Claude as if he were an ordinary guy. I could imagine having sex with him, but not dating. The thought of him picking me up at eight, dropping me off, and being satisfied with a good-night kiss seemed ridiculous.

I stayed kneeling in the seat, staring down at Louie. I was afraid to turn around and get comfortable, afraid I'd fall asleep and not wake up. I wasn't really afraid, but I was worried. A trip to the hospital might not be a bad idea, but first I had to tell Jean-Claude about Richard. And keep him from killing him.

I laid my face on my arms, and a deep, throbbing pain started behind my forehead. Good. My head should hurt after the beating it had taken. The fact that it hadn't been hurting had worried me. A good headache I could live with.

How was I going to keep Richard alive? I smiled. Richard was an alpha wolf. What made me think he couldn't take care of himself? I'd seen what Jean-Claude could do. I'd seen him when he wasn't human at all. Maybe after I saw Richard change I'd feel differently about him. Maybe I wouldn't feel so protective. Maybe hell would freeze over.

I did love Richard. I really did. I'd meant that yes. I'd meant it before last night. Before I felt his power creep over my skin. Jean-Claude had been right about one thing. Richard wasn't human. The snuff film had excited him. Was Jean-Claude's idea of sex any stranger than that? I'd never let myself find out.

Someone knocked on the window. I jumped and whirled. My vision swam in black streamers. When I could see again, Richard's face was outside the window.

I unlocked the doors, and Richard opened one. He started to reach for me and stopped. The hesitation on his face was painful. He wasn't sure I'd let him touch me. I turned away from the hurt on his face. I loved him, but love isn't enough. All the fairy tales, the romance novels, the soap operas; they're all lies. Love does not conquer all.

He was very careful not to touch me. His voice was neutral. "Anita, are you all right? You look awful."

"Nice to know I look like I feel," I said.

He touched my cheek, fingers sliding just over the skin, a ghost of a touch that made me shiver. He traced the edge of the scrape. It hurt and I jerked away. A spot of blood decorated his fingertips, gleaming in the dome light. I watched his eyes stare at the blood. I saw the thought trail behind his true brown eyes. He almost licked his fingers clean, as Rafael had done. He wiped his fingers on his coat, but I'd seen the hesitation. He knew I'd seen it.

"Anita . . ."

The back door opened, and I whirled, going for the last knife I had on me. The world swam in waves of blackness and nausea. The movement had been too abrupt. Stephen the Werewolf stood in the half-open door staring at me. He was sort of frozen there, blue eyes wide. He was looking at the silver knife in my hand. The fact that I'd been blind and too sick to use it seemed to have escaped him. It might have been that I was kneeling, moving towards him. I'd been willing to strike blind as a bat, not considering that whoever it was had a right to be there.

"You didn't tell me you brought someone with you," I said.

"I should have mentioned that," Richard said.

I relaxed, easing back to kneel in the seat. "Yeah, you should have mentioned that." The knife gleamed in the dome light. It looked razor sharp and well tended. It was.

"I was just going to check on Louie," Stephen said. He sounded a little shaky. He had a black leather jacket with silver studding snapped tight around his throat. His long, curling blond hair fell forward over the jacket. He looked like an effeminate biker.

"Fine," I said.

Stephen looked past me to Richard. I felt more than saw Richard nod. "It's okay, Stephen." There was something in his voice that made me turn slowly to look at him.

He had a strange look on his face. "Maybe you are as dangerous as you pretend to be."

"I don't pretend, Richard."

He nodded. "Maybe you don't."

"Is that a problem?"

"As long as you don't shoot me, or my pack members, I guess not."

"I can't promise about your pack."

"They're mine to protect," he said.

"Then make sure they leave me the hell alone."

"Would you fight me over that?" he asked.

"Would you fight me?"

He smiled, but it wasn't happy. "I couldn't fight you, Anita. I could never hurt you."

"That's where we're different, Richard."

He leaned in as if to kiss me. Something on my face stopped him. "I believe you."

"Good," I said. I slipped the knife back in its sheath. I stared at his face while I did it. I didn't need to look to put the knife away. "Never underestimate me, Richard, and what I'm willing to do to stay alive. To keep others alive. I never want us to fight, not like that, but if you don't control your pack, then I will."

He moved away from me. His face looked almost angry. "Is that a threat?"

"It's out of control, and you know it. I can't promise not to hurt them unless you can guarantee that they'll behave. And you can't do that."

"No, I can't guarantee that." He didn't like saying it.

"Then don't ask me to promise not to hurt them."

"Can you at least try not to kill them, as a first option?"

I thought about that. "I don't know. Maybe."

"You can't just say, 'Yes, Richard, I won't kill your friends'?"

"It would be a lie."

He nodded. "I suppose so."

I heard the rustle of leather from the backseat as Stephen moved around. "Louie's out of it, but he'll be okay."

"How did you get him into the Jeep?" Richard asked.

I just stared at him.

He had the grace to look embarrassed. "You carried him. I knew that." He touched the cut on my forehead, gently. It still hurt. "Even with this, you carried him."

"It was either that or let the cops have him. What would have happened if they'd piled him into an ambulance and he'd started healing like that?"

"They'd have known what he was," Richard said.

Stephen was leaning on the back of the seat, chin resting on his forearms. He seemed to have forgotten that I'd nearly stabbed him, or maybe he was used to being threatened. Maybe. Up close his eyes were the startling blue of cornflowers. With his blond hair spilling around his face he looked like one of those china dolls that you buy in exclusive shops, that you never let children play with.

"I can take Louie to my place," he said.

"No," I said.

They both looked at me, surprised. I wasn't sure what to say, but I knew that Richard could not come with me to Guilty Pleasures. If I had any hope of keeping us all alive, Richard could not be on the spot when I broke the news.

"I thought I'd drive you home," Richard said, "or to the nearest hospital, whichever you need."

It would have been my preference to, but not tonight. "Louie's your best friend. I thought you might want to take care of him."

He was staring at me, lovely brown eyes narrowed into suspicious squints. "You're trying to get rid of me. Why?"

My head hurt. I couldn't think of a good lie. I didn't think he'd buy a bad one. "How much do you trust Stephen?"

The question seemed to throw him off balance. "I trust him."

His first reaction was to say yes, I trust him, but he hadn't thought about it first. "No, Richard, I mean do you trust him not to talk to Jean-Claude or Marcus?"

"I wouldn't tell Marcus anything you didn't want me to," Stephen said.

"And Jean-Claude?" I asked.

Stephen looked uncomfortable, but said, "If he asked a direct question, I'd have to give a direct answer."

"How can you owe more allegiance to the Master of the City than to your own pack leader?"

"I follow Richard, not Marcus."

I glanced at Richard. "A little palace revolt?"

"Raina wanted him in the movies. I stepped in and stopped it."

"Marcus must really hate you," I said.

"He fears me," Richard said.

"Even worse," I said.

Richard didn't say anything. He knew the situation better than I did, even if he wasn't willing to do the ultimate deeds.

"Fine, I'd planned to tell Jean-Claude that you proposed."

"You proposed," Stephen said. His voice held a lilt of surprise. "Did she say yes?"

Richard nodded.

A look of delight swept over Stephen's face. "Way to go." His face fell into sadness. It was like watching wind over a grassy field, everything visible on the surface. "Jean-Claude is going to go ape-shit."

"I couldn't have said it better myself."

"Then why tell him tonight?" Richard asked. "Why not wait? You're not sure about marrying me anymore. Are you?"

"No," I said. I hated saying it, but it was the truth. I loved him already, but if it went much further it would be too late. If I had any doubts I needed to work them out now. Staring into his face, smelling the warm scent of his aftershave, I wished I could have thrown caution to the wind. Falling into his arms. But I couldn't. I just couldn't, not unless I was sure.

"Then why tell him at all? Unless you're planning to elope and didn't tell me, we have some time."

I sighed. I told him why it had to be tonight. "You can't go with me."

"I won't let you go alone," he said.

"Richard, if you are Johnny-on-the-spot when he finds out, he'll try to kill you, and I'll try to kill him to protect you." I shook my head. "If the shit hits the fan, this could end up like *Hamlet*."

"How like *Hamlet*?" Stephen asked.

"Everybody dead," I said.

"Oh," he said.

"You'd kill Jean-Claude to protect me, even after what you saw last night?"

I stared at him. I tried to read behind his eyeballs to know if there was anybody home I could really talk to. He was still Richard. With his love of the outdoors, any activity that would get you messy, and a smile that warmed me to my toes. I wasn't sure I could marry him, but I was positive I couldn't let anybody kill him.

"Yes."

"You won't marry me, but you'll kill for me. I don't understand that."

"Ask me if I still love you, Richard. That answer's still yes."

"How can I let you face him alone?"

"I've been doing just fine without you."

He touched my forehead, and I winced. "You don't look fine."

"Jean-Claude won't hurt me."

"You don't know that for sure," he said.

He had a point there. "You can't protect me, Richard. Your being there will get us both killed."

"I can't let you go alone."

"Don't go all manly on me, Richard. It's a luxury that we can't afford. If saying yes to marriage is going to make you behave like an idiot, it can be changed."

"You took back your yes."

"It's not a definte no, either," I said.

"Just trying to protect you would make you say no?"

"I don't need your protection, Richard. I don't even want it."

He leaned his head against the headrest and closed his eyes. "If I play the white knight, you'll leave me."

"If you think you need to play the white knight, then you don't know me at all."

He opened his eyes and turned his head to look at me. "Maybe I want to be your white knight."

"That's your problem."

He smiled. "I guess so."

"If you can drive the Jeep back to my apartment, I'll take a cab."

"Stephen can drive you," he said. He volunteered him without even wondering what Stephen would say about it. It was arrogant.

"No, I'll take a cab."

"I don't mind," Stephen said. "I'm due back at Guilty Pleasures tonight anyway."

I glanced at him. "What do you do for a living, Stephen?"

He laid his cheek on his forearm and smiled at me. He managed to look winsome and sexy at the same time. "I'm a stripper," he said.

Of course he was. I wanted to point out that he'd refused to be in a pornographic movie, but he still stripped. But taking your clothes off down to tasteful undies was not the same thing as having sex on screen. Not even close.

23

LILLIAN WAS A small woman in her mid-fifties. Her salt-and-pepper hair was cut short and neat in a no-nonsense style. Her fingers were as quick and sure as the rest of her. The last time she'd treated my wounds, she'd had claws and greying fur.

I was sitting on an examining table in the basement of an apartment building. A building that housed lycanthropes and was owned by a shapeshifter. The basement was the makeshift clinic for the lycanthropes in the area. I was the first human they'd ever allowed to see the place. I should have been flattered, but managed not to be.

"Well, according to X-rays you don't have a skull fracture."

"Glad to hear it," I said.

"You may have a mild concussion, but a mild one won't show up on tests, at least nothing we have the equipment for here."

"So I can go?" I started to hop down.

She stopped me with a hand on my arm. "I didn't say that."

I eased back on the table. "I'm listening."

"Grudgingly," she said, smiling.

"If you want grace under pressure, Lillian, I'm not your girl."

"Oh, I don't know about that," she said. "I've cleaned the scrapes and taped up your forehead. You were very lucky not to need stitches."

I didn't like stitches, so I agreed with her.

"I want you to wake up every hour for twenty-four hours." I must not have looked happy, because she said, "I know it's awkward, and probably unnecessary, but humor me. If you go to sleep and are injured more severely than I think you are, you might not wake up. So humor an old rat lady. Set the alarm or have someone wake you every hour for twenty-four hours."

"Twenty-four hours from the injury?" I asked hopefully.

She laughed. "Normally I'd say from now, but you can do it from the time of the injury. We're just being cautious."

"I like being cautious." Richard pushed away from the wall. He came to stand with us under the lights. "I volunteer to wake you every hour."

"You can't go with me," I said.

"I'll wait for you at your apartment."

"Oh, no driving for the night," Lillian said. "Just as a precaution."

Richard's fingertips touched the back of my hand. He didn't try to hold my hand, just that touch. Comforting. I didn't know what to do. If I was going to say no, eventually, it didn't seem fair to flirt. Just the weight of his fingers was a line of warmth all the way up my arm. Lust, just lust. Don't I wish.

"I'll drive your Jeep to your apartment, if you agree. Stephen can drive you to Guilty Pleasures."

"I can take a cab."

"I'd feel better if Stephen took you. Please," he said.

The "please" made me smile. "All right, Stephen can drive me."

"Thank you," Richard said.

"You're welcome."

"I would recommend you go straight home and rest," Lillian said.

"I can't," I said.

She frowned at me. "Very well, but rest as soon as you can. If this is a mild concussion and you abuse yourself, it could worsen. And even if it isn't a concussion, rest will do you more good than gallivanting around."

I smiled. "Yes, Doctor."

She made a small umph sound. "I know how much attention you're going to pay to my orders. But go along with you, both of you. If you won't listen to good sense, then be gone."

I slid off the table, and Richard did not offer to help me. There were reasons why we had been dating this long. A moment of dizziness and I was fine.

Lillian didn't look happy. "You promise me that this dizziness is less than it was."

"Scout's honor."

She nodded. "I'll take your word for it." She didn't look really pleased about it, but she patted my shoulder and walked out. She had made no notes. There was no chart to check. Nothing to prove I'd ever been here, except for some bloody cotton swabs. It was a nice setup.

I had gotten to lie back and relax in the car on the way here. Just not having to tote around naked men or drive helped a lot. I really was feeling better, which was great since I had to see Jean-Claude tonight regardless of how I felt. I wondered whether Gretchen would have given me a night of grace if she had put me in the hospital. Probably not.

I couldn't put it off any longer. It was time to go. "I've got to go, Richard."

He put his hands on my shoulders. I didn't pull away. He turned me to look at him, and I let him. His face was very solemn. "I wish I could go with you."

"We've been over this," I said.

He looked away from my eyes. "I know."

I touched his chin and raised his eyes to mine. "No heroics, Richard, promise me."

His eyes were too innocent. "I don't know what you mean."

"Bullshit. You can't be waiting outside. You have to stay here. Promise me that."

He dropped his arms and stalked away from me. He leaned against the other examining table, palms flat, all his weight on his arms. "I hate you doing this alone."

"Promise me you will wait here, or wait at my apartment. Those are the only choices, Richard."

He wouldn't look at me. I walked over to him, and touched his arm. Tension sang through it. There was none of that otherworldly energy, yet, but it was there below the surface, waiting.

"Richard, look at me."

He stayed with his head bent, hair falling like a curtain between us. I ran my hand through that wavy hair, grabbing a handful close to the warmth of his skull. I used the hair like a handle and turned his face to me. His eyes were dark with more than just their color. Something was home in his eyes that I'd seen only last night. The beast was rising through his eyes like a sea monster swimming upward through dark water.

I tightened my grip on his hair, not to hurt, but to get his attention. A small sound escaped his throat. "If you fuck this up through some misguided male ego thing, you're going to get me killed." I drew his face towards me, hand tangled in his hair. When his face was only inches from mine, almost close enough to kiss, I said, "If you interfere, you will get me killed. Do you understand?"

The darkness in his eyes wanted to say no. I watched the struggle on his face. Finally he said, "I understand."

"You'll be waiting for me at home?"

He nodded, pulling his hair against my grip. I wanted to pull his face to me. To kiss him. We stood there frozen, hesitating. He moved to me. Our lips touched. It was a soft, gentle brush of lips. We stared at each other from an inch away. His eyes were drowning deep, and I could suddenly feel his body like an electric shock through my gut.

I jerked away from him. "No, not yet. I don't know how I feel about you anymore."

"Your body knows," he said.

"If lust was everything, I'd be with Jean-Claude."

His face crumbled as if I'd slapped him. "If you really aren't going to date me anymore, then don't tell Jean-Claude. It's not worth it."

He looked so hurt. That was one thing I'd never meant to do. I laid my hand on his arm. The skin was smooth, warm, real. "If I can get out of telling him, I will, but I don't think Gretchen will make that one of my choices. Besides, Jean-Claude can smell a lie. You did propose, and I said yes."

"Tell him you changed your mind, Anita. Tell him why. He'll love it. That I'm not human enough for you." He pulled away from my hand.

"Jean-Claude will just eat that up." His voice was bitter, angry. The bitterness was strong enough to walk on. I'd never heard him like that.

I couldn't stand it. I came up behind him and wrapped my arms around his waist. I buried my face in the line of his spine. Cheek cradled between the swell of his shoulders. He started to turn, but I held tighter. He stood very still in my arms. His hands touched my arms tentatively at first, then he hugged them to him. A shudder ran through his back. His breath came in a long gasp.

I turned him around to face me. Tears glistened on his cheeks. Jesus. I'd never been good around tears. My first instinct was to promise them anything if they would only stop crying.

"Don't," I said. I touched a fingertip to one tear. It clung to my skin, trembling. "Don't let this tear you up, Richard. Please."

"I can't be human again, Anita." His voice sounded very normal. If I hadn't seen the tears, I wouldn't have known he was crying. "I'd be human for you if I could."

"Maybe human isn't what I want, Richard. I don't know. Give me a little time. If I can't handle you being furry, better to find out now." I felt awful, mean and petty. He was gorgeous. I loved him. He wanted to marry me. He taught junior high science. He loved hiking, camping, caving. He collected sound tracks of musicals, for God's sake. And he was next in line to rule the pack. An alpha werewolf. Shit.

"I need time, Richard. I am so sorry, but I do." I sounded like a chump. I'd never sounded so indecisive in my life.

He nodded, but didn't look convinced. "You may end up turning me down but you're going to risk your life confronting Jean-Claude. It doesn't make sense."

I had to agree. "I have to talk to him tonight, Richard. I don't want another run-in with Gretchen. Not if I can avoid it."

Richard wiped the palms of his hands over his face. He ran his hands through his hair. "Don't get yourself killed."

"I won't," I said.

"Promise," he said.

I wanted to say, "Promise," but I didn't. "I don't make promises I can't keep."

"Couldn't you be comforting and lie to me?"

I shook my head. "No."

He sighed. "Talk about painful honesty."

"I've got to go." I walked away before he could distract me again. I was beginning to think he was doing it on purpose to delay me. Of course, I was letting him do it.

"Anita." I was almost to the door. I turned back. He stood there under the harsh lights, hands at his sides, looking . . . helpless.

"We've kissed good-bye. You've told me to be careful. I've warned you not to play hero. That's it, Richard. There is no more."

He said, "I love you."

Okay, so there was more. "I love you, too." It was the truth, damn it. If I could just get over his being furry, I would marry him. How would Jean-Claude take the news? As the old saying goes, only one way to find out.

24

GUILTY PLEASURES IS in the heart of the vampire district. Its glowing neon sign bled into the night sky, giving the blackness a crimson tint like a distant house fire. I hadn't come to the district unarmed after dark for a very long time. Okay, I had the knife, and it was better than arm wrestling, but against a vampire, not much better.

Stephen was beside me. A werewolf wasn't a bad bodyguard, but somehow Stephen didn't look scary enough. He was only an inch or two taller than me, slender as a willow with just enough shoulder definition to make him look masculine. To say his pants were tight wasn't enough. They were leather and looked painted on like a second skin. It was hard not to notice that his derriere was tight and firm. The leather jacket cut him off at the waist, so the view was unobstructed.

I was wearing my black trench coat again. It had a little bit of blood on it, but if I cleaned it, it would be wet. Wet would not keep me warm. My sweater, one of my favorite sweaters, was torn off one shoulder down to the line of my bra. Too cold without a coat. Gretchen owed me a sweater. Maybe after I got my guns back, we'd talk about that.

Three broad steps led up to closed doors. Buzz the Vampire was guarding them. It was the worst vampire name I'd ever heard. It wasn't great if you were human, but Buzz seemed all wrong for a vampire. It was a great name for a bouncer. He was tall and muscle-bound with a black crew cut. He seemed to be wearing the same black T-shirt he'd worn in July.

I knew vampires couldn't freeze to death, but I hadn't known they didn't get cold. Most vampires tried to play human. They wore coats in the winter. Maybe they didn't need them the same way Gretchen hadn't needed to take the knife from her throat. Maybe it was all pretend.

He smiled, flashing fangs. My reaction seemed to disappoint him. "You missed a set, Stephen. The boss is pissed."

Stephen sort of shrank in on himself. Buzz seemed to get larger, pleased with himself. "Stephen was helping me. I don't think Jean-Claude will mind."

Buzz squinted at me, really seeing my face for the first time. "Shit, what happened to you?"

"If Jean-Claude wants you to know, he'll tell you," I said. I walked past him. There was a large sign on the door: No Crosses, Crucifixes, or Other Holy Items Allowed Inside. I pushed the doors open and kept walking, my cross securely around my neck. They could pry it from my cold dead hands if they wanted it tonight.

Stephen stayed at my heels, almost as if he were afraid of Buzz. Buzz wasn't that old a vampire, less than twenty years. He still had a sense of "aliveness" to him. That utter stillness that the old ones have hadn't touched the bouncer yet. So why was a werewolf afraid of a new vampire? Good question.

It was Sunday night and the place was packed. Didn't anyone have work tomorrow? The noise washed over us like a wave of nearly solid sound. That rich murmurous sound of many people in a small space determined to have a good time. The lights were as bright as they ever got. The small stage empty. We were between shows.

A blond woman greeted us at the door. "Do you have any holy items to declare?" She smiled when she said it. The holy-item check girl.

I smiled when I said, "Nope."

She didn't question me, just smiled and walked away. A male voice said, "Just a moment, Shelia." The tall vampire that strode towards us was lovely to look at. He had high, sculpted cheekbones, and short blond hair styled to perfection. He was too masculine to be beautiful, and too perfect to be real. Robert had been a stripper last time I was here. It looked as though he'd moved up into management.

Shelia waited, looking from Robert to me. "She lied to me?"

Robert nodded. "Hello, Anita."

"Hello. Are you the manager here now?"

He nodded.

I didn't like it, him being manager. He'd failed me once, or rather failed Jean-Claude's orders. Failed to keep someone safe. That someone had died. Robert hadn't even gotten bloody trying to stop the monsters. He should at least have gotten hurt trying. I didn't insist he die to keep people safe, but he should have tried harder. I'd never completely trust him or forgive him.

"You are wearing a holy item, Anita. Unless on police business, you must give it to Shelia."

I glanced up at him. His eyes were blue. I glanced down, then up, and realized I could meet his eyes. He was over a hundred years old, not nearly as powerful as Gretchen, but I shouldn't have been able to meet his eyes.

His eyes widened. "You have to give it up. Those are the rules."

Maybe being able to look him in the eyes had given me courage, or maybe I had had enough for one night. "Is Gretchen here?"

He looked surprised. "Yes, she's in the back room with Jean-Claude."

"Then you can't have the cross."

"I can't let you in then. Jean-Claude is very clear on that." There was a hint of unease in his voice, almost fear. Good.

"Take a good look at my face, Bobby-boy. Gretchen did it. If she's here, I keep the cross."

Frown lines formed between his perfect brows. "Jean-Claude said no exceptions." He stepped closer, and I let him. He lowered his voice as much as he could and be heard above the noise. "He said if I ever fail him again in anything large or small, he'll punish me."

Normally, I thought statements like that were pitiful or cruel. I agreed with this one.

"Go ask Jean-Claude," I said.

He shook his head. "I cannot trust you to stay here. If you get past me with the cross, I will have failed."

This was getting tiresome. "Can Stephen go ask?"

Robert nodded.

Stephen sort of hung by me. He hadn't recovered from Buzz's remarks. "Is Jean-Claude mad at me for missing my set?"

"You should have called if you couldn't make your set," Robert said. "I had to go on in your place."

"Good to be useful," I said.

Robert frowned at me. "Stephen should have called."

"He was taking me to a doctor. You got a problem with that?"

"Jean-Claude may."

"Then bring the great man out and let's ask him. I'm tired of standing in the door."

"Anita, how good of you to grace us with your presence." Gretchen was practically purring with anticipation.

"Robert won't let me pass."

She turned her eyes to the vampire. He took a step back. She hadn't even unleashed any of that impressive magic yet. Robert scared easy for a century-old corpse.

"We have been awaiting her, Robert. Jean-Claude is most anxious to see her."

He swallowed hard. "I was told that no one came inside with a holy item other than the police. No exceptions were to be made."

"Not even for the master's sweetheart." She put a lot of irony in that last part.

Robert either didn't get it or ignored it. "Until Jean-Claude tells me differently, she doesn't go through with a cross."

Gretchen stalked around us all. I wasn't sure who looked more worried. "Take off the little cross and let us get this over with."

I shook my head. "Nope."

"It didn't do you a lot of good earlier tonight," she said.

She had a point. For the first time I realized I hadn't even thought of bringing out my cross earlier. I'd gone for my weapons, but not my faith. Pretty damn sad.

I fingered the cool silver of the chain. "The cross stays."

"You are both spoiling my fun," she said. The way she said it made that sound like a very bad thing. "I'll give you one of your weapons back."

A moment before I'd have agreed, but not now. I was embarrassed that I had not gone for my cross earlier. It wouldn't have kept her from jumping me at the beginning. She was too powerful for that. But it might have chased her off Louie. I was going to have to stop skipping church even if I didn't get to sleep at all.

"No."

"Is this your way of getting out of our bargain?" Her voice was low and warm with the first stirrings of anger.

"I keep my word," I said.

"I will escort her through, Robert." She raised a hand to stop his complaining. "If Jean-Claude blames you, tell him I was going to tear your throat out." She stepped into him until only a breath separated their bodies. It was only standing that close that you realized that Robert was taller by a head and a half. Gretchen seemed bigger than that. "It isn't a lie, Robert. I think you're weak, a liability. I would kill you now if our master did not need us both. If you still fear Jean-Claude, remember that he wants you alive. I do not."

Robert swallowed hard enough that it had to hurt. He didn't back up. Brownie point for him. She moved that fraction closer, and he jumped back as if he'd been shot. "Fine, fine, take her through."

Gretchen's lip curled in disgust. One thing we agreed on: we didn't like Robert. If we had one thing in common, maybe there'd be more. Maybe we could be girlfriends. Yeah, right.

The noise level had dropped to a background murmur. We had everybody's attention. Nothing like a floor show. "Is there supposed to be an act on stage right now?" I asked.

Robert nodded. "Yes, I need to introduce him."

"Go do your job, Robert." The words were thick with scorn. Gretchen gave good scorn.

Robert left us, obviously relieved. "Wimp," I said softly.

"Come, Anita, Jean-Claude is waiting for us." She stalked away, long pale coat swinging out behind her. Stephen and I exchanged glances. He shrugged. I followed her and he trailed behind as if he were afraid of losing me.

Jean-Claude's office was like being inside a domino. Stark white walls, white carpet, black lacquer desk, black office chair, black leather couch against one wall, and two straight-backed chairs sat in front of the desk. The desk and chairs were Oriental, set with enamel pictures of cranes and Oriental women in flowing robes. I'd always liked the desk, not that I would admit it out loud.

There was a black lacquer screen in one corner. I'd never seen it before. It was large, hiding one entire corner. A dragon curled across the screen in oranges and reds, with huge bulbous eyes. It was a nice addition to the room. It was not a comfortable room, but it was stylish. Like Jean-Claude.

He sat on the leather couch dressed all in black. The shirt had a high, stiff collar that framed his face. It was hard to tell where his hair left off and the shirt began. The collar was pinned at his throat, with a thumb-size ruby pendant. The shirt was open down to his belt, leaving a triangle of pale, pale skin showing. Only the pendant kept the shirt from opening completely.

The cuffs were as wide and stiff as the collar, nearly hiding his hands. He raised one hand and I could see the cuffs were open on one side so he could still use his hands. Black jeans and velvet black boots completed the outfit.

I'd seen the pendant before, but the shirt was certainly new. "Spiffy," I said.

He smiled. "Do you like it?" He straightened the cuffs, as if they needed it.

"It's a nice change from white," I said.

"Stephen, we were expecting you earlier." His voice was mild enough, but there was an undertaste of something dark and unpleasant.

"Stephen took me to the doctor."

His midnight blue eyes turned back to me. "Is your latest police investigation getting rough?"

"No," I said. I glanced at Gretchen. She was looking at Jean-Claude.

"Tell him," she said.

I didn't think she was referring to my accusing her of trying to kill me. It was time for a little honesty, or at least a little drama. I was sure Jean-Claude wouldn't disappoint us.

"Stephen needs to leave now," I said. I didn't want him getting killed trying to protect me. He wasn't up to being anything but cannon fodder. Not against Jean-Claude.

"Why?" he asked. He sounded suspicious.

"Get on with it," Gretchen said.

I shook my head. "Stephen doesn't need to be here."

"Get out, Stephen," Jean-Claude said. "I am not angry with you for missing your set. Anita is more important to me than your being on time to your job."

That was nice to know.

Stephen gave a sort of bob, almost a bow to Jean-Claude, flashed a look at me, and hesitated. "Go on, Stephen. I'll be all right."

I didn't have to reassure him twice. He fled.

"What have you been up to, *ma petite*?"

I glanced at Gretchen. She had eyes only for him. Her face looked hungry, as if she'd waited for this a long time. I stared into his dark blue eyes and realized that I could without vampire marks; I could meet his eyes.

Jean-Claude noticed it, too. His eyes widened just a bit. "*Ma petite*, you are full of surprises tonight."

"You ain't seen nothing yet," I said.

"By all means, continue. I do love a surprise."

I doubted he'd like this one. I took a deep breath and said it fast, as if that would make it go down better, like a spoonful of sugar. "Richard asked me to marry him, and I said yes." I could have added, "But I'm not sure anymore," but I didn't. I was too confused to offer up anything but the bare facts. If he tried to kill me, maybe I'd add details. Until then . . . we'd wait it out.

Jean-Claude just sat there. He didn't move at all. The heater clicked on, and I jumped. The vent was above the couch. The air played along his hair, the cloth of his shirt, but it was like watching a mannequin. The hair and clothes worked but the rest was stone.

The silence stretched and filled the room. The heater died, and the quiet was so profound I could hear the blood rushing in my ears. It was like the stillness before creation. You knew something big was coming. You just didn't know quite what. I let the silence flow around me. I wouldn't be the one to break it, because I was afraid of what came next. This utter calmness was more unnerving than anger would have been. I didn't know what to do with it, so I did nothing. A course of action I seldom regret.

It was Gretchen who broke first. "Did you hear her, Jean-Claude? She is to wed another. She loves another."

He blinked once, a long, graceful sweep of lashes. "Ask her now if she loves me, Gretchen."

Gretchen stepped in front of me, blocking Jean-Claude from view. "What does it matter? She's going to marry someone else."

"Ask her." It was a command.

Gretchen whirled to face me. The bones in her face stood out under the skin, lips thin with rage. "You don't love him."

It wasn't exactly a question, so I didn't answer it. Jean-Claude's voice came lazy and full of some dark meaning that I didn't understand. "Do you love me, *ma petite*?"

I stared into Gretchen's rage-filled face and said, "I don't suppose you'd believe me if I said no?"

"Can you not simply say yes?"

"Yes, in some dark, twisted part of my soul, I love you. Happy?"

He smiled. "How can you marry him if you love me?"

"I love him, too, Jean-Claude."

"In the same way?"

"No," I said.

"How do you love us differently?"

The questions were getting trickier. "How am I supposed to explain something to you that I don't even understand myself?"

"Try."

"You're like great Shakespearean tragedy. If Romeo and Juliet hadn't committed suicide, they'd have hated each other in a year. Passion is a form of love, but it isn't real. It doesn't last."

"And how do you feel about Richard?" His voice was full of some strong emotion. It should have been anger, but it felt different from that. Almost as if it were an emotion I didn't have a word for.

"I don't just love Richard, I like him. I enjoy his company. I . . ." I hated explaining myself. "Oh, hell, Jean-Claude, I can't put it into words. I can see spending my life with Richard, and I can't see it with you."

"Have you set a date?"

"No," I said.

He cocked his head to one side, studying me. "It is the truth but there is some bit of lie to it. What are you holding back, *ma petite*?"

I frowned at him. "I've told you the truth."

"But not all of it."

I didn't want to tell him. He'd enjoy it too much. I felt vaguely disloyal to Richard. "I'm not completely sure about marrying Richard."

"Why not?" There was something in his face that was almost hopeful. I couldn't let him get the wrong idea.

"I saw him go all spooky. I felt his . . . power."

"And?"

"And now I'm not sure," I said.

"He's not human enough for you, either." He threw back his head and laughed. A joyous outpouring of sound that coated me like chocolate. Heavy and sweet and annoying.

"She loves another," Gretchen said. "Does it matter if she doubts him? She doubts you. She rejects you, Jean-Claude. Isn't that enough?"

"Did you do all that to her face?"

She stalked a tight circle like a tiger in a cage. "She does not love you as I do." She knelt in front of him, hands touching his legs, face staring up into his. "Please, I love you. I've always loved you. Kill her or let her marry this man. She doesn't deserve your adoration."

He ignored her. "Are you all right, *ma petite*?"

"I'm fine."

Gretchen dug fingers into his jeans, grabbing at him. "Please, please!"

I didn't like her, but the pain, the hopeless pain in her voice was horrible to hear. She'd tried to kill me and I still felt sorry for her.

"Leave us, Gretchen."

"No!" She clutched at him.

"I forbade you to harm her. You disobeyed me. I should kill you."

She just stayed kneeling, gazing up at him. I couldn't see her expression and was glad of it. I wasn't big on adoration. "Jean-Claude, please, please, I only did it for you. She doesn't love you."

His hand was suddenly around her neck. I hadn't seen him move. It was magic. Whatever was letting me look him in the eyes, it didn't stop him playing with my mind. Or maybe he was just that fast. Naw.

She tried to talk. His fingers closed, and the words came out as small, choked sounds. He stood, drawing her to her feet. Her hands wrapped around his wrist, trying to keep him from hanging her. He kept lifting until her feet dangled in the air. I knew she could fight him. I'd felt the strength in those delicate-seeming hands. Except for her hand on his wrist she didn't even struggle. Would she let him kill her? Would he do it? Could I stand here and just watch?

He stood there in his wonderful black shirt, looking elegant and scrumptious, and holding Gretchen with one arm, straight up. He walked towards his desk still holding her. He kept his balance effortlessly. Even a lycanthrope couldn't have done it, not like that. I watched his slender body walk across the carpet and knew he could pretend all he wanted to, but it wasn't human. He wasn't human.

He set her feet on the carpet on the far side of the desk. He relaxed his grip on her throat but didn't let her go.

"Jean-Claude, please. Who is she that the Master of the City should beg for her attention?"

He kept his hand resting on her throat, not squeezing now. He pushed the screen back with his free hand. It folded back to reveal a coffin. It sat up off the ground on a cloth-draped pedestal. The wood was nearly black and polished to a mirrorlike shine.

Gretchen's eyes widened. "Jean-Claude, Jean-Claude, I'm sorry. I didn't kill her. I could have. Ask her. I could have killed her, but I didn't. Ask her. Ask her!" Her voice was pure panic.

"Anita." That one word slithered across my skin, thick and full of forboding. I was very glad that that voice was not angry with me.

"She could have killed me with the first rush," I said.

"Why do you think she did not do it?"

"I think she got distracted trying to draw it out. To enjoy it more."

"No, no, I was just threatening her. Trying to frighten her away. I knew you wouldn't want me to kill her. I knew that, or she'd be dead."

"You were always a bad liar, Gretel."

Gretel?

He raised the lid on the coffin with one hand, drawing her nearer to it.

She jerked away from him. His fingernails drew bloody furrows on her throat. She stood behind the office chair, putting it between her and him, as if it would help. Blood trickled down her throat.

"Do not make me force you, Gretel."

"My name is Gretchen and has been for over a hundred years." It was the first real spirit I'd seen in her against Jean-Claude anyway. I fought the urge to applaud. It wasn't hard.

"You were Gretel when I found you, and you are Gretel still. Do not force me to remind you of what you are, Gretel."

"I will not go into that cursed box willingly. I won't do it."

"Do you really want Anita to see you at your worst?"

I thought I already had.

"I will not go." Her voice was firm, not confident, but stubborn. She meant it.

Jean-Claude stood very still. He raised one hand in a languid gesture. There was no other word for it. The movement was almost dancelike.

Gretchen staggered, grabbing at the chair for support. Her face seemed to have shrunk. It wasn't the drawing down of power that I had seen on her earlier. Not the ethereal corpse that would tear your throat out and dance in the blood. The flesh squeezed down, wrapping tight on the bones. She was withering. Not aging, dying.

She opened her mouth and screamed.

"My God, what's happening to her?"

Gretchen stood clutching bird-thin hands on the chair back. She looked like a mummified corpse. Her bright lipstick was a gruesome slash across her face. Even her yellow hair had thinned, dry and brittle as straw.

Jean-Claude walked towards her, still graceful, still lovely, still monstrous. "I gave you eternal life and I can take it back, never forget that."

She made a low mewling sound in her throat. She held out one feeble hand to him, beseeching.

"Into the box," he said. His voice made that last word dark and terrible, as if he'd said "hell" and meant it.

He had beaten the fight out of her, or maybe stolen was the word. I'd never seen anything like this. A new vampire power that I'd never even heard whispered in folklore. Shit.

Gretchen took a trembling step towards the coffin. Two painful, dragging steps and she lost her grip on the chair. She fell, bone-thin arms catching her full weight, the way you're not supposed to. A good way to get your arm broken. Gretchen didn't seem to be worried about broken bones. Couldn't blame her.

She knelt on the floor, head hanging as if she didn't have the strength to rise. Jean-Claude just stood there, staring at her. He made no move to help her. If it had been anyone but Gretchen, I might have helped her myself.

I must have made some movement towards her because Jean-Claude made a back-away gesture to me. "If she fed on a human at this moment, all her strength would return. She is very frightened. I would not tempt her right now, *ma petite*."

I stayed where I was. I hadn't planned on helping her, but I didn't like watching it.

"Crawl," he said.

She started to crawl.

I'd had enough. "You've made your point, Jean-Claude. If you want her in the coffin, just pick her up and put her there."

He looked at me. There was something almost amused in his face. "You feel pity for her, *ma petite*. She meant to kill you. You know that."

"I'd have no problem shooting her, but this . . ." I didn't have a word for it. He wasn't just humiliating her. He was stripping her of herself. I shook my head. "You're tormenting her. If it's for my benefit, I've seen enough. If it's for your benefit, then stop it."

"It is for her benefit, *ma petite*. She has forgotten who her master is. A month or two in a coffin will remind her of that."

Gretchen had reached the foot of the pedestal. She had grabbed handfuls of the cloth but couldn't drag herself to her feet.

"I think she's been reminded enough."

"You are so harsh, *ma petite*, so pragmatic, yet suddenly something will move you to pity. And your pity is as strong as your hate."

"But not nearly as fun," I said.

He smiled and lifted the lid of the coffin. The inside was white silk, of course. He knelt and lifted Gretchen. Her limbs lay awkwardly in his arms as if they didn't quite work. As he lifted her over the lip of the coffin, her long coat dragged against the wood. Something in her pocket clunked, solid and heavy.

I almost hated to ask—almost. "If that's my gun in her pocket, I need it back."

He laid her almost gently in the silk lining, then rifled her pockets. He held the Browning in one hand and began to lower the lid. Her skeletal hands raised, trying to stop its descent.

Watching those thin hands beat at the air, I almost let it go. "There should be another gun and a knife."

He widened his eyes at me, but nodded. He held the Browning out to me. I walked forward and took it. I was standing close enough to see her eyes. They were pale and cloudy, like the eyes of the very old, but there was enough expression left for terror.

Her eyes rolled wildly, staring at me. There was a mute appeal in that look. Desperation was too mild a word for it. She looked at me, not Jean-Claude, as if she knew that I was the only person in the room that gave a damn. If it bothered Jean-Claude, you couldn't tell it by his face.

I tucked the Browning under my arm. It felt good to have it back. He held the Firestar out to me. "I cannot find the knife. If you want to search her yourself, feel free."

I stared down at the dry, wrinkled skin, the lipless face. Her neck was as skinny as a chicken's. I shook my head. "I don't want it that bad."

He laughed, and even now the sound curled along my skin like velvet. A joyous sociopath.

He closed the lid, and she made horrible sounds, as though she were trying to scream and had no voice to do it with. Her thin hands beat against the lid.

Jean-Claude snapped the locks in place and leaned over the closed coffin. He whispered, "Sleep." Almost immediately the sounds slowed. He repeated the word once more, and the sounds ceased.

"How did you do that?"

"Quiet her?"

I shook my head. "All of it."

"I am her master."

"No, Nikolaos was your master, but she couldn't do that. She'd have done it to you if she could have."

"Perceptive of you, and very true. I made Gretchen. Nikolaos did not make me. Being the master vampire that brings someone over gives you certain powers over them. As you saw."

"Nikolaos had made most of the vampires in her little entourage, right?"

He nodded.

"If she could have done what you just did, I'd have seen it. She'd have shown it off."

He gave a small smile. "Again perceptive. There are a variety of powers that a master vampire can possess. Calling an animal, levitation, resistance to silver."

"Is that why my knife didn't seem to hurt Gretchen?"

"Yes."

"But each master has a different arsenal of gifts."

"Arsenal, it is an appropriate word. Now, where were we, *ma petite*? Ah, yes, I could kill Richard."

Here we go again.

25

"DID YOU HEAR me, *ma petite*? I could kill your Richard." He pulled the screen back into place. The coffin and its terrible contents gone just like that.

"You don't want to do that."

"Oh, but I do, *ma petite*. I would love to tear out his heart and watch him die." He walked past me. The black shirt fanned around him, exposing his stomach as he moved.

"I told you, I'm not sure I'm going to marry him. I'm not even sure I'm going to be dating him anymore. Isn't that enough?"

"No, *ma petite*. You love him. I can smell his scent on your skin. You have kissed him tonight. With all your doubts, you have held him close."

"Hurt him and I'll kill you, simple as that." My voice was very matter-of-fact.

"You would try to kill me, but I am not so easily killed." He sat down on the couch again, shirt spreading out around him, leaving most of his upper body exposed. The cross-shaped burn scar was a shiny imperfection on his flawless skin.

I stayed standing. He hadn't offered me a seat anyway. "Maybe we'd kill each other. It's your choice of music, Jean-Claude, but once we start this dance, it doesn't stop until one of us is dead."

"I am not allowed to harm Richard. Is he allowed to harm me?"

Good question. "I don't think it'll come up."

"You have dated him for months, and I have said little. Before you marry him, I want equal time."

I looked at him. "What do you mean, 'equal time'?"

"Date me, Anita, give me a chance to woo you."

"Woo me?"

"Yes," he said.

I just stared at him. I didn't know what to say. "I've been trying to avoid you for months. I'm not just going to give in now."

"Then I will start the music, and we will dance. Even if I die, and you die. Richard will die first, that I can promise you. Surely dating me is not a fate worse than that."

He had a point, and yet . . . "I don't give in to threats."

"Then I appeal to your sense of fair play, *ma petite*. You have allowed Richard to win your heart. If you had dated me first, would it be my heart you hold so dear? If you had not fought our mutual attraction, would you even have given Richard a second glance?"

I couldn't say yes, and be honest. I wasn't sure. I had refused Jean-Claude because he wasn't human. He was a monster and I didn't date monsters. But last night I'd had a glimpse of what Richard might be. I'd felt a power that rivaled Jean-Claude's creep along my skin. It was getting harder to tell the humans from the monsters. I was even beginning to wonder about myself. There are more roads to monsterdom than most people realize.

"I don't believe in casual sex. I haven't slept with Richard, either."

"I am not blackmailing you into sex, *ma petite*. I am trying to get equal time."

"If I agree, then what?"

"Why, I pick you up on Friday night."

"Like a date-date?"

He nodded. "We might even discover how you are meeting my eyes with impunity."

"Let's just stick to as normal a date as we can."

"As you like."

I stared at him. He looked at me. He would pick me up on Friday. We had a date. I wondered how Richard would feel about that.

"I can't date both of you indefinitely."

"Allow me a few months, as you have given Richard. If I cannot win you from him, then I will retire from the field."

"You'll leave me alone and you won't harm Richard?"

He nodded.

"You give me your word?"

"My word of honor."

I took it. It was the best offer I was going to get. I wasn't sure how much his word of honor was worth, but it gave us time. Time to work something else out. I didn't know what else, but there had to be something. Something besides dating the freaking Master of the City.

26

THERE WAS A knock on the door. It opened without Jean-Claude's giving permission. Somebody was pushy. Raina stalked in through the door. Pushy was one word for it.

She was wearing a rust-collared trench coat with the belt tied very tight at her waist. The buckle flopped loosely as she glided into the room. She undid a multicolored scarf and shook her auburn hair. It shimmered in the light.

Gabriel followed at her back in a black trench coat. His-and-her outfits. His hair and strange grey eyes looked as good with his coat as Raina's did with hers. Earrings glittered from the earlobe to the curl at the top of his ear. Every piece of metal was silver.

Kaspar Gunderson followed at their heels. He was wearing a pale tweed coat and one of those hats with a little feather in the band. He looked like an elegant version of everybody's 1950s dream dad. He didn't look happy to be here.

Robert stood sort of hovering in the doorway. "I told them you were busy, Jean-Claude. I told them you didn't want to be disturbed." He was practically wringing his hands with anxiety. After what I'd seen done to Gretchen I didn't blame him for being afraid.

"Come in, Robert, and close the door behind you," Jean-Claude said.

"I really need to oversee the next act. I . . ."

"Come in and close the door, Robert."

The century-old vampire did as he was told. He closed the door and leaned against it, one hand on the doorknob as if that would keep him safe. The right sleeve of his white shirt was sliced up, and blood trickled out of fresh claw marks. His throat showed more blood, as if a clawed hand had lifted him by the throat. Like Jean-Claude had done to Gretchen, but with talons.

"I told you what would happen if you failed me again, Robert. In anything, large or small." Jean-Claude's voice was a whisper that filled the room like wind.

Robert dropped to his knees on the white carpet. "Please, master, please." He extended his hands towards Jean-Claude. A thick drop of blood plopped from his arm to the carpet. The blood seemed very red against the white, white carpet.

Raina smiled. I was betting I knew whose claw marks Robert was sporting. Kaspar went to sit on the couch, distancing himself from the show. Gabriel was looking at me. "Nice coat," he said.

We were both wearing black trench coats. Great. "Thanks," I said.

He grinned flashing, pointy teeth.

I wanted to ask him if the silver earrings hurt but Robert made a low whimpering noise, and I turned back to the main show.

"Come to me, Robert." Jean-Claude's voice had heat to it, enough to scald.

Robert went nearly prone on the carpet, abasing himself. "Please, master. Please don't."

Jean-Claude stalked towards him, fast enough to have his black shirt sweeping behind him like a miniature cape. His pale skin flashed against the black cloth. He stopped beside the cowering vampire. Jean-Claude's shirt swirled around the suddenly quiet body. Jean-Claude stood utterly still. The cloth had more life to it than he did.

Jesus. "He tried, Jean-Claude," I said. "Leave him alone."

Jean-Claude stared at me, his eyes a bottomless blue. I looked away from those eyes. Maybe I could meet his gaze with impunity, but then again . . . He was always full of surprises.

"I was under the impression, *ma petite*, that you did not like Robert."

"I don't, but I've seen enough punishment for one night. They blood-ied him just because he wouldn't let them in your office a few minutes early. Why aren't you mad about that?"

Raina walked over to Jean-Claude. The spiked heels of her metallic copper pumps made indents in the carpet. A trail of stab wounds.

Jean-Claude watched her come. His face was neutral but there was something about the way he held himself. Was he afraid of her? Maybe. But there was a wariness to his body as she moved closer. He wasn't happy. More and more curious.

"We had an appointment with Jean-Claude. It would have hurt my feelings to be turned away at the door." She stepped over Robert, flash-ing a lot of leg. I wasn't sure she was wearing anything under the trench coat. Robert did not try to sneak a peek. He froze, flinching as her coat brushed his back.

Raina stood with her shapely calves, nearly touching Robert. He didn't move away from her. He seemed to just freeze as if he could pre-tend he wasn't there and everyone would forget about him. He wished.

She was standing so close to Jean-Claude that the length of their bod-ies touched. She was sort of wedged between the two vampires. I expected Jean-Claude to step back, give her a little room. He didn't.

She ran her fingers under his shirt, laying her hands on either side of his naked waist. Her lipsticked mouth parted and she leaned into him. She kissed him, and he stood like a statue under her hands. But he didn't tell her to go to hell.

What the hell was going on?

Raina raised her face enough to speak. "Jean-Claude doesn't wish to offend Marcus. He needs the pack's backing to hold the city. Don't you, love?"

He put his hands on her slender waist and stepped back. Her hands trailed along his skin until he was completely out of reach. She watched him the way snakes watch small birds. Hungry. You didn't have to be a vampire to feel her lust. Obvious was putting it kindly.

"Marcus and I have an arrangement," Jean-Claude said.

"What sort of arrangement?" I asked.

"Why do you care, *ma petite*? You are going to be seeing Monsieur

Zeeman. Am I not allowed to see other people? I have offered you monogamy and you have turned me down."

I hadn't thought about it. It did bother me. Damn. "It's not the sharing that bothers me, Jean-Claude."

Raina walked up behind him, long painted nails tracing his skin. Hands curling up his chest until her chin rested on his shoulder. Jean-Claude relaxed in her arms this time. He leaned his back against her, pale hands caressing her arms. He stared at me while he did it.

"What does bother you, *ma petite*?"

"Your choice of playmates."

"Jealous?" Raina asked.

"No."

"Liar," she said.

What was I supposed to say? That it bothered me to see her hanging all over him? It did. Which bothered me more than her groping him.

I shook my head. "Just wondering how far you'll go to secure the pack's favor."

"Oh, all the way," Raina said. She moved around to stand in front of him. She was taller than he was in her heels. "You are going to come play with me." She kissed him, one quick movement. She dropped to her knees in front of him, gazing upward.

Jean-Claude stroked her hair. His pale graceful hands raising her face upward. He bent towards her as if to kiss her, but he stared at me while he did it.

Was he waiting for me to say, no, don't? He'd seemed almost afraid of her at first. Now he was utterly comfortable. I knew he was taunting me. Trying to make me jealous. It was sort of working.

He kissed her long and lingering. He looked up from it with her lipstick smeared on his lips. "What are you thinking, *ma petite*?"

He couldn't read my mind anymore, one point for not having vampire marks. "That I think less of you for having sex with Raina."

Gabriel gave a warm, rolling laugh. "Oh, he hasn't had sex with her, not yet." He walked towards me in a long, gliding stride.

I flashed the trench coat showing the Browning. "Let's not get crazed."

He undid the trench coat's belt, and raised his hands in surrender. He wasn't wearing a shirt. He had a silver ring through his left nipple, and the edge of his belly button.

It made me wince just to see it. "I thought silver hurt a lycanthrope, like an allergy."

"It burns," he said. His voice had a soft huskiness to it.

"And this is a good thing?" I asked.

Gabriel put his hands down slowly and shrugged the coat off his shoulders. He turned slowly as the cloth fell like a striptease. I didn't see any other silver rings. He whirled as it came off his arms, and at the apex of the turn he flung it on me. I batted at the coat, knocking it away from me. That was the mistake.

He was on me, body flattening me to the floor. My arms ended up pinned to my chest, trapped under his coat. His waist had the Firestar trapped. I went for the Browning and his hand tore through the coat like paper, ripped the gun out from under my arm. He damn near took the holster and my arm with it. For a second my left arm was just one raw pain. When I could feel my arm again the Browning was gone and I was staring up into Gabriel's face from three inches away.

He wriggled his hips, grinding the Firestar into both of us. It had to hurt him more than it hurt me.

"Doesn't that hurt?" I asked. My voice was surprisingly calm.

"I like pain," he said. He put the tip of his tongue on my chin and licked across my mouth. He laughed. "Struggle harder. Push those little hands."

"You like pain?" I said.

"Yeah."

"You're gonna love this." I shoved the knife into his upper stomach. He gave a small sound between a grunt and a sigh. A shudder ran the length of his body. He reared up over me, still pinning me from the waist down, like he was doing girl's push-ups.

I raised myself up with him, shoving the knife in deeper, drawing the blade upward through the meat of his body.

Gabriel ripped the coat into pieces but didn't try to grab the knife. He braced an arm on either side of me, staring downward at the knife and my bloody hands.

He rested his face in my hair, slumping just a little. I thought he'd pass out. He whispered, "Deeper."

"Oh, Jesus." The blade was almost at the bottom of his sternum. When I got to it one upward thrust would give me his heart.

I lay back on the floor to get a better angle for the killing blow.

"Don't kill him," Raina said. "We need him."

We? The knife was on its way to his heart when he rolled off me in a blinding blur of speed. He ended up lying on his back not too far away. He was breathing very fast, his chest rising and falling. Blood poured down his naked skin. His eyes were closed, lips curled in a half smile.

If he'd been human he might have died later tonight. Instead he lay on the carpet smiling. He rolled his head to one side and opened his eyes. His strange grey eyes looked at me. "That was wonderful."

"Jesus H. Christ," I said. I got to my feet using the couch for support. I was covered in Gabriel's blood. The knife was thick with it.

Kaspar was sitting on the corner of the couch staring at me. He huddled in his coat, eyes wide. I didn't blame him.

I wiped my hands and blade on the black couch. "Thanks for the help, Jean-Claude."

"I was told that you are a dominant now, *ma petite*. Struggles of internal dominance are not to be interfered with." He smiled. "Besides, you did not need my help."

Raina knelt beside Gabriel. She lowered her face to his bleeding stomach and began to lick it. Long, slow movements of her tongue. Her throat convulsed as she swallowed.

I would not be sick. I would not be sick. I looked at Kaspar. "What are you doing with these two?"

Raina raised a blood coated face. "Kaspar is our sample."

"What's that supposed to mean?"

"He can shapeshift back and forth as often as he wants to. He doesn't pass out. We use him to test potential stars of our movie productions. To see how they react to somebody changing shape in the middle of things."

I was going to be sick. "Please tell me you don't mean he changes in the middle of sex as a sort of screen test."

Raina cocked her head to one side. Her tongue rolled around her mouth, licking the blood clean. "You know about our little films?"

"Yeah."

"I'm surprised Richard told you. He doesn't approve of our fun."

"Are you in the movies?"

"Kaspar won't play on film," Raina said. She stood up and walked towards the couch. "Marcus won't force anybody to be on film. But Kaspar helps us audition people. Don't you, Kaspar?"

He nodded. He was staring at the carpet, working very hard at not looking at her.

"Why are you all here tonight?" I asked.

"Jean-Claude promised us some vampires for our next movie."

"That true?" I asked.

Jean-Claude's face was blank, lovely but unreadable. "Robert needs to be punished."

I frowned at the change of subject. "The coffin's full."

"There are always more coffins, Anita."

Robert crawled forward. "I'm sorry, master. I'm sorry." He didn't touch Jean-Claude, but he crept close to him. "I can't bear the box again, master. Please."

"You're afraid of Raina, Jean-Claude. What do you expect Robert to do with her?"

"I am not afraid of Raina."

"Fine, but Robert was overmatched. You know he was."

"Perhaps you are right, *ma petite*."

Robert looked up. A moment of hope flashed across his handsome face. "Thank you, master." He looked at me. "Thank you, Anita."

I shrugged.

"You can have Robert for your next film," Jean-Claude said.

Robert grabbed his leg. "Master, I . . ."

"Oh, come on, Jean-Claude, don't give him to her."

Raina plopped down on the couch between Kaspar and me. I stood up. She put an arm over Kaspar's shoulders. He flinched.

"He's handsome enough. Any vampire can take a great deal of punishment. Most acceptable," she said.

"You saw them here tonight," I said. "Do you really want to do that to one of your own people?"

"Let Robert decide," Jean-Claude said. "The box, or Raina?"

Robert looked up at the lycanthrope. She smiled at him with her bloody mouth.

Robert lowered his head so he could see her, then nodded. "Not the box. Anything is better than that."

"I'm out of here," I said. I'd had all the interpreternatural politics that I could stand for one night.

"Don't you want to see the show?" Raina said.

"I thought I'd seen the show," I said.

She tossed Kaspar's hat across the room. "Strip," she said.

I'd sheathed the knife and retrieved the Browning from the carpet where Gabriel had thrown it. I was armed. For what good it did me.

Kaspar sat there on the couch. There was a pink flush to his white skin. His eyes glittered. Angry, embarrassed. "I was a prince before your ancestors discovered this country."

Raina propped her chin on his shoulder, still hugging his shoulders. "We know how blue your pedigree is. You were a prince and you were such a big, bad hunter, such a wicked boy that a witch cursed you. She turned you into something beautiful and harmless. She hoped you'd learn how to be gentle and kind." She licked his ear, running her hands through his feathery hair. "But you aren't gentle or kind. Your heart is just as cold and your pride just as impervious as it was centuries ago. Now, take off your clothes and turn into a swan for us."

"You don't need me to do it for the vampire," he said.

"No, do it for me. Do it so Anita can see. Do it so Gabriel and I don't hurt you." Her voice was going lower. Each word more measured.

"You can't kill me, not even with silver," he said.

"But we can make you wish you could die, Kaspar."

He screamed, a low, ragged cry of frustration. He stood up abruptly and pulled on his coat. The buttons snapped and fell to the carpet. He flung the coat into Raina's face.

She laughed.

I started for the door.

"Oh, don't leave yet, Anita. Kaspar may be a pain in the ass, but he's really quite beautiful."

I glanced back.

Kaspar's sport jacket and tie lay on the carpet. He unbuttoned his white dress shirt with quick, angry movements. There was a line of white feathers down the middle of his chest. Soft and downy as an Easter duck.

I shook my head and kept going for the door. I did not run. I did not walk faster than normal. It was the bravest thing I'd done all night.

27

I TOOK A taxi home. Stephen stayed behind to strip or just to lick Jean-Claude's boots, I wasn't sure which and I wasn't sure I cared. I'd made sure Stephen wasn't in trouble. It was the best I could do. He was Jean-Claude's creature, and I'd had about enough of the Master of the City for one night.

Killing Gretchen was one thing, tormenting her was another. I kept flashing on the sound of her frantically beating hands. I'd like to believe that Jean-Claude would keep her asleep, but I knew better. He was a master vampire. They ruled, in part, through fear. Gretchen seemed like a real good threat. Displease me and I'll do that to you. Worked for me.

I was standing outside my apartment when I realized I didn't have a key to it. I'd given Richard my car keys, which had my house keys on the ring.

It felt silly standing out in the hallway about to knock on my own front door. The door opened without me touching it. Richard stood in the doorway. He smiled. "Hi," he said.

I found myself smiling back. "Hi, yourself."

He stepped back to one side, giving me room. He hadn't tried to kiss me in the door like Ozzie meeting Harriet after work. I was glad. It was too intimate a ritual. If we ever did this for real, he could molest me at the door, but not tonight.

He closed the door behind me, and I half expected him to take my coat. Wisely, he did not.

I took off my own coat and laid it across the couch, where all good coats go. The warm smell of cooking food filled the apartment. "You've been cooking," I said, not entirely pleased.

"I thought you might be hungry. Besides, all I had to do was wait. I cooked. It filled the time."

I could understand that. Though cooking would never have occurred to me unless forced.

The only lights were in the kitchen. It looked like a lighted cave from the darkened living room. If I wasn't mistaken, there were candles on the table.

"Are those candles?"

He laughed. It had an embarrassed edge to it. "Too hokey?"

"It's a two-seater breakfast table. You can't possibly serve a fancy dinner on it."

"I thought we'd use the divider as a buffet and just have plates on the table. There's room if we're careful where we put our elbows." He walked past me into the light. He started puttering with a saucepan, sloshing something around in it.

I stood there staring at my kitchen, watching my possible fiancé cooking my dinner. My skin felt tight and itchy. I couldn't draw a complete breath. I wanted to go right back out the door. This was more intimate than a kiss at the door. He'd moved in, made himself at home.

I didn't leave. It was the bravest thing I'd done all night. I checked the lock on the door automatically. He'd left it unlocked. Careless.

I didn't know what to do next. My apartment was my refuge. I could come here and just kick back. I could be alone. I liked being alone. I needed some time to unwind, regroup, think how to tell him Jean-Claude and I had a date.

"Will dinner be spoiled if I clean up first?"

"I can reheat everything when you're ready. I planned the meal so it wouldn't ruin no matter how late you were."

Great. "I'm going to go clean up then."

He turned to me, framed by the light. He'd tied his hair back, but it was coming loose in long, curling strands. His sweater was a burnt orange that made his skin look golden highlighted. He was wearing an apron that said, Mrs. Lovett's Meatpies on it. I didn't own an apron, and I certainly wouldn't have chosen one with a logo from *Sweeney Todd*. A musical about cannibalism seemed inappropriate for an apron. Delightfully so, but still . . .

"I'm going to go clean up."

"You said that."

I turned on my heel and walked to the bedroom. I did not run, though the temptation was great. I closed the door to my bedroom and leaned against it. My bedroom was untouched. No signs of invasion.

There was a love seat under the room's only window. Stuffed toy penguins sit on the love seat and spill down onto the floor. The collection was threatening to take over half the floor like a creeping tide. I grabbed the nearest one and sat on the corner of the bed. I hugged it tight, burying the upper half of my face in its fuzzy head.

I'd said I would marry Richard, so why was I so bugged about his sudden domestic turn? We downgraded the yes to a maybe, but even if it had still been a yes it would have bugged me. Marriage. The implications of that hadn't really sunk in. It wasn't fair to ask questions like that when he was half-naked and looking yummy. If he'd dropped to one knee over a fancy restaurant dinner, would my answer have been different? Maybe. But we'd never know, would we?

If I'd been alone, I wouldn't have eaten at all. I'd have taken a shower, thrown on an oversize T-shirt, and gone to bed surrounded by a few select penguins.

Now I had a fancy dinner to eat, by candlelight nonetheless. If I said I wasn't hungry, would he be insulted? Would he pout? Would he yell about all the work going to waste and tell me about starving kids in Southeast Asia?

"Shit," I said softly and with feeling. Well, hell, if we ever were going to cohabitate, he'd have to know the truth. I was unsociable, and food was something you ate so you wouldn't die.

I decided to do what I'd have done if he hadn't been here, sort of. I really disliked feeling uncomfortable in my own home. If I'd known it was going to feel like this, I'd have called Ronnie to wake me every hour. I was fine. I didn't need the help, but Ronnie would have been more comfy, less threatening. Of course, if Gretchen got out of her box, I trusted Richard would survive an attack, but wasn't so sure about Ronnie. One good point in Richard's favor. He was damn hard to kill.

I put the Browning in the holster built into the bed. I stripped off the sweater and let it fall to the floor. It was ruined and sweaters didn't wrinkle anyway. I laid the Firestar on the back of the toilet. Then I stripped off and got in the shower. I didn't lock the bedroom door. It would seem insulting, as if, if I didn't lock the door, he'd be naked in the bed with a rose in his teeth when I came out.

I locked the bathroom door. I'd done it when I was home with my father. Now I did it so if someone busted down the door, I'd have time to grab the Firestar off the toilet.

I turned the shower on as hot as it would go and stayed under it until my fingers started to prune. I was scrubbed clean and had delayed as long as I could.

I wiped the steam from the mirror with a towel. The top layer of skin was gone from my right cheek. It would heal just fine, but a scrape looks like hell until it heals. There was a small scrape on my chin and the side of my nose. A knot was blossoming into brilliant color on my forehead. I looked as though I'd been hit by a train. It was amazing that anyone wanted to kiss me.

I peeked out the door into the bedroom. No one was waiting for me. The room was empty and full of the whir of the heater. It was quiet, peaceful, and I couldn't hear any noises from the kitchen. I let out a long sigh. Alone, for a little while.

I was vain enough that I didn't want Richard to see me in my usual nighttime attire. I had had a nice black robe that matched a tiny black teddy. An overly optimistic date had given it to me. He never got to see me wear it. Fancy that. The robe had died a sad death covered in blood and other bodily fluids.

Wearing the teddy seemed cruel since I didn't plan on having sex with him. I stood in front of my closet and didn't have a thing to wear. Since I consider clothes something you wear so you won't be naked, that was pretty sad.

I put on an oversize T-shirt with a caricature of Mary Shelley on it, a pair of grey sweatpants—not the fancy ones, either, the kind with a drawstring in them. The way God intended sweatpants to be. A pair of white jogging socks, the closest thing I owned to slippers, and I was ready to go.

I looked at myself in the mirror and wasn't happy. I was comfortable, but it wasn't very flattering. But it was honest. I've never understood those women who wear makeup, do their hair, and dress wonderfully until after they're married. Suddenly, they forget what makeup is and lose all their thin clothes. If we did marry, he should see what he'd be sleeping beside every night. I shrugged and walked out.

He'd combed his hair out. It foamed around his face, soft and inviting. The candles were gone. So was the apron. He stood in the entryway between kitchen and living room. His arms were crossed over his chest, shoulder leaning against the doorjamb. He smiled. He looked so scrumptious, I wanted to go back in and change, but I didn't.

"I'm sorry," he said.

"What about?"

"I'm not completely sure, but I think for presuming I could take over your kitchen."

"I think it's the first meal that's ever been cooked in it."

His smile widened, and he pushed away from the door. He walked towards me. He moved in the circle of his own energy. Not that otherworldly power, but just Richard. Or was it? Maybe a lot of his drive was from his beast.

He stood staring down at me, close enough to touch but not doing it. "I was going crazy waiting for you. I got this idea to cook a fancy meal. It was stupid. You don't have to eat it, but it kept me from running down to Guilty Pleasures and defending your honor."

It made me smile. "Damn you, I can't even pout around you. You always jolly me out of it."

"And this is a bad thing?"

I laughed. "Yes. I enjoy my bad moods, thank you very much."

He traced fingers down my shoulders, kneading the muscles in my upper arms. I pulled away from him. "Please, don't." Just like that, the cozy domestic scene was ruined. All my fault.

His hands dropped to his sides. "I'm sorry." I didn't think he meant the meal. He took a deep breath and nodded. "You don't have to eat a bite." I guess we were going to pretend he had meant the meal. Fine with me.

"If I said I wasn't hungry at all, you wouldn't be mad at me?"

"I fixed the meal to make me feel better. If it bothers you, don't eat it."

"I'll drink a cup of coffee and watch you eat."

He smiled. "It's a deal."

He stayed standing, looking down at me. He looked sad. Lost. If you love someone, you shouldn't make them miserable. It's a rule somewhere, or should be.

"You combed your hair out."

"You like it loose."

"Just like this is one of my favorite sweaters," I said.

"Is it?" His voice held a teasing edge to it. I could have the lightness back. We could have a nice relaxing evening. It was up to me.

I looked up into his big brown eyes and wanted it. But I couldn't lie to him. That would be worse than cruel. "This is awkward."

"I know. I'm sorry."

"Stop apologizing. It's not your fault. It's mine."

He shook his head. "You can't help how you feel."

"My first instinct is to cut and run, Richard. Stop seeing you. No more long conversations. No touching. Nothing."

"If that's what you want." His voice sounded sort of strangled, as if it cost him dearly to say those words.

"What I want is you. I just don't know if I can handle all of you."

"I shouldn't have proposed until you'd seen what I really was."

"I saw Marcus and the gang."

"It's not the same as seeing me go beastly on you, is it?"

I took a deep breath, and let it out slowly. "No," I said, "it isn't."

"If you have someone else you can call to wait with you tonight, I'll go. You said you needed time and I practically move in. I'm pushing."

"Yeah, you are."

"I'm scared that I'm losing you," he said.

"Pushing won't help," I said.

"I guess not."

I stood there staring at him. The apartment was dark. The only light from the kitchen. It could have been, should have been, very intimate. I told everybody that lycanthropy was just a disease. It was illegal and immoral to discriminate. I didn't have a prejudiced bone in my body, or so I told myself. Staring up into Richard's handsome face, I knew it wasn't true. I was prejudiced. I was prejudiced against monsters. Oh, they were good enough to be my friends, but even my closest friends, Ronnie and Catherine, were human. Good enough to be friends, but not good enough to love. Not good enough to share my bed. Is that really what I thought? Was that who I was?

It wasn't who I wanted to be. I raised zombies and slew vampires. I wasn't clean enough to throw stones.

I moved closer to him. "Hold me, Richard. Just hold me."

His arms enfolded me. I wrapped my arms around his waist, pressing my face against his chest. I could hear his heart beat, fast and strong. I held him, listening to the beat of his heart, breathing his warmth. For just an instant I felt safe. It was the way I'd felt before my mother died. That childish belief that nothing can hurt you while Mommy and Daddy hold you tight. That utter faith that they can make everything all right. In Richard's arms, for brief moments, I had that again. Even though I knew it was a lie. Hell, it had been a lie the first time. My mother's death had proven that.

I pulled away first. He didn't try and hold on. He didn't say anything. If he'd said anything remotely sympathetic I might have cried. Couldn't have that. Down to business. "You haven't asked how it went with Jean-Claude."

"You were almost mad at me when you came through the door. I thought if I started questioning you right off the bat, you might yell at me."

He'd made coffee all on his own. That earned him at least two brownie points. "I wasn't mad at you." I poured coffee into my baby penguin mug. Regardless of what I take to work, it is my favorite mug.

"Yes, you were," he said.

"You want some coffee?"

"You know I don't like it."

How do you trust a man that doesn't like coffee? "I keep hoping you'll come to your senses."

He started dishing out his meal. "Sure you don't want some?"

"No, thanks." It was some small brown meat in a brown sauce. Looking at it made me nauseous. I'd eaten later than this with Edward, but tonight, food just didn't sound good. Maybe getting my head bashed into concrete had something to do with that.

I sat down in one of the chairs, one knee drawn up to my chest. The coffee was Viennese cinnamon, one of my favorites. Sugar, real cream, and it was perfect.

Richard sat down opposite me. He bowed his head and said grace over his meal. He's Episcopalian, did I mention that? Except for the furry part, he really is perfect for me.

"Tell me what happened with Jean-Claude, please," he asked.

I sipped my coffee and tried to think of a short version. Okay, a short version Richard wouldn't mind hearing. Okay, maybe just the truth.

"He took the news better than I thought he would, actually."

Richard looked up from his meal, silverware poised. "He took it well?"

"I didn't say that. He didn't burst through a wall and try to kill you immediately. He took it better than I expected."

Richard nodded. He took a sip of water and said, "Did he threaten to kill me?"

"Oh, yeah. But it was almost like he saw this coming. He didn't like it, but it didn't catch him by complete surprise."

"Is he going to try and kill me?" He asked it very calmly, eating his meat and brown sauce.

"No, he isn't."

"Why not?"

It was a good question. I wondered what he'd think of the answer. "He wants to date me."

Richard stopped eating. He just looked at me. When he could speak, he said, "He *what*?"

"He wants a chance to woo me. He says that if he can't win me from you in a few months, he'll give up. He'll let us go our merry way, and he won't interfere."

Richard sat back in his chair. "And you believe him?"

"Yeah. Jean-Claude thinks he's irresistible. I think he believes that if I let him use all his charms on me, I'll reconsider."

"Will you?" His voice was very quiet when he asked.

"No, I don't think so." It wasn't a rousing endorsement.

"I know you lust after him, Anita. Do you love him?"

The conversation was becoming déjà-vuish. "In some dark, twisted part of my heart, yeah. But not the way I love you."

"How is it different?"

"Look, I just had this conversation with Jean-Claude. I love you. Can you see me setting up house with the Master of the City?"

"Can you see setting up house with an alpha werewolf?"

Shit. I stared across the table at him, and sighed. He was pushing, but I didn't blame him. If I'd been him, I'd have dumped me. If I didn't love him enough to accept all of him, then who the hell needed me? I didn't want him to dump me. I wanted to be indecisive but I didn't want to lose him. Talk about having your cake and eating it, too.

I leaned across the table and held my hand out to him. After a moment he took it. "I don't want to lose you."

"You won't lose me."

"You are a hell of a lot more tolerant than I would be."

He didn't smile. "I know I am."

I would have liked to argue, but truth is truth. "I'd be bigger about this if I could."

"I understand your having reservations about marrying a werewolf. Who wouldn't? But Jean-Claude . . ." He shook his head.

I squeezed his hand. "Come on, Richard. This is the best we can do right now. Jean-Claude won't try and kill either of us. We still get to date and see each other."

"I don't like you being forced into dating him." He rubbed his fingers across my knuckles, caressing. "I like it even less that I think you'll enjoy it. In that small dark part of yourself, you'll be having a very good time."

I wanted to deny it, but it would be a total lie. "You can smell it if I lie?"

"Yep," he said.

"Then it's intriguing and terrifying."

"I want you safe so the terrifying part bothers me, but the intriguing part bothers me more."

"Jealous?"

"Worried."

What could I say? So was I.

28

THE PHONE RANG. I groped for it and found nothing. I raised my head and found the nightstand empty. The phone was gone. It had even stopped ringing. The radio clock was still there, glowing red. It read 1:03. I stayed propped on my elbow blinking at the empty space. Was I dreaming? Why would I dream that someone had stolen my phone?

The bedroom door opened. Richard stood framed in the light beyond. Ah. Now I remembered. He'd taken the phone into the living room so it wouldn't wake me. Since he was having to wake me every hour, I'd let him do it. When you're only sleeping an hour, even a short phone call can screw things up.

"Who is it?"

"It's Sergeant Rudolph Storr. I asked him to wait until I had to wake you, but he was pretty insistent."

I could imagine. "It's all right."

"Would fifteen minutes have killed him?" Richard asked.

I swung my legs out from under the covers. "Dolph's in the middle of a murder investigation, Richard. Patience isn't his strong suit."

Richard crossed his arms over his chest, leaning against the doorjamb. The light from the living room made strong shadows on his face. The shadows cut huge square shapes on his orange sweater. He radiated displeasure. It made me smile. I patted his arm as I went past. I seemed to have inherited a watchwolf.

The phone was sitting just inside the front door, where the other phone jack was. I sat down on the floor, putting my back to the wall, and picked up the phone. "Dolph, it's me. What's up?"

"Who's this Richard Zeeman that's answering your phone in the middle of the night?"

I closed my eyes. My head hurt. My face hurt. I hadn't had a hell of a lot of sleep. "You're not my father, Dolph. What's up?"

A moment of silence. "Defensive, aren't we?"

"Yeah, want to make something of it?"

"No," he said.

"You call just to catch up on my personal life or is there a reason you woke me up?" I knew it wasn't another murder. He was being too cheerful for that, which made me wonder if it couldn't have waited a few hours.

"We found something."

"What exactly?"

"I'd rather you just come and see it for yourself."

"Don't do this to me, Dolph. Just tell me what the fuck it is."

Another silence. If he was waiting for me to apologize, he was in for a long wait. Finally. "We found a skin."

"What kind of skin?"

"If we knew what the hell it was, would I be calling you at one o'clock in the freaking morning?" He sounded angry. I guess I couldn't blame him.

"I'm sorry, Dolph. I'm sorry I snapped at you."

"Fine."

He hadn't exactly accepted my apology. Fine. "Is it connected to the murder?"

"I don't think so, but I'm not some hotshot preternatural expert." He still sounded pissed. Maybe he wasn't getting much sleep, either. Of course, I bet no one had smashed his head into a sidewalk.

"Where are you?"

He gave me the address. It was down in Jefferson County, far away from the murder scene.

"When can you be here?"

"I can't drive," I said.

"What?"

"Doctor's orders, I'm not to get behind the wheel of a car tonight."

"How bad are you hurt?"

"Not too bad, but the doctor wanted me woken up every hour, and no driving."

"That's why Mr. Zeeman is there."

"Yeah."

"If you're too hurt to come tonight, it can wait."

"Is the skin where it was found? Nothing disturbed?"

"Yeah."

"I'll come. Who knows? There might be a clue."

He let that go. "How are you going to get here?"

I glanced at Richard. He could drive me, but somehow I didn't think it was a good idea. He was a civvie, for one thing. He was a lycanthrope, for another. He answered to Marcus, and to a degree to Jean-Claude. Not a good person to bring into a preternatural murder investigation. Besides, if he'd been human, the answer would have been the same. No deal.

"Unless you can send a squad car, I guess I'll take a taxi."

"Zerbrowski didn't answer his first page. He lives in St. Peters. He'll have to come right by you. He can pick you up."

"Is that okay with him?"

"It will be," Dolph said.

Great. Trapped in a car with Zerbrowski. "Fine, I'll be dressed and waiting."

"Dressed?"

"Don't even start, Dolph."

"Touchy, very touchy."

"Stop it."

He laughed. It was good to hear him laugh. It meant not many people had died this time. Dolph didn't laugh much during serial-killer cases.

He hung up. So did I.

"You have to go out?" Richard asked.

"Yeah."

"Do you feel well enough to go?"

"Yes."

"Anita . . ."

I leaned my head against the wall and closed my eyes. "Don't, Richard. I'm going."

"No debate allowed?"

"No debate," I said. I opened my eyes and looked at him.

He was staring down at me, arms crossed.

"What?" I said.

He shook his head. "If I told you that I was going to do something, no debate, you'd be mad."

"No, I wouldn't."

"Anita." He said my name the way my father use to say it.

"I wouldn't, not if your reasons were valid."

"Anita, you'd be pissed, and you know it."

I wanted to deny it but couldn't. "All right, you're right. I wouldn't like it." I stared up at him. I was going to have to give him reasons why I was going to go out and do my job. It wasn't a pretty sight.

I stood. I wanted to say I didn't have to explain myself to anyone, but if I meant this marriage thing, it wasn't true anymore. I didn't like that much. His being a werewolf was not the only hurdle to domestic bliss.

"This is police business, Richard. People die when I don't do my job."

"I thought your job was raising zombies and executing vampires."

"You sound like Bert."

"You've told me enough about Bert that I know that is an insult."

"If you don't want to be compared, then stop saying one of his favorite things." I walked past him towards the bedroom. "I've got to get dressed."

He followed me. "I know that helping the police is very important to you."

I turned on him. "I don't just help the police, Richard. The spook squad is just over two years old. The cops on it didn't know shit about preternatural creatures. It was a garbage detail. Do something to piss off your superiors and you get transferred."

"The newspapers and TV said it was an independent task force like the major task force. That's an honor."

"Oh, yeah, right. The squad gets almost no extra funding. No special training in preternatural creatures or events. Dolph, Sergeant Storr, saw me in the paper and contacted Bert. There was no training in preternatural crime for law officers in this country. Dolph thought I could be an adviser."

"You're a heck of a lot more than an adviser."

"Yes, I am." I could have told him that earlier in the summer Dolph had tried not calling me in right away. It had seemed like a clear-cut case of ghouls in a cemetery getting a little ambitious and attacking a necking couple. Ghouls were cowards and didn't attack able-bodied people, but exceptions to the rule and all that. By the time Dolph called me in, six people were dead. It hadn't been ghouls. So lately Dolph had started calling me at the beginning before things got too messy. Sometimes I could diagnose a problem before it got out of hand.

But I couldn't tell Richard that. There might have been a lower kill count if I'd been called in this summer, but that was no one's business but Dolph's and mine. We'd spoken of it only once, and that was enough. Richard was a civvie, werewolf or not. It wasn't any of his business.

"Look, I don't know if I can explain this so you'll understand, but I have to go. It may head off a larger problem. It may keep me from having to go to a murder scene later on. Can you understand that?"

He looked perplexed, but what came out of his mouth wasn't. "Not really, but maybe I don't have to. Maybe seeing it's important to you is enough."

I let out a deep breath. "Great. Now I've got to get ready. Zerbrowski will be here any time. He's the detective giving me a ride."

Richard just nodded. Wise of him.

I went into the bedroom and closed the door. Gratefully. Would this be a regular occurrence if we married? Would I be forever explaining myself? God, I hoped not.

Another pair of black jeans, a red sweater with a cowl neck, so soft and fuzzy that it made me feel better just to wear it. The Browning's shoulder holster looked very dark and dramatic against the crimson of the sweater. The red sweater also brought out the raw-meat color of the scrapes on my face. I might have changed it, but the doorbell rang.

Zerbrowski. Richard was answering the door while I stared at myself in the mirror. That thought alone was enough. I went for the door.

Zerbrowski was standing just inside the door, hands in the pockets of his overcoat. His curly black hair with its touches of grey was freshly cut. There was even hair-goop in it. Zerbrowski was usually lucky if he remembered to comb his hair. The suit that showed from his open coat was black and formal. His tie was tasteful and neatly knotted. I glanced down, and yes indeed, his shoes were shined. I'd never seen him when he didn't have food stains on him somewhere.

"Where were you all dressed up?" I asked.

"Where were you all undressed?" he asked. He smiled when he said it.

I felt heat rush up my face and hated it a lot. I hadn't done anything worth blushing for. "Fine, let's go." I grabbed my trench coat from the back of the couch and touched dried blood. Shit.

"I've got to get a clean coat. I'll be right back."

"I'll just talk to Mr. Zeeman here," Zerbrowski said.

I was afraid of that, but I went for my leather jacket anyway. If we ended up engaged, Richard would have to meet Zerbrowski sooner or later. Later would have been my preference.

"What do you do for a living, Mr. Zeeman?"

"I'm a schoolteacher."

"Oh, really."

I lost the conversation then. I grabbed the jacket from the closet and walked back out. They were chatting along like old buddies.

"Yes, Anita is our preternatural expert. Wouldn't know what to do without her."

"I'm ready. Let's go." I walked past them and opened the door. I held the door for Zerbrowski.

He smiled at me. "How long have you two been dating?"

Richard looked at me. He was pretty good at picking up when I wasn't comfortable. He was going to let me answer the question. Good of him.

Too good. If he would only be completely unreasonable and give me an excuse to say no. This isn't worth it. But damn if he didn't work really hard at keeping me happy. Not an easy task.

"Since November," I said.

"Two months, not bad. Katie and I were engaged two months after our first date." His eyes sparkled, his grin was mocking. He was pulling my leg, he didn't know it was coming off in his hands.

Richard looked at me. The look was long and serious. "Two months isn't very long, really."

He'd given me an out. I didn't deserve him.

"Long enough if it's the right one," Zerbrowski said.

I tried to get Zerbrowski through the door. He was grinning. He had no intention of being hurried. My only hope was for Dolph to page him again. That'd light a fire under his butt.

Dolph didn't call. Zerbrowski grinned at me. Richard looked at me. His big brown eyes were deep and wounded. I wanted to take his face in my hands and wipe that hurt from his eyes. Oh, hell.

He was the right one—probably. "I've got to go."

"I know," he said.

I glanced at Zerbrowski. He was grinning at us, enjoying the show.

Was I supposed to kiss him good-bye? We weren't engaged anymore. Quickest engagement in history. But we were still dating. I still loved him. That deserved a kiss if nothing else.

I grabbed the front of his sweater and pulled him down to me. He looked surprised. "You don't have to do this for show," he whispered.

"Shut up and kiss me."

That earned me a smile. Every kiss was still a pleasant shock. No one's lips were this soft. No one else tasted this good.

His hair fell forward and I grabbed a handful of it, pressing his face to mine. His hands slid around my back, underneath the leather jacket, hands kneading the sweater.

I pushed away from him, breathless. I didn't want to go now. With him staying overnight maybe it was a good thing I had to leave for a while. I meant it about no premarital sex, even if he hadn't been a lycanthrope, but the flesh was more than willing. I wasn't sure the spirit was up to the fight.

The look in Richard's eyes was drowning deep and worth anything in the world. I tried to hide a rather sappy smile but knew it was too late. I knew I would pay for this in the car with Zerbrowski. I would never hear the end of it. Staring up into Richard's face, I didn't care. We'd work out everything, eventually. Surely to God we could work it out.

"Wait 'til I tell Dolph we were late because you were smooching with some guy."

I didn't rise to bait. "I may not be home for hours. You might want to go home instead of waiting here."

"I drove your Jeep here, remember? I don't have a ride home."

Oh. "Fine, I'll be back when I can."

He nodded. "I'll be here."

I walked out into the hallway, not smiling anymore. I wasn't sure how I felt about coming home to Richard. How was I ever going to come to a real decision if he kept hanging around, making my hormones run amok?

Zerbrowski chuckled. "Blake, I have seen everything now. The heap-big vampire slayer in luuv."

I shook my head. "I don't suppose it would help to ask you to keep this to yourself?"

He grinned. "Makes the teasing more fun."

"Damn you, Zerbrowski."

"Loverboy seemed sort of tense, so I didn't say anything before, but now that we're alone, what the hell happened to you? You look like someone took a meat cleaver to your face."

Actually, I didn't. I'd seen that done once and it was a lot messier. "Long story. You know my secret. Where were you tonight all dressed up?"

"Married ten years tonight," he said.

"You're kidding?"

He shook his head.

"Big congrats," I said. We clattered down the stairs.

"Thanks. We hired a baby-sitter and everything. She made me leave my beeper home."

The cold bit into the sores on my face and made my head ache worse.
"Door's not locked," Zerbrowski said.

"You're a cop. How can you leave your car unlocked?" I opened the
door and stopped. The passenger seat and floorboard were full. McDon-
ald's take-out sacks and newspapers filled the seat and flowed onto the
floorboards. A piece of petrified pizza and a herd of pop cans filled the
rest of the floorboard.

"Jesus, Zerbrowski, does the EPA know you're driving a toxic waste
dump through populated areas?"

"See why I leave it unlocked. Who would steal it?" He knelt in the
seat and began shoveling armfuls of garbage into the backseat. It looked
like this wasn't the first time he'd cleaned out the front seat by shoveling
things in back.

I brushed crumbs from the empty seat onto the empty floorboard.
When it was as clean as I could get it, I sat down.

Zerbrowski slid into his seat belt and started the car. It coughed to
life. I put on my seat belt, and he pulled out of the parking lot.

"How does Katie feel about your job?" I asked.

Zerbrowski glanced at me. "She's okay with it."

"Were you a cop when she met you?"

"Yeah, she knew what to expect. Loverboy didn't want you to come
out tonight?"

"He thought I was too hurt to go out."

"You do look like shit."

"Thanks."

"They love us, they want us to be careful. He's a junior high school
teacher, for God's sake. What does he know about violence?"

"More than he'd like to."

"I know, I know. The schools are a dangerous place nowadays. But it
isn't the same, Anita. We carry guns. Hell, you kill vampires and raise the
dead, Blake. Can't get much messier than that."

"I know that." But I didn't know that. Being a lycanthrope was
messier. Wasn't it?

"No, I don't think you do, Blake. Loving someone who lives by violence is a hard way to go. That anybody'll have us is a miracle. Don't get cold feet."

"Did I say I was getting cold feet?"

"Not out loud."

Shit. "Let's drop it, Zerbrowski."

"Anything you say. Dolph is going to be so excited that you've decided to tie the noose . . . ah, knot."

I sank down into the seat as far as the belt would let me. "I am not getting married."

"Maybe not yet, but I know that look, Blake. You are a drowning woman, and the only way out is down the aisle."

I would have liked to argue, but I was too confused. Part of me believed Zerbrowski. Part of me wanted to stop dating Richard and be safe again. Okay, okay, I wasn't exactly safe before, what with Jean-Claude hanging around, but I wasn't engaged. Of course, I still wasn't engaged.

"You okay, Blake?"

I sighed. "I've lived alone a long time. A person gets set in her ways." Besides he's a werewolf. I didn't say that part out loud, but I wanted to. I needed a second opinion, but a police officer, especially Zerbrowski, wasn't the person to ask.

"He crowding you?"

"Yeah."

"He want marriage, kids, the whole nine yards?"

Kids. No one had mentioned children. Did Richard have this domestic vision of a little house, him in the kitchen, me working, and kids? Oh, damn, we were going to have to sit down and have a serious talk. If we did manage to get engaged like normal people, what did that mean? Did Richard want children? I certainly didn't.

Where would we live? My apartment was too small. His house? I wasn't sure I liked that idea. It was his house. Shouldn't we have our house? Shit. Kids, me? Pregnant, me? Not in this lifetime. I thought furriness was our biggest problem. Maybe it wasn't.

29

THE RIVER SWIRLED black and cold. Rocks stuck up like the teeth of giants. The bank behind me was steep, thick with trees. The snow between the trees was trampled and slicked away to show the leaves underneath. The opposite bank was a bluff that jutted out over the river. No way down from there unless you were willing to jump. The water was less than five feet deep in the center of the river. Jumping from thirty feet wasn't a good idea.

I stood carefully on the crumbling bank. The black water rushed just inches from my feet. Tree roots stuck out of the bank, tearing at the earth. The combination of snow, leaves, and nearly vertical bank seemed destined to send me into the water, but I'd fight it as long as I could.

The rocks formed a low, broken wall into the river. Some of the stones were barely above the swirling water, but one near the center of the river stuck up about waist high. Draped over that rock was the skin. Dolph was still the master of understatement. Shouldn't a skin be smaller than a breadbox, not bigger than a Toyota? The head hung on the large rock, draped perfectly as if placed. That was one of the reasons the thing was still in the middle of the river. Dolph had wanted me to see it in case there was some ritual significance to the placement.

There was a dive team waiting on the shore in dry suits, which are bulkier than wet suits and better at keeping you warm in cold water. A tall diver with a hood already pulled up over his hair stood by Dolph. He'd been introduced as MacAdam. "Can we go in after the skin now?"

"Anita?" Dolph asked.

"Better them in the water than me," I said.

"Is it safe?" Dolph asked.

That was a different question. Truth. "I'm not sure."

MacAdam looked at me. "What could be out there? It's just a skin, right?"

I shrugged. "I'm not sure what kind of skin it is."

"So?" he asked.

"So, remember the Mad Magician back in the seventies?"

"I'd think you wouldn't remember it," MacAdam said.

"I studied it in college. Magical Terrorism, senior year. The Magician specialized in leaving magical booby traps in out-of-the-way places. One of his favorite traps was an animal skin that would attach itself to whomever touched it first. Took a witch to remove it."

"Was it dangerous?" MacAdam asked.

"One man suffocated when it attached itself to his face."

"How the hell did his face touch it first?"

"Hard to ask a dead man. Animating wasn't a profession in the seventies."

MacAdam stared off across the water. "Okay, how do you find out if it's dangerous?"

"Has anyone been in the water yet?"

He jerked a thumb at Dolph. "He wouldn't let us, and Sheriff Titus said to leave everything for some hotshot monster expert." He looked me up and down. "That you?"

"That's me."

"Well, make like an expert so my people and I can get in there."

"You want the spotlight now?" Dolph asked. They'd had the place lit up like an opening night at Mann's Chinese Theatre. I'd made them turn off the lights after I'd gotten the first glance. There were some things that you needed light to see, other things only showed themselves in the dark.

"No light yet. Let me see it in the dark first."

"Why no light?" Dolph asked.

"Some things hide from light, Dolph, and they might still take a chunk out of one of the divers."

"You're really serious about this, aren't you?" MacAdam asked.

"Yeah, aren't you glad?"

He looked at me for a moment, then nodded. "Yeah. How are you going to get a closer look? I know the weather just got cold the last few days, so the water should be about forty degrees, but that's still cold without a suit."

"I'll stay on the rocks. I might dip a hand in to see if anything rises to bait, but I'll stay as dry as I can."

"You take the monsters serious," he said, "I take the water serious. You'll get hypothermia in about five minutes in water this cold. Try not to fall in."

"Thanks for the advice."

"You're going to get wet," Aikensen said. He stood just above me, leaning against a tree. His Smokey Bear hat was pulled low over his head, thick woolly collar pulled up near his chin. His ears and most of his face were still bare to the cold. I hoped he got frostbite.

He put his flashlight under his chin like a Halloween gag. He was smiling. "Didn't move a thing, Miss Blake. Left it just where we found it."

I didn't correct him on the "miss." He'd done it just to irritate me. Ignoring it irritated him. Great.

The Halloween smile faded, leaving him frowning in the light.

"What's the matter, Aikensen? Didn't want to get your delicate toes wet?"

He pushed away from the tree. The movement was too abrupt. He slid down the bank, arms windmilling, trying to slow his fall. He fell to his butt and kept scooting. He was coming straight for me.

I took a step to one side and the bank crumbled underfoot. I gave a hop and ended up on the nearest stone in the river. I huddled on it, nearly on all fours to keep from falling into the water. The stone was wet, slick, and bone-deep cold.

Aikensen landed in the river with a yell. He sat on his butt, freezing water swirling to nearly the middle of his chest. He beat at the water with his gloved hands, as if punishing it. All he was doing was getting wetter.

The skin didn't slide off the rock and cover him. Nothing grabbed him. I couldn't feel any magic on the air. Nothing but the cold and the sound of water.

"Guess nothing's going to eat him," MacAdam said.

"Guess not," I said. I tried to keep the disappointment out of my voice.

"God's sake, Aikensen, get out of the water," Titus's voice boomed from the top of the hill. The sheriff, along with most of the other policemen, were at the top of the bank, along the gravel road that led back to the place. Two ambulances were sitting up there, too. Since Gaia's law went into effect three years ago, an ambulance had to be on the scene if there was any chance the remains were humanoid. There were ambulances being called to take away coyote carcasses, as if they were dead werewolves. The law had gone into effect, but no extra money had been put into the emergency systems across the country. Washington did like to complicate things.

We were in the backyard of someone's summer house. Some of the houses had landings or even small boathouses, if they had deep enough water at the base of their land. The only boat you were taking off through this rocky channel was a canoe, so no landing, no boathouse, just the cold black water and a very wet deputy.

"Aikensen, get your butt up on one of those rocks. Help Ms. Blake out, since you're already wet."

"I don't need his help," I called back to Titus.

"Well, now, Ms. Blake, this is our county. Wouldn't want you getting eaten by some beastie while we stayed nice and safe on shore."

Aikensen stood, nearly falling again when his boots slid on the sandy bottom. He turned to glare at me as if it were all my fault, but he scrambled up on the rock on the side opposite the skin. He'd lost his flashlight. He was dripping wet in the dark, except for his Smokey Bear hat which he'd managed to keep above water. He looked as sullen as a wet hen.

"Notice you're not offering to climb out on this particular limb," I said.

Titus started down the bank. He seemed to be a lot better at it than I had been. I'd staggered like a drunk from tree to tree. Titus kept his hands out ready to catch himself, but he pretty much walked down. He stopped beside Dolph.

"Delegation, Ms. Blake. What made the country great."

"What do you think of that, Aikensen?" I said more softly.

He glared at me. "He's the boss." He didn't sound like he was happy with it, but he believed it.

"Get on with it, Anita," Dolph said.

Translation, stop yanking everybody's chain. Everybody wanted out of the cold. Couldn't blame them. Me, too.

I stood ever so carefully on the slick rock. My flashlight reflected off the choppy water like a black mirror, opaque and solid.

I shone the flashlight on the first stone. It was pale and shining with water, and probably ice. I stepped onto it carefully. The next stone, still okay. Who knew Nike Airs were good for icy rocks?

MacAdam's warning about hypothermia ran through my head. Just what I'd need, to be hospitalized from exposure. Didn't I have enough problems without having to fight the elements?

There was a gap between the next two stones. It was a tempting distance. Almost stepping distance but just an inch out of comfort range. The stone I was on was flat, low to the water, but solid underfoot. The next one was sort of curved on one side with a point.

"Afraid you're going to get your feet wet?" Aikensen flashed a smile that was more a baring of white teeth in the dark.

"Jealous that you're wet and I'm not?"

"I could get you wet," he said.

"Only in my nightmares," I said. I had to leap for it and hope some miracle of balance kept me safe. I glanced back at the bank. I thought about asking the divers if they had an extra dry suit for me, but it seemed cowardly with Aikensen shivering on the rocks. Besides, I could probably make the jump. Probably.

I backed to the edge of the rock I was standing on, and jumped. There was a second of being airborne, then my foot hit the rock. My foot slid off to one side. I collapsed onto the rock hugging it with both hands and one leg. The other leg ended up thigh deep in ice cold water. The shock of it left me cursing.

I struggled back up on the rock, water streaming from the jean's pants leg. My foot hadn't touched bottom. The water on either side of the rocks would come up to my waist, if Aikensen's little wading show was a good indication. I'd found a sinkhole deep enough to have doused every inch of me. Lucky it was just my leg.

Aikensen was laughing at me. If it had been anyone else, we might have laughed together at how ridiculous all this was, but it was him, and he laughed at me.

"At least I didn't drop my flashlight," I said. It sounded childish even to me, but he stopped laughing. Sometimes childish will get you what you want.

I was beside the skin now. Up close, it was even more impressive. I'd known it was reptilian from the bank. Standing next to it, I could see it was definitely a snake. The largest scales were the size of my palm. The empty eye sockets were the size of golf balls. I reached out to touch it. Something swirled against my arm as I reached for it. I screamed before I realized it was the undulating snakeskin spreading out in the water. When I could breathe again, I touched the skin. I expected it to be light, a sloughed skin. It was heavy, meaty.

I turned the edge of it to the light. It wasn't a sloughed skin. The snake had been skinned. Whether it had been alive when the skinning started was a moot point. It was dead now. Very few creatures can survive being skinned alive.

There was something about the scales and shape of the head that reminded me of a cobra, but the scales, even in the light of a flashlight, gleamed with opalescence. The snake wasn't any one color. It was like a rainbow or an oil slick. The color changed depending on the angle of the light.

"You going to play with it, or can the divers come and get it?" Aikensen asked.

I ignored him for the moment. There was something on the snake's forehead, almost between the eyes. Something smooth and round and white. I ran my fingers over it. It was a pearl. A pearl the size of a golf ball. What the hell was a giant pearl doing embedded in the head of a snake? And why hadn't whoever skinned the creature taken the pearl with him?

Aikensen leaned forward running a hand over the skin. "Yuck. What the hell is it?"

"Giant snake," I said.

He jerked back with a yell. He started scraping at his arms as if he could wipe off the feel of it.

"Afraid of snakes, Aikensen?"

He glared at me. "No."

It was a lie, and we both knew it.

"The two of you enjoy being out on those rocks?" Titus asked. "Get a move on."

"You see anything significant about the placement of the skin, Anita?" Dolph asked.

"Not really. The thing might have just gotten hooked on the rocks. I don't think it was purposefully placed here."

"We can move it then?"

I nodded. "Yeah, the divers can come in. Aikensen's already tested the water for predators."

Aikensen looked at me. "What the hell does that mean?"

"It means there might have been creepy-crawlies in the water, but nothing tried to eat you, so it's safe."

"You used me for bait."

"You fell in."

"Ms. Blake say we can move the thing?" Titus asked.

"Yes," Dolph said.

"Go to it, boys."

The divers all looked at each other. "Can we have the spotlight now?" MacAdam asked.

"Sure," I said.

The light smashed into me. I put a hand up to shield my eyes and nearly slipped off the rock. Jesus it was bright. The water was still opaque, black, and choppy, but the rocks glistened and Aikensen and I were suddenly center stage. The bright light washed all the color from the snakeskin.

MacAdam slipped his face mask on, regulator secure in his mouth. Only one other diver followed his lead. Guess they didn't need four to go in after the skin.

"Why're they putting on tanks just to wade out here?" Aikensen asked.

"Insurance in case the current gets them, or they find a sinkhole."

"Current's not that bad."

"Bad enough that if it catches the skin, the skin's gone. With tanks you can follow something in the water all the way down, wherever it goes."

"You sound like you've done it."

"I'm certified."

"Well, aren't you multitalented," he said.

The divers were almost out to us. Their tanks looked like the backs of whales sticking out of the water. MacAdam raised his face mask out of the water, and put a gloved hand on the rocks. He took the regulator out of his mouth, hugging the rock and paddling with his legs to keep free of the current. The other diver moved over by Aikensen.

"There a problem if we tear the skin?" MacAdam asked.

"I'll unhook it from this side of the rock."

"You'll get your arm wet."

"I'll live, right?"

I couldn't see his face well enough under all the equipment, but I'd bet he was frowning at me.

"Yeah, you'll live."

I moved my hand down the front of the skin until I hit water. The cold made me hesitate, but only for a heartbeat. I reached down, soaking myself to the shoulder to untangle it. My hand touched something slick and solid that wasn't skin. I gave a small yip and jerked back, nearly falling. I got my balance and went for my gun.

I had time to say, "Something's down there." It surfaced.

A round face, with a screaming lipless mouth, shot upward, hands reaching for MacAdam. I had a glimpse of dark eyes before it fell back into the water.

The divers got the hell out of there, swimming with strong sure strokes for shore.

Aikensen had stumbled back, falling into the water. He came up sputtering, gun in hand.

"Don't shoot it," I said. The thing surfaced again. I slid in beside it. It shrieked, its human-shaped hand groping for me. It grabbed a handful of jacket and pulled itself to me. My gun was in my hand, but I didn't shoot.

Aikensen was aiming at it. Shouts from the shore. The other cops coming, but there was no time. There was just Aikensen and me in the river.

The creature clung to me, not screaming now, just clinging as if I were the last thing in the world. It buried its earless face into my chest. I pointed my gun at Aikensen's chest.

That seemed to get his attention. He blinked, focusing on me. "What the hell are you doing?"

"Point it somewhere else, Aikensen."

"I'm tired of looking down the barrel of your gun, bitch."

"Ditto," I said.

Voices shouting, movement on the bank, people coming, almost there. Only seconds left until someone came. Someone saved us. Seconds too late.

A shot exploded next to Aikensen. Close enough to spray him with water. He jumped, and his gun fired. The creature went wild, but I was already moving, diving for the rocks. It clung to me as if attached. We floated by the big rock, swirling in snake skin, but I managed to point the Browning at Aikensen. The sound of his Magnum vibrated in the air, echoing down my bones. If Aikensen had turned towards us, I'd have fired.

"Goddamn it, Aikensen, put that damn gun away!" The splashing was heavy, and it was probably Titus wading into the water, but I couldn't look away from Aikensen.

Aikensen was looking away from me towards the splashing. Dolph got there first. He loomed over Aikensen like the vengeance of God.

Aikensen's gun started to swing towards him, as if he sensed his danger.

"You point that gun at me and I will feed it to you," Dolph said. His voice was low and reverberated even through the ringing in my ears.

"If he points it at you," I said, "I'll shoot him."

"Nobody's shooting him but me." Titus waded up. He was shorter than everyone but me, so he was struggling in the water. He grabbed Aikensen by the belt and pulled him off his feet, tearing the gun from his hand as he fell into the water.

Aikensen surfaced choking and mad. "What the hell did you do that for?"

"Ask Ms. Blake why I did it. Ask her, ask her!" He was short and wet, and still managed to browbeat Aikensen.

"Why?" Aikensen said.

I'd lowered the Browning, but hadn't put it away. "Trouble with carrying a big gun, Aikensen, is that it goes through a hell of a lot of flesh."

"What?"

Titus pushed him, making him stumble. Aikensen struggled to stay on his feet. "If you'd pulled that trigger, boy, with the creature pressed right up against her, you'd have killed her, too."

"I thought she was just protecting it. She said not to shoot it. Look at it!"

Everyone turned to me then. I used the rocks to leverage to my feet. The creature was dead weight, as if he'd passed out with his hands locked in my jacket. I had more trouble putting the gun away than I had getting it out. Cold, adrenaline, and the man's hand stuck on my jacket, covering the holster.

Because that's what I was holding. A man, a man who had been skinned alive, but somehow wasn't dead. Of course, it wasn't exactly a man.

"It's a man, Aikensen," Titus said. "It's a hurt man. If you weren't so damn busy pulling your gun and shooting at things, you might see what's in front of ya."

"It's a naga," I said.

Titus didn't seem to hear me. Dolph asked, "What did you say?"

"He's a naga."

"Who is?" Titus asked.

"The man," I said.

"What the hell is a naga?"

"Everybody out of the water now," a voice from shore yelled. It was a paramedic with an armload of blankets. "Come on folks, let's not have to run everybody into the hospital tonight." I wasn't sure, but I thought I heard the paramedic mutter under his breath, "Damn fools."

"What the hell is a naga?" Titus asked again.

"I'll explain if you can help me get him to shore. I'm freezing my ass off out here."

"You're freezing more than your ass off," the paramedic said. "Everybody to shore, now. Move it, people."

"Help her," Titus said. Two uniformed deputies were in the water. They splashed up. They lifted the man, but his fists had locked into my jacket. It was a death grip. I checked the pulse in his throat. It was there, faint but steady.

The medic was folding blankets around everybody as they hit shore. His partner, a slender woman with pale hair was staring at the naga, glistening like an open wound in the spotlight.

"What the hell happened to him?" one of the deputies asked.

"He's been skinned," I said.

"Jesus Christ," the deputy said.

"Right thought, wrong religion," I said.

"What?"

"Nothing. Can you pry his hands loose?" They couldn't, not easily. They ended up carrying him cradled between them. I sort of stumbled to the shore with his fingers still locked in my clothes. None of us fell. A second miracle. The first was that Aikensen was still alive. Staring at the raw bluish skin of the man, maybe the miracle count was higher than just two.

The medic with the pale hair knelt by the naga. She let out her breath in a great whoosh of air. The other medic threw blankets around me and the two deputies.

"When you get him pried off of you, you get your butt up to the ambulances. Get out of those wet clothes, ASAP."

I opened my mouth and he pointed a finger at me. "Clothes off and sit in a warm ambulance, or a trip to the hospital. Your choice."

"Aye, aye, Captain," I said.

"And don't you forget it," he said. He moved off to spread blankets and orders to the rest of the cops.

"What about the skin?" Titus asked. He had a blanket wrapped around him.

"Bring it to shore," I said.

MacAdam said, "You sure this is the only surprise out there in that sinkhole?"

"I think this is our only naga for the night."

He nodded and slipped back into the water with his partner. It was nice not to be argued with. Maybe it was the naked ripped body of the naga.

The paramedics had to pry the naga's hands from my jacket a finger at a time. His fingers didn't want to uncurl. They stayed bent like the fingers of the dead after rigor had set in.

"Do you know what he is?" the paramedic with pale hair asked.

"A naga."

She exchanged glances with her partner. He shook his head. "What the hell is a naga?"

"A creature out of Hindu legend. They're mostly pictured in serpent form."

"Great," he said. "Will he react like a reptile or a mammal?"

"I don't know."

The medics from the other ambulance were setting up a pulley system and directing everybody up to the warmth of the ambulances. We needed more medics.

The paramedics spread a warm saline solution on a soft cotton sheet and wrapped the naga in it. His whole body was an open wound with all that that implied. Infection was the big threat. Could immortal beings get infections? Who knew? I knew about preternatural creatures, but first aid for the immortal? That wasn't my area.

They bundled him in layers of blankets. I looked at the drill sergeant paramedic. "Even if he's reptilian blankets can't hurt."

He had a point.

"His pulse is weak but steady," the woman said. "Should we risk trying an IV or . . ."

"I don't know," her partner answered. "He shouldn't be alive at all. Let's just move him. We'll keep him alive and get him to the hospital."

The distant whoop of more ambulances sounded. Reinforcements were on the way. The medics put the naga on a long spine-board and fit it in a Stokes basket, attached to the ropes the other paramedics had set up at top of the hill.

"You got any other information that'll help us treat him?" the paramedic asked. His eyes were very direct.

"I don't think so."

"Then get your butt up to an ambulance, now."

I didn't argue. I was cold, and my clothes were beginning to freeze to my body even under the blanket.

I ended up in a warm ambulance wearing nothing but a blanket while more paramedics and EMTs forced heated oxygen on me. Dolph and Zerbrowski ended up in the ambulance with me. Better them than Aikensen and Titus.

While we waited for the medics to tell us we would all live, Dolph got back to business.

"Tell me about nagas," Dolph said.

"Like I said, they're creatures from Hindu legend. They're mostly pictured as snakes, particularly cobras. They can take human form. Or appear as snakes with human heads. They're the guardians of raindrops and pearls."

"Say the last again?" Zerbrowski asked. His neatly combed hair had dried in messy curls. He'd jumped in the river to save little ol' me, even though he couldn't swim.

I repeated it. "There's a pearl embedded in the head of the skin. I think the skin was the naga's. Someone skinned him, but he didn't die. I don't know how the skin ended up in the river, or how he did."

Dolph said, "You mean he was a snake and they skinned him, but it didn't kill him."

"Apparently not."

"How is he in man form now?"

"I don't know."

"Why isn't he dead?" Dolph asked.

"Nagas are immortal."

"Shouldn't you tell the paramedics that?" Zerbrowski said.

"He's been completely skinned and is still alive. I think they're going to figure it out on their own," I said.

"Good point."

"Which of you fired the shot at Aikensen?"

"Titus did it," Dolph said.

"He cussed him out, and took his gun away," Zerbrowski said.

"Hope he doesn't give it back. If anyone shouldn't be armed, it's Aikensen."

"You got an extra change of clothes with you, Blake?" Zerbrowski asked.

"Nope."

"I've got two pairs of sweats in the trunk of my car. I want to get back to what's left of my anniversary."

The thought of wearing a used pair of sweats that had been sitting in Zerbrowski's car was too much for me. "I don't think so, Zerbrowski."

He grinned at me. "They're clean. Katie and I were going to exercise today but never got around to it."

"Never made it to the gym, huh," I said.

"No." Color crept up his neck. It must have been something really good, or really embarrassing to get to Zerbrowski that quickly.

"What kind of exercise were you two doing?" I asked.

"A man needs exercise," Dolph said solemnly.

Zerbrowski looked at me, eyebrows going up. "And how much of a workout is your sweetie giving you?" He turned to Dolph. "Did I tell you that Blake's got herself a boyfriend? He's sleeping over."

"Mr. Zeeman answered the phone," Dolph said.

"Isn't your phone right beside your bed, Blake?" Zerbrowski asked. He was giving me his best wide innocent brown eyes.

"Get the sweats and get me out of here," I said.

Zerbrowski laughed, and Dolph joined him.

"These are Katie's sweats so don't get anything on them. If you really want to work out, do it nude."

I flashed him a one-fingered salute.

"Oh, do that again," Zerbrowski said, "your blanket gaped."

I was just amusing the hell out of everyone.

30

I WAS STANDING in my hallway at four o'clock. I was dressed in a very pink sweatsuit. My wet clothes were held sort of gingerly in a bundle under my left arm. Even with the new pink sweats, I was cold. The paramedics had only let me go because I promised to drink hot fluids and take a hot bath. I'd run up the stairs in a pair of gym socks. I could wear Katie's sweats, but not her shoes.

I was cold, tired, and my face hurt. The headache was gone, though. Maybe it was being dunked in ice-cold water. Maybe it was the touch of a naga. I couldn't recall any stories associating them with spontaneous healing, but it had been a long time since I read up on nagas. They'd been on the final in preternatural bio class. The big clue had been the pearl and the cobra skin. I was going to have to dig up my textbook and reread the section. Though the doc on call at whatever hospital they went to was going to have to read up faster than I was. Would nagas be in their computers? By law, they'd better be. Would the naga have anyone to sue for him if they didn't? Would he rise from his deathbed and sue himself?

I stood in front of my apartment for the second time in six hours and had no key. I leaned my head against the door for just a second and felt sorry for myself. I didn't want to see Richard again tonight. We had a lot to talk about that had nothing to do with his shapeshifting. I wished I hadn't thought of children. I didn't want to discuss the little tykes tonight. I didn't want to discuss anything. I wanted to drag off to bed and be alone.

I took a deep breath and stood straight. No need to look as woebegone as I felt. I rang my own doorbell and vowed to get an extra set of keys made. No, one of them wasn't for Richard. They were both for me.

Richard opened the door. His hair was sleep tousled, falling in a heavy, wavy mass around his face. He was shirtless and barefoot. The top button of his jeans was undone. I was suddenly glad to see him. Lust is a wonderful thing.

I grabbed the top edge of his jeans and drew him to me. He jumped when my wet clothes touched his bare chest, but he didn't pull away. His body was almost fever warm from sleep. I warmed my hands along his spine and he twitched, writhing against the cold but never pulling away. I dropped the wet clothes on the floor.

We kissed. His lips were gentle. My hands traced the edge of his waistband, fingers dangerously low. He spoke low and soft next to my ear. I expected sweet nothings or dirty promises. What I got was, "We have company."

I sort of froze. I had this image of Ronnie, or worse Irving, sitting on the couch while we groped each other. "Shit," I said softly and with feeling.

"Home at last, *ma petite*." It was much worse than Irving.

I stared up at Richard with my mouth hanging open. "What's going on?"

"He came in while I was asleep. I woke up when the door opened."

I was suddenly cold again, down to my sodden toes. "Are you all right?"

"Do you really want to discuss this in the hall, *ma petite*?" Jean-Claude's voice was oh so reasonable.

I wanted to stand in the hall just because he'd said not to, but that was childish. Besides, it was my apartment.

I stepped through the door, Richard a warm presence at my side. I kicked my wet clothes through the door, keeping my hands free. The gun was in plain sight over the sweats. The holster flapped loose without a belt, but I could draw the gun if I needed it. I probably didn't need it, but it was good to keep reminding the master that I meant business.

Richard closed the door and leaned against it, hands behind his back. His face was nearly hidden by a spill of hair. The muscles in his stomach bunched and just seemed to invite caressing, which was what we'd probably have been doing if there hadn't been a vampire in my living room.

Jean-Claude sat on my couch. The black shirt was spread around his naked torso. His arms were straight out along the back of the couch, raising the shirt, revealing nipples that were only two shades darker than his white skin. A slight smile curled his lips. He was dramatic and perfect on the white couch. He matched the decor. Shit. I was going to have to buy new furniture, something not white, not black.

"What are you doing here, Jean-Claude?"

"Is that any way to greet your new suitor?"

"Don't be a pain in the ass tonight, please. I'm too tired and too sore to mess with it. Tell me why you're here and what you want, then get out."

He rose to his feet as if pulled by strings, all boneless ease. At least the shirt closed on most of the pale perfection of his body. That was something.

"I am here to see you and Richard."

"Why?"

He laughed, and the sound rolled over me like a wave of fur, soft and slick, tickling, and dead. I took a deep breath and stripped the holster off. He wasn't here to hurt. He was here to flirt. I walked past both of them and draped the holster on the back of a kitchen chair. I felt their eyes follow me as I moved. It was both flattering and uncomfortable as hell.

I glanced back at them. Richard was still by the door, looking unclothed and inviting. Jean-Claude stood by the couch utterly still, like a three-dimensional picture of a wet dream. The sexual potential in the room was astronomical. The fact that nothing was going to happen was almost sad.

There was still coffee in the pot. If I drank enough hot coffee and took a really hot bath, maybe I'd thaw out. My preference would have been a hot shower, quicker at four o'clock in the morning. But I'd promised the paramedics. Something about my core temperature.

"Why did you want to see Richard and me?" I poured coffee into my freshly washed penguin mug. Richard was good at being domestic.

"I was told that Monsieur Zeeman planned to spend the night."

"If he did, what of it?"

"Who told you?" Richard asked. He'd pushed away from the door. He'd even buttoned the top button of his pants. Pity.

"Stephen told me."

"He wouldn't have volunteered the information," Richard said. He was standing very close to Jean-Claude. Physically, he was looming above him, just a bit. Half-dressed. He should have looked uncertain, hesitant. He looked completely at home. The first time I'd met Richard, he'd been naked in a bed. He hadn't been embarrassed then, either.

"Stephen did not volunteer it," Jean-Claude said.

"He is under my protection," Richard said.

"You are not pack leader yet, Richard. You can protect Stephen within the pack, but Marcus still rules. He has given Stephen to me, as he gave you to me."

Richard was just standing there. He hadn't moved, yet suddenly, the air around him swam. If you blinked, you'd have missed it. A creeping edge of power fanned out, prickling along my skin. Shit.

"I belong to no one."

Jean-Claude turned to him. Face pleasant, open, voice conversational. "You do not acknowledge Marcus's leadership?" It was a trick question, and we all knew it.

"What happens if he says no?" I asked.

Jean-Claude turned back to me. His face was carefully blank. "He says no."

"And you tell Marcus, and then what?"

He smiled then, a slow curve of lips that left his perfect blue eyes glittering. "Marcus would see it as a direct challenge to his authority."

I set down the cup of coffee and came around the island. Standing nearly between them, Richard's energy crawled over my skin like insects on the march. From Jean-Claude there was nothing. The undead make no noise. "If you get Richard killed, even indirectly, the deal is off."

"I don't need you to protect me," Richard said.

"If you get yourself killed fighting Marcus, that's one thing, but if you get killed because Jean-Claude is jealous of you, that's my fault."

Richard touched my shoulder. His power was like a rush of electricity down my body. I shivered, and he dropped his hand. "I could just give in to Marcus, just acknowledge his leadership, then I'd be safe."

I shook my head. "I've seen what Marcus considers acceptable. It's not even close to being safe."

"Marcus didn't know they filmed two endings," Richard said.

"So you have talked to him about it?"

"Are you referring to the delightful little films that Raina master-minded?" Jean-Claude asked.

We both looked at him. A brush of power lashed out, growing stronger. It was hard to breathe standing next to him, like trying to swallow a thunderstorm.

I shook my head. One problem at a time. "What do you know about the films?" I asked.

Jean-Claude looked at us, one and then the other. He ended staring into my eyes. "Your voice makes it sound more important than it should be. What has Raina done now?"

"How do you know about the films?" Richard asked. He moved a step closer. His chest touched my back, and I gasped. The skin up and down my back tingled as if someone had touched a live wire to the skin, but it didn't hurt. It was just an almost overwhelming sensation. Pleasurable, but you knew if it didn't stop soon, it would begin to hurt.

I stepped away from him, standing between both of them, giving my back to neither. They both looked at me. Almost identical expressions on their faces. Alien, as if they were thinking thoughts that I'd never dreamed of, listening to music that I could not dance to. I was the only human in this room.

"Jean-Claude, just tell me what you know about Raina's movies. No games, okay."

He stared at me for a heartbeat, then gave a graceful shrug. "Very well. Your alpha female invited me to join her in a dirty movie. I was offered a starring role."

I knew he'd turned her down. He was an exhibitionist, but he liked a certain decorum to his sideshow. Dirty movies would have been beyond the pale for him.

"Did you enjoy having sex with her on screen?" Richard asked. His voice was low, and that energy flooded into the room.

Jean-Claude turned to him, anger dancing in his eyes. "She brags about you, my furry friend. Says you were magnificent."

"Cheap shot, Jean-Claude," I said.

"You don't believe me. You are that sure of him?"

"That he wouldn't have sex with Raina, yeah."

A strange look crossed Richard's face.

I stared at him. "You didn't?"

Jean-Claude laughed.

"I was nineteen. She was my alpha female. I didn't think I had a choice."

"Yeah, right."

"She has her pick of the new males. It's one of the things I want to stop."

"You're still sleeping with her?" I asked.

"No, not once I had a choice," Richard answered.

"Raina speaks so fondly of you, Richard. In such loving detail. It can't have been that long ago."

"It's been seven years."

"Really?" That one word held a universe of doubt.

"I don't lie to you, Anita," said Richard.

Richard took a step forward. Jean-Claude moved towards him. The testosterone was rising higher than the supernatural powers. We were going to drown in both.

I stepped between them, bodily, putting a hand on each chest. The minute my hand touched Richard's bare skin, the power poured down my arm, like some cool electric liquid. My hand touched Jean-Claude a second later. Some trick of cloth, or vampire, put my hand on his bare skin, too. The skin was cool and soft, and I felt Richard's power cross my body and smash into that perfect skin.

The moment it touched, an answering roll of power spilled out of the vampire. The two energies did not fight each other, they mingled inside me, spilling back on each of them. Jean-Claude's power was a cool, rushing wind. Richard was all warmth and electricity. Each one fed the other like wood and flame. And under it all I could feel myself, that thing inside me that allowed me to call the dead. Magic for lack of a better word. The three powers melded into one skin-curling, heart-pumping, stomach-clenching rush.

My knees buckled, and I was left gasping on the floor on all fours. My skin felt as if it were trying to pull away from my body. I could taste my heart in my throat and couldn't breathe past it. Everything was sort of golden around the edges, and spots of light danced before my eyes. I was in danger of passing out.

"What the hell was that?" It was Richard. His voice seemed to come from farther away than it should have. I'd never heard him cuss before.

Jean-Claude knelt beside me. He didn't try to touch me. I looked into his eyes from inches away. The pupils were gone, nothing but that lovely midnight blue remained. It was the way his eyes looked when he was getting all vampiric on me. I didn't think he'd done it on purpose this time.

Richard knelt on the other side. He started to reach out to touch me. When his hand was an inch away, a little jump of power ran between us, like static electricity. He jerked his hand back. "What is that?" He sounded a little scared. Me, too.

"*Ma petite*, can you speak?"

I nodded. Everything was in hyperfocus, the way the world gets on an adrenaline high. The shadows on Jean-Claude's chest where his shirt spilled around him were solid and touchable. The cloth looked almost metallic black, like the back of a beetle.

"Say something, *ma petite*."

"Anita, are you all right?"

I turned in almost slow motion to Richard. His hair had fallen over one eye. Each strand was thick and perfect like a line drawn apart. I could see every eyelash around his brown eye in startling contrast.

"I'm all right." But was I?

"What happened?" Richard asked. I wasn't sure who he was asking. I hoped it wasn't me because I didn't know.

Jean-Claude sat beside me on the floor, back against the island. He closed his eyes and took a deep, shuddering breath. When he let it out, his eyes opened. They were still that drowning deep color as if he were about to feed on something. His voice came out normal, or as normal as it ever got. "I have never tasted such a rush of power without spilling blood first."

"Trust you to think of the perfect thing to say," I said.

Richard sort of hovered over me as if he'd like to help but was afraid to touch me. He glared at Jean-Claude. "What did you do to us?"

"I?" Jean-Claude's beautiful face was nearly slack, eyes half-closed, lips parted. "I did nothing."

"That's a lie," Richard said. He sat Indian fashion a little ways from me, far enough away to make sure we didn't accidentally touch but close enough that that lingering power crawled between us. I inched away and found that closer to Jean-Claude wasn't much better. Whatever it was, it wasn't a one-time deal. The potential was still there in the air, under our skins.

I looked at Richard. "You sound awfully sure that he's up to something. I'm willing to believe it. But what do you know that I don't?"

"I didn't do it. You didn't do it. I know magic when I smell it. It had to be him."

Smell it? I turned back to Jean-Claude. "Well?"

He laughed. The sound trailed down my spine like the brush of fur, soft, slick, startling. It was too soon after the rushing power we'd shared. I shuddered, and he laughed harder. It hurt and you knew you shouldn't be doing it, but it felt too good to stop. His laughter was always dangerously delicious, like poisoned candy.

"I swear by whatever oath you would trust that I did nothing on purpose."

"What did you do by accident?" I asked.

"Ask yourself the same question, *ma petite*. I am not the only master of the supernatural in this room."

Well, he had me there. "You're saying one of us did it."

"I am saying that I do not know who did it, nor do I know what *it* is. But Monsieur Zeeman is correct; it was magic. Raw power to raise the hackles on any wolf."

"What's that supposed to mean?" Richard asked.

"If you could harness such power, my wolf, even Marcus might bow to it."

Richard pulled his knees up, hugging them to his chest. His eyes looked distant, thoughtful. The thought intrigued him.

"Am I the only person in this room not trying to consolidate my kingdom?"

Richard looked at me. He looked almost apologetic. "I don't want to kill Marcus. If I could make a great enough show of power, he might back down."

Jean-Claude smiled at me. It was a very satisfied smile. "You admit he is not human, and now he wants power, so he can be leader of the pack." His smile widened just this short of a laugh.

"I didn't know you were a fan of sixties music," I said.

"There are many things you do not know about me, *ma petite*."

I just stared at him. The image of Jean-Claude boogying down to the Shangri-Las was stranger than anything I'd seen tonight. After all, I believed in nagas, I didn't believe that Jean-Claude had hobbies.

31

A HOT BATH. Once more in the oversize T-shirt, sweatpants, and socks. I was going to be the worst-dressed person in the room. I was planning to replace that black robe at the first opportunity.

They were sitting on the couch, each as far away from the other as they could get. Jean-Claude was sitting like a mannequin, one arm on the back of the couch, the other on the arm of the couch. One foot rested atop his knee showing his soft boots to perfection. Richard was curled on his side of the couch, one knee clutched to his naked chest, the other knee curled on the couch.

Richard looked comfortable. Jean-Claude looked as if he were waiting for a roving photographer to come by. The two men in my life. I could barely stand it.

"I've got to get some sleep, so everybody who isn't staying, out."

"If you are referring to me, *ma petite*, I have no intention of leaving. Unless Richard goes with me."

"Stephen told you why I'm here," Richard said. "She's hurt and doesn't need to be alone."

"Look at her, Richard. Does she look hurt?" He held up a graceful hand. "I admit she has sustained some damage. But she does not need your help. Perhaps she doesn't even need mine."

"I invited Richard to stay over. I did not invite you."

"But you *did* invite me, *ma petite*."

"First, please stop calling me that. Second, when did I invite you?"

"The last time I was here. In August I believe."

Shit, I'd forgotten. It was beyond careless. I'd endangered Richard. Things were working out, but I hadn't known that when I left him here alone, alone in a place where Jean-Claude could come and go at will.

"I can take care of that right now," I said.

"If a dramatic gesture will please you, then be my guest. But Richard must not spend the night."

"Why not?"

"I think you are one of those women that where you give your body, there, too, is your heart. If you sleep with our Monsieur Zeeman, I think it might be the point of no return."

"Sex isn't a commitment," I said.

"For most people, no, but for you, I think it is."

The fact that he knew me that well brought heat in a rush up my face. Damn him. "I don't plan on sleeping with him."

"I believe you, *ma petite*, but I see the way your eyes follow him. He sits there looking luscious and warm and very alive. If I had not been here when you came home, would you have resisted?"

"Yes."

He shrugged. "Perhaps. Your strength of will is frightening, but I cannot take that chance."

"You don't trust me not to molest him?"

Again that shrug that could have meant anything. His smile was inviting and condescending.

"Why? You got the hots for him yourself?"

The question caught him off guard. The surprise on his face was worth the outraged look on Richard's face. Jean-Claude looked at Richard. He gave him his full attention. He stared at Richard, eyes roaming his body in a slow, intimate dance. His gaze ended not on his groin or his chest, but on his neck. "It is true that the blood of shapeshifters can be sweeter than human blood. It is a wild ride if you can manage it without getting torn apart."

"You sound like a rapist," I said.

His smile blossomed in a surprised flash of fangs. "It is not a bad comparison."

"That was an insult, you know," I said.

"I know it was meant as such."

"I thought we had an agreement," Richard said.

"We do."

"You can sit there and talk about taking me for food, and we've still got an agreement."

"It would be enjoyable to take you for many reasons, but we have an agreement. I won't go back on it."

"What agreement?" I asked.

"We are exploring our mutual powers," Jean-Claude said.

"What does that mean exactly?" I asked.

"We're not sure," Richard said. "We haven't worked out the details yet."

"We've just agreed not to kill each other, *ma petite*. Give us a little time to plan beyond that."

"Fine. Then both of you get out."

Richard sat up straighter on the couch. "Anita, you heard Lillian. You need to be woken every hour just in case."

"I'll set an alarm. Look, Richard, I'm fine. Get dressed and go."

He looked puzzled and a little hurt. "Anita."

Jean-Claude didn't look hurt or puzzled. He looked smug.

"Richard's not spending the night. Happy?"

"Yes."

"And you're not spending the night, either."

"I had not planned to." He stood, turning to face me. "I will leave as soon as I've had my good-night kiss."

"Your *what*?"

"My kiss." He came around the couch to stand in front of me. "I will admit I had envisioned you wearing something a little more"—he tugged on my sleeve—"salacious, but one takes what one can get."

I jerked the sleeve out of his fingers. "You haven't gotten anything yet."

"True, but I am hopeful."

"I don't know why," I said.

"The agreement between Richard and me is predicated on the fact that we are all dating. You date Richard, and you date me. We both woo you. One cozy little family."

"Can you speed this up? I want to get to bed."

A slight frown appeared between his eyes. "Anita, you are not making this easy."

"Hurrah," I said.

The frown smoothed out as he sighed. "You would think I would give up on you ever being easy."

"Yes," I said, "you would."

"A good-night kiss, *ma* . . . Anita. If you truly intend to date me, it will not be the last."

I glared up at him. I wanted to tell him to go to hell, but there was something about the way he stood there. "If I say no kiss, what then?"

"I go away for tonight." He took that step closer to me that put us almost touching. The cloth of his shirt brushed the front of my T-shirt. "But if you give Richard kisses and do not allow me such privileges, then the agreement is off. If I cannot touch you, and he can, it is hardly fair."

I'd agreed to the dating because it seemed like a good idea at the time, but now . . . I hadn't really thought through all the implications. Dating, kissing, making out. Yikes! "I don't kiss until after the first date."

"But you have already kissed me, Anita."

"Not willingly," I said.

"Tell me you did not enjoy it, *ma petite*."

I'd have loved to lie, but neither of them would have bought it. "You are an intrusive bastard."

"Not as intrusive as I would like to be," he said.

"You don't have to do anything you don't want to do," Richard said. He was on his knees on the couch, hands gripping the back.

I shook my head. I wasn't sure I could explain it out loud, but if we were really going to do this, Jean-Claude was right. I couldn't hold Richard's hand and not his. Though it did give me a real incentive not to go all the way with Richard. Tit for tat and all that.

"After our first date you can have a willing kiss, not before," I said. I was going to give it the old college try.

He shook his head. "No, Anita. You yourself told me you liked

Richard, not just loved him. That you could see spending your life with him, but not with me. Perhaps he is a more likable fellow. I cannot compete in niceness."

"That's certainly gospel," I said.

He stared down at me with his blue, blue eyes. No drag of power, but there was a weight to his gaze. Not magic, but dangerous all the same.

"But in one area I can compete." I could feel his gaze on my body as if he'd touched me. The weight of his gaze made me shiver.

"Stop it."

"No." One word, soft, caressing. His voice was one of his best things. "One kiss, Anita, or we can end it here, tonight. I will not lose you without a struggle."

"You'd fight Richard tonight, just because I won't kiss you."

"It is not the kiss, *ma petite*. It is what I saw tonight when you met him at the door. I see you forming a couple before my eyes. I must interfere now, or all is lost."

"You'll use your voice to trap her," Richard said.

"I promise, no tricks tonight."

If he said no tricks, he meant it. Once he gave his word he kept it. Which also meant he would fight Richard tonight over a kiss. I'd left both guns in the bedroom. I thought we were safe for tonight. I was too damn tired to do this tonight.

"Okay," I said.

"You don't have to do anything you don't want to, Anita," Richard said.

"If we are all going to go down in a bloody mess, let it be over something more important than a kiss."

"You want to do it," Richard said. "You want to kiss him." He didn't sound pleased.

What was I supposed to say? "What I want most right this moment is to go to bed, alone. I want some sleep." That at least was the truth. Maybe not all of the truth, but enough to earn me a puzzled frown from Richard, and an exasperated sigh from Jean-Claude.

"Then if it is such a distasteful duty, let it be done quickly," Jean-Claude said.

We were standing so close, he didn't have to make a full step to press the line of his body against mine. I tried to put my hands up, to keep our bodies apart. My hands slid over the bare skin of his stomach. I jerked back from him, balling my hands into fists. The feel of his skin clung to my hands.

"What is it, *ma petite*?"

"Leave her alone," Richard said. He was standing beside the couch, hands in loose fists. Power prickled along my skin. His power creeping outward like a slow-moving wind. His hair had spilled over one side of his face. He looked out through a curtain of hair. His face had fallen into shadows. Light gleamed along his naked skin, painting it in shades of grey, gold, and black. He stood there looking suddenly primal. A low, spine-brushing growl trickled through the room.

"Stop it, Richard."

"He is using his powers on you." His voice was unrecognizable. A low, bass growl that was sliding away from human. I was glad for the shadows. Glad I couldn't see what was happening to his face.

I'd been so worried about Jean-Claude starting a fight, it hadn't occurred to me that Richard might pick one. "He isn't using powers on me. I touched his bare skin. That's all."

He stepped forward into the light, and his face was normal. What was happening inside that smooth throat, behind those kissable lips, to make his voice sound monstrous?

"Get dressed and get out."

"What?" His lips moved but that growling voice rolled out. It was like watching a badly dubbed movie.

"If Jean-Claude isn't allowed to attack you, then you sure as hell aren't allowed to attack him. I thought he was the only monster I had to deal with. If you can't behave like a human being, Richard, get out."

"What of my kiss, *ma petite*?"

"You have both pushed it about as far as it's going to go tonight," I said. "Everybody out."

Jean-Claude's laugh filled the shadowed dark. "As you like, Anita Blake. I am suddenly not so worried about you and Monsieur Zeeman."

"Before you start congratulating yourself, Jean-Claude—I revoke my invitation."

There was a sound like a low sonic pop. A great roaring filled the room. The door smashed open, banging against the wall. A wind rushed in like an invisible river, tugging at our clothes, flinging our hair across our eyes.

"You don't have to do this," Jean-Claude said.

"Yes," I said, "I do."

It was as if an invisible hand shoved him through the door. Slamming the door shut behind him.

"I'm sorry," Richard said. The growl was slipping away. His voice was almost normal. "It is too close to the full moon to get this angry."

"I don't want to hear it," I said. "Just go."

"Anita, I am sorry. I don't usually lose control like this. Even this close to the full moon."

"What was different tonight?"

"I've never been in love before. It seems to break my concentration."

"Jealousy will do that to you," I said.

"Tell me I don't have reason to be jealous, Anita. Make me believe it."

I sighed. "Go away, Richard. I've still got to clean my guns and knife before I can go to bed."

He smiled and shook his head. "I guess tonight didn't reassure you about how human I am." He walked around the couch and bent over, retrieving his sweater from the floor, where it lay neatly folded.

He pulled the sweater over his head. He pulled a ponytail holder from his jeans pocket, and tied his hair back. I could see the muscles in his arms work even through the sweater. He slipped his shoes on, bending over to tie them.

His coat was long, falling to his ankles. In the half light it looked like a cape.

"I don't suppose I get a kiss, either."

"Good night, Richard," I said.

He took a deep breath and let it out slowly. "Good night, Anita."

He left. I locked the door. I cleaned my weapons and went to bed. After the show that Richard and Jean-Claude had put on, the Browning was about the only thing I wanted in bed with me tonight. All right, the gun and one stuffed penguin.

32

THE PHONE WAS ringing. It seemed to have been ringing a long time. I lay in bed listening to it ring, wondering when the hell the machine would pick up. I rolled over, reaching for the phone. It was missing. The ringing was coming from the other room. Shit. I'd forgotten to bring it back in last night.

I crawled out of the warm covers and staggered into the living room. The phone must have rung fifteen times before I got to it. I sank to the floor with the receiver clutched to my ear. "Who is it?"

"Anita?"

"Ronnie?"

"You sound awful."

"I look worse," I said.

"What's up?"

"Later, why are you calling at"—I glanced at my wristwatch—"seven o'clock in the freaking morning. This better be good, Ronnie."

"Oh, it's good, all right. I thought we should catch George Smitz before he goes to work."

"Why?" My face was throbbing. I lay down on the carpet, cradling the phone against my ear. The carpet was very soft.

"Anita, Anita, are you there?"

I blinked and realized I'd fallen asleep. I sat up and leaned against the wall. "I'm here, but I didn't hear a word you said after something about needing to talk to Smitz before work."

"I know you're not a morning person, Anita, but you've never fallen asleep on me before. How much sleep did you get last night?"

"About an hour."

"Oh, God, I am sorry. But I knew you'd want to know. I've found the smoking gun."

"Ronnie, please, what are you talking about?"

"I have pictures of George Smitz with another woman." She let that sink in for a moment or two. "Anita, are you there?"

"I'm here. I'm thinking." The last was harder to do than I wanted it to be. I am never at my best first thing in the morning. After an hour's sleep I wasn't even close to my best. "Why do you say it's a smoking gun?"

"Well, a lot of times a spouse will report the other spouse missing to divert suspicion."

"You think Smitz offed his wife?"

"How poetically you put it, but yes, I do."

"Why? A lot of men cheat on their wives, most of them don't kill them."

"Here's the clincher. After I took the pictures, I talked to a few gun stores in the area. He'd bought some silver bullets at a store near the butcher shop."

"Not very bright," I said.

"Most murderers aren't."

I nodded, realized she couldn't see it, and didn't care. "Fine, looks like Mr. Smitz isn't the grieving widower he pretended to be. What do you want to do about it?"

"Confront him at home."

"Why not go to the cops?"

"The store clerk isn't exactly positive it was George."

I closed my eyes. "Great, just great. You think he'll confess to us?"

"He might. He's shared a bed with her for fifteen years. Mother of his children. There's got to be a lot of guilt there."

I don't think real well on an hour's sleep. "Cops, we should have the cops waiting in the wings, at least."

"Anita, he's a client of mine. I don't turn clients over to the cops unless I have to. If he confesses, I'll bring them in. If he doesn't confess, I'll hand over what I have. But I've got to try it my way first."

"Fine, do you call him and tell him we're coming or do you want me to?"

"I'll do it. I just thought you'd like to be there."

"Yeah, let me know when."

"He hasn't gone to work yet. I'll call him and be over to pick you up."

I wanted to say, "No, I have to go back to sleep," but what if he had killed her? What if he'd taken the others? George hadn't struck me as dangerous enough to take out shapeshifters, but then I'd thought he was genuinely grieving. Genuinely worried about his wife. What the hell did I know?

"I'll be ready," I said. I hung up without saying good-bye. I was getting as bad as Dolph. I'd apologize when Ronnie got here.

The phone rang before I could crawl to my feet. "What is it, Ronnie?"

"Anita, it's Richard."

"Sorry, Richard, what's up?"

"You sound awful."

"You don't. You didn't get much more sleep than I did. How come you sound so much better? Please tell me you aren't a morning person."

He laughed. "Sorry, guilty as charged."

Furry I could forgive; a morning person, I'd have to think about that. "Richard, don't take this wrong, but what do you want?"

"Jason's missing."

"Who's Jason?"

"Young male, blond, crawled all over you at the Lunatic Cafe."

"Ah, I remember him. He's missing."

"Yes. Jason is one of our newest pack members. Tonight is the full moon. He wouldn't risk going out alone today of all days. His sponsor went over to his house, and he was gone."

"Sponsor like in AA?"

"Something like that."

"Any signs of a struggle?"

"No."

I stood up dragging the phone in one hand. I tried to think past the leaden tiredness. How dare Richard sound so cheerful. "Peggy Smitz's husband—Ronnie caught him with another woman. A clerk may have sold him silver bullets."

There was silence on the other end of the phone. I could hear his soft breathing, but that was all. The breathing was a little fast.

"Talk to me, Richard."

"If he killed Peggy, then we'll handle it."

"Has it occurred to you that he could be behind all the disappearances?" I asked.

"I don't see how."

"Why not? A silver bullet will take care of any shapeshifter. No great skill involved. You just need to be someone that the shapeshifter trusts."

More silence finally. "Okay, what do you want to do?"

"Ronnie and I were going to confront him this morning. With Jason missing we don't have time to pussyfoot around. Can you supply me with a shapeshifter or two to help threaten Smitz? Maybe with a little muscle power we can get to the truth faster."

"I have to teach school today, and I can't afford for him to know what I am."

"I didn't ask for you to come. Just for some of you to come. Make sure they look intimidating, though. Irving may be a werewolf, but he isn't very scary."

"I'll send someone. To your apartment?"

"Yeah."

"When?"

"Soon as you can. And, Richard."

"Yes."

"Don't tell anybody what we suspect about George Smitz. I don't want to find him clawed up when we get there."

"I wouldn't do that."

"You wouldn't, but Marcus might, and I know Raina would."

"I'll tell them you have a suspect and want some backup. I won't tell them who."

"Great, thanks."

"If you find Jason before they kill him, I'll owe you one."

"I'll take the payment in carnal favors," I said. The minute I said it, I wished I hadn't. It was sort of true, but after last night, not down to my toes.

He laughed. "Done. I've got to go to work. I love you."

I hesitated just a second. "I love you, too. Teach the kiddies well today."

He was quiet for a space of heartbeats. He'd heard the hesitation. "I will. Bye."

"Bye." When I'd hung up, I stood there for a minute. If someone was just walking up and shooting shifters, then Jason was dead. The best I'd be able to do would be to locate the body. It was better than nothing, but not much.

33

WE PULLED UP in front of George Smitz's house at a little after nine that morning. Ronnie was driving. I was riding shotgun. Gabriel and Raina were in the backseat. If asked, I would have chosen different people for backup. I also wouldn't have chosen my boyfriend's old lover for backup. What had Richard been thinking? Or maybe Raina hadn't given him a choice. Her coming today, not the sex. I still wasn't sure how I felt about that. All right. I knew how I felt. I was pissed. But I'd slept with someone else. Glass houses and all. In any case, Richard had given me exactly what I'd asked for: scary, intimidating shapeshifters. I wasn't used to getting exactly what I asked for. Next time I'd be more specific.

Gabriel was dressed in black leather again. It could almost have been the same outfit I'd first seen him in, down to the metal-studded gauntlet on his right hand. Maybe his whole closet was one great big leather fest. The earrings were gone. The holes even in the harder cartilage of the ears had healed.

Raina was dressed normally enough. Sort of. She was wearing an ankle-length fur coat. Fox. Cannibalism is one thing, but wearing the skin of your dead? It seemed a little cold blooded even for the psycho bitch from hell. All right, she was a wolf, not a fox, but heck, I didn't wear fur on moral grounds. She flaunted it.

She leaned over the back of the seat. "What are we doing in front of Peggy's house?"

It was time to spill the beans. Why didn't I want to do it? I undid the seat belt and turned to face her. She was looking at me, face pleasant enough. On her lycanthrope bone structure she had all high cheekbones and a luscious mouth. Maybe she planned on doing something nefarious today.

Gabriel had draped himself over the backseat. The gauntleted hand trailed down Ronnie's arm. Even through her suede coat she shivered. "Touch me again, and I am going to feed you that hand." She'd scooted away from him as far as the steering wheel would allow, which wasn't far. Gabriel had touched her several times on the drive over. Teasing, nothing embarrassing, but it was bothersome.

"Hands are very bony. I prefer a more tender cut of meat. Breast or thigh is my preference," Gabriel said. His grey eyes were startling even in sunlight, maybe more so. They had a quality of light to the grey that was almost luminous. I'd seen eyes like that before, but I still couldn't place it.

"Gabriel, I know you are a pain in the ass. I know you're enjoying the hell out of teasing Ronnie, but if you don't stop it we're going to see just how good your recuperative powers are."

He slid across the seat, closer to me. Not necessarily an improvement. "I'm yours anytime you want me."

"Is coming that close to dying really your idea of sex?"

"As long as it hurts," Gabriel said.

Ronnie looked at us with wide eyes. "You have got to tell me about your evening."

"You really don't want to know," I said.

"Why are we here?" Raina asked again. She wasn't going to be distracted by Mr. Leather. Good for her. Bad for me. Her gaze was intense, as if my face were the most important thing in the world. Was this what Marcus saw in her? A lot of men are very flattered by undivided attention. Then aren't we all?

"Ronnie?"

She got the pictures out of her purse. They were the kind of pictures that didn't need any explanation. George had left his drapes up, very careless.

Gabriel curled back into the seat, flipping through the shots, a big smile on his face. He got to one particular shot, and laughed. "Very impressive."

Raina's reaction was very different. She wasn't amused. She was angry. "You brought us out here to punish him for cheating on Peggy?"

"Not exactly," I said. "We think he is responsible for her disappearance. If he's responsible for one disappearance, he could be responsible for more."

Raina looked at me. The concentration was just as pure but now I had to fight an urge to squirm. Her rage was pure and simple. George had hurt a pack member. He would pay for that. There was no uncertainty in her gaze, only an instant rage.

"Let Ronnie and I do the talking. The two of you are here to intimidate him if we need it."

"If there is any chance he has Jason, we don't have time to be subtle," Raina said.

I agreed with her, but not out loud. "We talk, you stay in the background and look menacing. Unless we ask. Okay?"

"I'm here because Richard asked me," Raina said. "He's an alpha male. I obey his orders."

"Somehow I don't picture you obeying anybody's orders," I said.

She flashed me a very nasty smile. "I obey the orders I want to obey."

That I believed. I jerked a thumb at Gabriel. "Who called in him?"

"I chose him. Gabriel is very good at intimidation."

He was big, leather clad, metal studded, and had sharp, pointy teeth. Yeah, I'd say that was intimidating.

"Your word that you'll stay in the background unless we need you."

"Richard said we are to obey you as we would obey him," Raina said.

"Great. Since you obey Richard only when it suits you, what does that mean?"

Raina laughed. It had a hard, brittle edge to it. The kind of laughter that made you think of mad scientists and people locked too long in solitary. "I will let you handle it, Anita Blake, as long as you are doing a good job. Jason is my pack member. I will not let your squeamishness endanger him."

I was liking this less and less. "I'm not squeamish."

She smiled. "That is true. My apologies."

"You're not a wolf," I said. "What are you getting out of this?"

Gabriel smiled, flashing sharp, pointy teeth. He was still flipping through the pictures. "Marcus and Richard will owe me a favor. The whole damn pack will owe me one."

I nodded. It was a motive I believed. "Give the pictures back to Ronnie. No smart remarks, just do it."

He pouted, sticking out his lower lip. It would have worked better without the fangs. But he handed the pictures to Ronnie. His fingertips brushed her hand, lingering a little, but he didn't say anything. That had been what I asked. Were all shapeshifters so damn literal?

His strange eyes stared at me. I suddenly remembered where I'd seen those eyes. Behind a mask in a film that I'd rather not have seen. Gabriel was the other man in the snuff film. I hadn't had enough sleep to hide the shock. I felt my face crumble with it and couldn't stop it.

Gabriel turned his head to one side, like a dog. "Why are you looking at me like I just sprouted a second head?"

What could I say? "Your eyes. I just figured out where I've seen them."

"Yes." He moved closer, putting his chin on the back of the seat, letting me have a good look at those luminous eyes. "Where?"

"The zoo. You're a leopard." Liar, liar, pants on fire, but I couldn't think of a better one, not this quick.

He blinked, staring at me. "Meow, but that wasn't what you were thinking." He sounded very sure of himself.

"Believe it or not, I don't give a damn. It's the best answer you're getting."

He stayed there, chin indenting the upholstery. You couldn't see his shoulders, so his head looked disembodied, like a head on a pike. Accurate, if Edward found out who he was. And Edward would find out. I'd tell him, gladly, if it would stop any more of those films from being made. Of course, I wasn't sure it would stop them. They were Raina's brainchild. Supposedly, she didn't know about the alternate ending. Yeah, right, and I moonlighted as the Easter Bunny.

Ronnie was staring at me. She knew me too well. I hadn't told her about the snuff film. Now I'd introduced her to two of the stars. Shit. We got out of the car into the bright, chilly winter sunlight. We walked up the sidewalk with a shapeshifter following at our backs that I had seen murder a woman on screen and feed from her still-twitching body. God help George Smitz if he was guilty. God help us all if he wasn't. Jason was missing. One of the newest pack members, Richard had said. If George Smitz didn't have him, who did?

34

RAINA GRABBED MY hand before it could touch the doorbell. Her grip had been very fast. I hadn't had time to react at all. Her nails were long and perfectly manicured with nail polish the color of burnt pumpkins. Those orange-brown nails dug into my wrist just enough to indent the skin. She let me feel the strength in that delicate hand. She didn't hurt me, but the smile on her face said she could. I smiled back. She was strong, but she wasn't a vampire. I was betting I could get to a gun before she could finish crushing my wrist.

She didn't crush my wrist. She let go. "Perhaps Gabriel and I should go in the back way. You did say you wanted us to stay in the background." She was smiling and looking oh, so reasonable. The nail marks in my skin hadn't filled out yet.

"I mean, look at us, Ms. Blake. Even if we say nothing, he can't ignore us."

She had a point. "How will the two of you get in the back door if it's locked?"

Raina gave me a look worthy of Edward, as if I'd asked a very stupid question. Was I the only one who didn't know how to pick a lock? "Fine, go to it."

Raina smiled and walked off through the snow. Her auburn hair gleamed against the fox fur coat. Her high-heeled brown boots left sharp little prints in the melting snow. Gabriel trailed after her. The chains on his leather jacket jingled as he walked. His metal-studded cowboy boots smashed over Raina's daintier prints almost as if it were purposeful.

"Nobody's going to mistake them for door-to-door salespeople," Ronnie said.

I glanced at our jeans, my Nikes, her snow boots, my leather jacket, her long suede coat. "Us either," I said.

"Good point."

I rang the bell.

We stood on the little front porch listening to the eaves drip. We were having one of those strange winter thaws that Missouri is famous for. The snow was all soft and fading like a snowman in the sunshine. But it wouldn't last. Getting this much snow at all in December was unusual here. We usually didn't get real snow until January or February.

It was taking a long time for Mr. Smitz to come to the door. Finally I heard movement. Something heavy enough to be a person moving toward the door. George Smitz opened the door in a bloodstained apron over jeans and a pale blue T-shirt.

There was a bloodstain on one shoulder, as if he'd lifted a side of beef and it had bled on him. He wiped his hands on his apron, palms flat, skin stretching along the fabric as if he couldn't get them clean. Maybe he just wasn't used to being covered in blood. Or maybe his palms were sweating.

I smiled and offered him my hand. He took it. His palm was sweaty. Nervous. Great. "How are you, Mr. Smitz?"

He shook hands with Ronnie and ushered us inside. We were standing in a little entryway. There was a closet to one side, a mirror on the opposite wall with a low table. A vase full of yellow silk flowers sat on the table. The walls were pale yellow and matched the flowers.

"May I take your coats?"

If he was a murderer, he was the most polite one I'd ever met. "No, thanks, we'll keep them with us."

"Peggy always got on to me if I didn't ask for people's coats. 'George, you weren't raised in a barn, ask them if you can take their coats.'" The imitation sounded accurate.

We stepped out into the living room. It was wallpapered in pale yellow with brown flowers done very small. The couch, the love seat, the recliner were all a pale, pale yellow, almost white. There were more silk flowers on the pale wood end table. Yellow.

The pictures on the wall, the knickknacks on the shelves, even the carpet underfoot was yellow. It was like being inside a lemon drop.

Either it showed on my face or George was used to it. "Yellow was Peggy's favorite color."

"Was?"

"I mean is. Oh, God." He collapsed on the pale lemon couch, face hidden in his big hands. He was the only thing in the room that didn't match the yellow lace curtains. "It's been so awful, wondering." He looked up at us. Tears glistened in his eyes. It was Academy Award caliber.

"Ms. Sims said she had news about Peggy. Have you found her? Is she all right?" His eyes were so sincere it hurt to look into them. I still couldn't tell he was lying. If I hadn't seen the pictures of him with another woman, I wouldn't have believed it. Of course, adultery wasn't murder. He could be guilty of one and not the other. Sure.

Ronnie sat on the couch, as far away from him as she could get but still rather companiable. Cozier than I was willing to be with the son of a bitch. If I ever managed to get married and my husband cheated on me, it wouldn't be me to go missing.

"Please sit down, Ms. Blake. I'm sorry, I'm not being a very good host."

I perched on the edge of the yellow recliner. "I thought you worked construction, Mr. Smitz. What's with the apron?"

"Peggy's dad can't run the store by himself. He deeded it to her years ago. I may have to quit working construction. But you know, he's family. I can't leave him in the lurch. Peggy did most of the work. Dad's almost ninety-two. He just can't do it all."

"Do you inherit the butcher shop?" I asked. We'd automatically gone into good cop, bad cop. Guess which one I was.

He blinked at me. "Well, yes. I suppose so."

He didn't ask if she was all right this time. He just looked at me with his soulful eyes.

"You love your wife?"

"Yes, of course. What kind of question is that?" He looked less sad and more angry now.

"Ronnie," I said softly.

She took the pictures out of her purse and gave them to him. The front picture showed him embracing the dark-haired woman. Peggy Smitz had been a blond.

Color crept up his face. Not so much red as purplish. He slammed the pictures down on the coffee table without looking at the rest. They slid across the table, images of him and the woman in various states of undress. Kissing, groping, nearly doing it standing up.

His face went from red to purplish. His eyes bulged. He stood up, his breath coming in fast, harsh gasps. "What the hell are these?"

"I think the pictures are self-explanatory," I said.

"I hired you to find my wife, not to spy on me." He turned on Ronnie, towering over her. His big hands balled into even bigger fists. The muscles in his arms bulged, veins standing out like worms.

Ronnie stood up, using her five feet and nine inches to good advantage. She was calm. If she was worried about facing down a man that outweighed her by a hundred pounds, it didn't show.

"Where's Peggy, George?"

He glanced at me, then back to Ronnie. He raised a hand as if he would strike her.

"Where'd you hide the body?"

He whirled on me. I just sat there and looked at him. He'd have to come over or around the coffee table to get to me. I was pretty sure I could be out of reach. Or have a gun. Or put him through a window. That last was sounding better and better.

"Get out of my house."

Ronnie had stepped back out of reach. He stood there like a purple-faced mountain, swaying between us.

"Get out of my house."

"Can't do that, George. We know you killed her." Maybe *know* was too strong a word, but "we're pretty sure you killed her" didn't have the right ring. "Unless you really plan to start swinging, I'd sit down, Georgie-boy."

"Yes, by all means sit down, George." I didn't look behind me to see where Raina was. I didn't think George would really hurt me, but better to be cautious. Taking my eyes off a guy who weighed over two hundred pounds sounded like a bad idea.

He stared at Raina. He looked confused. "What the hell is this?"

Ronnie said, "Oh, my God." She was staring behind me with her mouth open.

Something was going on behind my back, but what? I stood, eyes all for George, but he wasn't looking at me anymore. I stepped away from him just to be safe. When I had enough distance to be safe. I could see the doorway.

Raina was wearing a brown silk teddy, high heeled boots and nothing else. The fur coat was held open, the bloodred lining outlining her body dramatically.

"I thought you were going to stay in the background unless I called for you."

She dropped the fur into a fuzzy puddle on the floor. She stalked into the room, swaying everything that would move.

Ronnie and I exchanged glances. She mouthed the words, "What's going on?" I shrugged. I didn't have the faintest idea.

Raina bent over the silk flowers on the coffee table, giving George Smitz a long, thorough view of her slim backside.

The color was draining from his face. His hands were slowly unclenching. He looked confused. Join the club.

Raina smiled up at him. She stood up very slowly, giving George a good view of her high, tight breasts. His eyes were glued to her décolletage. She stood up, running her hands down the teddy, ending with a pass over her groin. George seemed to be having a little trouble swallowing.

Raina walked up to him until she was just a finger's pull away from him. She looked up at him and whispered out of full, sensuous lips, "Where's Jason?"

He frowned. "Who's Jason?"

She caressed his cheek with her painted nails. The nails slid out of her skin long and longer, until they were great hooking claws. The tips were still the color of burnt pumpkins.

She hooked those claws under his chin, putting them just enough in not to break the skin. "The tiniest bit of pressure and you'll have a howling good time once a month."

It was a lie. She was still in human form. She wasn't contagious. All the color had drained from his face. His skin was the color of unbleached paper.

"Where's your wife's body, Mr. Smitz?" I asked. It was a good threat worth more than one question.

"I don't . . . don't know what you mean."

"Don't lie to me, George, I don't like it." She raised her other hand in front of his face, and the claws slid out like unsheathed knives.

He whimpered.

"Where's Peggy, George?" She whispered it. The voice was still seductive. She might have been whispering, I love you, instead of a threat.

She kept her claws under his jaw and lowered the other hand slowly. His eyes followed that hand. He tried to move his head down, but the claws stopped him. He gasped.

Raina sliced through the bloody apron. Two quick, hard slices. The clothes underneath were untouched. Talent.

"I . . . killed her. I killed Peggy. Oh, God. I shot her."

"Where's the body?" I asked that. Raina seemed to be enjoying her game too much to pay attention to all the details.

"Shed out back. It's got a dirt floor."

"Where's Jason?" Raina asked. She touched claw tips to his jeans, over his groin.

"Oh, God, I don't know who Jason is. Please, I don't know. I don't know." His voice was coming in breathy gasps.

Gabriel walked into the room. He'd lost the jacket somewhere and wore a tight black T-shirt with his leather pants and boots. "He doesn't have the guts to have taken Jason or the others."

"Is that right, George? You don't have the guts?" Raina pressed her breasts against his chest, claws still at his jawline and groin. The lower claws pressed into the jean fabric, not quite tearing.

"Please, please don't hurt me."

Raina put her face very close to his. Claws forcing him to stand on tiptoes or have his chin spitted. "You are pathetic." She shoved the claws into his jeans, tearing into the fabric.

George fainted. Raina had to pull her hands away to keep from slicing him up. She kept a near perfect circle of jeans. His white briefs showed through the hole in his pants.

Gabriel knelt by the body, balancing on the balls of his feet. "This human did not take Jason."

"Pity," Raina said.

It was a pity. Somebody had taken eight, no seven shapeshifters. The eighth had been Peggy Smitz. We had her murderer on the carpet with his fly torn out. Who had taken them, and why? Why would anybody want seven lycanthropes? Something clicked. The naga had been skinned alive. If he'd been a lycanthrope instead of a naga, a witch could have used the skin to become a snake. It was a way to be a shape-shifter with all the advantages and none of the bad stuff. The moon didn't control you.

"Anita, what is it?" Ronnie asked.

"I have to go to the hospital and talk to someone."

"Why?" A look was enough for Ronnie to say, "Fine, I'll call the cops. But I drove."

"Damn." I glanced up and caught sight of a car driving by on the street. It was a Mazda, green. I knew that car.

"I may have a ride." I opened the door and walked down the sidewalk, waving. The car slowed, then double-parked beside Ronnie's car.

The window whirred down at the press of a button. Edward sat behind the wheel, a pair of dark glasses covering his eyes. "I've been following Raina for days. How'd you spot me?"

"Dumb luck."

He grinned. "Not so dumb."

"I need a ride."

"What about Raina and her little leather friend?"

It occurred to me to tell him that Gabriel was the other lycanthrope in the snuff film, but if I did that now, he'd go in and kill him. Or at least wouldn't want to take me to the hospital. Priorities.

"We can either give them a ride home or they can take a taxi."

"Taxi," he said.

"My preference, too."

Edward drove around the block to wait for me. Raina and Gabriel were persuaded to call a taxi to pick them up in front of another house. They didn't want to talk to the police. Fancy that. George Smitz came to, and Raina convinced him to confess to the police when they arrived. I apologized to Ronnie for deserting her and walked down the block to meet Edward. We were off to the hospital to talk to the naga. Here's hoping he'd gained consciousness.

35

THERE WAS A uniformed officer standing outside the naga's room. Edward had stayed in the car. After all, he was wanted by the police. One of the bad things about working with Edward and the cops is that you can't necessarily work with them at the same time.

The cop at the door was a small woman with a blond ponytail. There was a chair beside the door, but she was standing, one hand on her gun butt. Her pale eyes squinted suspiciously at me.

She gave a curt nod. "You Anita Blake?"

"Yeah."

"See some ID?" She said, real tough, no nonsense. Had to be a rookie. Only a rookie had that hard-on attitude. Older cops would have asked for ID, but they wouldn't have tried to make their voices lower.

I showed her my plastic ID badge. The one I clipped to my shirt when I had to cross a police line. It wasn't a police badge, but it was the best I had.

She took it in her hand and looked at it for a long time. I fought the urge to ask if she was going to be tested later. It never helps to piss the police off. Especially over trivialities.

She finally gave the badge back to me. Her eyes were blue and cold as a winter sky. Very tough. Probably practiced that look in the mirror every morning. "No one can question the man without police being present. When you called up to ask to speak with him, I contacted Sergeant Storr. He's on his way."

"How long will I have to wait?"

"I don't know."

"Look, a man's missing, any delay could cost him his life."

I had her attention now. "Sergeant Storr didn't mention a missing person."

Shit. I'd forgotten that the cops didn't know about the missing shapeshifters. "I don't suppose that you'd buy time is of the essence. How about lives are at stake?"

Her eyes went from hard to bored. She was impressed. "Sergeant Storr was very specific. He wants to be present when you question the man."

"Are you sure you spoke with Sergeant Storr, and not Detective Zerbrowski?" It would be like Zerbrowski to screw this up for me, just to irritate.

"I know who I spoke with, Ms. Blake."

"I didn't mean to imply that you didn't, Officer. I just meant that Zerbrowski could have gotten confused about how much access I'm allowed to the . . . ah, witness."

"I talked to the sergeant, and I know what he told me. You're not going in until he gets here. Those are my orders."

I started to say something unpleasant and stopped. I glanced at her nameplate. Officer Kirlin was right. She had her orders, and she wasn't going to budge from them.

"Fine, Officer Kirlin. I'll just wait around the corner in the patient waiting room." I turned and walked away before I said something not so nice. I wanted to push my way into the room, pull rank. But I didn't have any rank. It was one of those times when I was forcibly reminded that I was a civilian. I didn't like being reminded.

I sat down on a multicolored couch that backed a raised area of real plants. The chest-high planting area gave the illusion of walls, dividing the waiting room into three pseudo rooms. The illusion of privacy if you needed it. A television set was mounted high on one wall. No one had bothered to turn it on yet. It was hospital quiet. The only noise was the heater coming through the wall registers.

I hated waiting. Jason was missing. Was he dead? If he were alive, how much longer would he be alive? How long would Dolph keep me waiting?

Dolph came around the corner. Bless his little heart, he hadn't kept me waiting long at all.

I stood. "Officer Kirlin says you mentioned a missing person to her. Are you holding out on me?"

"Yeah, but not by choice. I've got a client that won't go to the police. I've tried to persuade them . . ." I shrugged. "Just because I'm right and they're wrong doesn't mean I can spill their secrets without clearing it with them first."

"There's no client-animator privilege, Anita. If I asked for the information you're legally obligated to give it to me."

I hadn't had enough sleep to deal with this. "Or what?"

He frowned. "Or you go to jail for obstruction of justice."

"Fine, let's go," I said.

"Don't push me, Anita."

"Look, Dolph, I'll tell you everything I know when they give me the okay. I may tell you anyway because they're being stupid, but I won't tell you shit because you bullied me."

He took a deep breath through his nose and let it out slow. "Fine, let's go talk to our witness."

I appreciated the naga still being "our" witness. "Yeah, let's go." Dolph motioned me out of the waiting room. We walked down the hallway together in silence. But the silence was companionable. No need to fill it with idle chitchat or accusations.

A doctor in a white coat with a stethoscope draped over his shoulders like a feather boa opened the door. Officer Kirlin was still at her post, ever vigilant. She gave me her best flinty steel look. It needed work. But when you're small, blond, female, and a cop, you have to at least try to look tough.

"He can talk for a very short time. It's a miracle that he's alive, let alone talking. I'll monitor the questioning. If he gets upset, I'll stop the interview."

"That's fine with me, Dr. Wilburn. He's a victim and a witness, not a suspect. We don't mean him any harm."

The doctor didn't look completely convinced but he stepped back into the room, and held the door for us.

Dolph loomed up behind me. He was like an immovable force at my back. I could see why the doctor thought we might browbeat the witness. Dolph couldn't look harmless if he tried, so he just didn't try.

The naga lay in the bed, thick with tubes and wires. His skin was growing back. You could see it spreading in raw, painful patches, but it was growing back. He still looked as though he'd been boiled alive, but it was an improvement.

He turned his eyes to look at us. He moved his head very slowly, the better to see us. "Mr. Javad, you remember Sergeant Storr. He's brought some people to talk with you."

"The woman . . . ," he said. His voice was low and sounded painful. He swallowed carefully and tried again. "The woman at the river."

I walked forward. "Yes, I was at the river."

"Helped me."

"I tried."

Dolph stepped forward. "Mr. Javad, can you tell us who did this to you?"

"Witches," he said.

"Did you say 'witches'?" Dolph asked.

"Yes."

Dolph looked at me. He didn't have to ask. This was my area. "Javad, did you recognize the witches? Names?"

He swallowed again and it sounded dry. "No."

"Where did they do this to you?"

He closed his eyes.

"Do you know where you were when they . . . skinned you?"

"Drugged me."

"Who drugged you?"

"Woman . . . eyes."

"What about her eyes?"

"Ocean." I had to lean forward to hear that last. His voice was fading.

He opened his eyes suddenly, wide. "Eyes, ocean." He let out a low guttural sound, as if he were swallowing screams.

The doctor came up. He checked his vitals, touching the ruined flesh as gently as he could. Even that touch made him writhe with pain.

The doctor pressed a button on the bedside. "It's time for Mr. Javad's medication. Bring it now."

"No," Javad said. He grabbed my arm. He gasped, but held on. His skin felt like warm raw meat. "Not first."

"Not first? I don't understand."

"Others."

"They did this to others?"

"Yes. Stop them."

"I will. I promise."

He slumped back against the bed but couldn't hold still. It hurt too much for that. Every movement hurt, but he couldn't hold still against the pain.

A nurse in a pink jacket came in with a shot. She put the needle into his IV. Moments later he began to ease. His eyes fluttered shut. Sleep came and something in my chest loosened. That much pain was hard to endure, even if you were only just watching.

"He'll wake up and we'll have to sedate him again. I've never seen anyone that could heal like this. But just because he can heal the damage doesn't mean it doesn't hurt."

Dolph took me to one side. "What was all that about eyes and others?"

"I don't know." Half-true. I didn't know what the eye comment meant, but I suspected the others were the missing shapeshifters.

Zerbrowski came in. He motioned to Dolph. They walked out into the hall. The nurse and doctor were fussing with the naga. No one had invited me out into the hall, but it was only fair. I wasn't sharing with them, why should they share with me?

The door opened, and Dolph motioned me out into the hall. We went. Officer Kirlin wasn't at her post. Probably told to leave for a little while.

"Can't find any missing-person case that has your name associated with it," Dolph said.

"You had Zerbrowski check me out?"

Dolph just looked at me. His eyes had gone all cool and distant—
cop eyes.

"Except for Dominga Salvador," Zerbrowski said.

"Anita said she didn't know what happened to Mrs. Salvador," Dolph
said. He was still giving me his hard look. It was a hell of a lot better than
Officer Kirlin's.

I fought the urge to squirm. Dominga Salvador was dead. I knew that
because I'd seen it happen. I'd pulled the trigger, metaphorically speaking. Dolph suspected I had something to do with her disappearance but
he couldn't prove it, and she had been a very evil woman. If she'd been
convicted of everything she was suspected of doing, it would have been
an automatic death penalty. The law doesn't like witches much better
than it likes vampires. I'd used a zombie to kill her. It was enough to earn
me my own trip to the electric chair.

My beeper sounded. Saved by the bell. I checked the number. I didn't
recognize the number, but no need sharing that. "An emergency, I've got
to find a phone." I walked off before Dolph could say anything else.
Seemed safer that way.

They let me use the phone at the nurses' station. Kind of them.
Richard picked up the phone on the first ring. "Anita?"

"Yeah, what's up?"

"I'm at school. Louie never showed up for his morning classes." He
lowered his voice until I had to plug one ear just to hear him. "Tonight is
full moon. He wouldn't miss classes. It raises suspicions."

"Why call me?"

"He said he was going to meet your writer friend, Elvira something."

"Elvira Drew?" As I said her name, I could picture her face. Her
green-blue eyes the color of ocean water. Shit.

"I think so."

"When was he supposed to meet her?"

"This morning."

"Did he make the meeting?"

"I don't know. I'm at work. I haven't been by his place yet."

"You're afraid something happened to him, aren't you?"

"Yes."

"I didn't set up the meeting. I'll call work and find out who did. Will you be at this number?"

"I've got to get back to class. But I'll check back with you as soon as I can."

"Okay. I'll call you as soon as I know anything."

"I've got to go," he said.

"Wait, I think I know what happened to the missing shapeshifters."

"What!"

"This is an ongoing police investigation. I can't talk about it, but if I could tell the police about the missing shapeshifters, we might find Louie and Jason faster."

"Marcus said not to tell?"

"Yeah."

He was quiet for a minute. "Tell them. I'll take the responsibility."

"Great. I'll get back with you." I hung up. It wasn't until I heard the dial tone that I realized I hadn't said, I love you. Oh, well.

I dialed work. Mary answered. I didn't wait for her to get through her greeting. "Put me through to Bert."

"Are you all right?"

"Just do it."

She didn't argue. Good woman. "Anita, this better be important. I've got a client with me."

"Did you speak with someone about finding a wererat today?"

"As a matter of fact, I did."

My stomach hurt. "When and where was the appointment set up?"

"This morning, about six. Mr. Fane wanted to get it in before he had to go to work."

"Where?"

"Her house."

"Give me the address."

"What's wrong?"

"I think Elvira Drew may have set him up to be killed."

"You are kidding me, right?"

"Address, Bert."

He gave it to me.

"I may not be in for work tonight."

"Anita . . ."

"Save it, Bert. If he gets killed, we set him up."

"Fine, fine. Do what you have to."

I hung up. It was a first, Bert giving in. If I hadn't known that visions of lawsuits were dancing in his head, I'd have been more impressed.

I went back to our little group. No one was talking to anyone. "There have been seven shapeshifters taken in this area."

"What are you talking about?" Dolph asked.

I shook my head. "Just listen." I told him everything about the disappearances. Ending with, "Two more shifters have gone missing. I think whoever skinned the naga thought he was a lycanthrope. It is possible by magic to take a shifter's skin and use it to shapeshift yourself. You get all of the advantages, greater strength, speed, etc. . . . and you are not tied to the moon."

"Why didn't it work with the naga?" Zerbrowski asked.

"He's immortal. The shifter has to die at the end of the spell."

"We know why. Now, where the hell are they?" Dolph asked.

"I've got an address," I said.

"How?"

"I'll explain on the way. The spell doesn't work until dark, but we can't take the chance they'll keep them alive. They have to be worried that the naga healed enough to talk."

"After seeing him last night, I wouldn't be," Zerbrowski said.

"You're not a witch," I said.

We left. I would have liked Edward at my back. If we did find renegade witches and a few shapeshifters on the night of the full moon, Edward at my back was not a bad idea. But I couldn't figure out how to manage it. Dolph and Zerbrowski were no slouches, but they were cops. They aren't allowed to shoot people without giving them every opportunity to give up. Elvira Drew had skinned a naga. I wasn't sure I wanted to give her an opportunity. I wasn't sure we'd survive it.

36

ELVIRA DREW'S HOUSE was a narrow two-story set off from the road by a thick line of bushes and trees. You couldn't even see the yard before you turned into the driveway. Woods stretched out all around the small yard, as if someone had put the house here and forgotten to tell anybody.

A patrol car followed us down the gravel driveway. Dolph parked behind a vivid green Grand Am. The car matched her eyes.

There was a For Rent sign in the yard. Another lay beside it, waiting to be stuck in the ground. It would probably go out by the road.

Two clothes bags hung inside the car. The backseat was packed with boxes. A quick getaway was in the offing.

"If she's a murderer, why'd she give you her actual address?" Zerbrowski asked.

"We check out clients. They have to have a place of residence or some way of proving who they are. We demand more ID than most banks."

"Why?"

"Because every once in a while we get a crazy. Or a tabloid reporter. We have to know who we're dealing with. I bet she tried to pay cash with no ID and when asked for three forms of it, she wasn't prepared."

Dolph led the way to the door. We followed behind like good soldiers. Officer Kirlin was one of the uniforms. Her partner was an older guy with greying hair and a round little belly. I bet it didn't shake like a bowlful of jelly. He had a sour expression on his face that said he'd seen it all and didn't like any of it.

Dolph knocked on the door. Silence. He knocked harder. The door trembled. Elvira opened the door. She was wearing a brilliant green robe, tied at the waist. Her makeup was still perfect. The polish on her finger-nails matched the robe. Her long blond hair was combed straight back, held from her face with a scarf that was just a touch bluer green than the robe. Her eyes blazed with the color.

Dolph muttered, "Eyes like the ocean."

"Excuse me, what's all this about?"

"May we come in, Ms. Drew?"

"Whatever for?"

There hadn't been time to get a warrant. Dolph wasn't even sure we could have gotten one with what we had. The color of someone's eyes wasn't exactly proof.

I sort of peeked around Dolph, and said, "Hello, Ms. Drew, we need to ask you a few questions about Louis Fane."

"Ms. Blake, I didn't know you were with the police."

She smiled, I smiled. Was Louie here? Was she stalling while some-one killed him? Dammit. If the police hadn't been here, I'd have pulled the gun and gone in. There are disadvantages to being law abiding.

"We're checking into the disappearance of Mr. Fane. You were the last one to see him."

"Oh, dear." She didn't back away from the door.

"May we come in and ask you a few questions?" Dolph asked.

"Well, I don't know what I can tell you. Mr. Fane never made our meeting. I didn't see him at all."

She stood there like a pretty smiling wall.

"We need to come in and look around, Ms. Drew, just in case."

"Do you have a warrant?"

Dolph looked at her. "No, Ms. Drew, we do not."

Her smile was dazzling. "Then I'm sorry, but I can't let you in."

I grabbed the front of her robe, yanking it tight enough to know she wasn't wearing a bra. "We either go past you or through you."

Dolph's hand descended on my shoulder. "I'm sorry, Ms. Drew. Ms.

Blake gets a little overzealous." The words were squeezed out between his teeth, but he said them.

"Dolph . . ."

"Let her go, Anita, right now."

I looked up into her strange eyes. She was still smiling but there was something else there now. Fear. "If he dies, you die."

"They don't put you to death for suspicions," she said.

"I wasn't talking about a legal execution."

Her eyes widened. Dolph jerked back on my shoulder. He pushed me down the steps. Zerbrowski was already apologizing for my faux pas.

"What the hell do you think you're doing?" Dolph asked.

"He's in there, I know it."

"You don't know it. I've called in for a warrant. Until we get it, unless she lets us in or he comes to a window and yells for help, we can't go in. That's the law."

"Well, it sucks."

"Maybe, but we're the police. If we don't obey the law, then who else will?"

I hugged myself, fingers digging into my elbows. It was either that or run up and smash Elvira Drew's perfect face in. Louie was in there, and it was my fault.

"Take a walk, Anita, cool off."

I looked up at him. He could have told me to sit in the car, but he hadn't. I tried to read his face, but it had gone cop blank. "A walk, good idea."

I walked towards the trees. No one stopped me. Dolph didn't call me back. He had to know what I'd do. I walked into the winter-bare trees. Melt fell in droplets onto my head and face. I walked out until I couldn't see them clearly anymore. In winter you can catch glimpses of things for yards, but it was far enough for our little game of pretend.

I angled back for the back of the house. The melting snow soaked into my Nikes. The leaves were a soggy mat underfoot. I had both guns and two knives. I'd replaced the one that Gretchen never returned. They were a set of four that I'd had made for me. Hard to find a knife with a high enough silver content to kill monsters and still take a hard edge.

But I couldn't kill anyone. My job was to get inside, find Louie, and yell for help. If someone in the house yelled for help, the police could come in. Those were the rules. If Dolph hadn't been scared they'd kill Louie, he wouldn't have let me do this. But law or no law, sitting outside while your suspect kills her next victim was hard to swallow.

I hunkered down at the tree line looking at the back of the house. A back door led onto an enclosed porch. There was a door with glass in it that led into the house, and a second door off to one side. Most houses in St. Louis have basements. Some of the older houses originally had only outside access to them. Add a little porch, add a little door. If I was hiding somebody, a basement sounded like a good place. If it was a broom closet, I just wouldn't go in.

I checked the upper-story windows. The drapes were closed. If there were people up there watching, I couldn't see them. Here was hoping they couldn't see me.

I crossed the open ground without getting out a gun. They were witches. Witches didn't shoot you, as a general rule. In fact, witches, real witches, didn't practice a lot of violence. A Wiccan wouldn't have had anything to do with human sacrifice. But the word *witch* means a lot of different things. Some of them can get pretty scary, but they seldom shoot you.

I knelt by the screen door that led onto the porch. I held my hand as close to the door handle as I could without touching it. No heat, no . . . hell there's no word for it. But there was no spell on the handle. Even good witches will sometimes bespell their outer doors so they're either alerted to a burglar's presence or some attachment occurs. Say, you break in and don't take a thing. The spell will stick to you and let the witch and friends find you. Bad witches can put worse things on their doors. We'd already established what sort of witches were inside, so caution seemed best.

I slipped the tip of my knife through the edge of the door. A little jiggling and the door opened. No breaking yet, but I had definitely entered. Would Dolph arrest me for it? Probably not. If Elvira forced me to shoot her out of sight of witnesses, he might.

I went to the second door. The one I hoped led to the basement. I ran my hand over it, and there it was. A spell. I'm not a witch. I don't know how to decipher spells. Sensing them is about my limit. Oh, one other thing. I can break them. But it's a raw burst of power directed at the spell. I just call up whatever it is that allows me to raise the dead and grab the doorknob. It's worked up to this point, but it's like kicking in a door without knowing what's on the other side. Eventually, you're going to get a shotgun blast in your face.

The real problem was even if I got past it safely, whoever laid the spell would know it. Hell, a good witch would feel the buildup of power before I touched it. If Louie was behind this door, great. I'd go in and keep him safe until my screams brought the cavalry. If he wasn't behind this door, they might panic and kill him.

Most witches, good or bad, are nature worshipers to a certain extent. If it had been Wiccans, their ceremonial area would have been outside somewhere. But for this, darkness and an enclosed space might suffice.

If I had a human sacrifice lying about, I'd want him stored as close to the ceremonial area as possible. It was a gamble. If I was wrong and they killed Louie . . . No. No dwelling on worst-case scenarios.

It was still daylight. It was afternoon. The winter sunlight was grey and soft, but it wasn't dark. My abilities don't come out until after dark. I can sense the dead and certain other things in daylight, but I'm limited. The last time I did this, it had been dark. I approached magic the same way I did everything else. Straight ahead, brute force. What I was really gambling on was that my powers were greater than whoever laid the spell. Sort of the theory that I could take a better beating than she or he could dish out.

Was that true in daylight? We'd find out. Question, was the spell just on the doorknob? Maybe. I'd have locked the door, spell or no spell. Why not just cut out the middle man?

I drew the Browning and backed up. I centered myself, concentrating on a point near the lock but not on it. I waited until that piece of wood was all there was. There was a quality of silence in my ears. I kicked it with everything I had. The door shuddered but did not open. Two more kicks and the wood splintered. The lock gave.

It wasn't a burst of light. If someone had been watching, they wouldn't have seen a damn thing but me falling backwards. My whole body tingled as if I'd put my finger in an electric socket.

I heard running footsteps in the house. I crawled to the open door. I dragged myself to my feet using the banister. A wash of cool air swept against my face. I started down the steps before I was sure I could walk. I had to find Louie before Elvira caught me. If I didn't find proof, she could have me arrested for breaking and entering and we'd be worse off than we were before.

I stumbled down the stairs, one hand in a death grip on the banister, gun in the other. The darkness was velvet black. I couldn't see a damn thing beyond the finger of daylight. Even my night vision needs some light. I heard footsteps behind me.

"Louie, are you down here?"

Something moved in the darkness below me. It sounded big. "Louie?"

Elvira was standing at the head of the stairs. She was framed by the light, as if standing in a body-sized halo. "Ms. Blake, I must insist you get off my property this moment."

My skin was still twitching with whatever had been on the lock. Only my hand on the banister kept me standing. "You do the spell on the door?"

"Yes."

"You're good."

"Not good enough apparently. Now, really I must insist you come up the stairs and get off my property."

A low growl came up from the darkness. It didn't sound much like a rat, and it certainly didn't sound human.

"Come out, come out, wherever you are," I said.

The growling got louder, closer. Something large and furry darted across the pale band of light. The glimpse was enough. I could always say I thought it was Louie. I leaned against the banister and screamed. I screamed for help with every ounce of sound I could make.

Elvira darted a look behind her. I heard the distant yells of police coming in the front door.

"Curse you."

"Words are cheap," I said.

"It will be more than words when I have the time."

"Knock yourself out."

She ran into the house, not away. Was I wrong? Had Louie been inside all along, and I was down here with a different fur ball? Was it Jason?

"Jason?"

Something came to the stairs and peered up into the dim light. It was a dog. A big, furry mutt dog, the size of a pony, but it wasn't a shapeshifter.

"Damn."

It growled at me again. I got up and started to back up the stairs. I didn't want to hurt it if I didn't have to. Where was Dolph? He should have been back here by now.

The dog let me ease back up the steps. Apparently it was only supposed to protect the basement. Fine with me.

"Nice doggy."

I eased up until I could touch the broken door. I slammed it shut, holding the doorknob. The dog hit it with a roaring crash. Its own weight kept the door closed.

I opened the back door, slowly. The kitchen was long, narrow, and mostly white. Voices came from farther in the house. A low growl filled the house, reverberating. The sound raised the hair on my neck.

"No one has to get hurt here," Dolph said.

"That's right," Elvira said. "Leave now, and no one gets hurt."

"We can't do that."

A hallway made up of one wall and the stairs led out of the kitchen towards the living room and the voices. I checked the stairs, empty. I kept going, easing towards the voices. The growl came again, closer.

Dolph yelled, "Anita, get your butt up here!"

It made me jump. He couldn't have seen me yet. The entrance to the living room was an open doorway. I went to one knee and peered around the wall. Elvira stood facing them. A wolf the size of a pony was at her side. If you just glanced at them, you might mistake it for the big dog. It was a good cover. Neighbors see it and think the wolf is a dog.

The other one was a leopard. A black leopard that put every Halloween kitty-cat to shame. It had backed Zerbrowski into a corner. Its slick, furred back came to his waist. Big as a hellcat. Jesus.

Why hadn't they shot? Police were allowed to shoot for self-protection.

"Are you Louie Fane or Jason?" Dolph asked. I realized he was asking the shapeshifters. I hadn't told him what kind of shifter Louie was, and Jason was a wolf. The wolf could be Jason. Though why he'd be helping Elvira I did not know. Maybe I didn't have to know.

I stood up and came around the corner. Maybe the movement was too sudden. Maybe the cat had just grown impatient. The leopard leaped at Zerbrowski. His gun fired.

The wolf turned on me. It all slowed down. I had forever to look down the barrel and pull the trigger. Every gun in the room fired. The wolf went down with a bullet in its brain from me. I wasn't sure who else had gotten a piece of it.

Zerbrowski's screams filled the echoing silence. The leopard was on him, slashing at him.

Dolph fired one more time, then threw the gun to the floor and waded in. He grabbed for the cat and it turned on him, slashing with daggerlike claws. He screamed but didn't back off.

"Dolph, down, and I'll nail it." He tried to get out of the way but the cat leaped on him, carrying them both to the floor. I walked forward, gun extended. They were a rolling mass. If I shot Dolph, he'd be just as dead as the leopard would make him.

I knelt by them and shoved the gun into that warm, furred body. Claws slashed my arm, but I pulled the trigger twice. The thing slumped, twitched, and died.

Dolph blinked up at me. There was a bloody slash on his cheek. But he was alive. I got to my feet. My left arm was numb, which meant it was really hurt. When the numbness wore off, I'd want to be somewhere with doctors.

Zerbrowski lay on his back. There was a lot of blood. I fell to my knees beside him. I laid the Browning on the ground and searched for the big pulse in his neck. It was there, thready, but there. I wanted to cry with relief, but there was no time. There was a black stain of blood near the lower center of his body. I pulled his coat back and nearly threw up on him. Wouldn't he laugh at that? The cat had damn near eviscerated him. His intestines bulged out at the tear.

I tried to pull my jacket off to hold over the wound, but my left arm didn't want to work. "Someone help me." No one did.

Officer Kirlin had Ms. Drew handcuffed. Her green robe was gaping open and it was clear she had nothing on under it. She was crying, crying for her fallen comrades.

Dolph said, "He alive?"

"Yeah."

"I've called for an ambulance," the male uniform said.

"Get over here and help me stop the bleeding."

He just looked at me, sort of shamefaced but neither he nor Kirlin moved to help.

"What the fuck is the matter with you two? Help them."

"We don't want to get it."

"It?"

"The disease," he said.

I crawled back to the leopard. It looked big, even dead. Nearly three times the size of a natural cat. I fumbled at its belly, and found the catch. Not a button, not a belt, but a catch where the fur peeled away. Inside was a naked human body. I pulled the skin back so they could see. "They're shapeshifters but not lycanthropes. It's a spell. It's not contagious, you chicken-shit son of a bitch."

"Anita, don't pick on him," Dolph said. His voice sounded so strange, so distant that I minded him.

The man pulled off his own jacket and sort of laid it on top of Zerbrowski. He pressed down, but gingerly, as if he still didn't trust the blood.

"Get away from him." I leaned on the coat, using my body weight to hold his intestines inside. They moved under my hand like something alive, sqishy and so warm they were hot.

"When the hell are you going to get some silver bullets for your squad?" I asked.

Dolph almost laughed. "Soon, I hope."

Maybe I could buy them a few boxes for Christmas. Please, dear God, let there be a Christmas for all of us. I stared at Zerbrowski's pale face. His glasses had fallen off in the struggle. I looked around and couldn't see them. It seemed important to find his glasses. I knelt there in his blood and cried because I couldn't find his damn glasses.

37

ZERBROWSKI WAS BEING sewn back together. None of the doctors were telling us anything. Guarded. His condition was guarded. Dolph was also in the hospital. Not as bad off but enough to stay for a day or so. Zerbrowski hadn't regained consciousness before they took him away. I waited. Katie, his wife, arrived sometime in the middle of all that waiting.

It was only the second time we'd ever met. She was a small woman with a mane of dark hair tied in a loose ponytail. Without a spot of makeup she was lovely. How Zerbrowski had managed to snag her I'd never figured out.

She walked towards me, dark eyes wide. She was clutching her purse like a shield, fingers digging into the leather. "Where is he?" Her voice was high and breathy, like a little girl's. It always sounded like that.

Before I could say anything, the doctor came out of the swinging doors at the end of the hall. Katie stared at him. All the blood had drained from her face.

I stood up and moved to stand beside her. She stared at the approaching doctor like he was some monster in her worst nightmare. Probably more accurate than I wanted it to be.

"Are you Mrs. Zerbrowski?" the doctor asked.

She nodded. Her hands where they gripped the purse were mottled, trembling with tension.

"Your husband is stable. It looks good. He's going to make it."

Christmas was coming after all.

Katie gave a small sigh and her knees buckled. I caught her and stood there supporting her dead weight. She couldn't have weighed ninety pounds.

"We've got a lounge in here if you can . . ." He looked at me, then shrugged.

I lifted Katie Zerbrowski in my arms, got the balance of it, and said, "Lead on."

I left Katie sitting by Zerbrowski's bedside. His hand wrapped around hers, like he knew she was there. Maybe he did. Lucille, Dolph's wife, was there now to hold her hand just in case. Staring down at Zerbrowski's pale face, I prayed that there was no "just in case."

I wanted to wait until Zerbrowski woke up, but the doctor told me it would probably be tomorrow. I couldn't go without sleep that long. My new stitches made the cross-shaped burn scar on my left arm crooked. The claw marks twisted to one side, missing the mound of scar tissue at the bend of my arm.

Carrying Katie had broken some of my stitches, and they bled through the bandage. The doctor who had operated on Zerbrowski resewed it personally. He looked at the scars a lot.

My arm hurt and was bandaged from wrist to elbow. But we were all alive. Yea.

The taxi dropped me off at my apartment building at what would have been a decent hour. Louie had been drugged and tied in the basement. Elvira had admitted to taking the skins of a werewolf, a wereleopard, and trying for the naga. Jason hadn't been in the house. She denied ever having seen him. What did she need with another werewolf skin? The wererat skin would have been for her, she said. When asked who the snake skin would have been for, she said her. There was at least one other person involved that she wasn't willing to give up.

She was a witch and had used magic to kill. It was an automatic death sentence. Once convicted, the sentence would be carried out within forty-eight hours. No appeals. No pardons. Dead. The lawyers were trying to get her to admit to the other disappearances. If she'd admit to it they might commute her sentence. Might. A killer witch. I didn't believe they'd lighten her sentence, but maybe they would.

Richard was sitting outside my apartment door. I hadn't expected to see him, night of the full moon and all. I'd left a message on his answering machine about finding Louie and him being all right.

The police were trying to keep it all quiet, especially Louie's secret identity. I hoped they could manage it. But at least he was alive. Animal control had the dog.

"I got your message," he said. "Thanks for saving Louie."

I put my key in the lock. "You're welcome."

"We haven't found Jason. Do you really think the witches took him?"

I opened the door. He followed me in and closed the door. "I don't know. That's been bothering me, too. If she'd taken Jason he should have been there." The wolf, once out of its skin, had been a woman that I didn't know.

I walked into the bedroom as if I'd been alone. Richard followed me. I felt light and distant and faintly unreal. They'd cut off the sleeve of my jacket and sweater. I'd tried to save the jacket but I guess it had been ruined anyway. They'd also cut through the left arm sheath. I had it and the knife shoved in my jacket pocket. Why do they always cut everything off in the emergency room?

He came up behind me, not touching, hands hovering over my arm. "You didn't tell me you were hurt."

The phone rang. I picked it up without thinking.

A man's voice said, "Anita Blake?"

"Yes."

"This is Williams, the naturalist at the Audubon Center. I played back some of my owl tapes that I'd recorded at night. One of them has what I'd swear was hyenas on it. I told the police, but they didn't seem to understand the significance. Do you understand what it might mean to have hyena sounds out here?"

"A werehyena," I said.

"Yes, I thought so, too."

No one had told him the killer was a probably a werewolf. But one of the missing shifters was a hyena. Maybe Elvira really didn't know what happened to all the missing lycanthropes.

"Did you say you told the police?"

"Yes, I did."

"Who'd you tell?"

"I called Sheriff Titus's office."

"Who'd you speak to?"

"Aikensen."

"Do you know if he told Titus?"

"No, but why wouldn't he?"

Why indeed.

"Someone's at the door. Can you hold on a minute?"

"I don't think . . ."

"I'll be right back."

"Williams, Williams, don't answer the door." But I was talking to empty air. I heard him walk across the floor. The door opened. He made a surprised sound. Heavier footsteps came back across the floor.

Someone picked up the phone. I could hear them breathing. They didn't say anything.

"Talk to me, you son of a bitch."

The breathing got heavy.

"If you hurt him, Aikensen, I will feed you your dick on knife point."

He laughed and hung up. And I'd never be able to testify in court who was on the other end of that phone.

"Dammit, damn it, damn it."

"What's wrong?"

I called information to get the number for the Willoton Police Department. I pressed the button that dialed it automatically for a small fee.

"Anita, what is it?"

I held up a hand, telling him to wait. A woman answered. "Is this Deputy Holmes?"

It wasn't. I got Chief Garroway after impressing on the dispatcher that this was a matter of life and death. I did not scream at her. I deserved mucho brownie points for that.

I gave Garroway the *Reader's Digest* version. "I can't believe even Aikensen would be involved in something like this, but I'll send a car."

"Thanks."

"Why didn't you just call 911?" Richard asked.

"They'd call the county police. Aikensen might even be assigned the call."

I was struggling out of my butchered jacket. Richard eased it off my left shoulder or I might never have gotten it off. When it was off, I realized I was out of coats. I'd ruined two in as many days. I grabbed the only coat I had left. It was crimson, long and full. I'd worn it twice. The last time was Christmas. The red coat would show up even at night. If I needed to sneak up on anybody, I could take it off.

Richard had to help me get my left arm in the sleeve. It still hurt.

"Let's go get Jason," he said.

I looked at him. "You're not going anywhere but wherever lycanthropes go when there's a full moon."

"You can't even put your own coat on. How are you going to drive?"

He had a point.

"This may put you in danger."

"I'm a full-grown werewolf and tonight is the full moon. I think I can handle it." He had a faraway look in his eyes as if he were hearing voices I would never know.

"All right. Let's go, but we're going to save Williams. I think the weres are close to his place, but I don't know exactly where."

He was standing there with his long duster coat on. He was wearing a white T-shirt, a pair of jeans with one knee gone, and a pair of less than reputable shoes.

"Why the scuffy clothes?"

"If I shift in my clothes, they're always torn apart. Precaution. You ready?"

"Yeah."

"Let's go," he said. There was something about him that was different. A waiting tension like water just before it spills over the edge. When I looked into his brown eyes, something slid behind them. Some furred shape was inside there, waiting to get out.

I realized what I was sensing from him. Eagerness. Richard's beast was looking out of his true brown eyes, and it was eager to be about its business.

What could I say? We went.

38

EDWARD WAS LEANING against my Jeep, arms crossed, breath fogging in the air. The temperature had dropped by twenty degrees with the dark. The freeze was back on. All the meltwater had turned to ice. The snow crunched underfoot.

"What are you doing here, Edward?"

"I was about to come up to your apartment when I saw you coming down."

"What do you want?"

"I want to play," he said.

I stared at him. "Just like that. You don't know what I'm involved in, but you want a piece of it."

"Following you around lets me kill a lot of people."

Sad, but true. "I don't have time to argue. Get in."

He slid in the backseat. "Who exactly are we going to kill tonight?"

Richard started the engine. I buckled up. "Let's see. There's a renegade policeman, and whoever's kidnapped seven shapeshifters."

"The witches didn't do it?"

"Not all of it."

"You think I'll get to kill any lycanthropes tonight?" He was teasing Richard, I think.

Richard wasn't offended. "I've been thinking about who could have taken them all without a struggle. It had to be someone they trusted."

"Who would they trust?" I asked.

"One of us," he said.

"Oh, boy," Edward said, "lycanthrope on the menu for tonight."

Richard didn't correct him. If it was all right with him, it was all right with me.

39

WILLIAMS LAY CRUMPLED on his side. He'd been shot at close range through the heart. Two shots. So much for the doctorate.

One hand was wrapped around a .357 Magnum. I was even betting that there would be powder on his skin, as though he'd really fired the gun.

Deputy Holmes and her partner, whose name I couldn't remember, were lying in the snow dead. The Magnum had taken most of her chest. Her pixielike features were slack and not half so pretty. With her eyes staring straight up she didn't look asleep. She just looked dead.

Her partner was missing most of his face. He was collapsed in the snow, blood and brains melting through the frozen snow. His gun was still gripped in his hand.

Holmes had gotten her gun out, too. For what good it did her. I doubted either one of them had shot Williams, but I'd have bet a month's pay that one of their guns had.

I knelt in the snow and said, "Shit."

Richard stood by Williams. He was staring at him as if he'd memorize him. "Samuel didn't own a gun. He didn't even believe in hunting."

"You knew him?"

"I'm in Audubon, remember."

I nodded. None of it seemed real. It looked staged. Would he get away with it? No. "He's dead," I said, softly.

Edward came to stand beside me. "Who's dead?"

"Aikensen. He's still walking and talking but he's dead. He just doesn't know it yet."

"Where do we find him?" Edward asked.

Good question. I didn't have a good answer. My beeper went off, and I screamed. One of those little yip screams that are always so embarrassing. I checked the number with my heart thundering in my chest.

I didn't recognize the number. Who could it be, and could it possibly be important enough to call back tonight? I'd left my beeper number with the hospital. I didn't know their number, either. I had to answer it. Hell, I needed to call Chief Garroway and tell him his people had walked into an ambush. I could make both calls from Williams's house.

I trudged towards the house. Edward followed. We were on the porch before I realized that Richard wasn't with us. I turned back. He had knelt down beside Williams. I thought at first he was praying, then realized he was touching the bloody snow. Did I really want to know? Yeah.

I walked back over. Edward stayed on the porch without being asked. Point for him. "Richard, are you all right?" It was a stupid question with a man he knew dead at his feet. But what else was I supposed to ask?

His hand closed over the bloody snow, crushing it. He shook his head. I thought he was just angry, or grief stricken, until I saw the sweat on his face.

He turned his face upward, eyes closed. The moon rode full and bright, heavy and silver white. The light was almost daylight bright this far away from the city. Wisps of cloud rode the sky, made luminous with moonshine.

"Richard?"

"I knew him, Anita. We've gone birding together. We talked about his doctorate thesis. I knew him, and now all I can think of is the smell of blood and how warm he still is."

He opened his eyes and looked at me. There was sorrow in his eyes, but mostly there was darkness. His beast was looking out through his eyes.

I turned away. I couldn't hold his gaze. "I've got to make this phone call. Don't eat any of the evidence." I walked away across the snow. It had been too long a night.

I called from the phone in Williams's kitchen. I called Garroway first, told him what we'd found. Once he could breathe, he cursed a bit and said he'd come himself. Probably wondering if things would have turned out differently if he'd come in the first place. Command decisions are always hard.

I hung up and dialed the number on my beeper. "Hello."

"This is Anita Blake. This number was left on my beeper."

"Anita, this is Kaspar Gunderson."

The swan man. "Yes, Kaspar, what is it?"

"You sound awful. Has something happened?"

"Lots, but why did you beep me?"

"I found Jason."

I stood a little straighter. "You're kidding."

"No, I found him. I've got him at my house now. I've been trying to contact Richard. Do you know where he is?"

"With me."

"Perfect," he said. "Can he come take charge of Jason before he changes?"

"Well, yeah, I guess so, why?"

"I'm just a bird, Anita. I'm not a predator. I can't control an inexperienced werewolf."

"Okay, I'll tell him. Where's your house?"

"Richard knows where it is. I've got to get back to Jason, keep him calm. If he loses it before Richard arrives, I'm running for cover. So if I don't answer the doorbell, you'll know what happened."

"Are you in danger from him?"

"Just hurry." He hung up.

Richard had come inside. He was standing in the doorway looking bemused, as if listening to music only he could hear.

"Richard?"

His head moved slowly towards the sound of my voice like a video running on slow speed. His eyes were pale golden yellow, the color of amber.

"Jesus," I said.

He didn't look away. He blinked his new eyes at me. "What is it?"

"Kaspar called. He found Jason. He's been trying to get you. Says he can't control him once he changes."

"Jason's all right," he said. He gave it that questioning lilt.

"Yes, are you all right?"

"No, I have to change soon or the moon will pick the time for me."

I didn't exactly understand that statement, but he could explain in the car. "Edward can drive, in case the moon picks going down Highway Forty-four as the perfect time."

"Good idea, but Kaspar's house is just up the mountain."

"What do you mean?"

"Kaspar lives just up the road."

"Great, let's go."

"You'll have to leave Jason and me up there," he said.

"Why?"

"I can make sure he doesn't hurt anybody, but he has to hunt. I'll take him out here. There are deer in the woods."

I stared at him. He was still Richard. Still my sweetie, but . . . His eyes were the color of pale amber, startling in his dark face.

"You're not going to change in the car, are you?" I asked.

"No. I would never endanger you. I have complete control over my beast. It's what being an alpha wolf means."

"I wasn't worried about being eaten," I said. "I just didn't want you to get that clear junk all over my new seats."

He flashed a smile. It would have been more comforting if his teeth hadn't been just a little pointier than usual.

Jesus H. Christ.

40

KASPAR GUNDERSON'S HOUSE was made of stone, or at least sided with it. Pale chunks of granite formed the walls. The trim was white, the roof shingles pale grey. The door was white as well. It was clean, neat, and still managed to be rustic. It sat in a clearing at the top of the mountain. The road stopped at his house. There was a turnaround but the road didn't go past.

Richard rang the bell. Kaspar opened it. He looked very relieved to see us. "Richard, thank God. He's managed to hold on to human form so far, but I don't think he can last much longer." He held the door for us.

We walked in and found two strange men sitting in his living room. The man to the left was short, dark, and had wire-framed glasses on. The other man was taller, blond, with a reddish beard. They were the only things that didn't match the decor. The entire living room was white—carpet, couch, two chairs, walls. It was like standing in the middle of a vanilla ice-cream cone. He had the same couch that I did. I needed new furniture.

"Who are they?" Richard asked. "They aren't one of us."

"You could say that." It was Titus. He stood in the doorway leading to the kitchen, a gun in his hand. "Don't anybody move," he said. His southern accent was thick as corn pone.

Aikensen stepped out of the door leading to the rest of the house. He had another big Magnum in his hand.

"You buy those by the caseload?" I asked.

"I liked your threat on the phone. It got me hot."

I took a step forward, hadn't meant to. "Please," Aikensen said. He was pointing the big gun at my chest. Titus was pointing at Richard. The two men in the chairs had guns out now, too. One big happy party.

Edward was very still at my back. I could almost feel him weighing the odds. A bolt action on a rifle shot back behind us. We all jumped, even Edward. Another man was behind us in the door. His solid grey hair was balding. The grey man had a rifle in his hands, pointed at Edward's head. There wouldn't be enough left to pick up in a baggie.

"Hands up, y'all."

We put our hands up. What else could we do?

"Lace your fingers atop your head," Titus said.

Edward and I did it like we'd done it before. Richard was slower.

"Now, wolfman, or I will drop you where you stand, and your little girlfriend might get all shot up in the bargain."

Richard laced his fingers. "Kaspar, what's going on?"

Kaspar was sitting on the couch, no, reclining was the word. He looked comfortable, happy as a well-fed cat . . . er, swan.

"These gentleman here have paid a small fortune to hunt lycanthropes. I supply them prey and a place to hunt."

"Titus and Aikensen make sure that no one finds out, right?"

"I told you I did a little hunting, Ms. Blake," Titus said.

"The dead man one of your hunters?"

His eyes flicked, not exactly looking away but flinching. "Yes, Ms. Blake, he was."

I looked at the two men with their guns out. I didn't turn around to see Grey Hair at the door. "You three think that hunting shapeshifters is worth dying over?"

The dark-haired one looked at me from behind his round glasses. His eyes were distant, calm. If it bothered him to be pointing a gun at fellow human beings, it didn't show.

The bearded man's eyes flicked around the room, never settling on anything. He wasn't having a good time.

"Why didn't you and Aikensen clean up the mess before Holmes and her partner saw the body?"

"We were out hunting werewolf," Aikensen said.

"Kaspar, we're your people," Richard said.

"No," Kaspar said. He stood. "You aren't. I am not a lycanthrope. I'm not even an inherited condition. I was cursed by a witch so long ago that I don't care to remember how long."

"Is that supposed to make us feel sorry for you?" I asked.

"No. In fact, I don't suppose I have to explain myself. You have both been decent to me. I suppose I feel guilty about that." He shrugged. "This will be our last hunt. One big gala event."

"If you had slaughtered Raina and Gabriel, I could almost understand it," I said. "But what did the lycanthropes you helped murder ever do to you?"

"When the witch told me what she had done, I remember thinking that being a great ravening beast would be a fine thing. I could still hunt. I could even slay my enemies. Instead she made . . ." He spread his hands wide.

"You kill them because they are what you want to be," I said.

He gave a small smile. "Jealousy, Anita, envy. They are very bitter emotions."

I thought about calling him a bastard, but it wouldn't help. Seven people had died because this son of a bitch didn't like being a bird. "The witch should have killed you, slowly."

"She wanted me to learn my lesson and repent."

"I'm not real big on repentance," I said. "I like revenge better."

"If I wasn't confident you would die tonight, that might worry me."

"Worry," I said.

"Where's Jason?" Richard asked.

"We'll take you to him, won't we, boys," Titus said.

Edward hadn't said a word. I wasn't sure what he was thinking, but I hoped he didn't go for a gun. If he did, most of the people in this room were dead. Three of them would be us.

"Pat 'em down, Aikensen."

Aikensen grinned. He holstered his big gun. That left one revolver, two automatics, and a high-powered rifle. It was enough. Dream team that we are, Edward and I had our limits.

He patted Richard down, a quick search. He was having a good time until he got up to where he could see Richard's eyes. He paled just a little looking into those wolf eyes. Nervous was good.

He kicked my legs farther apart. I glared at him. His hands hovered over my breasts, not where you start a search. "If he does anything but search me for weapons, I am going to draw a gun and take my chances."

"Aikensen, you treat Ms. Blake here like a lady. No hanky-panky."

Aikensen dropped to his knees in front of me. He ran just the palm of his hand over my breast, lightly just over the nipples. I smashed my right elbow into his nose. Blood sprayed outward. He rolled around on the ground, hands to his busted nose.

The dark-haired man was standing. He was pointing his gun very steadily at me. His glasses reflected the light hiding his eyes.

"Everybody calm down, now," Titus said. "Aikensen deserved that, I guess."

Aikensen came up off the floor, blood covering the lower half of his face. He fumbled for his gun.

"If that gun clears your holster, I will shoot you myself," Titus said.

Aikensen was breathing fast and heavy through his mouth. Little bubbles of blood showed at his nose when he tried to breathe through it. It was definitely broken. It wasn't as good as eviscerating him, but it was a start. He kept his hands on his gun, but he didn't pull it. He stayed on his knees for a long time. You could see the struggle in his eyes. He wanted to shoot me almost enough to try for it. Great. The feeling was mutual.

"Aikensen," Titus said softly. His voice was very serious, as if he were just realizing that Aikensen might go for it. "I mean what I say, boy. Don't you be toying with me."

He got to his feet, spitting blood, trying to get it away from his mouth. "You're going to die tonight."

"Maybe, but it won't be by you."

"Ms. Blake, if you could refrain from teasing Aikensen long enough for me to get him away from you, I'd appreciate it."

"Always glad to cooperate with the police," I said.

Titus laughed. The bastard. "Well, now the criminals pay better, Ms. Blake."

"Fuck you."

"No need to get abusive." He tucked his own gun into his side holster. "Now, I'm not going to do a thing but search you for weapons. Any more of this nonsense and we're going to have shoot one of you to prove we're serious. You don't want to lose your sweetheart here. Or your friend here." He smiled. Just good ol' Sheriff Titus. Friendly. Jesus.

He found both guns, then patted me down a second time. I must have winced, because he said, "How'd you hurt your arm, Ms. Blake?"

"I was helping the police on another case."

"They let a civvie get hurt?"

"Sergeant Storr and Detective Zerbrowski are in the hospital. They were injured in the line of duty."

Something passed over his chubby face. It might have been regret. "Heroes don't get anything but dead, Ms. Blake. You best remember that."

"Bad guys die, too, Titus."

He pushed the sleeve of the red coat up and took the knife. He hefted it, testing its balance. "Custom made?"

I nodded.

"I do admire good equipment."

"Keep it. I'll get it later."

He chuckled. "You have guts, girl, I'll give you that."

"And you're a fucking coward."

The smile vanished. "Always needing to have the last word is a bad trait, Ms. Blake. Pisses people off."

"That's the idea."

He moved to Edward. I'd give Titus one thing, he was thorough. He took two automatics, a derringer, and a knife big enough to pass for a short sword from Edward. I had no idea where he'd been hiding the knife.

"Who do the two of you think you are? The freaking cavalry?"

Edward didn't say a thing. If he could be quiet, so could I. There were too many guns to make one of them angry and try to jump the rest. We were outnumbered and outgunned. It was not a good way to start the week.

"Now we are all going to go downstairs," Titus said. "We want you all to join us in the hunt. You will be let out into the woods. If you can get away from us, then you are free. You can run to the nearest police and turn us in. You try anything funny before we let you go, and we will just kill you. You all understand that?"

We just looked at him.

"I can't hear you."

"I heard what you said," I said.

"How 'bout you, blondie?"

"I heard you, too," Edward said.

"Wolfman, you hear me?"

"Don't call me that," Richard said. He didn't sound particularly scared, either. Good.

If you're going to die, at least die brave. It pisses your enemies off.

"Can we put our hands down now?" I asked.

"No," Titus said.

My left arm was beginning to throb. If that was the most painful thing that happened to me tonight, I'd be ahead of the game.

Aikensen went first. Richard next with the dark-haired man and his calm eyes at his back. The bearded man. Then me. Titus. Edward. Grey Hair and his rifle next. Kaspar brought up the rear. It was a parade.

The stairs led into a natural cavern below the house. It was about sixty by thirty feet, with a ceiling that wasn't higher than twelve feet. A tunnel led out the far wall. Electric lights gave a harsh yellow glow to everything. Two cages were set into the granite walls. In the far cage Jason was huddled into a fetal ball. He didn't move as we all trooped in.

"What have you done to him?" Richard said.

"Tried to get him to change for us," Titus said. "Birdie here said he'd be an easy mark."

Kaspar looked uncomfortable. Whether it was the Birdie remark or Jason's stubbornness, it was hard to tell. "He will change for us."

"So you say," Grey Hair said.

Kaspar frowned at him.

Aikensen opened the empty cage. His nose was still bleeding. He had a wad of Kleenex held to it, but it wasn't helping much. The Kleenexes were crimson.

"In ya go, Wolfie," Titus said.

Richard hesitated.

"Mr. Carmichael, the boy, if you please."

Dark Hair put up his 9mm, and got out a .22 from his waistband. He pointed it at Jason's huddled form.

"We'd been discussing putting a bullet in him anyway. See if it would help persuade him to change for us. Now get in the cage."

Richard stood there.

Carmichael pointed the gun through the bars, sighting down his arm.

"Don't," Richard said. "I'll do it." He walked into the cage.

"Now you, Blondie."

Edward didn't argue. He just walked in. He was taking this a lot better than I thought he would.

Aikensen shut the door. He locked the door, then walked across to the second cage. He didn't unlock it. He waited with the soggy Kleenex pressed to his nose. A drop of blood fell to the floor.

"You get to share accommodations with our young friend."

Richard gripped the bars of his cage. "You can't put her in there. When he changes, he'll need to feed."

"Two things help the change happen," Kaspar said, "sex and blood. I saw how much Jason likes your lady friend."

"Don't do this, Kaspar."

"Too late," he said.

If I went in the cage, I was going to end up eaten alive. That was actually one of my top five ways not to die. I wasn't going in the cage. I'd make them shoot me first.

"Aikensen is going to open the cage, then you step inside, Ms. Blake."

"No," I said.

Titus looked at me. "Ms. Blake, Mr. Fienstien here will shoot you, won't you, Mr. Fienstien?"

The bearded man, uncertain eyes and all, pointed a 9mm Beretta at me. A nice gun, if you didn't insist on buying American. The barrel looked very big, and solid from the wrong end.

"Fine, shoot me."

"Ms. Blake, we are not joking."

"Neither am I. My choices are being eaten alive or being shot. So shoot me."

"Mr. Carmichael, if you will point your .22 over here." Carmichael did. "We can wound you, Ms. Blake. Put a bullet in your leg and then shove you in that cage."

I looked into his beady little eyes and knew he would do it. I didn't want to go into the cage, but I really didn't want to go in wounded.

"I'm going to count to five, Ms. Blake, then Carmichael here is going to wound you and we will drag you into that cage. One . . . two . . . three . . . four . . ."

"All right, all right, damn you. Unlock the damn door."

Aikensen did. I walked in. The door clanged shut behind me. I stood there near the door. Jason was shivering as if he had a fever, but he never moved otherwise.

The men outside seemed disappointed. "We paid good money to hunt a werewolf," Grey Hair said. "We are not getting our money's worth."

"We've got all night, gentleman. He won't resist this luscious tidbit forever," Kaspar said.

I didn't like being called a tidbit. Luscious or otherwise. "I called Garroway before we drove up here. I told him about his deputies getting ambushed. I told him it was Aikensen."

"Liar."

I looked straight at Titus. "You think I'm lying?"

"Maybe we'll just shoot all of you now, and flee, Ms. Blake."

"You going to give these gentlemen their money back?"

"We want a hunt, Titus." The three armed men didn't look like leaving before the fun was an option. "The police don't know about the bird-man's involvement," Carmichael of the .22 said. "He can stay upstairs. If they come asking questions, he can answer them."

Titus wiped his palms against his pants. Sweating palms, nerves? I hoped so.

"She didn't call. She's just bluffing," Aikensen said.

"Make him change," Carmichael said.

"He's not paying any attention to her," Grey Hair said.

"Give it time, gentlemen."

"You said we don't have time."

"You're the expert, Kaspar. Thinka something."

Kaspar smiled, staring at something behind me. "I don't think we'll have to wait much longer."

I turned around slowly, looking behind me. Jason was still huddled on the ground but his face was turned to me. He rolled onto all fours in one easy motion. His eyes flicked to me, then stared at the men on the outside of the cage. "I won't do it. I won't change for you." His voice was strained but normal. Human sounding.

"You've held out a long time, Jason," Kaspar said, "but the moon is rising. Smell her fear, Jason. Smell her body. You know you want her."

"No!" He bowed his head to the ground, hands and arms flat to the floor, knees drawn up. He shook his head, face pressed into the rock. "No." He raised his face up. "I won't do it like some sideshow freak."

"Do you think giving Jason and Ms. Blake here a little privacy would help matters along?" Titus asked.

"It might," Kaspar said. "He doesn't seem to like an audience."

"We'll just give you a little breathin' space, Ms. Blake. If you aren't alive when we get back, well, it's been nice meetin' ya."

"I can't say the same, Titus," I said.

"Well, now that is the God's honest truth. Good-bye, Ms. Blake."

"Rot in hell, bitch," was Aikensen's parting shot.

"You'll remember me every time you look in a mirror, Aikensen."

His hand went to his nose. Even that touch hurt. He scowled at me, but it's hard to look tough with Kleenex sticking out of your nose. "I hope you die slow."

"Same to you," I said.

"Kaspar, please," Richard said. "Don't do this. I'll change for you. I'll let you hunt me. Just get Anita out of there."

The men stopped and looked at him.

"Don't help me, Richard."

"I'll give you the best hunt you've ever had." He was pressed against the bars, hands wrapped around them. "You know I can do it, Kaspar. Tell them."

Kaspar looked at him for a long moment. He shook his head. "I think you'd kill them all."

"I'd promise not to."

"Richard, what are you saying?"

He ignored me. "Please, Kaspar."

"You must love her a great deal."

Richard just stared at him.

"No matter what you do, Richard, they're not going to let me go."

He wasn't listening to me.

"Richard!"

"I'm sorry," Kaspar said. "I trust you, Richard, but your beast . . . I think your beast isn't so trustworthy."

"Come on, we're wasting time. Garroway doesn't know where to look but he might come up here. Let's give 'em some privacy," Titus said.

They all trooped out after the chubby sheriff. Kaspar was last up the stairs. "I wish it were Gabriel and Raina in the cages. I am sorry about that." The swan man disappeared into the rock tunnel.

"Kaspar, don't leave us like this. Kaspar!" Richard's yells echoed in the cavern. But nothing answered the echoes. We were alone. Scuffling sounds made me whirl. Jason was on his knees again. Something moved behind his pale blue eyes, something monstrous and not friendly at all. I wasn't half as alone as I wanted to be.

41

JASON TOOK ONE crawling step towards me and stopped. "No, no, no." Each word was a low moan. His head fell forward. His yellow hair swept forward not long enough to touch the ground, but thick. He was wearing an oversize blue dress shirt and jeans. Clothes you wouldn't mind ruining if you happened to shapeshift in them.

"Anita," Richard said.

I moved so I could see the other cage, without losing sight of Jason.

Richard was reaching through the bars. One hand stretching out towards me as if he could bridge the space and somehow drag me to him.

Edward crawled to the door and began running hands over the lock. He couldn't really see the lock from inside the cage. He pressed his cheek to the bars and closed his eyes. When you can't use your eyes they become a distraction.

He leaned back and drew a slender leather case from his pocket. He unzipped it to reveal tiny tools. From this distance I couldn't really see them clearly but I knew what they were. Edward was going to pick the lock. We could be out in the woods before they knew we were missing. The night was looking up.

Edward settled back against the bars, one arm on either side of the lock, a pick in each hand. His eyes were closed, his face blank, all concentration to his hands.

Jason made a small sound low in his chest. He crawled towards me, two slow, dragging steps. His head flung upward. His eyes were still the innocent blue of spring skies but there was nobody home now. He looked at me as though he could see inside my body, watch my heart thudding in my chest, smell the blood in my veins. It was not a human look.

"Jason," Richard said, "hold on. We'll be free in a few minutes. Just hold on."

Jason didn't react. I don't think he heard.

I thought the few minutes was being overly optimistic, but hey, I was willing to believe it if Jason would.

Jason crawled towards me. I plastered my back against the cage bars. "Edward, how are you coming with that lock?"

"These are not the tools I would have chosen for this particular lock, but I'll get it."

There was something in the way Jason crawled towards me, as if he had muscles in places that he shouldn't have. "Make it soon, Edward."

He didn't answer me. I didn't have to look to know that he was working at the lock. I had every faith that he'd unlock the door. I backed down the bars, trying to keep an even distance between me and the werewolf. Edward would get the door open, but would it be in time? That was the $64,000 question.

A sound at the entrance caused me to glance back. Carmichael stepped into the cavern. He had the 9mm in his hand. He smiled. It was the happiest I'd seen him.

Edward ignored him, working at the lock as if an armed man hadn't stepped into the room.

Carmichael raised the gun and pointed it at Edward. "Get away from the lock, now." He cocked the hammer back, not necessary, but always dramatic. "We don't need you alive. Stop . . . working . . . on . . . the . . . lock." He stepped closer with each word.

Edward looked up at him. His face was still blank, as if his concentration were still in his hands, not quite focused on the gun being pointed at him.

"Throw the tools away from you. Right now."

Edward stared at him. His expression never changed but he tossed the two small tools away.

"Take the complete kit out of your pocket and toss it out of the cage. Don't even try to say you don't have one. If you've got those two pieces, you've got the rest."

I wondered what Carmichael did in the real world. Something not nice. Something where he knew what tools would be in a professional lock-picking kit.

"I won't warn you again," Carmichael said. "Throw it out or I pull the trigger. I am tired of screwing with this mess."

Edward threw out the slim leather pouch. It made a small slapping sound on the rock. Carmichael made no move to pick up the lock picks. They were out of our reach. That was what counted. He walked backwards, keeping us all in sight. He directed some of his attention to Jason and me. Oh, joy.

"Our little werewolf's awake. I was hoping he would be."

A low, ragged growl crawled up Jason's throat.

Carmichael gave a delighted bark of laughter. "I wanted to see him change. Good thing I checked back in."

"I'm thrilled that you're here," I said.

He came to stand just out of reach of our cage bars. He was staring at Jason. "I've never seen one of them change."

"Let me out and we'll watch him together."

"Now, why would I do that? I paid to see the whole show."

His eyes were sparkling with anticipation. Bright and shiny as a kid on Christmas morning. Shit.

A growl brought my attention completely back to Jason. He was crouched on the rock floor, hands and legs bunched under him. Watching that growl trickle from between his human lips raised the hair on the back of my neck.

He wasn't looking at me. "I think he's growling at you, Carmichael."

"But I'm not in the cage," he said. He had a point.

"Jason, don't get angry at him," Richard said. "Anger will feed the beast. You can't afford to get angry." Richard's voice was amazingly calm, even soothing. He was trying to talk Jason down, or out, or in, or whatever word you used for keeping a werewolf from shifting.

"No," Carmichael said, "get angry, wolf. I'm going to cut your head off and mount it on my wall."

"He'll revert back to human form after he's dead," I said.

"I know," Carmichael said.

Jesus. "Police find you with a human head in your possession, they may get a little suspicious."

"I've got a lot of trophies that I wouldn't want the police to find," he said.

"What do you do in the real world?"

"This is as real as it gets."

I shook my head. It was hard to argue with him, but I wanted to.

Jason crawled towards the bars, in a sort of monkey crouch. It wasn't as graceful but it had an energy to it, as if he were about to launch himself into the air. As if when he jumped he could fly.

"Calm, Jason, easy," Richard said.

"Come on, boy, try it. Rush the bars and I'll pull the trigger."

I watched him bunch every muscle and launch himself at the bars. He clung to the bars, hands clawing between them. Arms stretched as far as they would go. He wedged a shoulder between the bars as if he'd slip through. For one moment Carmichael looked uncertain, then he laughed.

"Shoot me," Jason said. His voice was more growl than words. "Shoot me."

"I don't think so," Carmichael said.

Jason gripped the bars with his hands and slid down to his knees, forehead pressed to the bars. His breathing was fast, panting, as if he'd run a mile in a minute flat. If he'd been human he'd have hyperventilated and passed out. His head turned slowly towards me, painfully slow, as if he didn't want to do it. He'd tried to force Carmichael to shoot him. Risked being killed to keep from turning on me. He didn't know me well enough to risk his life. It got him a lot of points in my book.

He looked at me, and his face was naked, raw with need. Not sex, not hunger, both, neither, I didn't understand the look in his eyes, and didn't want to.

He scrambled towards me. I backed away, almost running backwards. "Don't run," Richard called. "It excites him."

Staring into Jason's alien expression, it took everything I had to stand still. My hands gripped the bars behind me hard enough to hurt, but I stopped running. Running was bad.

Jason stopped when I did. He crouched just out of reach. He put one hand on the ground and crawled towards me. It was slow, as if he didn't want to, but he kept coming.

"Any more bright ideas?" I asked.

"Don't run. Don't struggle. It's exciting. Try to be calm. Try not to be afraid. Fear is very exciting."

"Speaking from personal experience?" I asked.

"Yes," he said.

I wanted to turn, see his face, but I couldn't. I had eyes only for the werewolf that was crawling towards me. The werewolf in the other cage could take care of himself.

Jason knelt on all fours by my legs, like a dog awaiting a command. He raised his head and looked at me. A spot of pale green color spilled into his eyes. The blue of his irises drowned in a swirl of new color. When it was done his eyes were the color of new spring grass, pale, pale green, and not human at all.

I gasped. I couldn't help it. He moved closer, sniffing the air around me. His fingertips brushed my leg. I jerked. He let out a long sigh and rubbed his cheek against my leg. He'd done more than this at the Lunatic Cafe, but his eyes had still been mostly human. And I had been armed. I'd have given nearly anything for a gun right now.

Jason grabbed the hem of my coat, balling his hands into fists, tugging at the cloth. He was going to pull me to the ground. No way. I shrugged the coat off my shoulders. Jason pulled it off me. I stepped out of the circle of cloth. He bundled the coat to his face with both arms. He rolled on the ground with it pressed to his body like a dog with a piece of carrion. Wallowing in the scent.

He came to his knees. He stalked towards me, moving with a liquid grace that was unnerving as hell. Human beings did not crawl gracefully.

I backed up, slowly, no running. But I didn't want him to touch me again. He moved faster, each movement precise. Pale green eyes locked on me as if I were all that existed in the world.

I started backing up faster. He moved with me.

"Don't run, Anita, please," Richard said.

My back thunked into the corner of the cage. I gave a little yelp.

Jason covered the distance between us in two smooth movements. His hands touched my legs. I swallowed a scream. My pulse was threatening to choke me.

"Anita, control your fear. Calm, think calm."

"You think fucking calm." My voice sounded strident, panicked.

Jason had his fingertips hooked in my belt. He pressed his body into my legs, pinning me to the bars. I made a small gasp and hated it. If this was going to be it, then dammit, I wasn't going to go out whimpering.

I listened to my heart pounding in my ears, and took slow, even breaths. I stared into those spring green eyes and relearned how to breathe.

Jason pressed his cheek against my hip, hands sliding around my waist. My heart gave a little pitty-pat and I swallowed it. I concentrated on my own heart until my pulse slowed. It was the kind of concentration that let you do that new throw in judo. The concentration that fed a zombie raising.

When Jason lifted his head and looked at me again, I gave him calm eyes. I felt my face blank, neutral, calm. I wasn't sure how long it would last but it was the best I could do.

His fingers slid under my sweater, up my back. I swallowed and my heartbeat sped up. I tried to slow it down, tried to concentrate, but his hands slid around my waist over my skin. His fingers traced my ribs moving upward. I grabbed his wrists, stopping his hands short of my breasts.

As he rose, my hands stayed on his arms. Standing with his hands still under my sweater raised the cloth, baring my stomach. Jason seemed to like the sight of bare skin. He knelt again, letting me keep hold of his arms. I felt his breath almost burning warm on my bare stomach. His tongue flicked out, a quick touch to one side of my belly button. His lips brushed my skin, soft, caressing.

I felt him take a deep, shaking breath. He pressed his face into the soft flesh of my belly. His tongue lapped my stomach, mouth pressing hard. His teeth grazed my waist. It made me squirm, and not with pain. His hands balled into fists under my sweater, hands convulsing. I didn't really want to let go of his wrists but I wanted him away from me.

"Is he going to eat me or . . ."

"Fuck you," Carmichael added. I'd almost forgotten him. Careless forgetting the man with the gun. Maybe it was the realization that he wasn't a danger to me. The danger was kneeling at my feet.

"Jason's only been one of us for a few months. If he can channel the energy into sex instead of violence I'd take it. I'd try to keep him away from killing zones."

"What's that supposed to mean?"

"Keep him away from your throat and your stomach."

I stared down at Jason. He looked up at me, rolling his eyes. There was a darkness in those pale eyes, a darkness deep enough to drown in.

I drew Jason's hands out from under my sweater. He slid his hands into mine, fingers interlocking. He nuzzled my stomach, trying to bury his face where the sweater had slid over my skin. I raised him up with our hands still locked together.

He raised our hands upward, pressing my arms backwards against the bars. I fought the urge to struggle, to jerk away. Struggling was exciting, and that was a bad thing.

We were almost the same height. His eyes were too startling from an inch away. His lips parted and I caught a glimpse of fangs. Jesus.

He rubbed his cheek along mine. His lips moved down my jawline. I turned my head, trying to keep him away from the big pulse in my neck. He came up for air, and brushed his mouth against mine. He pressed his body against mine hard enough that I knew he was glad to be there. Or at least his body was. He buried his face in my hair and stood there pressed against me, our hands on the bars of the cage.

I could feel the pulse in his neck thudding against the bone of my jaw.

His breathing was too fast, his chest rising and falling as if he were doing a lot more than foreplay. Was I about to move from foreplay to appetizer?

Power prickled along my skin but it wasn't Jason. I'd tasted this particular power before. Was the show exciting Richard? Would watching me die like this be a thrill like the woman on the film?

"She's mine, Jason." It was Richard's voice but with a bass undertone. The change was coming.

Jason whimpered. It was the only word for it.

Richard's power rode the air like distant thunder, drawing close. "Get off her, Jason. Now!" That last word lunged out in something close to a scream. But it was the kind of scream that cougars gave; no fear, but warning.

I felt Jason shake his head against my hair. His hands convulsed against mine. The strength of it made me gasp. It was the wrong thing to do.

He let go of my hands so suddenly I would have stumbled, but the line of his body kept me upright. He jerked away from me and I did stumble. He grabbed me around the thighs and lifted me into the air, too fast for me to stop even if I could have. He smacked me back against the bars. I took most of the blow on my back. Bruised, but alive.

He supported me with one arm and shoved my sweater upward with the other. I shoved the sweater back down. He made a sound low in his throat and slammed me into the floor. Hitting the rock took all the fight out of me for just a minute. He ripped the sweater as if it were paper, spreading it away from my stomach. He threw his head skyward and screamed, but the mouth he opened wasn't human anymore.

If I'd had enough air I'd have screamed.

"Jason, no!" The voice wasn't human anymore. Richard's power flooded the cage, thick enough to choke on. Jason struggled almost as if the power were thicker than air. He swiped at nothing that I could see with hands that had claws for fingers.

"Back off," the words were a snarl, barely recognizable.

Jason snarled back, teeth snapping the air, but not at me. He rolled off me, crawling along the rock, growling.

I just lay there on my back, afraid to move. Afraid that any movement would tip the balance and make him finish what he'd started.

"Shit," Carmichael said. "I'll be right back, folks, and the birdman better think of something to make one of you change." He marched off, leaving us to a silence that was replaced with a low, steady growl. I realized that it wasn't Jason anymore.

I rose up slowly on my elbows. Jason didn't try to eat me. Richard was still standing by the bars of his cage, but his face had lengthened. He had a muzzle. His thick brown hair was longer. The hair seemed to have flowed down his back, as if attached to the spine. He was holding onto his humanity with a string. A weak, shiny string.

Edward was standing very still near the door. He hadn't tried to run when Richard went all spooky. Edward always did have nerves of steel.

42

TITUS WAS THE first one through the door. "I am mighty disappointed in you all. Carmichael here tells me you almost had it, and this one interfered."

Kaspar stared at Richard as if he'd never seen him before. Maybe he'd never seen half-human, half-wolf before, but something about the way he was staring said that wasn't it. "Marcus couldn't have done what you did."

"Jason didn't want to hurt her," Richard said. "He wanted to do the right thing."

"Well, Birdman," Carmichael said, "what next?"

I stayed sitting on the rock floor. Jason was huddled against the far wall on his hands and knees, rocking back and forth, back and forth. A low, moaning sound crawled out of his throat.

"He's near the edge," Kaspar said. "Blood will push him over. Not even an alpha can hold him in the presence of fresh blood."

I did not like the sound of that.

"Ms. Blake, could you come over to the bars, please."

I moved so I could keep an eye on the moaning werewolf and the armed camp outside. "Why?"

"Either do it or Carmichael will shoot you. Don't make me start counting again, Ms. Blake."

"I don't think I want to come over to the bars."

Titus took out his .45 and walked over to the other cage. Edward was sitting down. He looked at me across the room, and I knew that if we ever got out, they were all dead. Richard was still standing at the bars, hands wrapped around them.

Titus stared up at Richard's animalistic face and gave a low whistle. "Good lord." He pointed the gun at Richard's chest. "These are silver bullets, Ms. Blake. If you called Garroway, we don't have time for two hunts anyway. Garroway doesn't know you're here, so we have a little time, but we don't have all night. Besides, I think the wolfman here might be too dangerous. So if you keep pissing me off, I'll kill him."

I met Richard's new eyes. "They're going to kill us anyway. Don't do it," he said. His voice was still a growl that was such a deep bass that it crawled down my spine.

They were going to kill us. But I couldn't stand there and watch, not if I could prolong the inevitable. I walked to the bars nearest them. "Now what?"

Titus stayed with the gun pointed at Richard. "Put your arms through the bars, please."

I wanted to say no, but we'd already established that I wasn't willing to watch Richard die just yet. It made saying no sort of hollow. I slipped my arms through the bars, which put my back to the werewolf. Not good.

"Grab her wrists, gentlemen."

I balled my hands into fists but didn't pull back. I was going to do this, right.

Carmichael grabbed my left wrist. The bearded Fienstien took my right. Fienstien wasn't holding on very hard. I could have pulled away, but Carmichael's hand was like warm steel. I stared into his eyes, and found no pity there. Fienstien was getting squeamish. Grey Hair, with his rifle, was in the middle of the room, distancing himself from it. Carmichael was here for the whole ride.

Titus came over and started unwrapping the bandage on my arm. I fought the urge to ask what he was doing. I had an idea. I hoped I was wrong.

"How many stitches did you get, Ms. Blake?"

I wasn't wrong. "I don't know. I stopped counting at twenty." He let the bandages fall to the ground. He got out my own knife and held it up where it would catch the light. Nothing like a little showmanship.

I pressed my forehead to the cage bars and took a deep breath.

"I'm going to reopen some of this wound. Cut out your stitches."

"I figured that out," I said.

"No struggles?"

"Get on with it."

Aikensen came over. "Let me do it. I owe her a little blood."

Titus looked at me, almost as if asking permission. I gave him my best blank look. He handed the knife to Aikensen.

Aikensen held the point just over the first stitch near my wrist. I felt my eyes widen. I didn't know what to do. Looking seemed a bad idea. Not looking seemed worse. Begging them not to do it seemed futile and humiliating. Some nights there are no good choices.

He cut the first stitch. I felt it snap, but surprisingly it didn't really hurt all that much. I looked away. The stitches went snip, snip, snip. I could do this.

"We need blood," Carmichael said.

I looked back in time to see Aikensen put the point of the knife against the wound. He was going to reopen the wound, slowly. That was going to hurt. I caught a glimpse of Edward in his cage. He was standing now. Looking at me. He was trying to tell me something. His eyes slid right.

Grey Hair had walked away from the show. He was standing close to the other cage. Evidently, he could shoot you, but he didn't like torture.

Edward looked at me. I thought I knew what he wanted. I hoped so.

The knife bit into my skin. I gasped. The pain was sharp and immediate, like all shallow wounds, but this one was going to last a long time. Blood flowed in a heavy line down my skin. Aikensen pulled the point down a fraction of an inch. I pulled suddenly on my arms. Fienstien lost his grip. He grabbed for my flaying arm. Carmichael tightened his grip. I couldn't get free but I could drop to the floor and make my arm move too much to use a knife on it.

I started to scream and fight in earnest. If Edward needed a diversion, I could give him one.

"One woman in a cage and the three of you can't handle her." Titus waddled up. He grabbed my left arm while Carmichael had my wrist. My right hand was back in the cage with me.

Fienstien was sort of hovering near the cage, not sure what to do. If you were going to pay money to hunt monsters, you should be better at violence than this. His holster was close to the bars.

I screamed over and over, jerking at my left arm. Titus held my arm under his, pinned next to his body. Carmichael's grip on my wrist was bruising. They had me at last. Aikensen put the knife to the wound and started to cut.

Fienstien bent down as if to help. I screamed and leaned into the bars. I didn't draw his gun. I grabbed the trigger and pushed it into his body. The shot took him in the stomach. He fell backwards.

A second shot echoed in the cavern. Carmichael's head exploded all over Titus. His Smokey Bear hat was covered in blood and brains.

Edward was standing with the rifle to his shoulder. Grey Hair was slumped against the cage bars. His neck was at an odd angle. Richard knelt by the body. Had he killed him?

There was a sound behind me. A low guttural cry. Titus had his gun out. He still had my arm pinned. Fienstien was rolling around on the ground. His gun was out of reach.

There was a low growl coming from behind me. I heard movement. Jason was coming back to play. Great.

Titus jerked my arm forward, nearly wrenching it out of the socket. He shoved his .45 against my cheek. The barrel was cold.

"Put down the rifle or I pull this trigger."

My face was pressed into the bars and the gun. I couldn't look behind me, but I could hear something crawling closer.

"Is he changing?"

"Not yet," Richard said.

Edward still had the rifle up, sighted on Titus. Aikensen seemed frozen, standing there with the bloody knife.

"Put it down, blondie, right now, or she's dead."

"Edward."

"Anita," he said. His voice sounded like it always did. We both knew he could drop Titus, but if the man's finger twitched while he died, I died, too. Choices.

"Do it," I said.

He pulled the trigger. Titus jerked back against the bars. Blood splattered over my face. A glob of something thicker than blood slid down my cheek. I breathed in shallow gasps. Titus slumped along the bars, gun still gripped in his hands.

"Open her cage," Edward said.

Something touched my leg. I jerked and whirled. Jason grabbed my bleeding arm. The strength was incredible. He could have crushed my wrist. He lowered his face to the wound and lapped at the blood like a cat with cream.

"Open her door now, or you're dead, too."

Aikensen just stood there.

Jason licked my arm. His tongue caressed the wound. It hurt, but I swallowed the gasp. No sounds. No struggles. He'd done damn good not to jump me while I fought the men outside. But a werewolf's patience isn't endless.

"Now!" Edward said.

Aikensen jumped, then went for the door. He dropped my knife by the door and fumbled at the lock.

Jason bit into my arm, just a little. I did gasp. I couldn't help it. Richard screamed, wordless and thundering.

Jason jerked away from me. "Run," he said. He buried his face in a puddle of blood on the floor, lapping at it. His voice was strangled, more growl than word. "Run."

Aikensen opened the door. I crab-walked backwards.

Jason threw his head skyward and shrieked, "Run!"

I got to my feet and ran. Aikensen slammed the door shut behind me. Jason was writhing on the floor. He fell to the ground in convulsions. Foam ran from his mouth. His hands spasmed, reaching for nothing that I could see. I'd seen people shift before but never this violently. It looked like a bad *grand mal* seizure or someone dying of strychnine.

The wolf burst out of his skin in a nearly finished product, like a cicada pulling out of its old skin. The wolfman raced for the bars. Claws grabbed for us. We both backed up. Foam fell from the wolf jaws. Teeth snapped the air. And I knew that he'd kill me and eat me afterwards. It was what he did, what he was.

Aikensen was staring at the werewolf. I knelt and picked up the dropped knife. "Aikensen?"

He turned to me, still startled and pale.

"Did you enjoy shooting Deputy Holmes in the chest?"

He frowned at me. "I let you go. I did what he asked."

I stepped up close to him. "Remember what I told you would happen if you hurt Williams?"

He looked at me. "I remember."

"Good." I drove the knife upward into his groin. I shoved it hilt deep. Blood poured over my hand. He stared at me, eyes going glassy.

"A promise is a promise," I said.

He fell and I let his own weight pull the knife up through his abdomen. His eyes closed and I pulled the knife out.

I wiped the knife on his jacket and took the keys from his limp hand. Edward had the rifle slung over his shoulder by the strap. Richard was watching me as if he'd never seen me before. Even with his odd-shaped face and amber eyes I could tell he disapproved.

I unlocked their door. Edward walked out. Richard followed but he was staring at me. "You didn't have to kill him," he said. The words were Richard's even if the voice wasn't.

Edward and I stood there looking at the alpha werewolf. "Yes, I did."

"We kill because we have to, not for pleasure and not for pride," Richard said.

"Maybe you do," I said. "But the rest of the pack, the rest of the shifters, aren't so particular."

"The police may be on their way," Edward said. "You don't want to be here."

Richard glanced at the ravening beast in the other cage. "Give me the keys. I'll take Jason out through the tunnel. I can smell the outside."

I handed him the keys. His fingertips brushed my hand. His hand convulsed around the keys. "I can't last much longer. Go."

I looked into those strange amber eyes. Edward touched my arm. "We've got to go."

I heard sirens. They must have heard the gunshots.

"Be careful," I said.

"I will be." I let Edward pull me up the stairs. Richard fell to the ground, face hidden in his hands. His face came up, and the bones were longer. They flowed out of his face as if it were clay.

I tripped on the stairs. Only Edward's hand kept me from falling. I turned around and we ran up the stairs. When I glanced back, Richard wasn't in sight.

Edward dropped the rifle on the stairs. The door burst open, and the police came through the door. It was only then that I realized Kaspar was gone.

43

NEITHER EDWARD NOR I had to go to jail, even though the cops found the people we killed. Everyone pretty much thought it was a miracle that we had gotten away with our lives. People were impressed. Edward surprised me by showing ID for a Ted Forrester, bounty hunter. Slaughter of a bunch of illegal lycanthrope hunters enhanced the reputation of all bounty hunters, Ted Forrester's in particular. I got a lot of good press out of it, too. Bert was pleased.

I asked Edward if Forrester was his real last name. He just smiled.

Dolph was released in time for Christmas. Zerbrowski had to stay longer. I bought them both a case of silver bullets. It was only money. Besides, I never wanted to watch one of them drip their life away through tubes.

I made one last visit to the Lunatic Cafe. Marcus told me that Alfred had killed the girl all on his own. Gabriel hadn't known it was going to happen, but once she was dead, waste not, want not. Lycanthropes are nothing if not practical. Raina had distributed the film for the same reason. I didn't really believe them. Awful damn convenient to blame a dead man. But I didn't tell Edward. I did tell Gabriel and Raina that if any other snuff films surfaced, they could kiss their furry asses good-bye. I'd sic Edward on them. Though I didn't tell them that.

I got Richard a gold cross and made him promise to wear it. He got me a stuffed toy penguin that played "Winter Wonderland," a bag of black-and-white gummy penguins, and a small velvet box, like one for a ring. I thought I would swallow my heart. There was no ring in it, just a note that said, "Promises to keep."

Jean-Claude got me a glass sculpture of penguins on an ice floe. It's beautiful and expensive. I'd have liked it better if Richard had gotten it.

What do you get the Master of the City for Christmas? A pint of blood? I settled for an antique cameo. It'd look great at the neck of one of his lacy shirts.

Sometime in February a box arrived from Edward. It was a swan skin. The note read, "I found a witch to lift his curse." I lifted the feathered skin from the box, and a second note fluttered to the ground. This one said, "Marcus paid me." I should have known he'd find a way to make a profit from a kill he'd have made for free.

Richard doesn't understand why I killed Aikensen. I've tried to explain, but saying I killed a man because I said I'd do it does sound like pride. But it wasn't pride. It was for Williams, who would never finish his doctorate or see his owls again. For Holmes, who never got to be the first female chief of police. For all the people he killed who never got a second chance. If they couldn't have one, neither could he. I haven't lost any sleep over killing Aikensen. Maybe that should bother me more than the killing—the fact that it doesn't bother me at all. Naw.

I had the swan skin mounted in a tasteful frame, behind glass. I hung it in the living room. It matched the couch. Richard doesn't like it. I like it just fine.